The Commune

By the same author

Two Tales

With Brian Buckley

Challenge & Renewal: Lawrence and the Thematic Novel

Available from the Chrysalis Press

The Commune

Margaret Buckley

The Chrysalis Press

Published by The Chrysalis Press
7 Lower Ladyes Hills, Kenilworth, Warwickshire

British Library Cataloguing in Publication Data:
Buckley, Margaret (1930–1992)
The Commune
I. Title F

ISBN 1 897765 06 1

Printed and bound in Great Britain by
Redwood Books, Trowbridge, Wiltshire

For my two darlings

1

"I think I remember being introduced to him once." Mrs Redfern was showing less interest than she felt, remembering clearly both the occasion and the impact it made on her. She was fully attentive but managed to make it seem by the odd distracted gesture and accessibility to other things going on in the room that it was a form of politeness.

He didn't need more. Leaning back in his chair, legs crossed, he provided his own distance, instinctively co-operating with the need in others. In this case especially, partial attention was good and more likely to leave a guarded woman off-guard.

"So what made you decide on the whole summer?" He was curious about the length of her intended stay on Mark Lewis's smallholding. Two or three months was a lot longer than necessary for the article she'd said she was writing, and from what he'd seen of her it wouldn't be her kind of holiday.

"I'm interested in what he's hoping to put in the place of all this - " she spread her hand to the room.

He seemed surprised at her answer, then changed his approach. "As far as I can tell we're the only two going."

Joan saw his disappointment as he said it - she felt something similar herself: in an unsociable department this man was the least sociable. She'd decided early on that interest in people wouldn't be easy for Bates unless they promised or baulked something - and watching him now adjust his position, uncrossing and stretching his legs towards her, saw that he hadn't finished with her yet.

"Does Mark expect any more to turn up on spec?" As he said it excitement surged in his face at the thought of one or two of Mark's girls turning up. He remembered Mark had a clutch of them when he taught there, goodlooking some of them, one or two might still make it.

She shrugged her shoulders. "I don't know."

He'd have gone, like her, without the bait, out of sheer curiosity. Even so he wasn't satisfied with her reasons. What was the extra in her case, Mark? Considering Mark had been a social success he wasn't doing too well. Only himself and the unlikely Joan had taken up an offer made to the whole campus. He gave a smile as a stopgap till he made up his mind how to proceed.

Joan looked away over his shoulder to where Jackson was leaning over the new History professor and spilling coffee down his coat. Bates was much too sure of himself but then he'd been spoilt - high colouring, thick black hair, bright blue eyes, fresh complexion and there, under her nose, two wonderfully well-shaped legs. She knew better than to look too closely. In any case the suggestion of exuberance was countered by a small nose and mouth, so the pleasure was mixed - he'd only bring to passion the cold objectivity he brought to everything else, a withholder who used his endowments to advantage, dark trousers and rose shirt fitting close enough to show off the contents, inaccessible manner to make it clear he'd never part with them. A sudden contrast with her memory of Mark made her realise why, from the outset of the conversation, she'd protected it.

"You only met him the once then?" he asked.

"The afternoon he handed his office over to me."

"What did you make of him?"

"Warm, outgoing." It was getting more difficult to answer.

"He gives that impression but it can't be so."

"Why not?" She groped for her empty cup on the floor and stood up. He followed suit.

The afternoon she met Mark had become touched with nostalgia in her memory and she didn't want it tampered with - in it lay the hopes she had when she took the job. Since then the English department had shown her forms of 'self-sufficiency' that made Mark's look more attractive. When you were tired of standing on your own two feet here you stood on someone else's. She'd already retired from politics and personalities and had a reputation for being hardworking, serious- minded and boring. Mark's personality had cast a misleading light. He seemed to like the people and dismiss the system. She found herself depending on the system and mistrusting the people. She was filled with admiration for a nature that in rejecting the system left itself wide open.

Bates hadn't gone away but joined her going upstairs. "Think what's involved," he said. She struggled to remember what they'd been saying. "Secure income and lifestyle, lots of varied contacts given up for what? Surely not so much a protest as a desperate act - and sudden."

"What makes you think it was sudden?"

"No one here had an inkling."

"That doesn't mean anything!"

"You can live a long while with the possibility of doing something desperate but the form it takes might come as a big surprise to yourself as well as everyone else. No one here had the faintest idea he was even interested in farming."

"Why should they? We don't know much about each other."

"Mark wasn't quite like that, seemed to make himself known and seemed such a part of all this, more than most of us - committed!"

"You were wrong, then."

"All of us? We were all wrong. It was like a slap in the face."

"To the system, not the people."

"Oh come on - a way of life exists because we give it our support. If it cripples us it's our own fault for taking it too seriously or not being interested enough in other things or not trying to change it. He made it seem more than most of us that the system had his and showed a scrupulousness in his responsibility to it most of us fell short of. That indicates something more than devotion to individuals. But putting that aside, when you remember the extreme nature of the change and that it affects himself and his family more than us you wonder where the violence really comes from and what it's really directed against."

She looked up. "What violence?" Her tone made her dissociation offensively clear and his manner became conciliatory, even intimate.

Opening her study door he said gently, "It's unlikely his whole family is subject to the same pressures as himself, but we'll see." He paused to let her in. "Ignorance of the business, the complete change, the insecurity - wouldn't you find it threatening?"

"Not the way you're suggesting. It might be exciting - a shared dream."

"You can be sure it's a dream - only a dreamer rejects

totally! And how would you describe someone who destroys an entire way of life?"

"Confident?"

There was something in his amused smile as he was leaving that suggested he may have found out something he wanted to know.

When her divorce had become known the more life-conscious members of the department had embarrassed and confused her with an uneasy personal touch. The usual rhythm disturbed, they seemed to be wondering if compassion or fellow-feeling would help and whether she had a chip on her shoulder or just wanted to forget it. She didn't know herself. For a while even the contacts she'd made through departmental business were put under strain. Her feelings were still too private and hurt too much. She doubted their ability and her own to relax into real contact. She'd been increasingly restless over the last few months and when one of the papers she wrote reviews for gave her a chance to write articles on subjects of topical interest she thought instantly of Mark's smallholding - escape, adventure, work in one package. She'd not looked closer until now and the idea Bates planted that Mark's decision was sudden seemed suddenly to fit with her own experience. She'd overheard some colleagues discussing Mark's general invitation when it had gone up on the noticeboard. Jackson had muttered something about places like that making you work yourself to death just to stay alive. Someone else said Mark had always been keen on symbols. It struck her that self-sufficiency, organic farming, a pollution-free life might sound very attractive to a passionate purist, if that's what he was. She found herself suddenly very excited at the visit and in a new way.

It was near the end of the Spring term and she felt tired and stale. She wouldn't wait. A preliminary Spring visit would be perfect and increase the scope of her article so she wrote to Mark suggesting it and in a friendly reply and handwriting so large it took up three sides of foolscap he asked her to stay as long as she liked, told her some other guests would be there and that he was touched and encouraged at the seriousness of her intentions for the article.

The last part of her journey was on foot. It had been raining and racing wisps of dark cloud increased an excitement she hadn't bargained for. The metal blue sky in the distance suggested further rain and she transferred her suitcase from hand to hand in an attempt to pick up speed - increasing it when she met a warm acrid smell from the ditches like wet dog fur. On the journey her excitement had been feeding exclusively on the scenery but it was now running like a fire with a prepared course.

The first glimpse of his house was through a gap in a crumbling six foot wall. A nineteenth century three-storied building, it stood just outside the village and was big enough to have housed a large family and servants. The approach was open - bare except for some overgrown rhododendrons and made bleak by a wide gravel drive. She knocked at the front door, got no answer and turned to the right. There was a boy facing her at the other end of the path bracing himself against a wooden fence. As she came closer she saw he had his arms threaded through some broken slats and that his preoccupied stare had already taken in her presence and forgotten it except for a shadow of pleasure at having an audience. He ignored her and she found herself waiting for him to be ready.

He jerked his arms further in and after a moment said

without looking at her, "I don't cry." The childishness brought back her presence of mind.

"You'll hurt yourself."

He drew out an arm to show some bleeding scratches and red pressure marks. "Feel it, feel my arm!"

"Are you one of Mark's sons?"

"Go on, feel it."

She didn't want to - something in his eyes made it look as if it were the preface to something even less funful but she wanted to co-operate and put her arm round it tentatively. She felt sinews and a small ball of muscle slipping about while he clenched and unclenched his fist.

"Where's your Dad?"

"You don't want my Dad. You gonna stay with that lot next door?"

"I thought it was all one house." She turned back immensely relieved but looked back to say "Thanks" at the last minute.

The other path led to what was originally the back door and it was open, but there was no-one in the kitchen. She took in the room excitedly - the size, long wooden shelves packed with stuff from floor to ceiling, enormous Welsh dresser against the furthest wall - an attractive smooth-planed refectory table with benches looking handmade, and the warmth from the black solid-fuel cooker that looked as if it might have come with the house. Someone came in behind her. She turned to see a boy rushing out and seconds later Mark stood with him in the doorway, arms stretched out in welcome.

"How lovely to see you!" He turned first, yanked off his boots on the edge of the step then came over, hands raised to take her in his arms. He changed his purpose when he saw her nervous expression and reached for her coat.

"Let's have this - why didn't you say when you'd arrive? One of us would have met you. Did you find us easily?"

He took her case and put it on the floor. Joan, overcome, having given up her coat picked up the case again but smiled, waiting to be taken to the others which he did, shepherding her to the hallway with his free arm round her waist.

Sheila'd heard Mark's voice and was halfway down the stairs offering her hand friendlily but with the slight tension towards a stranger that Joan expected and that made her speak for the first time:

"What a wonderful kitchen and house!" She couldn't have said anything to please her more.

"We like it," she said and blushed, turning back upstairs to show Joan her room. The happy embarrassment that made her sound almost offensive gave Joan back a more predictable world. It was pleasant and reassuring but at the same time disappointing. She suddenly realised she didn't want it, or rather that there was a conflict. Following Sheila's worn jeans up the stairs she found herself fighting an onslaught of dismay and exhaustion as if the tiring aspects of the journey had caught up with her. Sheila noticed it when she opened the door to her room and suggested she have a rest before coming down for some coffee.

Left alone she sat on her bed, took off her shoes and pushed the pillows up the wall, resting against them. The moments of panic, of wondering why she'd come here to stay with strangers eased off as she began to take in the room. It was so light it demanded attention. White everywhere, white walls, chest of drawers painted white and a white folk-weave counterpane. The three-legged stool in the corner looked not comfortable but invitingly home-made, smooth unvarnished wood good to touch. A plain blue bowl on the chest gave an unexpectedly refreshing vividness to it all and Joan perked up.

The same evening more guests arrived. They were a married couple who had visited before and were introduced by Mark as old friends but Sheila's pursed mouth and head tipped expressively to one side qualified it. Tom and Elizabeth Blake were in their early forties, a few years older than the Lewises, and moved about with the trained suppression of curiosity you might expect to see in a pair of healthy, energetic, unleashed but well-behaved dogs. She pushed the idea further - goodlooking, ears back, fur sleek inviting intimacy, eyes immediately responsive to affection and equally given over to exploration. The comparison came to mind more perhaps from the manner of the woman than the man though they were very much a pair and a first impression suggested considerable similarity in their responses.

Tom shook Joan's hand warmly and asked if she were going to become a permanent member of the household.

She shook her head. "Are you?"

"Semi-permanent at least. I'm on sabbattical but we've almost finished our book so it's a chance to help Mark and see what the life's like" - he lowered his voice and came close in - "I'm genuinely curious but can't see myself giving up my job. Mark understands, though I'm not sure Sheila does."

"What's your book about?"

He paused, reluctant, then told her: "Modern English novels." He looked blank as if not paying attention but Joan felt she was being observed.

She was a little put out. "I don't like many" came out almost touchily.

He grinned, put his arm under her elbow and asked her to come and meet his wife.

Bess, as he called her, was listening to Sheila and apparently concentrating on every word. She looked nervous, desirous of pleasing and being pleased and as if she were waiting eagerly for a pause in Sheila's flow to add something of her own but when Joan came up she turned to face her with an equal interest and except that the sudden blankness was absent her expectant look reminded Joan of Tom's. She felt that in both cases the expectation was friendly and the word 'playful' came to mind but she avoided further contact for the moment by asking Sheila if she could help with the supper.

The meal did all it was meant to. The company came together and relaxed. Adults and children sat at the long table with three opened bottles of Mark's strawberry wine and two bowls, one of hot beef stew one of rice, in the centre. The kitchen was hot and towards the end of the meal the Lewises' three sons, seated at the end of the table, made their presence felt. Leaning over excitedly they were grabbing and asking for more of everything, especially wine. To satisfy them Sheila took new bread from the oven and Joan identified the appetising smell that had been blending with the meal. She was already full but wanted it and when it was put on the table with strawberry jam couldn't resist it. Her lifelong thinnness had much to do with a low-level interest in food so this was a fairly rare experience and she found her excitement poaching in the enclosure she'd reserved over the years for spiritual matters. The bread was hot, the outer crust hard and crumbly, the inside soft, wheaty and faintly salty and the jam tasted like syruped fruit. When she surfaced the new responsiveness stayed with her and the group was transformed. Tom's full and handsome mouth was set off by his dark beard, Bess's eyes shone in a red face and Mark moved round the table with a wine bottle, his eyes brimming with the satisfaction he felt. Putting the bottle down, he cocked his leg over the bench and with a slight knock and push from his thigh moved Bess up to sit between her and his eldest son.

"This is wonderful," he said and stared into Bess's face, "I feel that the main objective is in sight. You're here for the rest of the year - by which time you'll be converted." His elated smile won the same from her. He ducked forward to grin at Tom who raised his glass in acknowledgment. "Everything we do here can, if we let it, be like a passion - a drive and excitement that never lets up." He turned back to her. "Everything we do - and it's all action - has a longterm as well as instant meaning. You can fail and go on failing until you feel more dispirited and depressed than you've ever felt and then when you least expect it succeed." Joan was slowly clueing into the fact that he was talking about farming. "You're challenged at every level and all the time and totally responsible for your survival. Failure isn't an accepted possibility. If you don't learn, if you don't see things as they are, you're done for. I didn't come into it without studying it but found I knew more about it than I thought. I knew monoculture was out, for instance. That's what I was getting away from - that and the persistence of the diseases that go with it - almost impossible to get rid of, my personal blight had already got out of hand - prescribed cures made it worse." The emotion and sententiousness kept them quiet. He pushed his plate away, cupped his head in his hands then looked up. "I'm tight - but because of you - all of you!" He looked at Sheila for approval and got it. "Joan's going to write about us," he said to Bess, "it might be just what we need. Dozens of people will be interested - some might come to see for themselves, some might stay."

Anxious at the delight in his face, scared at its vulnerability Joan said, "You can't expand too much, can you? Someone else lives next door."

Mark's hand dismissed the neighbours. "I'd like to think this house would be just one in a village we could build ourselves. This whole place is mine you know and the fourteen acres that go with it. The Selbys were tenants when I bought it but plan to go eventually. I couldn't bring them in with us."

"Why not?" Bess asked.

"Frank Selby despises my inefficiency as he sees it. When I first came he gave me some cynical advice after his fashion - useless to me. He farms seven acres, mostly salad crops for the towns nearby. He and his family have nothing to do with us." He'd floated off, staring at a few grains of rice swimming in spilt wine. Sheila got up to clear the table and Joan with her.

Joan was tender towards him in a way she'd not felt for so long she'd believed herself free of it. She hated being woken up and looking for relief found it in the youngest son. He was about three years old with an inviting plump belly poking out of jumper and trunks, touchy, intelligent with large expressive eyes that showed him precociously conscious of himself in relation to the rest of the world. He was more than usually interested in people over objects, the private playworld that buffered most infants being in short supply. She'd watched him at the table scanning faces and feeling the temperature of situations and seen the mixture of vulnerability and hunger for contact that exposed him, short-fused, to dozens of potentially emotional situations. As he came up to her, her hand went out but when he was in reach she had a moment's vision of him as a man - someone women would find irresistible - and suddenly tense with memories of her husband and the anger and anguish that went with them watched him recoil and drift towards his mother. Relieved, she rejected him but Sheila fobbed him off, leaving a gravy mark on his face and before she knew what she was doing she'd picked him up and kissed the other cheek. He was surprised and uncomfortable and struggled to be put down, making straight for Bess who was still at the table. He'd been fascinated by her during the meal. Joan had recognised his father's assiduous expression, the deliberateness towards someone whose attention he wanted.

There was a crash and a curse. The middle son, Claude, a heavy-faced lad of seven had been carrying too many plates to the sink. Peter the eldest, tight-faced, superior, echoing the cold rebuke in Mark's eyes, started to clear up the mess and Claude thumped him with both fists calling him a bugger. Mark got up, grabbed Claude by the arm and forced him out of the room. He came back alone and sat in his old place. Sheila paid only superficial attention - her face reflecting one or two responses she kept private, leaving involvement to Mark. When Claude didn't come back she looked dissatisfied and coming over to the Welsh dresser where Joan was pretending to put the salt away took it from her and did the job herself.

"This is a marvellous dresser" - Joan was defensive - "I've been having a good look at it."

Sheila brightened. "It took me months to find." Her hand ran over the wood. "I wanted an old one. Mark offered to make me one but I was holding out for something like the one I remembered at my aunt's when I was a girl. I got this at an auction. That too - " she pointed to her breadbin, chipped, cracked earthenware but large and a warm terra-cotta colour. Joan looked appreciative. "Shall I show you the hessian I got at the same time for curtains, lovely thick stuff, really cheap - natural colour but I don't know whether to leave it or dye it."

Joan nodded, pretending it hadn't been an immediate invitation and that she was interested in the coloured posters on the free wall of Rossetti-ish women in Salome-ish postures.

"They add a dash to the kitchen, don't they?"

Joan nodded again, noticing properly for the first time the long cotton skirt with swirling pattern Sheila was wearing for the evening. She looked at her face, it was long, features regular, skin already lined, but not unlike the poster. The hand she was stretching towards it was rough and stained and had hardworking fingernails that made Joan come suddenly to her defence in a non-existent battle.

In the pause they heard Mark telling the Blakes something about the children's guineapig. Tom, with his arm round Bess, was taking it all in.

"You've not been telling them about the guineapig!" Sheila went over to them. "What did you tell them?" Her tone suggested he'd have got it wrong. "It's my story. I found it." She turned to Bess. "It was Claude's pet. I found it dead in our copse. The fur was muddy and wet and when I lifted it water trickled out of its mouth. That's all we know."

"Well, how do you think it got that way?" Mark asked.

"I don't know any more that you do - kids playing with it and it fell in the pond I expect. They'd be too scared to own up."

"Can't guineapigs swim?" Tom asked.

"Claude could have reached it," Mark said, looking up scornfully. "There's only one way it *could* have happened."

"Only in *your* mind." Sheila picked up the dishcloth Claude had left on the table and cleaned up in front of him, every move an assault.

"Why won't you face facts?" he said quietly watching her hand. "You've said yourself you're afraid of him."

"Rubbish."

"Who?" Tom asked.

"Selby's youngest. His father's the real villain of course. He's got his three kids still living with them even though the other two are grown up. The girl's in her late twenties, the second a lad a few years younger - that's Jim. David is only eleven. Jim's a near halfwit, grins and twitches all the time - seems harmless enough but not so the youngest. He's physically strong and skinny, resembles Jim in the face but that's all. He's even precocious in ways that make me uncomfortable."

Joan moved closer. Sheila broke in again: "You've no right to talk like that, he's only a child." The guests looked at her, half approving the sentiment while annoyed at the interruption. "Makes *you* uncomfortable! What about him? If your face shows your feelings every time you go near him it's not surprising."

"You don't feel easy with him yourself." Mark wanted it finished.

"I treat him like any other kid. He's got his problems. His dad's difficult. I don't expect to feel easy with everyone."

Bess got up from the table and finding Simon still near picked him up and carried him to the sink where she was going to start the washing up. Sheila followed.

"Mark told me you couldn't bear the Selbys," Bess said.

"He had no right to."

"But is it true?"

"I treat them as I would anyone else." She rolled up her sleeves and filled the sink with water.

2

The following morning when Joan found Mark mending some wire netting she found him changed. He was preventing the free-range hens from ranging anywhere but in the orchard where he'd built a henhouse. It was chilly, his lips had a mauve look in spite of his bright cheeks and she felt that if she were to reach him now it would have to be through his work. She offered help and he said it was a one person job. She watched the hens, forty or more fat confident-looking Rhode Island Reds eyeing her with a sharper, more objective curiosity than she eyed them. Finding her empty-handed they treated her as a tree stump till she moved. As sparing of words as he could be Mark answered her questions explaining that when he started he let them go anywhere on the farm but the egg loss had been too great and he'd penned them in.

"They laid their eggs under hedges, in the barn, anywhere, some were smashed, others bad when we found them and I lost some of the hens to foxes." He looked at them with an affectionate protectivity that made Joan see their fatness and confidence in a new light.

She persisted with questions, noticing that some of the evasiveness was caused by anxiety which he kept at bay with the nervous agility of an expert.

"We need people here, permanently I mean, there's too much work for Sheila and myself. A third of the seven acres we farm gets left fallow" - with a sudden smile - "the word does something for me. Instead of fretting I feel as the rich must with idle money accumulating interest in the bank - it's doing nothing at the moment but I'm getting richer by the day." He said he'd get the North field planted this year with the Blakes' help but if they didn't stay he still had contacts at the university, part-time help was better than nothing and he wasn't entirely dependent on that - he had schemes for buying it if all else failed. Joan began to relax and admire the mixture of practicality and dreams the move had originally suggested - but the information was hard won. He'd already worked several hours when she found him, though it wasn't tiredness she was conscious of. At the end of half an hour in which she followed him from the orchard to the barn she had only an outline notion of what he'd achieved and hoped for but a detailed awareness that his passion to get away from people this morning was as strong as his lust for them last night.

She wandered about afterwards taking in the home acre. The laurel hedges she'd seen from her window enclosed a neglected rose garden and shrubbery. About six feet high they boxed in four square rosebeds and a semicircle of shrubs, grass paths and a small lawn, all reached through one wooden gate fixed open with a brick. Last year's weeds had died down at the foot of the roses but were beginning to mass together and send new growth into the open spaces. Sodden brown undeveloped rosebuds overtopped new shoots and Joan was just beginning to wonder if she should offer to do some pruning when Bess came into the garden. At first she didn't notice Joan but hung around at the entrance with a look of relief before moving over to the shrubs. She fingered the new leaves, smelt the flowering currant and parting the branches looked for nests. Her movements were purposeful and her absorption almost complete but Joan felt she was mentally elsewhere. She moved closer, still not seeing Joan.

"Are you going to work here?" Joan asked.

Bess jumped so hard it produced an echo in Joan that broke through her reserve. "They won't think it necessary," she said grinning, "perhaps we could offer to do the whole of it - just tidy it up in one day - what do you think?"

"All of it?" Joan didn't fancy the idea of working flat out towards a fixed objective within a fixed time.

"Well, if we only take a day perhaps they'll think it worth it - after all they haven't ploughed it up or anything."

"There's plenty of ground they can't use without destroying this." Joan looked hurt.

"Have you seen the pond and stream further down?"

She followed Bess past the yard, cowshed, greenhouse, pasture on one side and copse on the other till they came to it - larger than she'd expected - hidden from the house and almost entirely covered by waterlilies. The water looked black and gave the impression of depth, the stone edge was buried under overhanging grass and was only visible in patches under woody shrubs competing with brambles. The outer limit of what was once a garden. The size, the remnants of design, the copse insisted on the presence of another lifestyle that gave Joan a new and uncomfortable view of the enterprise. Why this place? There must have been cheaper.

"I wouldn't like to undertake that lot," she said looking at the shrubs.

"No, it looks hopeless - but the other isn't - shall we offer?"

The idea of an objective suddenly became appealing. "We'll never get it finished!"

Bess had been right and Sheila wasn't enthusiastic, suggesting instead a number of jobs ranging from milling to mucking out the pig but Bess was gently and plausibly inflexible. A way of sweating herself in, she said, of limbering up with the kind of work she'd done before. Sheila grudgingly accepted the sideways approach though in fact for Bess there was considerably more to it. Clearing the garden was a completable objective, wasn't fraught with responsibility, wasn't mucky and smelly, and offered a visual reward, her sense of accomplishment wouldn't be destroyed next minute and she wouldn't be asked to do a dozen other jobs after the first was finished. Her objection to variety that might in fact be less tiring was that it lost another objective - the build up of excitement not achievable if the work was turned into chores. To end the day feeling she'd worked hard and usefully wasn't enough. Mark had said he was refreshed by a constant change of activity and the sense of continuity that came with it but she was exhausted by it, missing the emotional knitting together of an immediate objective. She'd come to this place because Tom wanted to and though fascinated by Mark and his aims knew that for her the stay would be difficult.

She brought a hoe, fork and shears from the toolshed, determined to make her own way. Joan brought secateurs, eased her fingers into some leather town-gloves and started pruning. At the first rosebed Bess dropped her tools, keeping the hoe, and started jabbing abstractedly in front of her. The ground was hard and grassy and showed no change. She stepped up the effort, saying "It's crazy to have bought this place." Joan tensed, watching her peck at a clump. "A denial of his conscious motives." Silence. "Over-grandiose for someone who wants the 'real thing' in everything."

"I can see why anyone would prefer it if it was going cheap."

"But it wasn't. Mark and Sheila were hooked on the place. Her family's well-off and when her grandmother left her £40,000 they added the bit Mark had in the bank and bought it. They sank everything but a little to see them through the first couple of years."

"I thought they were self-sufficient."

"How could they be, they've only just started. They run a landrover, use electricity, pay rates, they're not into making their own clothes with their own wool yet - they've got to have some money. If their plans come off and they get enough people to work the land they can sell the surplus off for cash, like a monastery. Otherwise it would mean specialising, I should think - chemical fertiliser - expensive machinery - some degree of competition anyway, which isn't what he wants."

"No."

"Did you know it was to be done with a horse-drawn plough?"

Joan said nothing.

"Several were interested but dropped out at the last minute. Mark's setting some store by your articles."

"Only one. I hope it does him some good." She stopped pruning and stared at Bess anxiously. "I hope he isn't depending on a big response to it."

"People will know he's there if they want him. It might give a push to one or two."

"I wouldn't want to do that. It'll only be an informative article."

"You just said you hoped it would do him some good."

"I hope it does - but I wouldn't want to be responsible for anyone's decision."

Bess looked at her worried face. "If you're that worried why write? Nobody'll read it if it's not interesting; if it is you'll have to have been interested yourself and since you can't be interested in everything equally or see everything that's involved it'll have a bias. If you're not willing to trust your readers to know that and make up their own minds you shouldn't go into print."

Joan had a surprised smile. "There are degrees, aren't there? You can do your best not to persuade anyone to anything - I suppose I'm not that anxious." She suddenly felt friendly, even confiding. "I know it's the reason I don't write books. I don't scare myself with imagining books have any other effect than thought-sharing but they strike me as too permanent even for a few years. I don't like the idea that they stand as delegates for the author. I'd feel cornered, probably disown everything as belonging to a former or marginal self."

Bess waited for more but that was it and Joan moved off to the shrubbery. She turned back to the rosebed but forgot the hoe and began snipping off old rose growth at a speed that to Joan suggested accidents. Joan had settled into a thoughtful rhythm and the snipping unnerved her. Anxious over Bess's shoots she became fussy about her own. Bess's snipping was followed by a quick, intense, unrhythmical activity with the spade and this by straddling and kneeling, an occasional curse and a not too slow emergence of three piles of weeds on the path. She left huge quantities of loam attached to the roots, but more disturbing than that was the speed with which her particular bed was taking on a look of parklike tidiness. Kept from the steady rhythm of her own work style Joan found herself disapproving of the way Bess sacrificed everything to quick aesthetic satisfaction. She was half inclined to offer help to slow her down - offer to beat some of the loam back on to the flowerbed. Bess's way of bringing air and light was by assault like a storm. Ashamed at her irritation and criticism, the only thing she could do was slow herself in compensation. The harder Bess worked the slower Joan did.

The indirect suggestion had no effect whatever on Bess who was unaware of anything outside the circle of her activity, but it gave Joan a sense of total defeat when she compared what they'd both done before going into lunch. Glad to get away she felt guilty now at not having kept up her end of the bargain and wondered if Bess would be disappointed or annoyed.

Bess came in late, having made herself later by a lengthy and meticulous scrubbing of hands and fingernails. She looked redfaced, satisfied, but with ominous white marks round the sides of her nose reaching to the corners of her mouth. Joan's hope that the slightly ill look might be hunger seemed justified when having pushed in next to Tom and nuzzled his shoulder briefly Bess set about her macaroni cheese with a relish she envied.

Anxiety gone Joan looked round the table, pleased again. It seemed she was friendlily accepted on whatever terms she chose. This in itself was a rare pleasure. Even rarer was the complete freedom it gave to take in an assortment of faces that interested her. Each made its own claim and she couldn't remember when she'd last felt so unaware of herself in relation to others and at the same time so sharply aware of her responses to their words and actions. This in spite of the fact that the meal was on the whole a silent one. There was a great quantity of food but this time its effect increased tiredness. It didn't apply to Mark and Sheila who didn't eat much - they were quiet because it wasn't an occasion, just a pause. There was a noisy insularity about the clack of knives and forks on plates.

In Tom's expression when he left the table rosy and relaxed there was evidence he'd changed gear. A touch of defensiveness and obstinacy in his manner as he caught him up at the door prepared Mark.

"Do you mind if I carry on with my work this afternoon?"

"Not at all." They went to the large room across the hall that was full of battered furniture. Mark leant back in an armchair, tried to get comfortable and giving up sat upright on the edge with his legs wide open as if on a stool. "How's it coming along?"

"So so. We wish we had a free hand." He paused to gauge Mark's interest and see if it were worth embarking on the irritations and anxieties close to his heart, especially as he wasn't sure of Mark's tastes. "It's this business of giving it a sociological and comparative slant. Generalisations so big they're meaningless or associated scraps so small they're worthless. We want to write about a few modern novels from a particular standpoint not about a standpoint with reference to novels."

Mark looked as if he were listening.

"We didn't want to write the damned thing in the first place -did it because the publishers wouldn't take the one we'd just written. They liked our style and this was a commission with a small downpayment, but you can't write to order and against the grain. What we're up against is the fashion for seeing everything from okay intellectual platforms. On the one side there's a demand for the kind of moral slant journalists and reviewers call 'committed,' which excuses banality and insensitivity for the sake of the novel's social or political pretensions, on the other a soul-destroying caution leaving a gap most academics fill with knowledgeable self-display."

Mark sat with his head down, arms resting on his thighs, hands dangling between his legs - impossible for Tom to interpret. It increased his need for a readable response.

"You see how you're trapped if you're excited by literature? The academic way out has become so pernicious that it's easier to be condemned for not having read enough contemporary criticism than for a superficial reading of the novel. A friend said jokingly, 'I don't have time to read the books, I spend all my time reading the articles.' What's more, having an excited response leaves you open to charges of being snooty or hard. It's ungentlemanly to be tough on a novel that shows an informed concern with social conditions, just because it's unthought, unfelt and pretentious. It's perfectly okay though to approach any work, good or bad, with a gimmick slant. 'Anal Eroticism in Paradise Lost' would be taken on like a shot.... They imagine informed impartiality can be established by reference to an assortment of other works and ideological standpoints. A baggy argument that fits only where it accidentally touches doesn't seem to bother them. A swamp of references vouchsafes the author's seriousmindedness, though what he's supposed to be seriousminded about other than promotion is anyone's guess. It makes the novels both a hunting and a parade ground and as novels they cease to exist. An interest in trying to work out a little of any good novel's unique relation to life seems naive, unoriginal, even unnecessary. Under the banner of information you can offer a bibliography of circumambient ideas but you can't, under the banner of involvement, offer a personal reading. Surely if some of that reading went over old ground, as it must, an eager lay-reader might be grateful for the inclusion of his own response just so long as something illuminating was added, but committing your own responsiveness to paper is out of favour for obvious reasons - most of us don't want others to know how little of it there is. Much safer to make a bid for approval among like minds in a theatre closed to the public. In my opinion the snobbish side of it involves the usual self-interest. If you belong to a club and want to stay in it, it's only the opinion of the members that counts. Closed ranks in education are as powerful as anywhere else. I still remember my amazement when a reviewer ran down Jane Austen for snobbery because she'd shown moods of intolerance in her letters. The point picked on was that she'd mentioned bad breath in the case of some visitors she'd disliked. They happened to be from a lower class. I could just as easily say it was the reviewer's snobbery that saw 'class' as everything and Jane Austen's lack of it that had seen them as unpleasant people. Using that to back an argument that she didn't have a wide enough social conscience was incredible. They want it all ways, you see. Bad breath in criticism now comes from writers trying to reach a wider market. You can be caught out in a couple of sins at the same time - a snobbish preference for good books aimed at a vulgar market."

"You make it sound as if all current criticism's self-serving or hypocritical." Mark didn't lift his head.

"No, it just looks that way." Mark's supportive smile as he got up did its best but Tom sensed enough reservation to put his hand out. "You know it's just irritability, don't you? Of course those approaches have their uses. I'm letting off steam against fashions that will let pass any old shit if it's packaged right and gets nervous if it isn't. The only way round, it seems, is to have a wellkown name that's already created its own fashion - and how do you do that without getting published?"

Mark felt guilty at his resistance, moved by the opennness he couldn't resist. There was something in Tom that went, in his mind, with the heavy walk and black beard and now, with his predispositions under attack, he wondered if he'd paid enough attention to its moral significance. 'Arrogant bigot!' stuck in his mental throat. He liked Tom and envied some aspects of his nature.

"I understand, I do. I've kept away from the business so far except for a few essays. I was shocked that you seemed to dismiss so much." It wasn't enough. To come over to his side even further he added: "I see the things you get angry with in a different light. Most of us struggle to be fair - writing isn't easy. We try to put down the bits we see as interestingly as possible. Surely the approach you're suspicious of shows a lack of self-assurance about expressing a personal response because we're uncertain it'll be fresh enough not to bore. The exploration of what you see as marginal factors, the hesitancy, seem to me good things, a real humility."

"Ideally it might be, though I'm not convinced, but as soon as we open our mouths the unideal takes over. Funk and showing off take up most of our energy, hard work - and by that I *don't* mean research but an expanding responsiveness - the least. It's what *actually* happens that irritates."

"We're all human," Mark smiled.

"Don't I know it, it's just that I don't see why one way of expressing it should be preferable to another, there's room for the lot!"

He saw that Tom wanted his good humour as much as he wanted to give it and surprised himself with his next urge to prove it. "Better not let Sheila hear you. She thinks certain attitudes are 'out' and she's a stickler."

"Oh, Sheila!" Tom looked happily reassured as if this were a 'joke' conclusion. Mark blushed, resisted the brief friendly pressure of Tom's hand on his shoulder and went back to the kitchen.

Slipping his arms round his wife's waist he asked her if she wanted help. Sheila was mesmerised by her work routine and whisked herself away, reaching for a tea-towel and shoving it in his hand. Flushed, masterful, she was in the world they'd agreed to, reminding him of his part in it and confident of his approval. Cheated, he approved. She might live in it as if it were a dream but it was real and he envied her. A drama restricted to the self, a private elation and disappointment - what else was there when you were living up to a self-imposed challenge? But he always needed the support of a larger group and needed their co-operation. Practising an ideal before the audience of yourself wasn't enough. Now and then he wondered if the idea they'd followed would turn out to be another ideological trap, wondered if any bid for more life could possibly be achieved by less - but others would come, dozens of them. He finished off the cutlery and went out to work.

Later in the day Sheila summoned them all to yoga. Both the Lewises were skilled in the physical exercises - the patient twisting, knotting, stretching and curving had, on the Blakes' previous stay, been a pleasure to watch - but only Sheila believed in the spiritual ones. They remembered her meditation on a stool, deep breathing at the most unlikely moments and that Bess had been chided for persistent curiosity about their personal 'notes'. Tonight Mark and Sheila said it was to be fun for all. Joan wouldn't join in, she'd learn more by watching she said and stuck to her point in spite of Sheila's claims that there was nothing to learn, "no competition, you just do what you can and feel better."

Bess, keen to join in the fun, threw herself into it a little too wholeheartedly and was reminded she was missing the point if she thought it was all working towards a quick sweat and a sigh of relief afterwards. She slowed down her twists, changed her snorts to a steady exhalation through one nostril after another and seriously attempted to balance her legs in an open scissors position in the air with her shoulders as pivot. The weight of her bottom made it difficult to keep her legs in the air without breaking her neck and the comic subversion caught from her by Tom reached Sheila and finally Mark who aware of the beauty and skill of his own actions was more reluctant to indulge her horsing around, not wanting the intimacy of these collective acts to be destroyed. He did the exercises solely as exercises but added his own metaphysic, he needed the sense of harmony with the others and the more than physical balance to be had from the mixture of self-surrender and self-control demanded by the slowness. But the relaxed deliberateness that did so much for him was entirely alien to Bess who felt that the self-suppression, or sedation in her case, that was necessary to do it naturally and beneficially was impossible. The idea that communal yoga must be a romp to be meaningful was ineradicable. In the end she was intolerant. Mark displayed his 'bows' and 'cobras' beautifully but Bess was irritated and disappointed. His handsome body was passive. His shape, health, flexibility suggested a spontaneous energy that the movements denied. That, it seemed, was one of the objectives. In him the removal or recircuiting of that energy was ugly. At his most anxious to please and invite he was most mastered and his body dead, a vehicle he took natural pride in keeping in good order.

Having decided that his appeal for generalised intimacy was a sad concomitant of the success of the mastery, she was shocked at the warmth and deliberateness of his hand when he put it on her thigh to help her tuck her foot in her groin. She was perched precariously on the other foot and tottered, achieving the right position only briefly and while his hands darted affectionately at the ready. She would have liked to leave to practise a private yoga on her responses but it was suppertime and Sheila asked for help in getting a quick meal because she had a surprise for them.

The surprise turned out to be a barn dance that was going to be held in the agricultural college a few miles away. In the flurry of affairs, preparing food, eating, getting the children ready and fetching babysitters Bess had no time to get herself in order but enough for tension and alarm. She fetched mugs that the children had left in the sitting room and saw Mark leaning over Joan talking intently to her, his face thrust down a few inches from hers. The fraction of a glance fixed the scene that she read compulsively while losing her effectiveness about the house. His body only from the waist upwards inclined towards her, the stiffness of the rest suggested tension and withholding. A fleeting impression of a false offer - tantalisation. In a flash of anger she saw it as narcissistic, a helpless craving for intimacy and admiration using sex as bait. Seen in time! - she determined to protect herself from the havoc he might work with her feelings while he was reassuring his own, and she was stiffly on guard when he came into the kitchen later dressed for the dance. In tight jeans and close-fitting open-necked shirt he was holding a leather jacket by a forefinger over his shoulder, and she interpreted dress and good looks alike as gratuitous assault.

Later, getting ready upstairs, she relaxed. Tom was with her. They kissed and cuddled to make up for the day's separation and she said what she thought of Mark. Tom was interested as always in whatever interested her and the intimacy gave him alternative checks on her. He suggested that what she saw in the scene with Joan was really nervous shyness and an eager but conventional desire to please. She was briefly disappointed then relieved and having played down her responsiveness by confessing it in generalities was more than ready to see Mark in this light and followed Tom happily downstairs leaping the last three as a foretaste of things to come.

Downstairs they were having a sherry before going. At first Bess refused one, not wanting a muzziness to spoil her excitement but later, seeing the others grow expansive, she asked for it and followed Mark to the kitchen in silence, standing in silence while he poured it. He was aware of her estrangement, brought the wine as if to speak of it but shied, leaving her to read his eyes. Search, question, with a certain pain at her coolness and stiffness - but she saw the directness and intensity as a personal characteristic like a fast walk, no more. She allowed herself to respond cautiously to the point he was making in holding on to the glass long enough to contact her fingers. He was released. "I like your skirt," he said and touched it briefly. Stiffening and turning away she carried her glass back to the others, head full of invective - 'lump of self, indiscriminate sod!' - but the sherry worked and so did the next that she fetched herself.

When they reached the college after a chilly journey in Mark's old landrover the dance was in full swing. The loud music, tables full of half-drunk beer pushed up against the walls, coats and sweaters booking chairs and the floor packed with dancers left them standing, waiting to see where there was space. The two men eyed the bar in the far corner assessing their chances of bringing back full glasses. Bess looked for an opportunity to join the dance and took Tom's hand but couldn't hear the caller's instructions. Sheila and Joan stood back.

In the car Sheila'd told them all how fond she was of "dance" and while explaining to Joan, who'd never been to a barn dance, how free and communal it was and how shyness and a sense of incompetence was irrelevant had managed, with friendly advice on how to "strip-the willow" and place your feet when swung, to fill her with such dread that she was standing now white, tense and deafened by the noise. She stared at the dust and the furious, barging musical activity - then it suddenly stopped. Laughing, sweaty dancers took their places at the tables. When their group was among the few left standing they found three spare chairs and took them to the table with most room, which was nearest the band. The women settled, Bess watching the band closely for the next dance, the men fetched drinks. On the fiddle a ginger-haired youth with red-gold sideboards gave a couple of bars' excited tuning, someone was exchanging jokes with the accordion player, a boosy laugh and simultaneous lifting of full pints and the joker came forward. The caller, tall, lean, middle-aged, put down his pint to test the microphone, kicked the lead to one side and set up an ear-cracking racket over the speakers, then bringing the mike to chest level stuck out his foot. A display of jeans, plaid shirt, scarf and toggle, a flick of his black hair and he announced "The Cumberland Reel."

Bess and Tom were on the floor in an instant, Mark and Sheila followed when Joan refused his offer. The caller shouted for more pairs to fill up the sets and the practice started. The groups, noisy and part-drunk, only half heard his only half-articulate instructions - these he mixed up and was corrected by knowledgeable dancers. Catcalls and laughter followed by varieties of happy incompetence, and the steps were suddenly concluded. The music started in earnest. The dancers warmed up - responses varying from self-conscious to reckless - through the 'stars' and the giggling riot of the 'baskets' to that moment in the beating, rhythmic, irresistible music when opposite pairs took their partners in a grip and hurled sideways across the group passing each other and flying out of the confines of the set. Stopped by an oncoming pair they were turned by the music back to their places. Energy released, it flooded into the reformation of the 'stars' where two couples pacing round in a circle, first in one direction then in the other, four arms at head level, hands at the hub waited, resting, before clutching each other round waists and shoulders to whirl in the 'basket.' Turning as fast as the music would let them men hoisted women off the ground. Flying legs, shoes in the air, shrieks of laughter mixed with delight, organised chaos changed by the music drove them to separate, clapping and waiting for another chance to break out of the set.

When the music stopped the dancers wanted more, Bess wanted more. The pace was right, the patterns were right. She couldn't wait to be lifted and whirled with her arms round, clutching the shoulders of two men. With the music dictating the change in her needs all sense of constraint was gone.

When it was finished the second time the dancers were hot and their throats full of dust and were glad to get back to their drinks. Bess and Tom were so refreshed it took time to realise Sheila and Mark hadn't felt the same but before they could ask them why, the music had started and again the Blakes were first on the floor. They danced continuously for more than an hour. Released by action and a chain of partners Bess was given up to hot sweaty faces, slipping spectacles, wet edges of hair, damp moustaches and grabbing arms, and drugged by the smell of their sweat concentrated little on the steps, dancing poorly.

Mark was her partner once or twice but she danced with him for a short time often, clutching him freely and enjoying it openly. He lost his stiffness and looked out for her, judging how far down the chain she was and the likelihood of reaching her before the dance was over. He was freer still when Joan reluctantly accepted his offer of a dance that he promised would be simple. Away from Sheila's immediate influence, freed and restricted by impersonal sound, he let himself go. When he swung with Bess or took her in an elbow link he gripped her hard and forced her to recognise him as separate from the others and when in answer she squeezed his hand he replied immediately with his own. A leap of exhilaration before they parted lost them their steps and confused their next moves leaving them to be rescued by fresh partners.

After the interval Bess noticed a change in Mark, a coldness that she related to herself. Disappointed and with a sense of shame she fought as unwarranted, she adopted a cooler manner herself but felt cheated by it of other pleasures so she partnered him, when she had to, passively - a moment's vacuum before others filled the space.

In a gap between dances Sheila's face announced trouble. Her eyes dark with anger, expression resentful she prompted in Bess a spasm of guilt that erupted in her question: "What's the matter, is anything wrong?"

"Is anything right, you might ask." She made a gesture

that included Mark. "This is appalling - we're thinking of leaving."

Bess said nothing but stared. Joan saw that Sheila, absorbed in her outrage, was going to confuse her further. "Sheila thinks the caller's bad. He gets the steps mixed up apparently, and you can't hear him."

"Oh, is that all? He's tight. So's everyone else."

"What do you mean, 'is that all?' Isn't that all we're here for? If he can't do his job properly he shouldn't be doing it."

"We're dancing."

"Call this dancing?"

Bess shrugged. "Why not? More accuracy - more selfconsciousness, less fun."

"Why should it be? Do you only get fun from things done sloppily? It's incompetence. He's let them fool around because he doesn't know his job."

"He's drunk and they are - he couldn't stop them. All that would happen is more people would be sitting at tables drinking and fewer dancing, only the sober and skilful would be on the floor."

"What else?" Sheila's incredulity triggered off Mark's support:

"It *is* a shambles." He felt he'd moved in with a conciliatory and incontrovertible judgment and was hurt by Bess's look.

She took Tom's arm and spoke to him: "If I ask around a bit I'm sure we can find someone to give us a lift back."

"You're keen to stay on?" Faced with a situation he felt he had no part in Tom was amenable to anything and was surprised at Bess's resistance. Joan hadn't been enjoying herself and if the other two felt like that it was alright with him but there was Bess nodding fiercely in answer.

Disappointment and anger drove her to the nearest table

and on to the next until she'd found a party that were going their way and would take them back. She came back with her new arrangements fixed. There was a moment of tension between the two women. Sheila having lost the lead justified her judgment at length. Bess having freed herself listened and agreed.

3

Joan lay in bed for a while the following morning dismissing the sounds of activity from downstairs and the pounding feet and childish shouts from the passage outside her door. The warmth of the bed and the room's bare calm had a stronger pull. She'd been puzzled by the tensions of the previous evening, not her own but the others, and afterwards at home with Sheila and Mark had enjoyed herself much more. Within an hour she'd almost forgotten the dance. Sheila'd enlisted her critical support on the way back and some elderberry wine and hot roll and butter had done the rest.

Getting up late she worked hard to make up for it and finding Mark alone for a while in the sitting room made enquiries for her article as if offering a double duty. She asked him how things were working out financially, whether they had hopes of becoming completely self-supporting and whether they might in time show a profit. This time he was ready and talked of problems of wastage he hadn't mastered, about the pig he'd bought to use up the surplus milk and the numberless mistakes he'd made in other areas that still distressed him. He argued with and qualified the idea of profit. If the commune continuously expanded as he hoped there would never be one. In the early stages they'd sell enough surplus to buy what they couldn't provide for themselves and when they'd built their own dynamo, made their own clothes and turned entirely to horse transport all the profits would be ploughed back into enlarging the commune - building more places and buying more land. He insisted he'd never specialise for a quick profit and faster growth:

"I've not left teaching to become a farmer. I want independence and association, or rather in association - in a small enough compass to feel a natural, not a 'moral' responsibility. A difficult balance. And I want a balance of activities - my own diversity answered by a diversity of action including intellectual action but with that reduced to its proper status. Almost all needs are potentially answerable as they arise if the circumstances are right - a natural order and a natural control." He talked of his passion for dolphins and the freedom implicit in their social behaviour. Their line of development was backed, he said, by a very high and co-operative intelligence that made them self-adapting, not adaptors of others or the outer world. It meant the volitions prompting it must be primarily outgoing and quite unlike the aspirations of an ego-centralised humanity - and something close to this was above all what he wanted from his commune. "I can only speak for myself, so answering questions about aims and achievements is difficult. The answer closest to the truth for me would be that in rejecting the usual concepts of achievement and most of all of definition - that is of myself, my aims and ambitions, all of which could change by the moment - I feel I stand some chance of tasting the freedoms of the dolphins' kind of adaptation. It's what I most want and seems to come hardest. This way of living forces my hand. I can't give you anything more specific. Being at the mercy of what happens here I haven't any shaped objectives. I don't want to sacrifice overall change for nervous specificness and lose everything - I already have a new and constructive as opposed to destructive relationship with my environment. All the paths opened up by both the commune and the self-sufficient way of life must stay open."

Joan had more than she bargained for. It both interested and distanced her. The personalised variation of old arguments came over with a cold passion that made her more fascinated by the man than his ideas and when he saw something lacking in her response he decided to let himself go. This time while he was speaking she was struck by what she'd heard many times before but now with the force of a revelation. Even failure, it seemed, and in a sense he was failing now, was convertible by a passion for the route.

"Being on the verge of disaster is essential to success. You're forced to give everything you've got, which means the struggle against physical odds holds the centre, with the moral/emotional ones leading off - they hold their proper place as a result, not minimised but changed and qualified. Most of our energy has to be put into answering our deepest selfish needs for staying alive wherever we are, and here this is at the same time directed largely outside the specifically human world and its values. The inner battles shade off. You achieve new and less personal perspectives."

"You mean it gives you a sense of proportion."

"It changes the proportion. It's one of the reasons why successive failures on a small scale can even be valuable. When you're personally and immediately responsible for your own and others' existence a crop failure is more than bad management, it's deprivation, physical and emotional, and even if you can put up with it yourself you feel the kick-back immediately and personally through them. You start again. Forced to. Take new risks and learn from the results, bearing all the responsibility while at the mercy of forces predominantly unrelated to your private needs. In this last respect no different from any other way of life, you'll think, but the really important thing is that success is related to the laws of the natural not the human world. That's where the freedom lies. To me, so far, that's been the revelation. There are new ingredients in this success, which is still competitive but not with people. Manual jobs I've succeeded in after endless failures have given me an unqualified sense of achievement more exhilarating and intense than I've ever felt before. In the beginning everything was an exercise in failure punctuated with sudden, almost unexpected, amazingly releasing success. Challenges in this world are pure, your joy in success pure and you're freed as a result. Here regular failure must become emotionally unimportant, endemic. The blind necessity to repeat until you succeed is all that counts - you can't back out."

Captured but still alienated Joan fell for the passion and some of its purposes while worrying about the sense of isolation coming from so many "associative" ideals. And the quest for purity looked strange in the light of his need for dolphin-like flexibility and being shaped by what was. He'd mentioned earlier that financial insecurity still scared Sheila, and Joan could see why. On the other hand the place itself represented an investment and from Mark's point of view that would certainly be an impediment. There was finally no "blind necessity" except what was dictated by his nature. Perhaps new ways of life were born like this - a universal imbalance spotted first and responded to hardest by neurosis. She hadn't expected to feel excited by some of the possibilities that excited him.

Later in the week Mark became inaccessible again. One day she didn't see him at all and the following morning she found Sheila in the kitchen, tense and pale with what looked like the residue of anger. Non-committal formality in answer to questions about the others reached its purest when Sheila gave her Mark's whereabouts. He'd walked into town about an hour ago taking the short cut.

This Spring morning - brilliantly clear and windy - had been too much for him. In spite of suggestions he go by car at least and get back sooner, he'd gone on foot, finally shrugging off the pressures Sheila'd put on him to stay. He conducted his business successfully - came to an understanding with two new shopkeepers interested in buying his free-range eggs, and bought a scythe. The successful outcome freed him. He liked Corfax - the town was jostled by hills and huddled round streams.

In the streets, looking up at small open bedroom windows with curtains blowing out he had the feeling he'd had many times before of their being almost low enough to walk into, but the keeping outside and glancing in (to the lower ones at least) excited him. As a guest he'd have been defeated. Eager curiosity was always seen as a threat. He got closer imaginatively. The rooms were all small, light in patches, but with a glimpse of carpet could explode into life. A sense of danger and rewards filled him with anticipation. New life. The commune was everything. At last there'd be no artificial barriers, no rules of association. New people to explore at close quarters, reassurance coming from endlessly changing contact and identification, not one or two dependencies. As a result less defensiveness and greater intimacy. Only confined relationships threatened.

From the main street he looked up at the ruined castle dominating the town from a hilltop, a fortress commanding a gap in a long range of hills stretching far inland and to the sea in the other direction. Climbing the seaward ridge from a footpath by one of the cottages he wanted the whole lot in view - castle, town, his own land, the hills and a sense of sea and heath beyond - but by halfway the feeling of power and achievement had changed. He was tired and stopped to look down at a landscape of grass and sheep, when from the corner of a field an upright animal strode with geometric accuracy diagonally across it. He turned his back, continuing the climb, and reached the top sweating, to face a second ridge. Bald-faced, furless, wrapped, he saw it again, this time outlined on the crest and riding on another animal's back. Panic and disgust laid him on the grass. People, himself, alien, finite-purposed, without contact or conception of it, dangerous, unassociative, concept-driven, ego-motivated - he turned his face down, sealing body to earth on a sloping world.

At home he kept away from the house as much as he could until he was thickened by work and isolation and longed for contact. After a few days' uncompromising separateness his family were resentful of the sudden demand for affection, so he looked for it where he thought he could find it. Bess's responsiveness seemed close to his own, but working for, not against her. It looked as if there was warmth, a capacity for love and a separateness - all of which he feared and longed for. To be near but not too close became a temporary objective. It was essential not to get too close. Keeping a balance, keeping involved, keeping things changing and alive without an integrating passion, sexual or ideological, meant militant self-watchfulness - a living tension that if sustained promised the world. He spent the day working with or close to Tom and Bess, not speaking much but relying on her quick response to what was wanted. She gave him, in her enjoyment of their clumsy work-conversation or his persistent but physically close silences, the attention and affection he needed.

To Joan, Bess and Tom seemed an inviolable unit when they were working together. Coming up to them planting out seedlings she saw them fresh, almost exhilarating, bending and crouching with a rhythmic ease quite different from Bess's gardening method, and it made her feel obtrusive, even unable to say hello as she passed. It was a relief to be working with Sheila who was private but in a businesslike way and gave unfussy advice. Just the same she was glad to have the afternoon off. One of the perks of being a newcomer was to spend most of them relaxing or at least in an upright position.

She'd offered to make beds and tidy up and found herself alone in the house and free to explore. There were three unused bedrooms and she opened one of the doors. A strong dry smell of apples burst out and she stepped in quickly to trap it. Light and small like her own, the room had been turned into a storeroom and the smell was coming from dozens of small newspaper parcels stacked in the corner. On one of the inner walls a row of plaited onions hung over six or seven demijohns of wine. One of these was plopping at regular intervals. The broad shelves on the other wall were only about a third full but the colours of preserves stood out from the empty bottles and jars, mostly pulped greens and browns of chutney. By now she found she was breathing deeply as if excited, the sweet air was breathtaking.

The next room was a disappointment. It was darker, stuffy and contained spare furniture. She picked up an unfinished seascape with its face to the wall and it revived her interest, so she opened a couple of drawers in a bedside unit. A picture in one of the newspaper linings caught her eye. It was of the then-new Science Block at Trowbridge where she'd got her first teaching job and met her husband. Taking it out to see the date she caught a sheet of letter paper as it fell from it and read the heading, 'Dearest Mark,' simultaneously. It wasn't intentional - it stood out like a headline - but having started she went on without stopping. The large open hand only managed three or four words to a line and was arranging a meeting. Even without the further endearments the flow and tone were unmistakable and brought back the memory of a plain but radiant face turned up to her husband's. She dropped the paper back into the drawer, then opened it to put the letter back in the paper.

Amazed at her calm she stood there recalling bitterly how after the divorce she seemed to hate him most for his inability to conceal it all from her. Instead he told her about it and about himself with a voracious innocence and a passion to be understood that frightened her more than deceit. She'd been deaf to a need she couldn't meet and stood now with her hand on the door, shame and fear blotting out everything but the memory of his flushed face. His mouth was beautiful, talking, insistent; her anger and longing turned vicious. Full of pain she'd hurled a book at it - her feeling now as vivid as if the events were ten minutes not ten years old.

Outside, the hall felt cold. In place of the thoughts she'd banned there was nothing. She noticed how dirty the walls were. At the top of the stairs she looked down at the thin Indian rug at the foot - on those polished floors an invitation to Simon to break his neck.

She went outside to be in the sun, avoiding the others but needing contact of some kind. She hurried past the cowshed where the acid dung and smell of urine was too strong, and stopped at the stable. The horse wasn't there. With the vague intention of finding it she followed the path alongside and found Tom and Mark instead. They were talking. She couldn't pass without acknowledging them but avoided immediate contact by bending to the sack of dry peas at Mark's feet and running her fingers through them.

"You'd be interested in all this, Joan," Tom said, "Mark's been telling me some of his ideas for making this a really paying concern."

She looked at him then at Mark, pretending to listen.

"Joan knows what I want to do with what we earn." He studied her for a moment and decided she needed the full picture. "The schemes for raising cash before the commune gets going involve getting 'next door' out - which doesn't seem likely. I was telling Tom, when I bought this place the agent told me Selby was looking for a place of his own. He boasts enough about his profits and the money he's put by, and from what I can gather in town he's doing pretty well. If that's true he's not going to be in a hurry to shift his glasshouses and start over again. Whenever I ask him when he's thinking of going he fobs me off. I can see he'll wait till it's worth his while but that could be never - in fact the whole thing could be just another boast, something he knows perfectly well won't come off. Sometimes I think the sod keeps up my hopes on purpose. He despised my attitudes to farming right off just as much as I despised his. We're natural enemies - it would suit him to see me come a cropper."

"What were the money-making schemes?" Joan asked when it seemed he wanted her to speak.

"Well, they all depended on his getting out. We were going to take in tourists in the summer. They pay well and Sheila says she could manage, with a bit of cleaning help from the village. There are five more bedrooms in the other half of the house. We could have students to stay - free so long as they worked full time - in fact a combination of the two would suit us best. When I've got all fourteen acres I can make more economical use of the land, sell more surplus and so on. I was fool enough to tell him my plans earlier on. I also said I wouldn't have bought the place If I'd thought he wasn't going."

"Do you think the agent was to blame?" Tom asked. "If he'd had the place on his hands a while he might be tempted to throw in a rumour as if it were fact."

"No. People in the village say he's been talking about it for the last few years. But it's more than just needing the house and land, it's actually difficult farming next to him. He's a classic example of what *not* to be. The land's over-worked, saturated with fertiliser and insecticide and I can't stop worrying about it, he's destroying it with chemicals - it could take years to reclaim when he does leave. From him I get a sneer every time I mention organic farming - it's worse than talking to a brick wall - everything you say and are is taken personally, he's only got two responses, contempt and hostility - I started off with one and have earnt the other. He doesn't give me any worse than he gives his own family - in fact it's probably a relief to let it out on someone else. For all I know my presence here might give him just the inducement he needs to stay!"

Tom laughed as if that were the point of the story but Joan was watching Mark, quick to respond to a hint of panic. It didn't matter if Mark was right or wrong, if he believed it the damage was done.

"I'm sure you're worrying unnecessarily" - the dismissal came out slowly, rather heavily and as reluctance to be drawn in. Mark felt he hadn't made his point strongly enough.

"You probably don't understand the sort of man we're dealing with here. He's dangerous. The youngest son's been in trouble with the police several times. I've seen bruises on him and the wife that are no accident and heard things I wasn't meant to. But it's more than putting two and two together, it's something you feel whenever you're with him - more than tension, more like a threat. He's not just a crude basher you can avoid while keeping a protective eye on his family. In his way he's quite subtle, even self-suppressive - he's no fool, it would be easier if he were. He's usually one jump ahead. If you think of all his responses as keyed to antagonism, or resentment at their mildest, and his idea of pleasure as scoring one off, you won't be far out. The all-round grudge isn't passive or active in an obvious or predictable way - more like an inflammation - almost any contact is acid. He calls his responses realistic."

"You think he'd deliberately cause you trouble if he felt like it?" Joan asked.

"No question. He's done it already but I can't prove it".

More than ever keen to get away she made a move but couldn't follow through. Walking off at this point was impossible. She refused to ask how Selby'd cause trouble, wondering if she were more afraid of the picture being true or of Mark's being manic.

Tom filled the gap but he didn't question him either: "I didn't know he was such a thorn in your side." His tone was open, curious and suggested he found the whole business interesting. Joan gave him an irritated glance. She felt as on the first meeting that he was ready to take part energetically and good-naturedly in anything but it would be perhaps not so much a game but a compulsive exercise - the ardent objectivity left part of him untouched. She could leave them to each other.

"I must go and find Sheila." She turned back to the house and passing the sitting room window saw Sheila on the floor exercising and Bess in the doorway. Bess waved and Joan went on to the orchard and the hens.

Bess had noticed her tension: "Joan looked tight-up, do you think she's enjoying it here?"

No answer. Sheila, face down on a white cotton rug, was trying to pull her feet towards her head.

"Doesn't it hurt being inside out?"

No answer. When she was ready, still lying on her stomach, she turned her head up: "Won't you join me?"

"I came in for a rest, I think I'm too tired for it."

"It'll make you feel better - I do it to refresh me among other things. It's not supposed to hurt, you know" - she grunted a laugh - "if it hurts you're doing wrong - you do it gently at your own pace - just stretching."

"You make it sound good but I don't think I know what my pace is."

Sheila turned, sat up cross-legged and stood up expertly from this position. "You have to link it up with everything else. Perhaps that would be difficult at this stage."

Bess had perched on the arm of the sofa to watch. She found her easy to be with, her face was stiller than most and reassuring. Incessant mood change - lightning fast and to be caught in flight if you wanted to understand the whole picture - she was used to, but even with calmer friends the stillness wasn't the same as this, she was generally restless with it, and wanting more had learned to pick a little at the seams of the sewed-up idea of self to see what else was there, or to interpret refraction in a reflecting pool. Sheila's stillness made her brown face look more functionally a face, with the eyes, nose and mouth reassuringly there in their own right and not as potential signal-makers. Expression erupted as a pleasant surprise, unchallengeably genuine and a fact of nature like her nose and chin.

"Why do you take Yoga so seriously?"

Sheila perked up - she liked sharing her enthusiasm and even more the prospect of a convert. "When I do enough of it I feel attuned to everything, patient with people, and work comes easily." She rested against the table opposite Bess. "It helps me sleep, I feel I couldn't do without it." Her look was a schoolgirl's, enthusiasm and conscientiousness referred to a higher authority - Yoga. She wanted to capture Bess's interest, Bess wanted it and said nothing, hoping she'd go on. She didn't.

"What else does it involve then?"

"It's a whole way of life, or can be if you're serious enough about it."

"You are?"

Sheila nodded several times and started to blush, then picked up her yoga mat and folded it. "I've been doing it long enough to know how it works." A sudden change in manner took Bess by surprise. "You'll have to take my word for it." She was angrily defensive, then changed her tone to one of superior experience: "You become more natural and confident - more ready to take things on." The emotional edge was unwarrantedly sharp, Bess felt, and it put her back up.

"Sounds like a good fuck," she said irritably.

Sheila smiled. "I'm used to that sort of thing. You don't *have* to understand."

This wasn't what Bess wanted, she leaned forward full of remorse. "I really want to know - I'm not prying or making fun. What made you believe in it enough to make you start?"

"I don't know. People talked about it and I thought I'd give it a try - I've always been interested in other cultures. Anyway I felt I needed something calming. It's slow and deliberate, it sounded right - a matter of gently training and mastering your body" - she smiled at Bess - "not taking it out for a romp."

"I like taking it out for a romp."

"Then you won't enjoy Yoga."

"A sense of fun can't be all that foreign to it."

"It can come as a result, it doesn't have to be part of the training. It's supposed to put you in touch with what you really want, so that would be one of the things for you."

"How does it do that?"

Sheila picked up a thread from her mat and glanced up at her. "Look, after exercising I sit and train myself to be quiet and meditate. Mark made me a special stool. It should be low so that you sit in a special way with a straight back."

Bess waited.

"Meditating makes my deeper urges and needs come to the top. I've only been doing this side of it for a year and it's working already. You're put in touch with yourself, the exercises do it physically, the meditation mentally. Afterwards I feel released."

"That wasn't a joke then, it *is* like a good time in bed."

"I suppose so - if that's how you see it." She tailed off, leaving Bess feeling she'd made the same mistake twice.

"I mean it - I feel wonderful. Light, at peace, even radiant - usually completely, sometimes painfully in touch with everything - air, light, colour, animals, people, music, everything. Sometimes it's too much and makes me feel tearful with pleasure and excitement."

"That's not quite the objective." Sheila smiled at her but looked saddened. "You've got a good relationship with

Tom."

"And you with Mark."

"He's more difficult."

"So was Tom once, we talked and fought a lot."

"You're very lucky."

"No - well, perhaps we are." Bess suddenly found the roles reversed. "I know generalisations don't cut any ice. Like you I can only say it works."

"I can see it does - but with some people, not us. Too much talk between Mark and me would ruin everything."

"Why?"

"We don't always see eye to eye, and why should we, we want our independence as people - we're ourselves."

Bess looked irritable again. "I'm glad you know what yourself is, surprised you need Yoga in that case. Do you think what you are now is you, and what you would be later wouldn't be?"

"Perhaps."

"That's rubbish! You're just used to what you are - and if you fix on it doesn't change - then you get bored and vicious. I mean 'one' does."

"I'd be afraid."

"What of? - of changing? You only change in a way that's natural to you and have a wider range of 'yous' - otherwise it's duty not change."

"But if my changes clash with his?"

"That's part of the understanding you get by talking and fighting, there's no reason why they shouldn't be totally different and totally acceptable."

"Ideally perhaps."

"No, actually. It's a matter of not having a special reverence or cast iron prejudice for what you think at the moment is you - of being more interested in what's going on than in your idea of yourself in the context. It's trainable, like Yoga. You don't mind freeing yourself with Yoga, do you, or the effort and self-discipline involved? I suppose you'd see that as done for the self by the self and all in your own territory and much less fearful a change. Why I don't know. I'm more frightened of what I am on my own than what I might be mixing. And you two feel you're such social people? I don't at all fancy a bunch of independent units all performing a private tight-rope."

"We can't be perfect together until we perfect ourselves!" Sheila was hurt and angry.

"You've got it the wrong way round."

Sheila wasn't having it. "I'm not interested in just a few more or a few better fucks." She was standing up now - like a block.

"Is that what we've been talking about? Well, don't knock it. It can seem like life itself sometimes - all the things you say Yoga does but not locked in yourself, so more than that."

Sheila looked hard at her. She meant it, she was a fanatic of a different sort. "It's not the same for us," she said gently, half wanting to go, half held by Bess. She ventured a practical question: "Do you always have a good time?"

"Always, *now.*"

Sheila looked sheepishly at her. "You must have a very good relationship with Tom."

"It doesn't belong to just him and me."

"It wouldn't work for us - I can't explain why." She paused, looking as if she had more to say, but when it came it disappointed Bess. "If I can get what I need from Yoga, that's all right for me."

"I suppose so." Bess was reluctant to be democratic on this issue.

In Sheila there was a fellow feeling that wasn't satisfied - she did want to explain further. "I get peace without starting up nasty battles and analyses - that's supposing I knew what to analyse. It would bust us up quicker than anything."

"It's not just peace you're after surely. Anyway you're wrong, you'd know what to say right enough. You're probably not afraid of busting the two of you up, just yourself. You'd have to see yourself as analytically, as you chose to call it, as you saw him."

"I can't do it."

"You're scared."

"Only a fool wouldn't be. Not everyone's as goodnatured as Tom."

"Doesn't everyone respond to goodnatured honesty?"

"How do I know I'll be goodnatured?"

"You'll see there's no point in being anything else. If you're really honest you won't offend as deeply as that because you'll have been just as honest about yourself. You both see quickly that the battle lies on a different plane from personalities and one-upmanship."

"I wish I could believe it."

"Why not? You think the urge to score would always get the better of you?"

Sheila studied Bess's face for hostility, then said quietly: "I don't know, or how I'd be if he did it. I obviously don't trust myself the way you do."

"I don't trust myself at all. It doesn't matter. You can dispose of it with the same honesty."

The two women stood silently in front of each other then Sheila, accepting her seriousness at least, grabbed Bess's arm. "Know anything about dreams?" The question, sudden and urgent, removed the last trace of suspicion between them.

Bess looked bewildered.

"Do you?" Sheila was set on an answer.

"What d'you mean?"

"Do you know what recurring dreams mean - things like that."

"No."

"I have them terribly often, sometimes they ruin my sleep - another reason I need Yoga. They're not exactly nightmares - not vicious ones anyway but disturbing. They spoil things and leave me restless."

"What are they?"

"They're all on the same theme"- the two women found chairs and drew them closer - "about water. Last night, for instance, I was crossing a dark lake again by a path of paving stones. The path goes like a path in a garden - no rails - and it lies on top of the water. I go across with no particular fear and in the middle it stops. In front of me is nothing but black moving water. I suddenly feel insecure, I haven't the faintest idea what I'm doing there, the water all round laps against the stones - there are no waves but it seems full of swirling movement even where it looks calm, sometimes there most of all. It looks dangerous as if the movement is made by the weight and depth of water. I'm too frightened to turn back because for the first time I properly realise where I am and exactly what I'm doing. Anyway I can't go on. I switch my dream or panic my way into another one depending on the kind of night I'm having. Sometimes it's a pool in a meadow where the same thing happens but the pool is surrounded by trees and hedges. Sometimes I'm crossing an enormously wide and swollen river with a swift current, this time I'm crossing by a suspension bridge that sags unnoticeably towards the middle and when I get there it disappears under a fierce current of water. It reappears four or five yards further on, rising at the same rate to supports on the opposite bank. It's all perfectly symmetrical but sagging, so there's no way to go up the other side without swimming the few yards between, but the current's too fast and the water too deep. I think about swimming but I'm too scared. I can't see the bridge just under the water when I look for it. Sometimes I visualise continuing to walk on it under water holding on to the sides but as soon as the water reaches my neck I switch my dream."

Sheila paused and looked for Bess to say something but Bess was rapt, waiting for more.

"Sometimes, and these are more beautiful and more frightening, I dream about the sea. I'm walking up a country road, hilly, the weather bright, I'm feeling perfectly normal or perhaps unusually happy when suddenly the countryside becomes mountainous or cliff-like and as I turn a bend in the road there's a huge sparkling wall of water heaved yards above my head, poised in the act of breaking over me - brilliantly blue, clear, sparkling with light on it. Or I've made a very difficult climb up a mountain that comes to a point. It's been very steep and I approach it from some green land and want to climb this and see from the top, it's just the next thing to do on my walk and when we get halfway up Mark and I find the rock crumbly, the shale keeps slipping under our feet - he's better than me, makes better progress - I try to keep up with him and start to panic then suddenly I'm at the top, and the top is a sharp point, Mark's nowhere to be seen and I look down and see a stream of shale and stones that I've disturbed sliding down into an enormous ocean that's blue, choppy, frothing at the foot of the mountain - I'm terrified and my feet move."

Sheila stopped talking, took a tissue out of her jeans and wiped her palms. "That's all - I seem to ring the changes on those - funny, aren't they?"

Bess was still in them.

"Perhaps I've made them sound more frightening than they are. I'm scared but not often sweaty scared like really horrible nightmares." She sat with her hands in her lap. "What do you think?"

"I'm picturing them."

"Well?"

"I want a drink, I'll get some."

4

For Bess, being happy wasn't enough - there was a surplus that wouldn't stay in the self or the pair or group that bred it but needed to express itself outside. It was a social achievement and the world had to go along, in theory at least, or she was trapped - if it only occurred in a protected area she'd stop feeling it. Intensely sociable, constantly leaping the blocks put up by aspects of her own personality or past experience, it looked for a similar success with others and this morning, in reaction to her conversation with Sheila, Bess felt outside their lives and that they were not all joined by common experience but separated by it. The combinations of difference and sameness in people that excited and made her feel alive, this morning made her unhappy. She couldn't throw off the mood and the effort made her irritable and jaundiced.

It was Sunday, a day the Lewises had decided to make as much as possible a traditional family day and the focus was on that. Bess watched Mark with his eldest son - he relied on him for help when he wasn't at school. Peter, only ten, seemed to have the sense of duty on these occasions one generally saw in hard-pressed middle age but he did everything with a quick, fluid, garrulous participation that suggested he enjoyed and needed the routines and rules that would be death to Simon, she imagined, when he got older. Peter was doing well at school and according to

Sheila read avidly any book given him. She'd proudly made much of the extra time it took to collect and take back the five or six library books a week he needed. She'd had, or was pretending to, some anxiety about his health on account of it - she'd often switched off his light at her own bedtime and sometimes found him reading when she got up at six. Anxiety had lost ground to pride in his insatiability. "Not all story books by any means. I sprinkle in History, Science and anything else I think might be useful." He looked fit enough on it, a lean lad with faint blue eyes that frequently wore a look Sheila described as remote and Bess interpreted as numbed.

This morning his father was showing him how to carve a whistle. They worked well together, impatience and excitement never gave rise to irritating snatching or lapses of concentration - he watched till Mark finished shaping the mouthpiece then took and examined it. He looked pleased and put out his hand for the knife to carve his own. There was a balance of patience, curiosity and eagerness that Mark loved in the boy as if to him it expressed the essence of intelligence. The pleasure of doing most jobs with Peter as apprentice was increased, with Claude it could turn into torment. He saw the younger boy as clumsy without obvious nervousness, practical and down-to-earth but without the skills to go with it - with his lack of facility a little patience and receptivity would have been useful but Claude reacted to challenge as if it were put there with ulterior motives. He was moody, doggedly obstinate, and never offered to help. Simon, not able to join in except as observer or anarchist, showed promise of being a far bigger problem to him. He wanted his own way and would bully for it - had a flaring temper that impressed the adults even at this age, and eyes that fluently expressed assessments of situations his tongue could not. With Peter and Mark working together more and more exclusively the other two went to look for Sheila, and Bess followed them.

She was in the kitchen rolling pastry - slapping it over sliced apple - trimming it to the edge of the plate - thumbing a pattern - striding to the hot oven and slamming its door with a speed and concentration that showed her firing in all cylinders. In that large kitchen Bess felt Sheila's energy had the displacement value of six people in a broom cupboard and her attention, as usual when Sheila was in top form, was wholly taken over by her. She excelled in rapid transitions both in jobs and mental attitudes and now, dusting her hands on her apron, her expression changed. Claude was sitting at the table - he'd got out his holiday homework, 'What I did in the holiday'. Simon was crayoning. Sheila drew back her head like a pecking hen and with a bird-like sharpness of interest spun Claude's book round while his pen was poised, judged he was "coming on", and taking his pen wrote letters on Simon's page telling him to look at the shape of Claude's "little b's".

"Do you feel you'll go mad doing several things at once?"

Sheila was delighted - "I'm used to it!" - and gathered her bowls up noisily.

When Joan came in and asked if there was something she'd like her to do and was given a job it occurred to Bess she should be doing something herself and she asked to wash up. The wave of a wet hand made her step back remembering her bad record - slow, obsessive - a working presence likely to blur anyone's sense of achievement - though as an audience she had her value. She felt Sheila wanted her to stay and was touched. It brought her instantly into Sheila's world but as the assertive overtones became increasingly antagonising she found herself fighting against loss of sympathy, against being on the outside again, and held tight to the idea that this whole way of life was a good one, especially for Sheila. The larger the group the higher the value put on her skills and indomitable sense of duty and the greater the possibilities for power and affection. All this in theory at least. In fact being a 'good sort' and a hard worker is undervalued at close quarters and gets mostly mental recognition especially when it comes across with a confidence just this side of self-righteous. When it's offered as an unarguably honourable claim to love, one can always think of a dozen dishonourable ones nicer. And she was undervalued. Her combination of brusque practicality with intensely romantic aspirations made it difficult, even for her family, to come very close and Sheila when not active seemed bewildered.

Mark breezed in and out of the kitchen and Bess changed her mind. Sheila had more than enough of both power and appreciation. He was aware of his wife's presence constantly. When Bess followed him back to the sitting room she saw his quiet activity with Peter as getting its balance largely from its context. A good part of the satisfaction seemed to depend on the relation it bore to their other activities and Sheila was the 'caller' in that dance. Was this why she often looked flushed and excited in her rôles?

She went to her own room and found Tom reading at the table. The place was already beginning to take on the quality of their own world, their books and clothes were everywhere naturalising the foreign objects they were scattered on. With the sun shining on Tom's black hair and glistening beard she stared at him. He was beautiful, the room was full of the smell of his sweat and she became looser in her movements, brighter and excited. Putting a hand on the shoulder furthest from her she pressed against the one closest and looked down to see what he was reading. He slid his hand, palm downwards, over a typewritten letter.

"I've been hiding this from you, it came yesterday." Bess came to and snatched at his hand but he leaned and she couldn't lift it. "I'll tell you what it says - you'll get upset."

"Is it from Macfaddien?"

"Yes. He says the same thing in different words. We've been too selective."

"Let me see it!"

"No, you'll get worked up about the way he expresses himself."

"What's he say then?"

Tom outlined what he said about the almost completed draft of their book and Bess pretended not to notice his carefully plotting a way through the tinder of emotive words left carelessly lying about by a complacent antagonist.

"Did I see 'opinionated'?"

"You may've done - it's not important - the message is the same as ever." Tom's calm had a momentarily pacifying effect.

"What was the word next to it, electric?"

Tom laughed. "Eclectic".

"What does he mean?" Bess looked shocked and sat down behind him on the bed. "I don't understand. What's he talking about?" She looked confused and hurt. Tom had turned round and taken her hands.

"I don't know why you react to these letters, he means nothing more than usual, we haven't toed the line enough, the book isn't sufficiently a handmaiden to the series - look, he uses the word 'handmaiden', see?"

He let Bess glance at the sentence he pointed out and

she made no effort to take the letter, it was already too much. Bitter disappointment that the passionate interest the book communicated was treated as arrogance, the excitement over some writers as eclecticism, the lesser interest in others as dismissiveness used up most of her energy - the rest suppressed tears. Their book had never been abusive - they hadn't often felt it - just not interested in the games some of the authors played. She tried to conceal the strength of her feelings from Tom because she needed the balanced view he had of it and a strong display on her part would destroy it.

"We go out of our way to be fair," she said tensely. "I've never known anyone be more fair - less in love with cheap point-scoring."

"Darling, that's not the issue - we show more interest in some books than others!"

"Of course we do, who doesn't?"

"But he doesn't want anything like that. What he'd really like is a mention of all the most widely read books nicely strung together with some smart talk."

"Why didn't he say so in the first place, we could've told him where to go."

He was staring at her hands. "We'll have to meet him and discuss it. These letters and drafts aren't doing any good." He looked downcast for the first time. "What a bloody nuisance it all is - why do they have such fixed ideas about the style they want? How do they expect different writers in the series to have the same approach? What attracted us meant nothing to him, he wasn't really giving us a chance to study the period thematically - for him that was just a fashionable idea - what he'd really like is an inspired directory. What he gets, if the one he showed us is anything to go by, is what he deserves - meretricious rubbish."

Bess drank in the balance of irritation and determination in his voice and remained silent long enough to hear his detailed plans for a re-writing that might be acceptable. At the end of it she'd come round to the new plans and for the next couple of hours - partly to satisfy their irritation, partly in submission to the inevitable - they made up first ribald then salesman-like headings to the new sections of the book. By the time lunch was ready they were into it enough to enjoy the game and accommodate the misery of rewriting. It was a private world, neither wanted to discuss it with the others at lunch time - they wanted to escape but equally, since the job had to be done, they avoided having its hold on them weakened by the varieties of comfort or indifference on offer from people fully engaged in affairs of their own.

Downstairs the cinnamon and apple smell coming from two hot cakes standing on the dresser was mixing with steam from potatoes and leeks. When they were eating Bess asked about them and was told they were for friends coming this evening and staying the night after a camping tour. There was an urgency and excitement during the meal. It was building up too fast for guests not due till evening and in any case the pressure seemed to be coming from the children. She picked up their odd remarks about rope ladders and rubber tyres and remembered there'd been a half promise earlier in the week to visit an adventure playground on Sunday. The sop for the adults was a country house attached to it and open at the weekends. Excited to be doing something fresh she packed down her dessert faster than Claude, finishing first and weakening the strength of Sheila's comment on his table manners.

When they were all in the back of the Landrover an

indecipherable mixture of smells dominated by oil and hay tipped the balance for the others. who became suddenly exposed and alert. The children insisted the playground come first. A high wooden fence made it look like a fort in Indian territory with the gates ripped off. Near the entrance was a look-out tower - Simon went for the ladder up to it, the other two were off in different directions with an instant, silent participation that scattered the adults in a similar way. The 'frontier' illusion was kept up by rope bridges and long ropes hanging from trees. There were logs supported five or six feet off the ground to be balanced on before reaching the tyre-swings. They were the only people there apart from two boys who retired to the edges as the group advanced.

The silence was broken first by Claude. They turned to see his sturdy brown face shouting for Mark from the middle of a rope bridge. Frightened and excited he got Mark to watch his progress, he was about fifteen feet in the air and the bridge spanned an eighteen-foot gap between wooden platforms. The three key ropes in the lacework were the ones underfoot and waist-high - the rest was like a safety net and from below he looked as if he were walking in a string bag.

"Oh, well done!" Mark's voice came from the swings and Claude blushed looking furiously determined. He made a fast crossing. Peter, now on the ground next to his father, had been watching.

"You going, Peter?"

"Not yet."

Claude, coming up to them, grinned, looked confidently into Mark's face and ran off to watch them from the hand-over-hand pole nearby.

Bess had also been watching from a distance and now

went over and climbed to the platform. She stood looking at it, then tested it. The swaying, jerking response to her full weight scattered all curiosity and the 'giving' and enmeshing filled her with panic. Clutching the side ropes was useless, they moved as she did. With nothing to brace herself against, it was impossible to keep up a heel-toe progress on the bottom rope since it wasn't taut enough to balance on without help. Her feet got trapped - then as she fell, her knees. She flopped back on to Sheila's feet on the platform and stared up, white-faced.

"Are you going?"

"I can't."

Sheila moved round her carefully and Bess went down. Like Claude, Sheila glanced every few seconds at Mark. Bess watched the first few steps, saw a flush of alarm, a tenser grip on the ropes that again gave instead of bracing. She beamed a strained smile at Bess. The glances at Mark increased as she neared the middle and the sagging and swinging was at its worst.

"Mark!" She suddenly opened her mouth with a grating shout that drew Joan and Tom to her too. Mark moved almost underneath. His smile, more complacent than reassuring, looked peculiarly unrelated to the struggle though that was obviously the cause.

Bess, suddenly anxious, shouted encouragement - "Oh, well done Sheila!" - and ran up the other ladder to meet her.

The relief of an excited terrier was the last thing Sheila wanted and she dismissed it, turning to Mark: "It was nothing, don't be silly, a kid's game and perfectly safe."

Once she was down Mark went over to Peter. Claude had crossed the pole several times, body swinging rhythmically like a pendulum. It was Peter's turn now. He was more unnerved by Claude's success and unspoken bombardment of self-confidence than the ordeal. Mark saw, sympathised and his face softened. The boy put his hands round the pole but was reluctant to let his feet swing off the ladder.

"Come on, I'll be close, you won't fall." He moved in closer, his hands jerking as if to catch him, as Peter swung free.

Bess, seeing Claude leave, turned in time to see his back change expression from erect confidence to tense independence. He must have sensed her attention and after a moment's indecision came back but to her, glancing only once to see Peter moving one hand gingerly away from the next, his thin body dangling, wriggling and kicking its legs to get a swing, like a dying man on a gallows. The sight gave the final release. He stared up at Bess wondering if he wanted to join her - she'd mounted a horizontal pole about four feet off the ground - but he thought better of it and moved off.

She balanced her way along to reach a dangling rope with a noose at the end - it was some distance off the ground and this looked like the only way to get to it. Slipping her foot in the loop she put the other foot on top and swung. The rope pinched viciously and she dropped to the ground. A second later she grabbed it, put back her foot and pulled herself up. She swung and let it hurt.

Sheila came over and trying the same found she couldn't reach. "How did you do that? You're shorter than me!"

The congratulation in her tone puzzled Bess: "I don't know." But thinking this was a friendship game and that she was repaying her own admiration over the bridge she reminded her of it. "I couldn't cross that bridge, though." She had her knuckles rapped:

"It isn't a competition!" Tense but not angry Sheila went

round to the log and Bess watched her balance her way along noting for the hundredth time the deep lines that ran from the sides of her nose almost unbroken to the corners of her mouth. She recalled Mark had the same lines - deeper, whiter, sometimes like scars focussing and bunching the large nose and down-turned mouth tight-closed in a characteristic expression of self-domination.

Joan stood by all this time - in part as Simon's custodian and entertainer though the entertainment hadn't been all his. She'd no interest in joining the climbing and swinging but a great deal in the high feeling running among the others. She noticed the men, unexpectedly, took very little part in the activity and wondered if it was too tame for them. Perhaps they felt they were too heavy, they looked interested but did nothing. Perhaps it was Mark's influence - she'd seen Tom look at one or two things with a gleam in his eye. Mark was the one behaving like a practised athlete in the feelings and skills involved, and his presence was intrusive. She was pleased when within the hour even the children had had enough and were ready to see the house.

They approached it through gardens laid out on a slope that used the house as its main ornament - a neat, unpretentious grey stone building large enough to have an interesting range of rooms and compact enough to retain some character. They waited outside for their guide and when she came she prepared them, and a number of others joining them from the gardens, in the gentle diction reserved for special occasions. The darkness inside collaborated and the density of air, smell of the wood and incense-like polish drugged them into an obedient flock while she shepherded them, without gesture or expression from her round dreamy face, to the long gallery. Here she pointed out the two ancestors painted by Holbein and

Rubens, and giving them just enough time to feel awe and pleasure carried her tone, with a passing reference to Van Eyck, to the feet of the current Earl whose picture hung at the far end. For her group the frame of mind wasn't transferable - they waited expectant, bunched up to be moved on.

Tom, penned in opposite the portrait, spent the time comparing it with the one next to it of the Earl's father. The former was cruder but he was irritated not just by the lack of skill and the garish paint but the present Earl's expression - cynical, effortfully contemptuous, and posed sitting and grey-suited as an unlikely tycoon. The portrait of the father in ceremonial military uniform focused not on the blaze of red, but on the flat, blue, dreaming eyes. Tom was suddenly obsessed with the fashions behind them and while moving with the others into the next room missed the objects in it. Apparently nothing was required from painter or poser but that they feed a fantasy. He found himself touched by their modesty. Suggestions of power and purpose had to be found somewhere - the faces were no help and the painter wasn't up to a reading of his own, so all that was left was what they thought they represented. One, his hand on his sword, dreamed of Empire and benevolent government - the other, turning disillusion to account, canny and informal sat cross-legged in a high-backed chair taken from the boardroom. Wrestling with worries about publishers and the hopelessness of a battle with prevailing taste, arguing concession to the hopes and fears that gave it power he pushed his way through the group looking for Bess, only to see her guided by Mark up a narrow flight of stairs. His attentive stoop had taken possession of her and annoyed Tom but he looked round for Joan who might be glad of company.

He came up to her in a bedroom where they were being shown some dull tapestries and a fourposter. The guide told them a story about a member of the family held prisoner for several years in the little room opened by one of the panels. It was empty, then as now, except for a single bed and two faded pictures. From the window of the larger room they could see where he was allowed to exercise "in the small enclosed garden below". Bess went to look and saw a wooden gate in a high wall and two trees in the enclosure. She found it difficult to feel the restraint she was meant to. Mark on the other hand, leaning over and stiffly pressed against her, took a swift startled glance and turned for the exit. The group had packed out the room so he couldn't leave without disturbance. The guide pointed out a secret niche in the cell wall, it held a chipped plaster Virgin Mary. White-faced he pushed his way through and out of the door. For the rest of the tour he was spotted only once, by Joan, reading the plaque at the side of a suit of armour.

They met up with him strolling up and down the gravel path at the exit. Tom, who'd been almost as keen to get out, came up to him. "Airless, disappointing place," he said and they walked off together. Joan saw Mark's head inclined eagerly towards Tom's speaking mouth and tried to catch them up but not hard enough - she was too tired to be curious.

When they reached home it was obvious they were all in the same condition except for Sheila and Mark who had a new lease of energy. They fed the children, put them to bed and prepared the table and evening meal on their own except for an occasional conscience-prompted gesture from the others.

"You'll like the couple coming tonight" Sheila told Bess,

who was dreaming first and peeling potatoes second. "We haven't seen them for ages, not that we know much about the man. I only saw him once at a bus stop, he's Beatrice's latest - a sort of gentleman farmer, I think. Anyway, Beatrice is great fun - you'll see."

She arrived an hour later and looked as if she might be. A pleasant looking woman nearly six feet tall and large boned who responded to the warm welcome so genuinely and with such assurance that she quickly made her hosts feel at home. Joan was thrown out by a contrast between the bold excited eyes and the fussy, wispy hair fluffed round her face. Her long loose blue dress suggested a pre-raphaelite ideal Sheila emulated in her few non-working moments. Her pale companion was introduced as "Jack" and looked more like a businessman than a farmer, slightly taller than Beatrice, thin and standing close, moving with her when she moved, behaving as if he saw present contacts as so temporary they didn't need him to be socially supple.

"Have you been in this part of the world before?" Mark asked him and put out a chair for Beatrice who smiled and answered:

"I didn't know what to make of it when we came through. Jack says my impressions are all wrong."

Her friend stood still waiting for her to sit, then when she'd done so sat by her, crossing his legs. Mark, partly embarrassed by Jack's stiffness, partly delighted to have Beatrice to himself as a result, drew his own chair round to face her. "What were they?"

Bess and Tom sat opposite and watched, Bess staring at Mark's tightly-trousered thighs and knees pointed determinedly towards Beatrice as if they had their own intentions. Beatrice was blossoming under their mute obsession.

"Well, it was an overcast evening wasn't it?" she said "so it looked very bleak and forbidding. Lots of chalky ploughed earth with the twilight making it look whiter, sterile-looking. The chalk made it look as if it had snow on it."

The information was given with shy sideways reference to Mark but ostensibly to the group in general. The furniture in the sitting-room had been shifted so the sofa and chairs formed an irresolute circle and the occupants faced each other. Jack muttered something at her side that nobody heard. Nobody questioned or argued. Sheila got up to start the meal and poured some wine before leaving.

"I've felt like that myself before now." Mark, taking the information to himself carried it gallantly to the rest of the company. "It's only one of its many moods, though, and certainly not the dominant one. It's the richest soil you could hope for."

"You've no regrets then?" Beatrice asked. Her question, apparently an invitation to tell her a little about the place and his life here had an urgency or privacy of tone that prevented him. His hesitation made the rest of the group wonder if he did have regrets and seeing it he was so emphatic he sounded insincere:

"It's the only place to live!"

Beatrice gave a loud laugh and Jack put his hand on her knee, at which the sound suddenly opened and relaxed. The release was infectious. This first sign of autonomous life from him, made with no change of expression and complete confidence in its effect, amused and charmed the others and when Mark handed round the wine telling them to drink it and come and eat, the atmosphere became lively, even funful, and it increased throughout the meal. Nothing much was said while eating but the women's eyes tried to ferret out the nature of the dominating physical presence, that Bess felt had a difficult time subduing itself and turning broad, eager gestures into ones adapted to polite eating and subtle sexual invitation. Men, food and women took on a new structural formula - an isomer of the original - the bonding changed only subtly with each atom playing roughly the same part while the molecule was behaving in an unusual and unpredictable way.

When Mark suggested they all go in the Landrover to town to have a look at it by night they felt it was the very thing they all wanted and the obvious choice for a cold spring evening. The supper things cleared, they crowded into the car with few protestations at Sheila's having to stay behind and babysit and Sheila looked cheerfully unperturbed, refusing Joan's offer to stay in her place. They made the five mile journey along pitch-black lanes, hugging themselves warm under blankets.

Mark parked in the central square and took them to his favourite pub, pushing open the door into a mass of bodies. He squeezed through, grinning and apologising. The noise, smoke, close brief physical contact with strangers and intercepted expressions from animated faces affected their heightened responsiveness, exciting and agitating them so much that they became immediately the noisiest and most active. One or two people unconsciously made way for them at the bar. They were clumsy - Beatrice shrieked with laughter as Bess knocked Mark's beer elbow upward and the foam hung in disconsolate clusters from his moustache. After a momentary stiffness he broke into clownish head-shaking, flinging them free to make them stick to her then, putting his beer down, flung his arms round her to keep the target still and his aim accurate. Tom and Joan who'd been shouting liquor preferences and changes of mind to each other broke off, watching and cheering her evasions until Mark, victorious, let her go. She leant round him, blushing, to put her hand in Tom's pocket for a handkerchief. Quieter after the skirmish and more mellowly themselves, the group stood pressed up against each other looking round over each others' shoulders but listening to Mark telling them he'd take them to the castle. The movement of another group pushed them closer and Bess with her right arm pressed into Mark's chest and stomach where his jacket hung open could feel his body's warmth and movement bearing in on her with a concentration that made her light-headed and half-drunk. Unaware of anything else, submerged in a sensual torrent let in by the open floodgate she looked into his face and seeing it rushing through him grabbed at consciousness. Now the group structure changed. Mark and Bess were at the centre and everything took place round them, the physical and emotional presence of the others containing and covering them.

The urge to leave was shared instantly and took them out into the night air where they felt they'd moved from one social centre to another. Parked cars blazed under the street lamps, their colours only softening near the windows of the pubs that gave out warmer light and muffled shouts and laughter. They buttoned up, skirted the cars and made for the only road out of the square that had street-lights. Here several of the shop windows were lit and they found themselves slowing down to stare at polished stone rings and necklaces that reflected back invitingly. The display had been cleverly arranged with the stones placed among shadow-casting wood carvings and when they were released it was only to other shop windows.

Joan found herself less captured than she wanted and grew conscious of the cold wind, the increased moisture in the air and the limits of the town. A couple of hundred yards further on the street lights finished. Obsessed with the presence of hills and the sea beyond she looked back and noticed how small and bunched the cottages were. The shops were only cottages with enlarged front windows. Some signs hung just below open bedroom windows and creaked out of tune with each other. The nearest had a painted loaf with "Duffy" printed under it and a newly-painted "Etheridge: Grocer" gleamed in the street-light but the intimacy and compactness betrayed the hills the more, she smelt the outside in everything. Looking back at the central square it had changed. The sports cars, no longer assertive, made suggestions of speed and metallic confinement that touched and panicked her.

The others were slowing down too. They'd come to an old curatage set back near the end of the road. It was like the rest in general appearance, grey-stone-walled and grey tiled, but arresting. It had a porch in deep shadow and larger windows, the walls looked built to last. Joan joined them now they'd stopped while they waited for Mark who'd moved in for a closer look.

He was framed against the window where curtains hung heavily either side over a low sill. When he pressed his face on the glass and shaded his eyes the street light showed up a round, polished table with papers on it and a high-backed chair turned a little towards the window, it was leather-seated and permanently indented as if the sitter had just left. Beyond, on two sides of the room, shelves of books ran from floor to ceiling. It was a sanctuary and acted on him like a drug. He saw it not as evading but fostering contact - it was only here and at this level it could be managed, and he'd dismissed it. He didn't answer when Tom spoke. Bess pulled at his jacket asking if he wanted to burgle the place. With his eyes fixed on the plain wooden cross on the empty wall, his feelings leapt towards the religion he'd dismissed and that belonged with the academic world holding him spellbound. In rejecting theory and the false confidence, the vulnerability that went with it, he felt he'd rejected achievable balance. The longing to be part of it again made him unable to move.

Tom shaded his eyes and looked in: "What is it?" Coming away he shrugged at Bess whose look made him say, "It's an attractive room."

The comment sank in slowly and filled Mark with rage. He moved away alarmed at the strength of it, forcing it unexplored underground.

The group followed him back to the centre, clearly wondering why they'd come this way in the first place if it didn't lead to the castle. Now they crossed the square and took the other half of the same road out of town and almost instantly turned left down a lane. It announced itself as total blackness suspended between two buildings and felt like walking into an invisible wall. Bess and Joan had second thoughts about going on. For a while the route led downhill - a short, steep, narrow descent in a cold, clinging mist - then turning a corner they saw the castle ruins on its rounded hill lit not by moonlight but a ground glow, a faint white light hanging through the mist and punctured with black, ill-defined masses of gorse. Objects were flattened and disconnected. With dimension and normal proportion gone the group slowed down and then stopped. They noticed silence, then the lack of it - a welter of small sounds of movement. There was air movement - some kind of wind in spite of the mist and a sudden fresh awareness that this air had texture made Bess shout to Tom who was ahead: "I'm not going on."

Mark coming up to her put his arm round her protectively. "Are you frightened? It's nothing really." He stroked her slightly as he spoke.

Tom turned at his wife's call and watched, looking at Mark's face bent towards hers - the white skin, obtrusive nose and heavy shoulders. With a sharp "Bess, come here!" he moved towards them with a quickness and lightness that was uncharacteristic and instantly effective in drawing her away and towards him. The group stood scattered down the hillside. Tom, diverting his anger, turned Bess sharply towards the castle. "Look, you fool - what's there to be frightened of, we're nearly there!"

"It's not just the castle" - she sounded plaintive. "I don't like the mist, I can't see where I'm walking."

"I'll go with you Tom if the others want to go back." Mark moved towards him. "We'll meet them back in the pub."

Tom looked bewildered and Bess, feeling for his hand, felt him go stiff. "It's not that important."

"But I want to. Why don't we go together?"

Tom dropped her hand. "If Bess is unhappy I'll go back with her. Perhaps one of the others'll go with you."

Mark smiled round the group and his teeth caught the light, the skin, stretched over nose and cheeks, whitened on the bone. The others, looking at a face like a fist, didn't think much of the idea. A movement to close ranks brought Beatrice to the fore: "I think we've probably had enough - let's go home."

In the kitchen their old mood flared again. Sheila had fed the cooker fire and its doors were open for them to warm themselves.

"I knew you'd be frozen on the way back - get some of

this into you." She poured a dull gold wine from a screw-topped bottle into glasses waiting for them; it tasted of pollen. Before finishing they drew the bench and chairs up to the cooker and Mark, who'd suddenly sprung into life, luxuriously handled the back of the chair he'd made himself before placing it nearest the fire for Joan. She'd been sitting next to him in the car and he'd heard her teeth chattering. He sat where he could watch her thaw and drank in gulps.

Joan found shc was hungry and ate three of the oatcakes Sheila passed round but sipped her wine. Eventually she relaxed and reddened in the warmth of the fire and with a second glass began to watch the others. What she saw delighted and amazed her. Friction had emphasised the unanimity. Their need for easy intercourse took precedence over everything. Beatrice's arrival had brought it out. They'd responded as a group. The collective picked up, used, overrode individual response and apparently, for the moment at least, without casualties. It seemed to promote only what kept it going, the lively and enriching. It blocked the rest with an unconscious ease and with an apparently casual responsiveness that left everything to chance. Mark was in his element now - eyes glowing, listening attentively to something that quiet friend of Beatricc's was saying. Tom's face was so red it looked inflamed. He was leaning forward to hear and Bess's face was underneath, she was on the floor between his legs, her face relaxed, his about to burst with wellbeing. Thoughts, some anxious, that had risen during the evening and been overlain came back but only to turn her to the group for answers and expose her to the same mesmeric absorption in it. She spread her legs secretly to the heat, rested her drink on the arm of her chair and turned her own red face towards those furthest from her. Beatrice's arm was bracing her on the bench and came into frequent contact with Mark's restless corduroyed bottom. His faded mauve trousers against the black sweater gave an impression of quickness about the hips and thighs that contrasted excitingly with his heavy shoulders. She'd missed the start of the conversation between him and Jack and tuned into it to hear Jack speak out Beatrice's full name, Beatrice Calder. Sheila had mentioned it earlier and it hadn't meant anything, but now in a short unexpected burst of furious research Joan came up with a memory: a writer of Women's Lib. and 'Leftish' articles in The Weekend Review. So that was it. It explained some of the willing suspension of self on the part of the others, she was an event in herself. The articles had been full of a crude and engaging energy. She stared at her now as if seeing her for the first time. Perhaps the fact that she was famous had some effect on Beatrice herself, at least as much as on the others, part of her had become public property and she was at ease in the open - that said a lot about her. Energy that expressed itself easily in a public form became in its willingness a separate, no longer personal commodity. There was certainly nothing spurious or fame-based in the general excitement. What went on in her company changed from second to second, tempo, grouping, action or withdrawal - all perhaps highlighted, but not held on course by a special image of her or themselves in relation to her. Joan began to listen attentively - Jack was filling in details about his life.

He'd inherited a farm from a childless uncle at a time when he said he was disillusioned at the use the Treasury was making of his Economics degree. The idea of running the farm rather than selling it had been too strong for him and he'd put into practice on a small scale theories of agriculture and economics that excited him, feeling he was freeing himself from the paralysing effects of office ritual, hierarchical relationships and an end product so insignificant he missed it. His farm manager taught him the ropes. He made a study of the business and increased the profit the farm was making by the end of the second year. For the next few years profits rose steadily and he started looking around for new ventures. He bought up a nearby smallholding which he decided to farm without specialising and had to learn all over again. More and more interested in the experiment he left the running of the other in the hands of his manager and having originally dismissed the idea of organic farming as financially unviable was now prepared to see what it had to offer in terms of quality of produce and perhaps of a different economy. He tried to run it self-sufficiently - using only its own animal and vegetable waste and growing crops to feed his stock as well as himself, living as far as possible off his own produce. It became an obsession. His manager thought of it as his toy - the hands even resented doing a stint of work on 'the patch' as they called it, catching the idea of it as a rich man's plaything. He found himself doing more and more on his own and working long hours. The hard labour he said he enjoyed and resented in equal proportions. It took up so much of him he didn't really want to let go. Sheila questioned the resentment.

"You must know what I mean," he said. "I was hooked. There were cold winter days when my fingers and feet were stiff and painful and every muscle tense with rejection but I stuck it to get through the stint I'd allotted - slave of a necessity I'd made myself. I was uneasy taking men off my farm too often and made do by working like three men myself!" He grinned at her. "I'm not a man who needs a lot of conversation or contact but like most people I need some." He smiled again but Sheila, her eyes widened with disturbed attentiveness, made no flicker of response and held him to his course. "It was no joke I can tell you. You can't even think. The work demands a kind of concentration and there's nothing left over. Physically it was a mistake as well. You might think a healthy open-air life is just what your body needs but mine didn't. A day's digging, hoeing and planting - the same the next and the next in cold spring weather and you can't lie straight in your bed though you pass out right enough. You can't keep changing your job if there aren't enough of you - certain things have to be done to time - in fact everything has, seasons won't wait neither will stock. I had a whip held over me but hard as I worked nothing was ever finally finished. We ate, me and the stock, in order to produce more to eat - end product more limited than the one I'd walked out on. It was a drug alright and I wasn't reacting well mentally or physically - aches, chills, worst of all black depressions and it didn't get better as time went on. I can honestly say I never once felt as physically fit nor anywhere near it as I had at college after a brisk game of tennis - not once!"

"So what happened?" Bess asked.

"So I got out." He was uncomfortable as the centre of attention and shifted his position on the bench, glancing irritably at the fire as the source of his overheating. He spoke again, just the same, and filled the silence they'd all left for him. "I developed a nasty side to my nature I hadn't suspected. To justify myself I must say that this kind of work can destroy your freedom rather more effectively than any other. It's totally confining - I would be very tired you see, and one whole side of me still unused. I got up petty grievances about people and really went to town on them - like old Bill's leaving me all the jobs he didn't like, pretending he'd not had time, or offering cack-handed help with something he could really do better than me. It put me in touch with what was happening though. About this time I started to pine to go into town - be served a meal by a waiter - go to a show and sleep in a place tarted up for comfort - a posh hotel, say. I did it once or twice - it didn't work - both sides seemed empty. It felt like suffering from a form of malnutrition but I couldn't clear my head enough to trace the deficiency - I was rejecting people like crazy unless they were at a distance and in special rôles. Finally I saw there was nothing to do but get out - I'd not really thought it out, I just went." Eased, he spread his hands to the fire. "I saw the point of towns and my old work after a year or so."

Nobody spoke, Mark raised his head as if he were about to but Jack forestalled him: "It became freedom for me - freedom from the awful bullying of survival. I'm not saying you can ever escape it but it felt as if I was - I was lucky and got back into the Ministry of Ag and Fish and it felt like childish irresponsibility by comparison - so much time off to think and feel, even change. I did the thing properly - sold the lot. I might still be in it if I hadn't tried that little side show - who knows? After all, the money-making concern had only been a business like any other and in that respect gave me a measure of freedom."

"But you were lonely" - Mark spoke as soon as he was finished - "no one can work like that."

Jack, uncomfortable again and apologetic said, "I don't really see how it can be otherwise, done on a small scale or on a large one, if you're a labourer - there are very few jobs you can do with others and that kind of work doesn't stimulate conversation, you get out of the habit. About the only thing you can communicate is your tiredness."

"No, I didn't mean that - it was the overall lack of company that was wrong, I'm sure of it - nobody with the same aims as your own. Your workmen were doing it for wages, wanting nothing from you but their paypacket and you nothing from them but their labour - no shared interest or responsibility for success or failure - that's why there must be a commune. The whole project here stands or falls by that - if that isn't successful there's nothing, but the commune can only be successful if there's a common focus."

Jack smiled doubtfully at the fire and said nothing.

"Suppose you're successful, what then?" Beatrice asked, turning to face Mark. "You make it sound as if your problems are over at that point. Much more likely to be just starting. You're confined with a large family group instead of a small one. As far as the energy drain is concerned I can't see how it could be different from what Jack describes until or unless you make a profit and that would apply however big the commune. You'll only be able to have more people and less work when you can feed and support a surplus. The next few years are going to be lean ones aren't they and even if you reach the stage where you've more free time will your larger family make you happier? You'll have more than an ordinary family's problems and less of its freedoms. For one thing you won't have got used to the members of it by living with them from birth. Without a subconscious acceptance of that sort you stand roughly the same chance of success as you would on the outside with people who've chosen the same job as yourself - that is when a choice is made that isn't based on the size of the paypacket but by people with similar attitudes and ambitions to yourself. Sharing the focus doesn't guarantee you'll get on. It's people not jobs that are the problem."

"Of course, but this way - sharing our private and working lives - you can't so easily operate different sets of values for each."

"If I thought it was the answer I'd be living with my family now and working on it and with it. Your system can't bridge the real gaps. For starters you'd have to build up a new code of relationships and expectations. If you tried to live by the old ones you'd find it tough going, probably end up shutting yourselves off from each other to protect your sanity or falling under the sway of the most powerful - which would you choose?"

"Neither - are those the only alternatives you see?"

"For most of us, yes. And the way to achieve anything better can be found with society as it is where there's a wider network for individual solutions."

"You think the structure of society as it is can't be bettered?" He looked surprised and disappointed.

"Oh no, but I think plans need to take in all society for them to be satisfactory to any part of it. Breakaway groups aren't the way."

"Unless they're the beginning of a new system - a large society made up of commune-like units."

"But we can't agree that systems are the answer."

Joan was puzzled, finding it difficult to square what Beatrice was saying with the 'definitely left' tone of her articles. Jack was uneasy and spoke up for Mark as well as Beatrice.

"It's like you said earlier, Mark, it's only a stress focus that would work. If the whole group were under constant stress to take their minds off each other it might be some kind of awful social problem solver."

"Is that what I said?" Mark, bewildered, shook his head like a wet dog. "Is that what you believe?"

"Of course not" - Bess came in for the first time. "They don't see the possibilities, that's all."

Mark smiled gratefully. "We might achieve a natural balance at a personal level" he said, turning back to Beatrice. "The system's only a means to that end. I feel we stand more chance living like this."

"What's so natural about balance?" Beatrice, her eyes glowing, issued her challenge like an invitation. "Soon you'll be telling me you want to dig a trench in the morning and strum your guitar in the evening."

Sheila's chair scraped back and set their teeth on edge - it was the first attack of the evening. "What do you know about it, Beatrice? We none of us know till we've lived it." She stood up, looking at the fire-and-wine-drenched group that with bodies immobilised were ready to wreak havoc with their minds. "What've you got against trying?"

"Nothing - nothing dear, honestly." She looked surprised, even hurt. "It's just my reaction to the ideas that moved you to do this. Opposite, you see. That doesn't make you wrong. It's just not right for me."

"How do you know?"

"We've all got to live and there's no easy way round it. Think of the pitfalls here, the opportunities for chaos, think of the villainous and delightful proximities. Think of trying to live by one code of behaviour when something different, perhaps destructive of your original expectations, might suit the system better - are you ready for that? I've sometimes thought - not about you, you must know by now how I feel about you" - she looked warmly at Sheila and put a hand on Mark's knee - "that communes are attractive to those who want to avoid closeness not achieve it." She looked hesitantly at Mark. "Think of the opportunities - the more people, the less close to any one of them, perhaps?

Evasion could be the objective, though it's not likely to be the outcome. It's not as straightforward as it looks. Suppose it's those who can't give up their dream of contact, yet can't really face it, who are attracted?"

Mark looked up at Sheila irritably and waved her down and she sat back in her chair. "Of course, in a sense that's right," he said, "they fail in the terms given them and try something new - that's how change comes about and it might not reflect so much on the people as the situation - the social code they're leaving. It wouldn't mean it wasn't a creative expression of the desire for more contact because it was a desire for different."

"You don't think it strange or cause for alarm," she persisted, "that people who've failed for whatever the reason in human terms, or social if you like the word better, should perpetrate their recoil in the name of greater togetherness?"

"Not at all." He looked pleased with her and spoke with the quiet emotional abstraction of the totally committed. "Someone who fails in that way - unless he's suicidal - will try to come back in another. Why should that be alarming?"

"So you're assuming only such people will be attracted to it. Difficult way to start a happy and flourishing society with all those who adapt most easily left out. You've not much chance of radically changing the structure of society as a whole, in which case essentially you're still left out or have left them out and have failed again surely?"

He looked on her without looking at her, his smile a muscular activity of easing, only accidentally social. "Failed? I thought we all failed in some ways and succeeded in others. Who knows how the kind of success we might achieve here, and there are other places like ours, might eventually affect the whole European way of life? If a small group of people fits better here than it would dispersed in a larger, that's success for them, not failure. Who's judging and from what standpoint?"

"The chances of their fitting better have to be small since they're the people they are. There's a good chance their problems will be intensified by the closer focus."

Joan, still watching Beatrice closely, noticed that although she was leaning back supporting herself on her arms in roughly the same way as earlier there was a softened outline. Her bright eyes and expression were roused by something more than the light of battle, something personal, something he seemed not to or not want to notice.

"I can't see the point of all this - I just can't. Why do you want to do it?" Sheila turned to Mark, leaning forward, still in her chair but with tears in her eyes. "Why encourage it?"

"Hear, hear!" Jack's quiet voice supported her without looking at her.

Bess, seeing her hurt and frightened, was tense at Mark's remoteness from both women and at the bullying that came naturally from this very dissociation. The more he moved away in spirit the more they, in their different ways, moved after him, bridging the gap. An additional strain was in finding she went along with much of what Beatrice said while denying her right to say it and she sat now, looking at the floor, chewing with small, snapping bites at a hangnail on her thumb. The feeling of being trapped transferred itself to her interest in Mark. Her compassionate identification with some aspects of his nature meant, for her, failure to keep a distance. What he was moved her more than it alienated. She heard Beatrice talking again - now it was about the necessity for action. She was sympathising, she believed in action herself, she wished them all the luck in the world.

"It's better to see all the traps as Mark does" - she was talking to Sheila - "you stand a good chance of making this work as a result."

"Ah, that's where contemplation comes in!" Sheila was delighted at the turn of events. "Transcendental meditation I mean - it strips away the irrelevant - puts you in touch with your real self and what really matters." In control again and to celebrate the passing of the crisis she suggested some music - should they sing?

There was a general groan and they looked up at a face too tired to do anything but fall into bed. Jack, wanting to go along with her, asked "Can we listen to records?"

"Messaien?" Beatrice added.

"No, I've nothing after Brahms and not much of that."

"I was like that a couple of years ago." Beatrice heaved her legs over the bench to get out and help choose. She stretched and went over to see what there was. When the others started to move Joan got away.

Halfway up the stairs, puzzled at the licence Beatrice had to do as she pleased, wondering if it was given or if she took it, she decided Beatrice knew her ground with the Lewises almost too well. She paused - the writer of that letter perhaps? Staring at the frayed carpet on the next stair her stomach knotted. If she were, at least she was no longer a threat. Going on to her room, suddenly clear of it, she locked the door behind her.

5

Dressing slowly and abstractedly the following morning Joan tried to track the change in herself since she'd arrived. A series of sharp emotional knocks like the one last night made it look as if she were losing her bearings. She understood clearly enough it was the group that fascinated her (she could have written her self-sufficiency article on the first day - had more or less done so) but being interested in it had made her responsive to the project behind it and emotionally involved in the outcome. If this particular group could be brought to live together permanently or even for a few years it would be an achievement that excited her so much she found herself thinking she might join them. The thought came, was dismissed as nonsense and came again. Her habitual manner was more and more difficult to retrieve, it had depended so much on the effort to make a wavering decision constant - that she could do without people and would make claims on no-one. She certainly wanted no more to be made on herself, but with this unexpected involvement she'd dropped her guard. Now what had felt like a cleansing, renewing freedom was beginning to look like loneliness.

Her anxiety about the previous evening came back. Beatrice wasn't a threat but may have been once, though even that was unlikely. Sheila was too easy even when cross with her - there was no evidence of anxiety or underlying resentment. Mark's womanising - interested, permissive, responsive to anything in any one of them - was such that it amounted to no more than exaggerated gallantry but this very fact, since you'd grow used to discounting it, could make it dangerous. Sheila would be unwary. It might have been Beatrice then!

It was late again when she got downstairs. They were all about their various jobs except for Beatrice who was finishing her porridge and offered to serve some to Joan. She thanked her, sat down with it and concentrated on the food, adjusting.

It was hot, thick, gritty and needed salt. Watching the milk make a hole in the centre and set the edges afloat she realised she wasn't ready to eat, on the other hand she wasn't ready to talk and sitting opposite Beatrice it seemed the only alternative. She took half-hearted spoonsful from the edge. Beatrice hardly noticed her and drank her coffee staring out of the window with tired eyes. When Joan was nearly finished she found a question and put it as if to pass the time:

"How long have you known the Lewises?"

"Ooh - several years." She turned her gaze to Joan, putting her chin on one hand. "Well, Mark anyway - we worked together."

Joan wasn't certain how to pick up from here. "Aren't you interested in his new way of life?"

"Interested but couldn't see myself doing it, could you?"

"No."

"I suppose there's a faint chance it might work." Joan noticed she was idly following her movements. When she got up for coffee Beatrice turned to her - half interested in being waylaid, certainly in no hurry to go outside.

"That's not how you sounded last night." She sat back in

her place.

"Well - I suppose I think it'd have a better chance if it were a bigger experiment. As it is it looks as if it's out to defeat its own best purposes."

"What are they?"

"To give people the room they think they need to express themselves."

"I thought it was an experiment in relating to others."

"That too, but how do you do that if you're knotted?"

Joan waited, her own elbows on the table.

"If you take your old attitudes into a new system it's not a new system. I'd be more optimistic if it were an experiment in recognising no restrictive family ties rather than in multiplying old ones - I mean sexually and parentally - if everything were on a sharing basis or at least on a free to come and go one. I'd like to see how communal children grew up - whether they'd be freer to be themselves."

"You'd be more optimistic, I'd be less." Joan wanted to keep her going. "Have you ever thought of having children?"

"Not really - if I did I wouldn't want them on the old terms. There's no way I'd be willing to use up all my energy in the one role or put my kids into such a pressure chamber. No fun for them burning themselves up to achieve the impossible. You can't satisfy a caged animal. I'd be quite interested in a marriageless society." She was looking out of the window again. The subject produced compulsive responses and, half detached, she began to leave more and more to her mouth. "My son needn't know I was his mother, needn't feel he was an extension of me, could belong to himself."

Joan smiled in her cup. It was a negligent resumé that didn't do justice to one of her articles. She remembered it as playful and utopian and the title had stuck: 'The Communal Advantages of Singularity'. She'd been attracted to the personality behind the pedantry. "Do any of us?" she said.

"What?"

"Belong to ourselves. Could we ever? You can't escape pressures even by avoiding people - lack of them shapes you another way."

"You can escape that kind of pressure!" Beatrice focussed her gaze for the first time. Funny she hadn't really noticed Joan properly. Not so reserved this morning. She racked her brains to remember what Sheila'd said about her when they were introduced. "Haven't you ever found family ties restrictive or got to the point where being too close seems more destructive than keeping your distance?"

"Yes, but only on the grounds of pain. I like the security of a family and find I don't really believe in the mythical 'self' we're supposed to be looking for. That's one of the ideas behind Mark's project that attracts me. Of course to some extent we're limited by our temperaments but we're not defined by them and whatever the limits are, exposure makes more of us. I've a good idea what my limitations are but if I get involved enough the barriers start to break. There mightn't be much of a change to an observer but to me it's one near-indefinable shift after another. The more I respond the less I'm aware of myself as having shape or definition, just human equipment, and I find myself chasing ideas and possibilities that would have been dead to me earlier. Looking for a final definition or freedom for 'me' seems to me madness or worse, an awful kind of ignorant self-protection and self-love. It's my particular nightmare and my particular sin if you'll forgive the word. I'm afraid both of protecting myself and of not."

Beatrice smiled and warmed to her. "Isn't the kind of experiment I was interested in worth a try on those grounds alone?"

"But you can't have no ties at all if you're living with others. I'd feel about it the same as you did last night about Mark's venture - it'd be substituting a large family group for a small one. There'd be as many restrictions of our own making and hardly different in kind. If your son's got lots of people to learn from he isn't necessarily going to pick on those who'll help him adjust any better to the whole group. He'll go for whatever appeals to his current development. Children do it in any society - friends, teachers, relatives are models for different things at different times. We're all so different, all any of us can hope for is a permanent source of contact - of accessibility, and this is more likely in a natural family group."

Beatice shifted her legs and put her cup down. "But we're not all that unlike each other. We respond to the same things and can take a few things for granted - no need to hold on that desperately to any group."

"But suppose those basics aren't enough? For a lot of natures they aren't. Some need a more intricate and constant intimacy to feel the reassurance they need to live. Or, on the other hand, suppose you did manage to transfer expectation and contact of this kind to a larger group, couldn't this make you more vulnerable to pressure, not less? If you avoided individual influences wouldn't you be more exposed to mass ones? I wouldn't like that. The truth is your own nature'll have to be satisfied whatever the size of the group you feel you belong to. If your son's nature for instance is intense he'll find when he gets into the larger society it's full of little units he can't break into and he'll have no skills for making his own. Another nature might happily take to diffuse relationships but outside his group be seen as only able to achieve casual contacts which'll put up different barriers - you can't change personal limits even in your kind of experiment and expanding them might be easier in a family group. After all how do you make yourself care enough in a large group to force you to use your imagination about individual cases? In a small one you've got to or go under - you've got to understand in detail and sympathise, there's nowhere else to go."

She paused, looking tense and miserable. The sudden tumult of remembered rows with her husband and worse suppressions shut her up. She'd done it, walked out, mindlessly self-protective and until she'd come here there'd seemed to be nowhere else to go.

"So, like me," Beatrice said, "you don't put faith in systems - but you've got to have social experiments or you're protecting the limits you're afraid of."

Joan nodded. "Mark's experiment is more likely to work though, isn't it?" It's such a good compromise."

Beatrice smiled again. "Sounds as if he's won you over anyway."

"Oh, no."

Another smile.

"I'm interested, like you."

"What a charmer the man is! When I worked with him he kept us all on our toes - the women, I mean - staff as well as students. I only just resisted being brought to heel." Joan frowned. "For a long time I wondered if it was just another expression of male ego, if we were all mirrors in which he could see his charms reflected."

"He gives me the impression of being a very genuine man."

"But genuine what? If you feel yourself falling under his

spell and show it - I mean really show it - he steps back."

"So he should."

"Should he?"

"I agree with him, I'm afraid - how can anyone deliberately invite that kind of chaos?"

"Doesn't look to me like a conscious decision, more like a reflex - but if it is it has to be based on something more interesting. A man who likes women, needs to get close to them and inspire their affection and who shies away when he does - who appears to be lonely while having intense friendships with several - may not be the old-fashioned moral stoic he appears to be."

"Almost bound to be since he's feeling the same feelings he's producing."

"Ah, but is he to any great degree? You might see him in a slightly different light if you'd met him before he got in to all of this. You probably see him as someone whose good sense and genuineness, not to mention intensity, makes it difficult for him to get easy solace from anything - someone not to be taken in by appearances and equally unlikely to show off - a man who seems to carry a natural or accidental loftiness into every aspect of his life. It's there even in the way he dresses - a totally characteristic naturalness and straightforwardness. It took me some time to feel his appearance was so magnificently unselfconscious it amounted to being dressy and probably took no end of conscious discrimination to achieve. Isn't naturalness essentially something you don't notice? Even his work clothes set him off."

"He's a handsome - "

"No, let me finish, I want to tell you a story. I began to see it fitting with other behaviour - his relationship with women, obviously, and even with ideas - in all cases his best purposes usurped by a hungry ego that was forced to obey the precepts of its own good sense but always kicked back - in this case with a pretentious lack of pretension. It began to look like a dangerous business and we women were some of the victims (I was still wriggling on the hook). It looked as if he were making no demands at all when in fact he was making too many. This view of him was strengthened when I met him accidentally once in a camping store. The place sold jeans and jackets and so forth and finding I didn't want anything I hung around with him while he tried on various trousers and jackets, drawing in his stomach, thrusting out a leg, examining thigh and buttock from one side then the other and trying on an assortment of colours and designs. Occasionally he was pleased at the effect and glanced over to me to be sure. He was totally preoccupied then suddenly dismissed the lot and walked out. Going along the road he was chatting as if we'd never been there, it'd all taken place at some other level of consciousness, but after a while he looked jaded. Thinking he was disappointed at not finding anything I said 'It wasn't a very good shop. Cheer up, better luck next time!' and he looked first surprised then furious."

Joan was silent until she realised Beatrice had paused for a response. "Sounds touching. We're all vainer than we think."

"Hold on. Everything he'd tried on in the shop he'd come out of his cubicle to look at in the outside mirror. With jackets he used me more openly, putting them on straight off the rack and asking me if I liked them without bothering with a mirror."

"Well?"

"But after he'd looked angrily at me and I'd said defensively 'Don't you like clothes?' he looked at me with an amused indulgence I could hardly believe. Over the years that and a lot of other equally small and touching things seemed to add up to something not so touching, a kind of victory parade over self and us. He was an old campaigner and wore whatever clothes, literally and metaphorically, were most effective in attack and had the advantage of all good battledress - camouflage. From top to toe a campaigner celebrating a life-long victory over 'the monstrous regiment of women'."

"Oh come off it Beatrice, who isn't vain, interested in the opposite sex and aware it causes problems?"

"Don't you see - women, ideas, systems - there's always as much self-love as self-hatred in taking them up or dropping them."

"No, I don't."

"He's trickier than he seems."

"Aren't we all."

Beatrice looked indifferent and stood up lazily stretching all six feet of herself in front of Joan who felt both cramped and insignificant but followed her outside. She was now taking deep breaths of air and said on an exhalation "Don't you honestly feel men have had the best of it? It's a man-made world, or rather was while childbirth took up all our time - and there's still a male ethic to break through." Joan didn't say anything. "Wife, lover, mother, stay in the background!"

"You call it background? Don't you think they might feel they've missed out somewhere?"

"I don't think so - not consciously anyway and it's their conscious behaviour making the trouble. I think for a couple of generations at least it's going to be a battle and Mark knows it. At least it is for people like him and me and surely we're not that different from everyone else. Mark and

I have a lot in common. I love men so much I'm afraid of them. What's more I wouldn't sacrifice my freedom to range, as he's done, for anything - I'm too greedy and that's one of the reasons why until now at least, I've not wanted to be pinned down by children."

Joan gave a brief sideways glance at her. "So your only lasting contact will be with yourself. Not much to be got out of that in the long run. I deeply wish I'd had children."

At that moment a sudden skirmish and foot-pounding to her right was followed by a male shout and explosion of childish crying. It was coming from Selby's path and as she turned Simon banged into her legs letting out screams of fright released by the collision. Claude just behind stared up with a white face.

"What's the matter?" She tried to pick Simon up but he flung himself away and stood facing and looking past her, suddenly quiet. He'd gone purple, arms slightly forward, back hunched waiting for breath, then the screams broke out again, effort and passion contorting his face and neck muscles as if his body were garotting him. His chest heaved so violently it made him totter and she picked him up, still resisting, deafening her with yells and squeals, pushing his squirming body away while she gripped it harder. She let the storm burst round her making unconscious sounds of soothing until the note of frenzy eased. When the sounds opened and released him to the ordinary business of crying she felt she was released too. The terror, the loss of self he'd felt she'd experienced herself and under its influence hadn't seen the stout figure of Mrs. Selby walking towards them. Beatrice went to meet her.

"Poor little chap, he does take on so!" Mrs. Selby's voice was on guard, bright eyes sharp and at-the-ready, red face defensive, bluster in stance and expression. Joan was first aware of her swollen legs and looked from knotted veins to a sturdy aproned body and black-grey hair. Simon's arms were in a choking grip round her neck, his body flattened against her like a wet leaf but pushing her back and she obeyed, turning and carrying him away until she came to a field where she spotted Mark's head turned towards them over a hedge.

"What's the bellowing?"

She handed the boy over and stood waiting. He squeezed out through the nearest gap with his son in his arms and put him down. "You hurt?" He examined him, holding him off while Simon cried and struggled to get closer, then letting him grab his leg he looked to Joan for an explanation.

"He was coming from the Selby's place."

With a mood change as fast as his son's he bent to pick him up. "Did he touch you?" A slight shake of angry impatience. "Did Mr. Selby hit you - did anyone hurt you?" The boy cried harder and clambered in to cling round his neck. Beatrice came up.

"It's all right now. Mrs. Selby says the three of them damaged some lettuce seedlings. Her husband lost his temper and belted his son and Simon got frightened."

"Murderous bastard!" He walked off and they watched him take Simon into the house.

The two women were still there when he came back and squeezed through the hedge without speaking. He bent out of sight and stood up holding something. Joan looked over and saw the plough and, for the first time, the horse which she now heard rhythmically tearing grass. She jumped when he shouted to make it move. The horse ignored him. He let go the plough and came over again.

"The man's a menace." He spoke quietly. Joan thought

it was time to go and it must have been reflected in her face. "I'm not exaggerating. There's a rumour he had another child - knocked it out of its highchair in one of his rages and killed it."

Joan wouldn't look at him.

"The say David, the next youngest, was there when it happened."

She glanced up. His presence, icier and tenser by the second, was even worse than his words. "The whole family's rotten."

Beatrice was attentive.

"His daughter was up to her tricks when she was thirteen, there was a scandal that got into the local papers about her. Did you know he was a chef before he came here? Had quite a reputation in a hotel in Wiltshire. He had a lunatic brother who used to visit him there. Scared the hell out of the kitchen staff - hairy, sloping forehead, the lot. He'd spent ten years in an asylum and when they found out about it the woman he'd paid most attention to left. On the whole he was the harmless one, he stood around and laughed mostly, but daughter and brother put paid to Frank. He'd never been popular. He was accused of stealing and fired."

"No wonder he's difficult," Beatrice said.

"You mean he's got an excuse for what he is? Don't you believe it. He thinks he has. Somebody staying at the Bull recognised him and told us the story. One thing stuck when I heard it. He'd been boastful at work, thought himself superior to both job and colleagues which didn't go down too well, but most of the time was morose and uncommunicative. What they loathed more than anything was the way he enjoyed their discomfort and anxiety. If he knew someone was anxious he'd be around saying or doing something to make it worse - usually under the guise of reassurance. One of the staff was pregnant and when she found she was going to have a breach confided it to her friends. He found out and became solicitous - told her how careful she'd have to be - that in cows it was always dangerous - that his family as farmers would expect to lose calf or cow or both - and kept up a persistent concern for as long as the torment pleased him. Eventually she left too." As he'd got under way he'd leant towards them. "I've discovered it's dangerous," he said pushing his face closer to Joan's averted one, "to play the liberal game in certain instances. Wisdom lies sometimes in letting instinct take over."

She didn't answer.

"If you've got madness masquerading as sanity it's a moral problem of a different kind. You can't deal with it point by point or with understanding because you don't understand. It's alien, unreachable, with its own momentum. In his case with an unlimited potential for harm. I'm frightened for my children and not just for their physical well-being. There's no solution but opposition. Fairness gets turned against you - becomes part of your weakness and his strength, all you can do is fight. Sometimes it worries me so much I'm afraid if I can't get rid of him I'll never make it here."

Beatrice put her hand out. "Don't, Mark, it'll do you more harm than he can."

She went through the gap to him and Joan, turning to go, saw them standing side by side with Beatrice patting the horse as if soothing Mark. After a moment he joined in. Within seconds he was murmuring "Beauty isn't she?" and Joan, still pushed by the momentum of his moods, studied the small Arab head, thick neck, barrel shape, long matted mane and unexpected fringe of chestnut hair above the hooves, then looked at Mark. He was looking round for her, his large clear eyes wanting to please and be pleased. She completed her turn and left.

When she'd gone a few yards she heard Beatrice coming up behind and as she reached the glasshouse felt her hand on her shoulder turning her to watch Mark. He was bracing his shoulders against the reins and effortlessly this time moving off with his horse.

"Wouldn't you know it was a female horse?" she said. "Look at him living his dream."

Joan, unnoticed, cast up her eyes and went to find Sheila.

In the kitchen order and efficiency at a spanking pace built up a barrier and a sense of achievement that eventually made Joan feel less vulnerable, but she still avoided Mark. During lunch she found herself watching and being charmed by Tom. He was fed up with seeds, he said. Mark offered him a chance to plough and his face lit up. Why didn't he attract attention as fast as Mark? There was something refreshing, confident and straightforward in his responses.

She found a job for the afternoon where she could watch him. Mark was teaching him how to handle the plough and gave careful instructions and demonstration but Tom was only half attentive, restlessly eyeing the horse and plough. Joan caught his excitement and looking up after he'd cut a furrow saw his face shining and rosy over a gleaming fold. He was more beautiful, more sensually exciting, more 'given' than Mark. But he gave little of it to her, that was the difference. Now he was trying to get the reins taut round his right shoulder and under his left arm. It seemed only to work until he took the plough, in attempts to move he lost the tension. Mark left the horse to her own devices and showed him some body movements to manipulate the reins without touching them. Tom ploughed a wavy furrow but at the end of it the horse wouldn't budge. He stood red-faced, willing her sturdy backside to move. When it did it was sideways and upset the plough. He persisted for the best part of the afternoon and eventually learnt to turn her and after a spectacular series of straight furrows handed her over to Mark. He looked relieved and happier to be lining the troughs with compost.

It was Mark who attracted her attention now in spite of herself - changed yet again and this time so relaxedly in tune with his work that she began to feel she'd made up the rest. If not that then she'd exaggerated the violence or suddenness of his moods through her own fears. Later she thought she sensed a kind of exhilaration in him that was parallel with or encouraged by Tom's willing and silent trekking backwards and forwards to the cart. Tom had moved into a steady pace without tension or boredom.

That Mark had been imagining the fulfilment of his hopes seemed clear when after supper Tom said, "I enjoyed this afternoon", and Mark, his expression happy and grateful, answered without misgiving, "A wonderful way to live!"

They were sitting in the lounge where Sheila'd built a log fire, and from their different angles they all faced it red-cheeked and heavy-eyed. Joan had a book she wasn't reading. Bess, on the floor, her head on Tom's knee, stared into it watching the sparks fly off a log. Only Mark wanted to talk, and to get encouragement turned to Beatrice and Jack on the sofa.

"I feel the opposite to you, you see, Jack. For me this is the only freedom worth having."

Jack smiled with no intention of arguing. Beatrice and he hadn't worked hard and there was a touch of friendly participation in it.

"It's so simple," he went on, "but such a mystery. The instinct's born in us and we've buried it alive." He paused, gathering his thoughts. "This way most of our objectives are physical and achievable and because of that we get back a sense of possibilities. As part of the other gargantuan system you lose all sense of what you yourself can do about your life - the system's too big to keep up more than token contact with the units that build and depend on it. A sense of impossibilities and defeat is the result. Here the powerlessness goes and because of that the objectives become not just physical but, once they're shared, carriers of emotional and imaginative connotations giving rise to new ideas and attitudes that might slowly affect the world. But nothing can be born, nothing can happen without others." He glanced over to Tom who was almost asleep, his eyes only as conscious as friendship demanded. "The personal rewards, all dreams aside, are enormous."

Tom smiled.

"Where else can you get something close to a child's sense of pleasing your group while doing what's necessary? If we lived like this there'd be no divorce between child and adult, no sudden onslaught of individual responsibility, no loss of the group we were committed to, and we'd be working physically, intellectually and imaginatively all at the same time like a child because effort and ambition would be related back to our group in an endless interchange. The split between mind and body, objective and love would disappear. The confinement of working in society as it is is brought about by its lovelessness."

Joan turned her head. Bess raised hers - still staring into the fire but not at it, a slight tension and dismissiveness in the angle.

"Outside it's all monotony dedicated either to cash or

hopelessly indistinct objectives. You tie yourself down with responsibilities you've made yourself simply to enable you to work with others in an artificial situation. Half the 'musts' and 'must nots' do no more than keep up appearances. Everyone knows it but agrees it's necessary while being frustrated and irritated by it. After all if you show the boredom you feel, you're slacking and if you're slacking you're leaving the stress to others. Secret slacking's a national pastime, open slacking's an offence. Colleagues get more outraged at it than at the system that makes it necessary. It's not their fault. Ego is most inflammable where it's under-expressed and if you can't ever feel your value and see its importance then everything becomes a competition for recognition. The way I see it you can't win in such a society. If you work really hard and lose yourself in the system it seals you off in spite of the fact that essentially you're doing it to please others as much as yourself. Your sense of achievement is based on a system's principles which in a complex society are too far removed from the motivations that give rise to them - too far removed, therefore too crude and too simplified. Following these routes leads you to more and more specialist abilities apparently less and less related to their overall purpose. You lose sight of the people it's designed for and neither system nor individual functions adequately. So, paradoxically, the harder you work the more isolated you become and the more confined to work as your only means of self-expression, at which stage you also become potentially dangerous. A threat to your work, your view of it, your position in it, becomes a threat to yourself. What can we do when so much of our life urge is being expressed and satisfied in abstract? We all need to feel excited and alive and that somehow we belong and are doing something worthwhile.

Submission *en masse* is the only way we've found to maintain our social relatedness and apart from the nervous life of the tasks that's all we've got left except for some jaded flank-rubbing. You don't really relate in such a system except by lucky accident. You've lost the setting for seeing and knowing you depend on each other."

"Have you got some political ideas at the back of all this?" Jack asked. "It doesn't sound as if this commune is all you want."

"Only political by accident - I've no party" - he paused a moment - "unless it's the Ecologists. Eventually if people take to it all over the country it'll take political shape." He looked over to Tom who was asleep.

"Can I tell you my overall dream?" he said turning to Jack again - "you could call it political if you like but I see it as a kind of inevitability." Jack nodded. "I've felt since my teens that a mood of disenchantment in society was a wonderful thing. Tension, misery, anxiety are the preludes to change - how else do you make the effort and risk the exposure involved? I felt we were in a renaissance greater and more far-reaching than any other. Here I'm close to one tiny aspect of it but it holds the seeds, along with similar settlements all over the country, of a new way of life. Think of the total reorganisation of social and economic life around small-scale units in some ways like a kibbutz, in others like a small town. Only the beginnings, mind you, a transitional society between what we know and are used to and what we might become. Anything new must be based on need - in this case for something we've lost. Hunger for life and love are synonymous - it's a biological fact like the fact of death. If we're forced into isolation we'll identify with anything - our surroundings, the elements, even a system. The definition of love has always been too small and local, that's all. Everything we do, believe and are depends on our society. What we consider to be 'abstracts' are the fumes of flesh and blood. Since we value ourselves as we're valued and take revenge on society when we aren't it's amazing to me we've never faced up to this properly as a practical and political issue. The new society will grow, as always, out of taking into account only the most obvious facts of our situation as they occur to us - out of taking the most convenient and least disturbing ways of solving the problems we recognise. A book I've been reading gives a general idea of the way thinking is going when it's not going backwards. After the year 2,000 for instance, the possible life of a European is pictured as one in which there'll still be major towns but outside them the hamlets emptied by the industrial revolution will be busy again. Strikes and discontent in urban factories will've made big flourishing ones decentralise many of the operations - they'll get done in small units in the new rural communes. Work roles and times will be very flexible and retirement abolished. I would think work would include other things than just the factory or office stint which might not amount to more than 2 or 3 days a week. Class barriers, pay differentials will've become less and less meaningful. Many places will be specially insulated against heat loss and have a windmill or some form of waterpower to generate electricity. Farm and human refuse will commonly be recycled for fuel, and solar energy increasingly adopted. Jobs, all of them, domestic and otherwise will be shared by men and women alike. The idea of equal responsibility and involvement between sexes and ages will be growing from now on. If a feeling of group centrality gets a chance to grow through the smaller working units and the leisure made by job-sharing then a new vision of the world gets a chance to be born. With time off in which to associate freely - to take part in sports and a diversity of social interests which will be seen as just as radical to our social structure as the nine-to-five slog is now - we'll develop a new idea of what it means, because inside an increased social awareness lies the most unexpected thing of all - an increased independence. It's the result of seeing, feeling, knowing your value, and this is fed back to society in fresher thinking. If real relationships with people are valued as an essential part of the social system then you're being both fully used and less threatened. The result is more energy, ideas and compassion at society's disposal."

Jack and Beatrice looked refreshed and touched by the insight into what powered him. There was nothing to argue with. Jack muttered something that sounded hesitant but approving and the whole thing hung intact like a suspension over their heads. It stayed with them for the next few days.

Bess, in spite of scepticism about his motives and ability to follow through without risking more than he was prepared to, found herself caught by it and when later in the week Beatrice happened to tell her about Simon and the seedlings found herself tense and anxious about the neighbours in a similar way to Mark.

She saw Claude dragging Simon, who was anxious and reluctant, up Selby's pathway one afternoon and followed them thinking to fetch them back without making an issue of it. Joan was working the patch next to the fence and watched them. Simon had started to cry and alerted Mrs. Selby who came out to face a group.

"Hello, you back again, nipper?" She opened the gate.

"They've got to go in for tea." Bess apologetically covered her determination. She turned Claude round briskly and picked Simon up.

"You've been 'ere a few days, 'aven't you?" Mrs. Selby ignored everything but the apology. "You gonna stay?"

"For a while anyway." She moved to go.

"Stay a minute - 'ave a cuppa tea. Go on you two, yer mum wants yer!" She'd put her hand on Bess's arm, Simon was struggling to get down and Bess felt captured.

"You too!" Mrs. Selby looked at Joan. "I never get a chance for a chat. 'E won't be in for 'alf hour." That made the difference, they felt easier - Bess was moved by the excitement and curiosity in her face but still dithered. Mrs. Selby looked to Joan who stood with her head down. "Oh come on for Christ's sake - they can't miss you for a few minutes." She turned down her path, the business settled.

Going indoors felt like entering a new world - the dark, the smells of dog, paraffin and a mixture of unknowns came over as alarming as well as alien. The passage gave on to a chilly kitchen as big as the one next door but with a flagstone floor that made it feel like a courtyard. The light was dim, the window too small and the only rug was on the other side of the room in front of the cooker. Joan was drawn to it and stood waiting to feel warmer. When she looked up Bess was nodding and smiling into a corner where there were two others sitting at the far end of a table. The plump young woman had one eye concealed by hair and the other fixed on her. The lad next to her was in the throes of a silent joke. Joan said hello and a nervous snort took him by surprise. He put his hand to his mouth and turned to his sister who, cocking her eye in his direction without spoiling her smile, caught and fixed his gaze which came to rest on her hair.

"These are the other two, Jim and Marion." There was a pause. "Get the biscuits, Jim." Mrs. Selby drew a couple of chairs from the table while Jim pushed his own back to the wall and stood up. A nervous twitching in his hands and arms spread to his whole body.

"Come on lad, we'll be 'ere till Christmas." The visitors watched him disengage, cross the room and come back with a rattling tin. "It's 'is nerves the doctor says." Tall and wiry, he rattled the tin at his mother. "What about cups and saucers?"

Bess made a dart to help but Mrs. Selby blocked her, gesturing them to the chairs she'd prepared. Marion got up, barged by her brother becalmed at the table, and finished the setting. Bess and Joan sat as directed. Joan, intensely nervous, searched round the room in a longing for objects. There was a 'rocker' next to the stove with a flattened cushion, a stone sink under the window, and a paraffin heater not in use. Why didn't they shut the back door? She brightened at the steaming tea-pot.

Bess was smiling up at Jim who was still standing, eyes on his mother, hands twitching gently on the table-cloth.

"Sit down boy and pass the biscuits." It took a few moments. Joan took one. Bess snatched one before it jerked out of reach. Jim, delighted at her eagerness, grinned at her, his high cheekbones and narrow eyes emphasizing the one expression his face looked built for - pleasure. Fresh-complexioned, rosy, a boy's innocence in a man's body he stood up again for no reason, brown curls and skinny body towering over them, not dressed so much as covered in sweater and jeans and looking, in suppressed leaps, for a way out. Bess gobbled her biscuit. Enjoying his enjoyment she took another. Joan, moving from objects to general structure, was noticing the frightening sameness this kitchen had to the one next door. Of course it had. She wasn't paying enough attention to the people in it. She picked up her biscuit.

Mrs. Selby encouraged her: "What about you? - you permanent?"

"No, a week or two, that's all."

"Sort of holiday, then."

Joan nodded.

"You find your jeans cut into you when you're bending?" Marion asked leaning towards her from the corner. "I've 'ad to give 'em up, I'm too fat. You'd be alright though." Joan grinned. "Either that or walk round with 'em undone and falling off me bum."

"That's enough, Marion. Fill up the cups." Mrs. Selby pushed hers towards her. Bess, wanting to make up for it, asked if she worked here all the time.

"Fat chance of anythin' else." Marion pulled a face and cocked her eye at her mum.

"Why not?" Bess asked.

Staring at her mother's neck: "Dad couldn't run the place without us."

"Do you grow for yourselves as well as the market?" Bess asked Mrs. Selby after a silence. "I mean do you farm all the stuff you need, like Mark?"

"Good Lord no!" she answered with a laugh as if Bess were comparing her husband to a nincompoop. "Frank's got 'eating in those glass'ouses. We aren't short of a bob."

"Alright if you're a lettuce," Marion muttered to Joan but Joan was distracted by a quick, soft padding and sudden appearance of a skinny mongrel. Seeing them he stopped in the doorway and barked - slowly moving inside, sharpening the aggression and building up the volume. Noise and stink rose to a pitch and Mrs. Selby shrieked "Get out, you bugger!" raising her hand. He stood stunned, trunk stiffly poised on legs stuck out like a new-born giraffe's and his head thrust forward. When the noise leapt out again it had a relentless mechanical build-up that terrified Joan and he spotted it, giving the sound a fiercer edge broken with squeals of frustration. He stood lurching his head at her.

"You don't wanna be afraid of 'im," Mrs. Selby said, "'e's mostly wind! 'E'd only bite if we weren't 'ere."

Joan whitened.

"'Ere, you bugger!" The heavy but gentler tone and a wave of her hand to her side stopped the noise. He cocked his eye receiving instructions, raised his top lip, lowered it, barked, stopped again, then with a high-pitched whine came over to sit by her. She gave him a biscuit that he scoffed with a noise like clearing his throat. Joan, peering over the table, saw the muzzle raised.

"How many times have I told you not to feed him from the table." A voice from the doorway took them completely by surprise. Quiet, toneless, a light disturbance of the silence that penetrated just as effectively as the noise. Instead of looking up curiously their first response was alarm at Mrs. Selby's disobedience. The visitors hadn't met Frank before and even allowing for the emotional stripping the dog had caused couldn't account for the naked insecurity they felt when they did.

It was an unexpectedly fine face. He was tall, thin, self-contained - there seemed little more than an expectation of response that was automatically given. Bess was curious. He walked past them to put something on the draining-board. His wife fetched a large mug and filled it. Joan, totally put out, would have liked to leave but couldn't - not paralysed by curiosity but involvement, being part of the unresolved situation that had a life of its own and that hadn't finished with her.

Bess needed to break the silence but not with him and tried to say something to Mrs.Selby. She found herself anxiously vetting the possible small-talk but ready to take a leap in the dark, when she was forestalled. He'd approached the table and was appraising her. She waited. David came in and walked past his father to the sink to examine what they now saw was an oily wheel. He showed no interest in the company. By now Bess had lost the urge to talk and was afraid whatever she said would betray something. Frank put out his hand for his tea and the dog ducked out.

"So you're helping Mr. Lewis." He addressed both but was looking at Bess. There was cool amusement in it that changed her feelings to resentment. She didn't answer. The question was general and he turned to Joan. Silence.

Feeling the pressure Bess finally said "yes" and smiled up, but at Jim who looked away and at the biscuits.

"Offer the lady the tin."

"I've had some," Bess said quickly this time to him, "thank you."

She needn't have bothered. Jim sat there stricken with the command, his hands twitching in his lap. Drawing them up and putting them round the box without lifting it, he paused. Suddenly it burst into life.

"'Old it still." His tone gently focussed attention on it. "'Ow can she take one?"

Bess looked up angry but her hand was reaching out.

"Now the other lady" - Joan shook her head - "and yer mother and sister." He offered to one after the other, both hands arresting the box. When they refused he put it down. "Yer brother and me?"

Bess snatched and offered it. He took one with a slight smile.

"So," chewing slowly, "do you like working for Mr. Lewis?" He drew his chair to her side.

"We work with him. Yes, we like it."

"Ah," pause, "and what sort of things do you do with him?"

Bess blushed and Joan answered, "Everything. It's interesting and rewarding. Mark's an unusual man." She stopped as suddenly as she'd started. In letting Bess off the hook she felt she'd exposed Mark.

"Unusually approved of by the ladies, anyway."

Silence, and no appreciable intensification of response.

"Tricky thing farming the way 'e does - needs all the support 'e can get in any shape or form. 'E's so gone on what's natural. Mind you the rest of us farm pretty naturally too, those of us 'oo can't afford to mix business with pleasure, I mean. The land 'asn't shown 'im 'oo's boss yet - give it time. 'E's lucky 'e's not dependent on it."

Bess was about to say he was and bit back.

"Yes. Good thing 'e doesn't need the cash. Nice to be able to throw up a job and indulge a fancy" - noticing Bess was hard-pressed - "'e's full of fancies of course- I've seen a number of 'em come and go." He turned to her, crossing his legs. She held on.

Joan, looking away, noticed the two adult children had retired so far into the darkening corner she'd forgotten they were there. They were close to each other, both looking at Marion's empty plate, negating all impulses, destroying all vital signs. Becoming forgettable they were almost invisible. Joan kept blinking to keep them in focus. Mrs. Selby sat with her elbows on the table clasping her chin, her mouth buried in her fingers.

"'E doesn't seem able to be able to get people to stay. I wonder why that is? Are you staying?"

Bess turned to face him. "For a term - my husband's on leave."

"Ah, married are you? Should've guessed. And to a soldier. What made you come?"

She hesitated, then: "It was my husband's idea." She wondered if the animosity would come across as disapproval of Tom's decision.

"Still, I expect there are compensations."

It wasn't working out. She was beginning to feel hysterical. He was fast on his feet, pursuing his course and always a step ahead. How was it she let him? Perhaps he wasn't doing it, perhaps she was doing it to herself. He was indifferent, bored - there wasn't enough of him backing it. Trying to make an impression, probably, like the cockney accent that came and went.

"You go along with all this organic farming?"

There it was again. She blushed. Did he know there was anything going on between her and Mark? She didn't herself. She forced a sentence: "It seems the best way."

"Best?" He considered it. "Depends what you want. I want cash, you see, can't afford to play about."

Not too bad. She spoke again: "I don't know why you think Mr. Lewis isn't serious." She glanced at Mrs. Selby to include her in the conversation but met a rigid profile.

"I wouldn't say 'e wasn't serious about 'is interests, whatever they are, just not about farming."

She wasn't up to it. If he was going to do what he wanted with or without her it would have to be without her. If she didn't respond he couldn't get very far unless he spelt it out and that way he wouldn't be able to get to her in the process.

"'E's got puzzling ideas about what's natural," he said, feeling he had a clear field. "Is it unnatural, would you say, to grow the stuff people want and get out an undamaged crop?" He paused but not for an answer. "'E's afraid of the chemicals. Okay. But 'ow does a man like 'im decide it's better to starve 'alf the world than damage the 'ealth of the lot?"

She'd mistaken the nature of his power, she thought, especially when his next words enhanced the note of patient reasonableness.

"'Is stuff'll be eaten up in the fields" - facing her attentively - "everything's got pests. They'll waste 'is crop and 'is effort and won't stop there. Some'll live in 'im as 'appily as off 'im." Pause. "'E's after picture book stuff." They slipped out as the facts he lived with in a tone that developed a note of pleasurable intimacy - the resignation was an undercurrent. There was even a touch of excitement in laying them bare. He looked roused. "All those quaint ideas" - he uncrossed his legs - "I've watched 'im. I think I know 'im and maybe that's why 'e don't like me. We both like our own way." Her mind raced ahead. "I know 'ow to get it - 'e bungles. What's more I 'co-operate' as 'e calls it more 'an 'e does." There was a long silence that no-one thought of breaking and when he was ready he picked up the old thread. "It's fascinatin' lookin' over 'is land knowing the millions of parasites on 'is grass 'ave all got 'is number. I can see the liver fluke - tiny white specks smaller than a pin's 'ead - spattered all over it." Pause. "'E'll 'ave to watch out for tapeworm in 'is pig. My father 'ad one. When they're ripe bits break off and pass out in yer motion."

'Ripe', 'motion', suddenly clinical - word-perfect for the shades of offence and contempt he wanted - she felt sick.

"And 'e better look out for stomach worms - inch or more long and look like thin twisted string, sometimes short and fine as thread so you can 'ardly see 'em. Lungworm's easier to find - two or three inches long and somewhere between thread and fine string. They're all coughed up or left in the dung and transferred in a lovely natural way." He paused again to look at her closely. "When you think of it we both 'co-operate' in our different ways but mine's more natural because I play by the rules and beat it at its own game - injections, pesticides, insecticides, fertiliser, the lot and no 'olds barred. But don't think I don't understand, I do."

Bess cut out. It wasn't her own fear and disgust she was feeling but his implantation. He was neither harmless nor ignorant but a specialist and the instrument and enemy of life as he saw it. He took power from what he reckoned with and others ignored. His offensive won victories and made victims - enough to obscure the victimisation he felt. If he saw himself as a purist he thought whatever knowledge the world possessed, his was deeper and it was this assurance he directed at her like a beam of light that made her blink in spite of herself. Wherever she turned it was in her eye.

"In a way 'e's achieved quite a name for 'imself for 'is naturalness. Most of us 'ave seen 'im at it in the East field. And 'e's got 'is wife and kids where 'e wants 'em. In many ways a man I can understand. Is the scrawny bird with black 'air still there? 'Aven't seen 'er since I spotted 'em in the grass. As I say 'e don't keep 'em long." Bess was hardly listening but the meaning came through. Twilight was making it impossible to distinguish faces. "Expect 'e's 'ad 'is 'ands on you a few times", he appraised her dismissively, "but that's not my scene. Financially independent, my game would be different."

She found she was standing clasping the table. Sick, hot, faint, she needed the lavatory so urgently she thought she wouldn't make it to the door but was terrified of being overcome by so much evidence of his triumph - so total a response and so totally fitted to his understanding. She leant slightly towards Mrs. Selby asking the way to the bathroom - "Something I've eaten!"

Mrs. Selby got up, switched on the light and seeing her drained face pointed quickly through the doorway. "Up the stairs and to the left."

Joan watched her walk with the exaggerated balance of someone afraid of fainting and leapt out of her seat to reach her at the door.

"I'm alright." It was urgent and irritable and made her step back. Bess climbed with one hand on the wall. There was still someone behind. She looked back to see David, his face grinning and informative. His hands were moving - plunging a forefinger rhythmically through a circle he'd made with forefinger and thumb of the other hand. Her bewildered look made him say, "The loving one." He looked expectant. As her face changed he gave a slow nod, but she hadn't understood.

"Go away." Quiet and vicious her tone made him pause. He assessed her then plunged his finger at face level a few times before turning back.

For a few seconds she'd been free of her symptoms, now they were back stronger than ever. At the top of the stairs she couldn't remember which way to go and groped in the dark for the door. She found it, opened it and ran her hand down the wall for the switch. She'd gone right in before adjusting to the light and seeing what was there. A naked couple on a single bed, brother on sister poised, dazed, skinny and sweaty, with her fingers clenched into his buttocks like a vice. He was looking up at Bess, dark under the eyes and blinking, his face radiant. Marion came to, looked pained, and glazed her out. Bess, collecting her wits, left and stood outside then ran downstairs and out of the house.

In the Lewises' garden she realised suddenly all symptoms had vanished. Relief and ease spread through her like a drug. When she stepped indoors the place was transfigured - the release of energy and sense of freedom turned every object into a stimulus that gave back in clarity and definition what her excitement used up. They focussed and sharpened her responses to a pitch where they needed physical release in laughter but were too surprised at themselves to give vent.

She heard music and followed the sound. Mark was practising in the living-room. The only light was over the music stand which made watching and listening one. He stopped, started, adjusted his strings, repeated the passage - waited for something good. An arm round her shoulder made her jump. Joan was there, frowning and solicitous, "You alright?"

"Sh! He doesn't know anyone's here."

Joan looked puzzled and dropped her arm. What was she up to? Was she ill or wasn't she? She looked over to Mark for explanation. At the fourth repetition of the same few bars she turned back to Bess. Whatever it was she was alright now. She turned back to Mark. Selby's remarks had gone home. He sat there oblivious. A navvy with a dwarf violin under his chin. She began to recognise snatches from "The Turkish". Mozart gutted. The wide shoulders and physical stiffness made it ridiculous, though there was no reason to suppose size made any difference, it was understanding that was missing. His only concern was the discipline. The repetitions were equally boring. Manuscript accuracy was everything. Fair enough if you couldn't play well but a poor skill ought to let some life through. Poor Mozart. Poor anyone. Wide shoulders, long thighs, impassive face, square-topped fingers clumsy and practical-looking, but they focussed attention and made the violin look like an exercise in carpentry.

He was playing better now and for longer. It didn't work. His power conflicted with the music's, a separate body-energy not assimilated in the playing and fighting the music. Separate, disturbing and focussing attention on him - an accident but as if designed and yet he loved and admired every phrase, which was one of the reasons for his missing the point. She wondered why she was seeing as assets the deficits she'd prepared for him. Limitations, after all, were the result of displacement by other forces. He moved like a turtle over a dolphin. ignoring or unconscious of difference, reacting with some and in opposition to most of its movements, and the interplay and contrast were exciting.

With a spasm of mistrust she left and Bess, sneaking in, found a chair at the back of the room to enjoy the intimacy he wasn't aware of and she'd only just realised she wanted. She wasn't listening but was disappointed whenever he stopped playing. The sound, like touch, stimulated and satisfied. The effect of Selby's accusations hadn't been lost but transmuted. Verification of what she knew made things at this moment clearer, easier and brought Mark closer.

"I didn't know you were here!" he said as he saw her. "Why didn't you tell me, I'd have played something for you." He turned on the centre light and came over. Delighted to see her, only his mouth made apologies, his eyes looked excited. "Weren't you bored?"

"No."

A leap of understanding, but he searched for reassurance: "I don't play well, I don't practice enough." He moved closer until she felt surrounded without being touched. Unthinkingly completing the experience she raised her hand to his face. He jerked back. When his eyes re-kindled it was with reproach. "I shouldn't have been doing it now but attending to Floss."

The coldness worked on her like an act of spite, the hypocrisy like a planned offence. No wonder he and Selby hated each other, too much alike. She hurried to find Tom. He wasn't upstairs but she passed the kitchen on her way outside and saw him peeling apples and talking to Sheila.

"Tom."

He turned, grinned, and there was a curl of green peel on the end of his knife. She smiled and went back to their room.

Mark filled a bucket with warm water and took it with an empty one to the cowshed. He shut the door and relaxed. Undoing Floss's rope and leading her to the clean concrete floor partitioned off from the rest of the stall he tied her to a post but before milking stroked her behind the ears putting an arm over her neck and patting and murmuring. She accepted him. The soft shades of gold and brown in the coat fascinated him, so did the delicacy of her head and large, gentle eyes. He ran his hand down to her nose but she whisked it up and away. He persisted, rubbing along her jaw nearer her mouth and she opened it exploratively. "Alright, it's here." He drew the small hay trough up to her and she started to eat. The next ritual he performed in a dream, washed his hands and her udders in warm water, dried her with a towel massaging at the same time, then cleaning down her haunches so no dirt or dung would fall into the milk, fetched his stool and sat with the empty bucket gripped at an angle between his knees. He took the top of the teats between thumbs and forefingers and with the rest of his fingers began the rhythmic squeezing downwards, listening for the splash of milk against the pail.

Within seconds he was suspended with her in a physical peace that removed the last vestige of guilt and fear.

Bess, who'd gone back to the kitchen to work with Tom, watched him come in later relaxed and business-like. He'd dismissed her completely. Hurt and angry she stood closer to Tom who was rummaging in the bread bin for the remaining rolls. Closer still his movements against her made her lean over his back kissing it, feeling the movements lift and stir. A moment later Mark, barging over to the sink, knocked into her. It was Tom who looked up. Mark's relaxed, apologetic smile, teeth alive eyes dead, did nothing for him but Bess, glancing up, sprang to life. Taking the rolls from Tom she arranged them on a baking tray. Seeing Mark's problem had released her from her own.

The meal before Beatrice's departure was another triumph of liveliness with Mark paying so much attention to Beatrice his eyes waited on hers for cues and for opportunities to release his responsiveness. He stacked presents of onions and preserves in the boot of their car.

After the flashing of lights and hooting the rest of them came back in a lively disorder that made Joan feel this was the most wholehearted celebration of a visit she'd experienced and her pleasure at being part of it made her think about Beatrice's insistent individualism with a touch of patronage. What on earth was the point of it if its biggest effort to come out of itself took the form of a cause - one that took the joy out of associating with others - feminism. Was that the closest she could get to belonging? What about all this?

Mark's vision of a new society was becoming so real to her it was more than a social theory. All that had been lost when she grew up was being offered back - that encircling world where thoughts, behaviour and ambitions of parents and friends, diverse as they were, had been integrated by what she'd felt to be her part in them and by her gymnastic ability to identify her interests with theirs. It was a world letting everything in and losing none of the uniqueness of the experiences at the same time as blending them with her own personal and subjective responses. If members of the group moved out the structure still remained intact. Unconscious reference to the remainder gave confidence to open up to newcomers. A fast, explorative identification with others was only possible with that kind of backing. A sense of permanent commitment was paramount, it didn't have to be in pairs but it did have to be taken for granted. If Mark wanted something not restrictive but reliable, with each member of the group balanced in dependence on the others while vigorously and independently in action - that was for her! It made her feel more excitedly alive and expansive than she had since she was a child.

She was clearing the table with Bess who asked her what she thought of Beatrice. Her thoughts broken into she didn't know where to begin or if she wanted to share any of them, but Bess wanted to talk - still excited by the liveliness of the meal. Bess felt generous towards a figure who, in the last instance at least, had claimed so much attention from Mark as a means of forgetting his response to herself and who, in any case, was leaving. As Joan was reluctant she pushed ahead with her own view: "I liked her energy!"

Joan nodded, "Lots of it." There was reservation in the tone.

Bess wasn't going to let her put an end to the excitement of the last couple of hours. "That's good, isn't it?"

"Depends what it's for."

Bess looked puzzled. "A good time? Women's Lib?"

Joan hesitated then looking at her determined face: "But

all that energy for defence purposes. She's sceptical about everything worth having - men, the possibility of successfully belonging to a group ... how do you base a life on manic suspicion of either?"

Bess was silenced. She hadn't expected criticism along those lines, especially from Joan. In any case her own view of Beatrice was almost the opposite. Eventually she said, "She seemed to be on the attack to me - but only to bring about closer relationships - attacking the things she feels might keep us apart."

Joan thought about it. "Well yes, attack, but for the purposes of defence surely, defence of her right to be exactly what she is and with minimal reference to others. She wants closeness on her terms. She's suspicious of Mark's kind of challenge. Doesn't seem open to change except where she's decided it's necessary. If she's mentally prepared for it okay, but then she's got the advantage. That's self-appointed scope to be different, isn't it? I got the impression a group or even one man on a permanent basis was a threat. Don't you feel all that energy's been restricted too much and could easily become restrictive - a good thing to stay clear of?"

Bess was quiet again. Joan was taking Mark's angles on trust which was exactly what he hoped for. She should have seen it coming. She was just the right sort, an isolate wanting association made easy. Even so how much of it was Mark's ideology and how much Mark? Was she under the spell? She waited, plates in hand.

Joan went on, "I can see all that power needed room and Women's Lib. is a demand for that, rightly, on behalf of herself and the rest of us - but if you try too hard you push out the things you need room for."

"She's got to sort things out."

"She's making a cause of it - that's something else. That can be a sort of leukaemia, you start attacking your life's blood."

Bess frowned - not so much in disagreement as anxiety. This wasn't just a convert but a possible fanatic. It wasn't like her.

"She's one of those people whose ability to analyse and neutralise is as strong as their responsiveness - it amounts to running on the spot."

Bess was working up the courage to turn the conversation directly to Mark and to probe when Tom came in and straight over to her. He took her plates and put them down and putting his arms round her smiled at Joan over her head. It was a friendly smile but business-like, he was pre-occupied.

"You were full of something this afternoon when I was in the kitchen," he said, pushing himself off and looking at Bess, "What was it?"

Bess raked her memory. "Oh, nothing much. A rotten experience next door. Got me unawares. Joan was there, weren't you?"

Joan nodded, amazed at the way she'd distanced it.

"There was something I've not told anyone yet," Bess went on, "the brother and sister - when I went upstairs to find the lavatory I barged in on them. They were stark naked making love!"

Joan blushed - a slow suffusion over neck and face. Tom's face opened and grinned with surprise: "You don't mean it!"

"And strangest of all it seemed right!"

He frowned but with some of the smile left over.

"It's a terrible house - dominated and terrorised by Selby. He's sinister and the youngest boy is too but what I stumbled on destroyed him. I suppose it was because even though they'd had to escape from the kitchen unseen it wasn't either nervous or furtive. Finding them was a shock that reversed everything. Their faces were rosy, blinded with life." Tom, stepping back, disapproved of the interpretation. She pushed it: "Don't you see he wants victims and he's failing, he wants fear round him and is failing - even the youngest's not a victim, just another predator."

"They're all victims," Joan murmured.

"In one way - in another they've shoved it back in his face. He's no more than a desert they've learnt to survive in. Sure he thinks he's won - that's his illusion. They've got their own ways out - each one different."

"Oh, Bess!" Joan said.

But Tom was with her again: "Vicious stupid brute -"

"Not stupid - that was the worst part of it - at least not the way you probably mean it. When I was there he was applying his intelligence very effectively - no effort at all to adapt his technique to what he thought would be my kind of weakness."

"She's right!" Mark came up. He'd been listening at the door. "He's no fool. As for the others I've seen 'em myself kissing and fondling in our boxed garden. He torments them right enough" - he looked down at Bess - "but degenerate genes make them what they are. He torments them because he feels superior to them - even to what he is himself. Feels he's cornered by life's dirty tricks but wouldn't have it any other way. Look at the fuel for revenge!"

Joan stepped back. Unsafe, alienated, she hated his hatred and Bess's instant perception of a balance. Both seemed dangerous and evasive.

"He's got a chip off the old block in David", Mark went

on, "he'd better watch his step, and not just when he grows up." He paused giving room to the next remark, "He's Marion and Jim's son not Frank's - at least so everyone says. How's that for poetic justice? His own bit of hot-house home-grown malice. Trouble is I'm lumbered with all three generations. What am I supposed to do?"

"Nothing," Bess answered.

"He's not going to let me live in peace" - looking at her - "he wouldn't need a reason but he's got one anyway. He could never overlook the fact I own his place. What would give him most pleasure would be to get rid of me. All his landlords perhaps, one by one. He's got his daily nuisance-value but that's small satisfaction against the big one - he knows my plans and knows his continued presence does the most damage. He didn't intend to stay when I bought the place - now I think he'll never go."

"Can't you get rid of him legally?" Tom asked - "say you want the house and land for dependents."

Mark looked worried. "I've thought about it. I've got to get advice, it's not promising according to a solicitor friend. When I bought the place it'd been held by joint tenants, Selby and Hardcastle. The owner sold up when Hardcastle left and Selby told him he was going too. Nothing in writing on Selby's part but the agent was verbal witness. This autumn the joint tenancy agreement with the old landlord runs out and there may be a chance. I've been warned it could lead to nothing. It might be impossible to get him out if he doesn't want to go unless I've somewhere else to offer him - which I haven't! The locals all thought he was going. Now he says he's not leaving this flourishing little business unless I make it worth his while. I've only the one hope. It had been a joint tenancy and I might be able to claim the original terms of the agreement don't apply."

"It's a good thing you won't need the space for a bit," Tom said.

"Even now I don't know if he means what he says. If he's genuinely got other plans he might still be going and think it a good idea to let me stew for a bit and perhaps pick up some compensation on the side. I've no way of finding out. All I can be certain of is whatever decision he makes it'll carry maximum suffering for the rest of us!"

"Perhaps he doesn't know himself," Joan said.

"Christ, I hope he does or he'll be tempted to stay for the fun of it. The only chance I've got is if there's something definite - a more profitable opportunity elsewhere. It's like being victim to the weather, you can't be sure what's going to make it do what it does or when." He looked tired. Joan thought it was over and made a move to go. He stopped her by continuing, "Of course David might solve all our problems. He's got arson on his record. They say he burnt down their house some years back. Mrs. Selby claims it was an accident, but there was also a 'badly placed' bonfire that burnt part of our fence a few months ago."

Sheila had seen the oldest boy to bed and came to join the others. She heard the last few remarks and came over with a sudden explosion of voice and gesture that for a split second reminded Joan of Mrs. Selby: "You do carry on!" She fell silent just as abruptly, battling with her feelings and her right to express them.

Mark ducked his head almost imperceptibly - it looked more like a new tension than a movement. Lowering his eyes he bent towards her as if offering help.

Confused she looked at the others and settled on Bess: "He's always judging! He's wrong nine times out of ten!"

Bess looked at Mark who was completing a semi-circle round her to the door. Turning back he lifted his hand. They all followed him out of the kitchen into the sitting-room.

Tom had been interested in Mark's practical problems. To avoid starting the subject up in Sheila's presence he crossed behind the sofa where Mark was now sitting, picked up a book and sat beside him. Within seconds they were absorbed in conversation. Bess went into the room and out again. Sheila got out her sewing. Joan thought she'd have to get a book but didn't feel like it. She watched the two men.

Selby was an obsession with Mark. Almost certainly not the villain he thought he was. She had an uncle a bit like him and used to make a similar mistake - a farmer like Selby, difficult and truculent - she hated him as a child but loved visiting the farm so it couldn't have been that bad. Later she saw he was in perpetual anticipation of ruin. Everything was a threat, too much rain, too little, a sudden wind when the plums were ripening. Her aunt and cousins seemed unhappy and bullied, her aunt especially. Her mother, championing her sister, hated him. The place had been nice when he was out, as he mostly was, because the family seemed to accept it all and she'd come to think they all understood him, that their submission was a sort of defence of him because looking after them was part of his stress. She recalled Mrs. Selby's acquiescent face, chin on hands. It wasn't quite the same. Selby had more power and, by the look of it, a meaner nature. But that was all, surely. His life as he saw it was a fight. His house had burned down, he'd lost his job because of his brother and daughter. It must have been difficult getting established again. He probably felt he had to frighten and bully to make people work and make a go of it. He'd been gifted. Mark said he'd made some small name for himself as a chef. In that case there'd be some perfectionism in his make-up making him harder on the opposition. Perhaps the only sinister factor was the intensity of Mark's, and in her own way Bess's, interpretation of it. If getting rid of Selby became a 'cause' for Mark why shouldn't it work the other way? Mark was ready to think of him as a force - he'd lost touch with his humanity. He was turning the whole thing into a crusade - half crusade, half nightmare - a testing ground for proving himself and standing or falling by the result - reliving the legendary and biblical ideas he'd discarded.

When she found herself worrying more about Mark's imbalance than Selby's she left the room.

6

The morning was damp and cool with an overcast sky and a wind strong enough to lift and stir the branches of trees without moving the hedge sprays under them to more than a solitary clapping from a bunch of new leaves. All the adults in the Lewis commune were lined up against the hedge with rainclothes on and buckets at their sides, ready for potato-planting. They'd breakfasted, come out together and were waiting on starter's orders. The shared sense of special occasion - this was the first time they'd all worked on the same job - was too much for Bess and Tom who, excited by the wet freshness in the air, started horsing around with the potatoes they'd filled their buckets with from sacks at the edge of the field. Mark, picking up the mood, shouted "Go". Grabbing and ducking went at the pace of a race broken only by split-second pauses to firm the potatoes a foot from each other. Starting at the heads of the furrows ploughed and lined the day before they kept together, working as a team, reaching into buckets and bending into furrows almost in time with each other until potatoes were dropped or people looked up, breaking the pattern.

After ten minutes Joan stood up to stretch, saw the others still at it and went down again, cursing her sedentary life and admiring Mark's easy swing. Sheila, standing, tightened her head-scarf, eyes blazing: "Isn't this fantastic?" Joan didn't look.

Within half an hour the stiffest had had enough and wanted a rest but didn't like to ask for it. Bess, who'd taken on the idea of a race was moving on not at a steady but erratic speed gained by veering between tiredness and the incentive of keeping up with Mark. She needed to stand and flex her back but couldn't in case she lost ground. Being left behind would have depressed her. Tom, knowing the power of a game over her, took action against the after-effects.

"Look at this" - the excitement in his voice brought her over - "is it a fossil?" She took and examined it but Mark's progress up the field still bothered her. She shouted to him to come and see.

He came and ran his finger over the shape. "It's a flint cast of a sea urchin", he gave the information like a present. "I've found others and checked on them" - turning it over and over in his hand. They passed it from one to the other, their heads closing over it and Joan came to see what was up. Sheila carried on. Mark delighted at their curiosity felt suddenly aware of the sea it had come from. Joy turned to fear - a weight of water made him press for reassurance on the ground that pressed him back. He went over to his furrow.

They kept at it but slower, each at his own pace, bodies marking progress like shapes on a graph. Joan became oblivious to everything but effort but did her best not to fall behind. In another twenty minutes she'd done so irretrievably and stood up. David was watching her from the other side of the hedge. He might have been pacing her for some time but was preoccupied with something at his chest - a kitten. Joan smiled.

"Pretty puss." He spoke to himself but for her benefit.

She was too tired to engage and bent down to work. "You like her?" She glanced sideways and nodded. "There are five - they've got to be drowned."

The cat leapt out of his arms as they reached a gap in the hedge and made a noise that was a cross between a purr and a chirrup, landing in Joan's furrow. It was too old to be drowned. She stopped. Its body was so small the extremities looked too much for it - round head and upright sinewy tail as big as her little finger. She was too tired for this but the urge to pick it up was almost stronger. "Its eyes are open!" she said heavily.

Reading her he put on his mother's business-like bustle: "Got to. Can't 'ave 'undreds of wild cats running around." The kitten stopped, doubled back and cuffed a potato twice.

She picked it up and gave it to him. "Let me get on." David followed her quietly for a bit, then left.

In the evening the group was tired but unusually pleased with itself. Being tired was now a permitted luxury. Joan was lower in spirits than the rest and felt left out but later the others came to it. In their case it was partly the result of Mark's phone call. His father rang him up in the middle of the evening and when he came back, though he said nothing about it he hung about long enough to infect them with his tension. Sheila was the last to go to bed, apart from Bess, and her fidgeting as if on the verge of talking but not sure what to say or if she wanted to gave Bess a chance to ask if anything was wrong.

"Mark's mother's very ill," came instantly.

The news burst like a fist through Bess's view of life here as a contained world. Until that moment she hadn't realised she had one. "I'm so sorry!"

Sheila looked at her and frowned. "Funny," she said,

"that's more than I got from him." She looked as if she were about to cancel the remark but didn't, then as if groping for a qualifying view or hoping Bess would provide it. In Bess's silence she offered a review of the facts: "She's had a stroke and it's left her right arm and leg paralysed. His father wants him to go and see her and help sort out the practical problems. They've always put great reliance on his suggestions. He wants to know if he should get a daily help or if that would make things seem too strange." She found she still hadn't come up with the relevant facts and added, "Mark dreads the visit, dreads the involvement and dreads seeing his mother."

"Of course he does," Bess said.

Sheila looked at her. "It's almost as if someone's played him a dirty trick - acts angry as well as hurt. Part of him refuses to take notice. He's stiff with anxiety and won't talk about it - I don't know if it's about her or about facing it."

"Both."

She stared at Bess. "What about them? I haven't seen a spark of gentleness or compassion!"

"He's too close to it. You've got to disengage for that."

Sheila thought for a bit. "I'm not so sure, they've not been all that close recently."

"That could be part of the difficulty."

Sheila didn't answer but seemed ready to postpone assessment - in any case something might happen that would overtake the need to make one. Bess saw her as having judged him but on the lookout to test it. Part of her mind would always have to be kept open if he regularly took her by surprise. The urge to pin him down wouldn't go, though. Some things had to be taken for granted in a relationship and gentleness and compassion would have been good ones.

"It's difficult with Mark to tell what he's feeling," Sheila said at last, "And I don't know what I'd be like in his position except it wouldn't be like that - but my parents are both strong thank God." The thought gave her so much relief she went on, "My mother's still very active at seventy - does Yoga," she smiled at Bess.

"Don't you want to go with Mark?"

"They want to see him, not me. Anyway, I've got to stay here, someone's got to run the place."

"How long's he going for?"

"A weekend I'd think."

"Couldn't the rest of us -" Sheila's snort and sudden movement to the door cut her short, but she changed her mind and came back:

"He'll deal with it in his own way. I'd like to see his mother but later - p'raps I'll go down alone for a day or two." She looked at Bess for the first time since the conversation started as if fully seeing her. "He's had a more difficult childhood than me I suppose, his father used to be very religious - a lay preacher. As a boy Mark never missed a Sunday listening to his Dad preaching hell-fire in church - till he found he kept his organist as mistress on week-days. He found that out when he was thirteen and at the same time as his mother so he had to deal with her shock as well as his own. She developed 'nerves' and fainting spells and leaned heavily on him as the oldest and favourite, the girls were much younger. He said what he found most difficult at the time was the unbelievable size of the hypocrisy. He'd had the fires of hell raging in his ears since he was old enough to understand."

"Poor Mark."

Sheila nodded, "I've sometimes thought it might explain the coldness in him."

"Coldness?"

"Distance then, he's got a way of keeping you at a distance however affectionate he is." She paused. "When I want to come closer he won't let me", she paused again, "if I ask him what to do in any situation he always tells me to make up my own mind and it's not always what you want is it? I'd like to share problems sometimes and work them out together."

"Well, you're doing that here, at least."

"Oh he's good at that - ideas, generalities, planning and putting them into practice. I meant things personal to me or the two of us. He's up against it now, you see, now his Mum's ill. Difficult to turn that into general issues."

Bess squeezed her shoulder on her way out. "Tell me if you change your mind and want to go with him - I promise to do everything you say, you've only to write a list."

Mark was missing for most of the following day and Bess saw him for the first time in the evening leaning over the back of Joan's chair. His head was lowered, body almost touching but not quite - bearing down on her. Joan's face was turned up to him brightly and his arm rested on the back of her chair - almost an embrace through the wood. With a flash of anger she sat as far away as she could, lolled back and shut her eyes. She studied them again through half-closed lids. Sheila was right. He's disposed of it for the time being anyway. He was back with the habit of a lifetime - touch and go - bestowing his favours. The pretext this time was in the Moth book they were looking at. He put his hand momentarily over hers to keep her from turning the page. Perhaps Sheila was right about the coldness too. It wasn't just that he didn't know what he wanted, he was excited by the double act. To be emotionally generous and self-contained gave him a sense of mastery. Fool. Long may it last! But the genuine side was the intensity which he couldn't help and that sometimes looked like desperation. From person to person, object to object - the Moth book was coming under the same scrutiny, the same pressure of interest. He stood upright now and noticed her, smiling. She accepted it as if too tired to respond. As he left the room his walk was full of energy. He'd done it then. No wonder he was in many ways so conventional. Society always thought of something to make things easier - "stiff upper lip" for insentience, "love of life" for fear of death - all the opportunities you need to ignore the reality and get on with the mechanics. It meant you were locked up forever, of course, with yourself, your anxiety, fear, shame, sudden childish acts of self-assertion - but presumably they were easier to deal with than exposure. What's more it let you accept defeat as a norm and build instead an ideal world you never could or would belong to.

With her chin sinking on to her chest, depression and exhaustion were tightening their grip when Joan, now sitting closer and in front of the fire, noticed her state and smiled. She responded before she'd had time to think but withdrew it immediately, lapsing into sleepiness.

Joan was changed and Mark was probably the reason. He worked hard at his ideals and some of them came off. He meant well, even though it meant having a crippling respect for his own inventions. He wanted love but also to be fair, put every drive at the service of the commune, and into being what he thought 'a good chap' - the destructive too, presumably. Too much dedication made it look as if you didn't have much faith. If he eased up a little it wouldn't fall apart but he might. Ideals served his purpose - that was the point of them - he'd always be tying himself to blind horses. But how could he? All that energy and curiosity given such limited expression and that not its own. Any ideal that couldn't accommodate its opposite was doomed. No wonder he spent his life frightened of sabotage. Tom had come in and she went over to sit by him needing his freshness and generosity.

Joan, seeing how tired Bess was, noticed her own for the first time and stretched out in front of the fire. Her back was stiff and tender but blended its sensations quite pleasantly into the vague-headed, fat-fingered, all-over paddedness she was experiencing more and resisting less with the increasingly heavy physical work. She began to enjoy the side effects. When not too exhausted she found she could 'float' in this condition and there would still be enough curiosity or involvement left to feel in touch, as just now with the strange-looking moth. As Mark suggested, the work offered its own peace and encouraged a different kind of curiosity and one she felt was on the whole more easily delighted and accepting. It wasn't just that physical energy was being used up on physical things as it should be but on things with a life of their own. Turning over in bed sometimes she'd have a vivid picture of a choice seedling she'd planted the day before - images with the freshness and excitement of themselves. It was the old world made new. She stretched out with an unusual sense of luxury, the fire's warmth enclosed her blood-padded body with a personalness she wasn't used to and felt was almost too strange to be trusted and that was disturbed suddenly by a light touch on her thigh. Simon stared up at her, dazed, sleepy and flushed from bed. With a rush of love she picked him up, dazed herself by his sweetish smell and softer body warmth and folded him gently against her, arranging his head and legs by shifting her position. The weight of his head on her breast and arm fixed her immovably. The suffusion and completeness not to be disturbed, she shut her eyes. His eyes rolled up, and they lay there till Sheila found them and took him back to bed.

Awake and refreshed Joan went to the window. Outside, beyond the house lights, she could just see the path along the edge of the boxed garden and fetched her coat. The cool, fresh air outside made its biggest impact when she got away from the house. Ahead, in the twilight, Mark's copse was outlined against the sky, the branches jostling as if in bodiless water, and inside, dark and damp, she was surrounded by trunks full of life exclusive of hers, touching them to establish connection and a right to be there. Cool, compact, rougher than she'd expected she was completely absorbed and became conscious there'd been a steady glow of light at ground level only after it had gone. She moved in its direction, curious, and saw the outline of a man. He was at the edge of the copse. The wind lifted a lock of hair and replaced it and she recognised the silhouette as Selby's. She hurried aside, waiting before turning back.

In the night she woke suddenly after a sound sleep convinced there was something to remember. When it came it was the image of Selby but with something in the ground at hip height, a spade.

Restless for the rest of the night she went back to the spot as soon as she'd had breakfast but there was nothing to see. She could smell wood smoke, thin, occasional, but pungent enough to track and came up to the source before seeing David full length on the ground puffing rhythmically to coax damp twigs. He barely noticed her. Was this it? Had Selby been correcting some of his mischief?

"What are you doing here? Don't you know that's dangerous?"

He went on till he'd got it to billow, then turned to her briefly: "Can't do any 'arm, it's wet."

"Why do it if it won't burn?"

He got to his feet and took her hand, drawing her over the twigs where the smell was strongest. She inhaled, coughed and stood back looking at the blue coils, puzzled. He was waiting.

"The smell's good."

He ignored it. "Matches, paper, wood - boom! All this wood lying about - I mean they're asking for it."

Shaking her hand free she kicked leaves over the smoke. "People don't leave it lying around, this is a wood - what d'you expect?"

He stared at the doused twigs and his face, generally shut and unreadable, became disarmingly childlike. "There was a whopper when I was a kid" - he glanced up to stare direct and to catch her reaction - "our house burned down." Her grimace encouraged him. "Lot of fuss and talk. I had to talk to a lot of people kept asking daft questions nothin' to do with it." After a pause: "There was this box of kindlin' - 'E kept it under the stairs with old newspapers. Bloody great box of matches on the mantelpiece - I ask yer!" Joan looked blank and he pushed on, "I've never seen flames like it - orange, jumpin' all over the place - fantastic!"

"Anyone in the house?"

"They all got out." After another pause: "You should've seen 'im. 'E sleeps like the dead when 'e goes off but 'e crawled on to the roof from 'is winder - nothin' on - arms, legs, dangler - slidin' and jumpin' like a monkey."

"Were you trying to scare them?"

He looked up, losing interest. "They asked the same questions."

"Who?"

"Where they put me. I kept tellin' 'em."

"What?"

"I wanted to go 'ome."

Joan moved away and sat on a stump - it was the right move and he went on:

"They let me go 'ome when we moved 'ere."

When she found he was finished she asked, "Why do you like fires?"

There was a long silence at the end of which she glanced up and saw him looking straight ahead, dismissive.

"Well?"

He looked sideways not bothering to turn, it was final in a way that made her feel she'd been caught out or failed a test.

Later the same day she told Mark about the conversation as a roundabout way of alerting him to Selby's night visit which was still worrying her. Telling him about David gave her a chance to put it in a good light and it didn't in fact produce the alarm she feared - he tucked the information into a mental pouch and left her feeling she'd spread malicious gossip rather than done an anxious duty. Somehow he'd shifted his position and couldn't be reached. She decided to do what the Blakes had done and go her own way.

The Blakes were hard to find since Mark had loosened his grip on them. They'd taken the opportunity to get on with their own work. Within a couple of days it had become a miserable obsession. The slant the publisher favoured couldn't be achieved just because he wanted it, and nothing they did came right. Bits of sociology, biography, history, reference to foreign literatures - there was no room for it in their conception of the book, it bored them and each new attempt to get it in produced a worse deformity. They'd agreed to write from the standpoint of 'themes' thinking it would give them the scope they wanted for short essays on a few representative books. They'd chosen themes that seemed to by-pass 'know all' surveys and leave room for something more exciting and were discovering it was almost impossible to square these with his directives. MacFaddien had his own fiction in mind - a many-faceted cosmopolitan reader who was totally uninformed, - someone multi-motivated but not towards literature. The book was to be both popular and academic. According to him almost everyone who'd written since 1900 merited a mention - especially his friends. He'd come up with themes like "city life" and "country life" and they'd pretended not to hear. They'd compromised on 'coverage' and included a number of authors they weren't interested in only to feel guilty afterwards because many of those would have responded better to a lighter touch. While they'd been writing they'd been irritable with them for not working the themes fully or interestingly and characteristics that might have appealed to them under other circumstances nearly drove them mad under these.

Bess was particularly sore on these issues. For her literature was both very exciting and a place to explore. Whenever she found the old social directives analysed and exploded and current ones obeyed she lost interest. In many as soon as something interesting appeared it disappeared just as quickly, heading away from people and situations to other people and other situations. She preferred television - there was more life in it - real faces, at least, and you weren't so aware of the political, social and literary moulds - expressions and gestures added by the actors deepened and personalised it. In the novels that gave her most trouble the ideological containers were all the same. If there was raw material to put in them they couldn't get it to ferment without the sugar of idealism or its invert, bitterness. They wanted the expansion of thought and feeling that she wanted but the effects they produced came from a special brew and she dismissed them accordingly, angry at having to drink. Often it was worse than that; when authors seemed to be asking to be seen in a certain light, even if it was no more than to be thought good and caring people, then the request and the invitation to us to be the same put her off. It made a club atmosphere she couldn't stand, made membership bids for admiration, even love - why not if the rules were obeyed? Neither admiration nor love came out of it. Self-absorbed, their imagination and outgoing feeling had to be in short supply despite reverence for the concepts. They seemed untouched and uninvolved when most appearing to be both. Her responses were deadened the more they tried to widen them.

On the second afternoon Tom threw his novel on the windowsill and left it there. He went to find the others. A physical life was good he'd decided and made things a lot easier, he found his body sprang to work after a rest - his legs had a life of their own. By the evening he was ready again to see something interesting in all the authors.

When Bess came in it was still early but she found him fast asleep and couldn't resist lying beside him. She'd been unsettled by yet another encounter with Mark outside her room. She'd brushed by him preoccupied but by the time she'd got to the door she remembered her notes were downstairs and went back for them. Coming back she found him kneeling and fiddling with a loose piece of skirting board and stood up as she reached him.

"You alright?"

"Fine." She moved to go round and he stepped out,

blocking.

"Different kinds of work too much for you?"

"No." She felt her face go stiff and brought some smiling flexibility into it, avoiding his eyes.

"You've been very quiet recently. I've not seen much of you."

She looked at him, saw imperious enquiry turn to appeal which her body interpreted as 'what's the matter, don't you like me?'

"No." She pushed by. He hadn't moved fast enough.

Still dealing with the effects of the collision she put her arms round Tom and he woke up full of life. They went downstairs transformed after making love. Bess was game for anything, in touch with everything and very pleased to find new people were coming for a 'singing' evening.

A solicitor friend turned up. Mark had taken financial advice from him in the first year and they'd discovered a mutual interest in madrigals and started monthly meetings. Sometimes he came alone, sometimes with friends. Tonight he was alone. A bachelor in his early forties, middle height, bald but with a lampshade fringe of longish blond hair - at the back it touched his shoulders - he had a slightly florid style of dress drawing attention to small bright eyes, shining frameless spectacles and a very red mouth. He looked like a decorative figurine much handled. Bess wondered if he over-celebrated his nights out - either that or his clients had to find a sense of security elsewhere - the black Porsche he'd arrived in might or might not qualify.

Lionel went straight into the kitchen and put his arms round Sheila. "How's my beauty?"

She blushed and bustled.

The had a light supper and sang first from a book of Victorian songs with Mark accompanying part of the time on his violin. They stuck to the well-known ones for the benefit of Bess and Tom who couldn't sight read and who, as they relaxed more and more into it found their fun-seeking gusto coming uppermost. It was out of line. The group was enjoying itself but not in the same way and they toned it down as potentially disruptive.

Sheila moved to the fore: "Let's have some of the less well known."

Those who could do it sight-read one called 'This is love'. Sheila's harsh voice ran excitedly across the blend as she leant against Lionel sharing his copy. Their voices balanced - not good to hear but good to be present in. Her confidence soared and sure of her pitch she asked Mark occasionally to check his strings. Bess and Tom had to assume the sounds she gave him were pitch-perfect and decided it was a good noise. Lionel raised his arm and put it round her shoulders closing his hand over the top of her arm, occasionally stroking it with his fingers and closing it again. Her face flaming with pleasure and bombarding them with delight offered Bess, no longer able to sing, a new scenario and she put all her enthusiasm into staring.

Lionel's red scarf was loosely tucked into his shirt. It framed a straining sinewy blood-roped neck, set off his mouth and lit up his face. He had a fine light tenor. Joan's thin face, pink with effort, looked for reassurance from one to the other as they stood strung out in a semicircle. Expression, clothes, music, enjoyment - sensual and non-sensual in equal proportions - personality etched into faces that gave themselves up to the business of singing - held Bess's attention for a long while before she properly noticed Mark in the middle. He was leaning with his violin first in one direction then in another but that was the limit of synchronisation. Cold fury at Lionel's familiarity with his wife recycled as vigour set a fast pace that finally tired them of Victorian songs.

They got down to the serious business of the evening - the madrigals. Sheila's face changed as she grouped them together according to voice and strung them out for Mark's instructions. When they'd been singing for a while her face like a schoolgirl's blanked and expanded - ready to learn but readier to please and keep her interests hidden. When pretence became purpose the didactic ingredient affected the others. Bess's mistakes became irritating and Tom's uncertain baritone a cause for mild rebuke. These two hung back singing less and less and soon they all stopped for a drink.

The Blakes were allowed to sit out the second half and the music took on a new life. As a delighted observer Bess thought she was safe. She found it a different exposure. Fascinated by Mark's movements she paid too much attention and he became aware of it placing himself favourably and intensifying both liveliness and control. He was turned slightly in her direction, chin pressed down hard, assiduous to the music. He lowered the violin to sing favourite snatches, his voice negatived to blend unnoticed. Delight and disappointment, rejection and desire drew her attention away and inwards. Her passion for Tom had sharpened not dulled her susceptibility.

Mark was bouncy after the singing and had fun with the ladies. The group sat where they were on the floor in the middle of the room and away from the fire. After a while he got up and fetching a plate of dark, sour-looking bread stepped over feet and interrupted conversations until he stood in front of Bess and said something she didn't hear.

"Did you hear what I said?" He was smiling, she looked anxious. "I said do you like brack bed?" She still wasn't sure.

He started to giggle. "I made a mistake, I said - "

"Yes I heard."

He went away still amused and tried it on Joan: "I must watch what I say - did you hear what I said? I said...."

Bess got up and went to the table bringing back two cakes, one for Tom. Mark sat at Joan's feet and leant on her legs while Joan chatted and smiled affectionately.

Lionel took his bread to the table, folded a large slice of salt beef on to it opened wide, bit, chewed, glanced sideways at Sheila then at Mark, rolled his eyes, swallowed and said:

"I never," emphatically, "ever enjoy food anywhere as much as here" - a pause - "was this your beef?"

Mark shook his head. "Part of an exchange with a neighbouring farmer."

"He farm the same way?" He opened again.

"Usual sort. We're the only 'health' nuts."

"Aaaw - you're spoiling my pleasure." He twisted his beaming face. "Full of stuff is it then - hormones and things?"

"Don't!" Mark ducked his head, only half fooling. He was suddenly subdued. A few seconds later he got up, duties as host foremost. When Bess noticed him again he was nodding mechanically to Joan's words.

The following morning he found a place to work on his own and out of sight. Everything was on top of him. Memories, of Sheila's glow, Bess's eyes and Lionel's comments on the meat made a visual/intellectual mix with anxiety at visiting his mother that intensified it all beyond endurance. Fear and anger turned to anxiety and indifference, when that too retreated it left a familiar survivor - an old argument with a new lease of life. It came when he was weakest and with the force of a nightmare - the destruction of us all. Panic was followed by submission then concession. Only immediate release mattered. A horde of anxieties fled to the only exit - to the things we could do something about. He gave himself the usual reassurance. He'd be alright, his family'd be alright. His knowledge protected them at least. For the careless and unenlightened there was no hope - greed manipulated judgment, we scoffed the poison that reached into our future, hormone-injected for mutation and death. We were dying. It wasn't enough for him to be saved.

The storm abated. Nothing was left. The invader stood unchallenged - his shadow over everything.

On the wall next to the patch he was digging he became aware of the Russian vine. The new tendrils kept lifting in the wind and touched him occasionally. They flicked in front of him, slender, searching, their fineness emphasised a succulent tension. One of them brushed the handle of his spade and paused through the next gust, ready. He stared in horror at the helpless submission to opportunity - at the vital indifference he couldn't bear, and running indoors fetched his shears. Savage pruning turned into a passion of concern. At the end, tender towards the heavier branches, he tied them to the wall.

That afternoon he had business in Kinemouth and was ready to re-establish contact with the others. He asked them if they'd like a trip and as they were keen suggested a walk along the cliffs. It turned into a holiday. He took them past the heath as neither Tom nor the Blakes had seen it. The bright day showed up everything - mile after mile of dead-looking heather, patches of sand and dazzling gorse. Half-way across he stopped the car and Sheila hauled Simon out of the back. Joan got out to look at the gorse and Mark followed. The land dipped away from the road, and out of sight from the car was a clump of silver birches about four feet high, bushy and delicate. She wondered what else she hadn't noticed - mounds of chalk and sand a little way off where the soil had been skimmed for gravel and on the horizon a small ridge of hills. Tributaries of streaming yellow blazed on the clefts stopping as suddenly as they started but even there the sense of sky and space took precedence over everything. She turned round to see unbroken heath. Suddenly she looked up for reassurance. The sky was exciting, intimately active and curious over the heather, clouding, lightening, selecting patches for scrutiny - the light intensifying on one spot and building up her urge to get to it until it was superseded by the shifting focus. The air was fresh and easy to breathe - an expression of the volatility and pulse that changed, illuminated and dominated the heath until it became part of its own argument. As she watched she felt she was being watched and turned to see Mark just behind her lifting his arm affectionately but not touching her.

"I'll take you right into it some time." He turned her back to the car.

From this point Joan was alerted to the countryside and preoccupied to the point of obsession. She was leaving in a few days and wanted the impact to stay. Mark, excited by her response, decided to start the walk early. He parked three miles out of town to walk in over the hills and they set off from a village squeezed into them. As they climbed, its surrounding fields looked like gardens - the borders thick with blackthorn blossom. Joan's excitement was marred by feeling Mark wanted her company. She wanted something else and dropped back. She looked evasively into the hedge but a flash of white wings broke out in front of her like a burst spray. It redirected her but not to him - to the bullocks on the other side of him following them to the stile. She put her hands behind her back. A bullock behind her pushed his sticky nose in her palm and, sensually excited, she dropped back again until there was a gap between herself and the rest of them.

Eventually the hedges disappeared. It was open ploughed earth all round, enhancing the contours of the hills and reflecting the clouds. Behind her the village looked as if it were in a rift. One of the cottages suddenly picked out by sunlight held on to a small triangle of land. It was surrounded by flowering fruit trees with daffodils at their feet. Gardens and fields had become a pattern of triangles and rectangles defended by glinting slate roofs. The sharp angles were softened here and there by moss and occasional thatch which led her eye to a solitary conical thatch on the outskirts. Changing her mind towards Mark she turned round and caught the others up only to find her privacy protected by the steep climb and head wind.

Mark was separating himself now and picking up speed. There was an assertion in the enormous sweeps of hillside that excited him. He felt the sea close. At the top of the next ridge he saw it. Ahead of him to the right the path he wanted crossed the foot of a hill that sloped green and precipitous almost to the water-line. His eye was caught by two trees stranded in the middle, stiff with tenacity, wind-carved but dominating the herd of scattered Friesians below them. Branching down he passed the herd at a pace that made them leap out of his way and clear his path.

Half an hour later he found himself waiting for the others on a bridge just outside Kinemouth. When they arrived he was sitting on the wall dreaming and banging a stick against his leg like a farmer waiting for his dog to bring up the herd. They had something to drink at the nearest café where he left them, wanting to get his business finished quickly and be on the move. He sold eggs and cheese in advance with the dispatch of an old hand and the excitement of a new but at the end, in spite of it, because of it, tiredness and a feeling of emptiness came with the sense of completed objective.

They took a new route back to the village, one that at the start followed the main coastal road. There he was robbed of all that remained of a sense of purpose. Everywhere the town insisted on its own preoccupation. Half the buildings were boarded up waiting for the tourists. He couldn't see the beach for dead shops and beach huts, and the blind-eyed look of the others irritated. When he reached the cliff path the sea was offensive in a similar way - a glittering calm, its passive pulse along the shore emphasizing its condition - laid out, garish, waiting, it connived with the town. He climbed and took to looking inland. The air off the fields was heavy and the ploughed earth no longer looked fresh. The sun was burning for the first time this year and there was a sting in it.

The trap was sprung. In a moment of panic he resisted - which was all that was needed. His heart raced, he poured with sweat, his skin pricked. It was far too early for this kind of heat and it was too penetrating. He emptied his mind. Sweating too much his throat dried out. No stopping it now. The facts coursed through him and met no resistance. Resistance, acceptance, it was all the same. Up to a quarter of the protective layer of ozone gone in half a century - ultra-violet exposure - stinging radiation. If they stopped it now the harm would still go on, nitrous oxide lived in the atmosphere more than thirty years. The earth was breathing it out while he looked - choked with nitrogenous fertiliser. He turned to the sea that was rotting its fish in glittering pollution. Why bother? Destruction on this scale took time, we wouldn't know all the effects for fifty years.

The sweat fell in drips from his chin and he opened his shirt. He'd once been fool enough to believe the effects of the build-up of carbon dioxide could be balanced out by industrial dust. In fact they joined forces. He remembered he'd thought it fair at the time that our dust should find a beneficial place. Man was a natural product, why shouldn't some of his by-products fit? But he wasn't natural, he was a freak - too much skill coupled to too little intelligence - skill wasn't related to understanding. Our dust didn't act like volcanic dust that was thrown high into the stratosphere and scattered solar radiation, it hung round us low and blanketing - appropriate testimony to a lack of imagination - it increased the surface temperature, reinforced the pattern.

He sat down to catch his breath. Forests. He wanted the world covered with green forests - life-giving protection. Looking down he saw dark hair - a face came into view and waving arms gleaming and extended. Bess. She'd caught him. It didn't matter. Resistance, acceptance, it was all the same. He stood up but couldn't move.

Bess had been amazed at his progress up the path and tried to catch him up to override her own tiredness. The more she flung herself into it the sooner it'd be over and it was more fun than hanging back.

"What a performance!" she said and seeing his exposed chest touched it. "You're icy!" He flattened her hand on him, holding it there. The melting look that accompanied the movement only made itself felt when he'd gone. She watched him wield his body away while the full force of it streamed back to her.

In a moment he stopped, waited and fell into a normal pace beside her. A little later he started talking about his 'game with the land'. She'd learnt earlier that this consisted of pitting one form of life against another and that it fascinated him. Some of the tricks he used were old ones, he told her, but though the idea of biological pest control wasn't new there were pioneers in the field and they were badly needed. Unfortunately their research had to be financed voluntarily. There was no money coming from sources whose profits might fall if they had much success. Grimness and excitement grew in equal proportions and transferred to his personal success stories; the interplanting of carrots and onions, he said, had avoided both carrot and onion fly, "the smell of one jams the smell of the other", and he described the experiment for this year which was to put bits of rhubarb in the holes before planting out his brassica seedlings. He hoped it would deter clubroot organisms.

Bess received the news in silence and he found his enthusiasm failing. He wondered what she was thinking and found himself in the opposite camp. Games? Jokes more like. Biology and control were contradictions in terms. If you imagined you had the measure of any living thing you were a half-wit. The restless hungers that kept it alive did their own jamming but finally overcame anything artificially introduced. There wasn't a solution. But it wasn't the fight or the hazards he feared - it was lack of motivation for surviving them. He needed more than this and would continue to even if the commune worked. More life, more association, more freedom. With constriction built in. Perhaps what he wanted was death. Death was the powerhouse. Unlimited freedom for change and association - unlimited potential of gases and minerals with the quick compassionate simplicity of the non-biological.

There was a reproachful poke on his shoulder that pulled him up. Sheila's red face behind him asked what he thought he was doing: "I've called you half a dozen times - I want you to deal with him." Bewildered he looked past her. Bess had disappeared. She was back walking with Tom. "It's Claude I'm talking about - he will keep going to the edge. I've told him it crumbles. I've been shouting for ages!"

He looked for Claude. "Come here!" He came. Claude's face was red, contorted with unshed tears. "Don't be such a baby!"

The three of them kept ahead with the others lagging behind and the gap wasn't closed till they crossed a stile.

They picked up the path in a sheltered hollow where it turned into a farm track. The sun was beating down on baked mud leading them down to an open gate and up again apparently to the cliff edge. In the near distance it was covered with a dark liquid they couldn't identify until almost on top of it when the blaze of green and black turned into a river of beetles. They were climbing over each other's backs copulating or attempting it while the females continued to move upward carrying their passengers.

Mark came to a standstill, adjusted, and walked alongside afraid of stepping on them. Their stiff mobility, fixity of case, flexibility of jointed legs, backs like nuts glittering together in black-blue fragments of one action flowed uphill. They were passing him. The soft liquid movement of the mass made him giddy and he re-focussed on individuals - on legs sensitively feeling out and hauling. Admiration and rejection spun him again and his feet stumbled sideways threatening the stream. When his head cleared the vertigo in his legs stayed on, so did the horror of stepping on them as strong as the urge to do it. Peter was shouting excitedly behind him and caught him up. His hands were proffered and slightly cupped:

"Thousands of 'em! Millions!" Dazzled with excitement he showed them in his hands - three of them scrabbling over each other and his palms.

Mark flung out his hand and the beetles shot on to the grass. Peter dropped down looking for them - Bess too instinctively helping but suddenly unable to control her anger she looked up with a sneer so heavily suppressed there was little room for the words: "And what was that for?" Mark made off.

For the next day or so he kept to himself except for Joan. She was leaving and it was safe to draw closer and feel the loss. She became his companion through most of his jobs and she asked the right questions. He felt he was feeding her reasons for returning as well as material for her articles. In the end unreserved in her admiration of his aims, involvement, and the way he was dealing with threats to his success, she felt the excesses that had frightened her earlier were the forbidding side of strength and perhaps the salvation of his cause. His personal balance of passion and intellect, involvement and control, made anything possible and her personal attachment became such that the pain of leaving was considerably eased when he said he would take her with him as far as London where he must visit his mother.

The unity in retreat they found in each other's company was threatened even so on the last afternoon. Joan was on her own and took a farewell stroll round the smallholding. She made for the pond and found Claude and David already in possession but at the moment of turning back she was arrested by Claude's expression. There was something about it both familiar and unpleasant. She came up unnoticed behind the bushes. Like Mark she generally paid less attention to him, he wasn't as obliging as Peter nor as enchanting as Simon but she knew him well enough to recognise the mood. It was an intense version of what she'd seen more than once - curiosity, alarm and indefinable satisfaction.

She looked across the pond to see what was causing it. David kneeling on the other side held his arm stiff and under water - it was vibrating a little. He took in her presence as he had before without ruffling his interest but it faintly increased a histrionic quality in the concentration that reminded her of the arm-threading episode on their first meeting. He pulled up his arm. A limp kitten dripped over his lap and was released over the grass. He glanced at his lacerated hand. When he looked at her she saw the thing was finished for him successfully. It was Claude's angry blush of betrayal when he discovered someone there that stayed with her.

In the evening she was tenser with Mark and made him feel there was more to it than her departure. He stepped back and so did she. It gave her the final push she needed to get back to her own world.

On the drive to London she established the balance she wanted, promising him she'd spend her summer vacation there while privately bristling with ideas and anxieties for the new term. The next day in the British Library she was happy to be with others about their business. Their absorption, obsessive and dismissive, reassured her. Coming out, mingling with the crowd and toying with the idea of going to a concert showed her how much she needed the retreat. She went straight home.

Mark had gone to his parents' house. His father opened the familiar yellow-gloss door and put his hand out smiling and relieved, then on a sudden impulse put both arms round him: "You're here then." Mark squeezed him.

Tottering slightly, pink, dazed, he disengaged himself. "Go and see your mother, she's been taken ill again, bad this one - they don't know if she'll pull through." He was concentrating on his delivery, not wanting to garble important news. Mark, rigid with panic and reluctance to understand, stood doing nothing. "Come on boy, she's in the bedroom."

He watched his father's thin body move ahead of him, he'd had a stroke two years before and it had left him stiff and with a faultily-locking kneecap that made him balance his walking action carefully like a robot. Thin skin over the skull shone through the floss of grey hair, one ear was higher than the other and lacked the defiance of symmetry. Mark couldn't look at it. He watched his own feet and kept well behind till the bedroom door where he caught him up and fixed his eyes on the back of his neck while he fiddled uncertainly with the door handle. As the door opened he was overcome by the familiar smells associated with his parents' old age - with their transformation from living people to terrifying, essentially uncommunicating frailties that he avoided. His own world, his life was blasted with a leprosy. Drained of energy he submitted to the sweetish, medicated, faintly unclean air of the sickroom as his father pushed it wide. The sun had been pouring into the room in the afternoon - the light still streamed through the thin, drawn curtains that moved sinuously in a gust that never reached him from the open window. His father waited for him to look, fixing his eyes hungrily on his face. With an effort that he felt left him witless Mark drew himself to the side of the bed and sat perched on the edge of the chair already placed there, still unseeing.

"Take her hand! We think she can feel it." Mark touched the hand lying near him on the bedspread. "Not like that,

Squeeze it so she knows."

He pressed his son's hand round his wife's and Mark stiffening with horror stared incredulously at the thin, panting, neatly-nightgowned twisted body of his mother lying on her side with the elbow under her, raised on a pillow, her eyes open and sightless. She panted as if all her energy were in the breathing, her mouth drawn sideways continuously as if sucking her teeth as he'd seen her do it often. It reminded him of the half soothing half irritable rhythmic foot-wagging he did himself when he had a stomach ache. For a moment he saw an expression of angry involvement in her eyes - her mouth emphatic and contemptuous was working as if arguing. He was sure she was remembering something.

"That happens sometimes. She seems to surface. We don't know if she can hear. Try shouting in her ear."

Mark sat there with tears streaming down his face, horror and compassion reduced him to near-childish hysteria that had to be let out. He riveted himself to her hand holding himself there as if he were submitting to death itself, forcing the hand to stay firm that if he could he'd have shed like a crab, while his spirit writhed and raged.

His father walked to the other side of the bed, leant over her, brushed the damp, thin hair from her ear and said loudly "Have you any pain?"

"No."

"Whenever I say that she seems to answer - but not to anything else. Speak to her - she can hear - at least in patches."

Mark gripped her hand tighter: "Mmm." He couldn't say it - this wasn't his mother - then he heard it break through - "Mum" - a pause - "Mum!" and felt shocked and relieved at the sound of it. Finding he could do it he burst into tears calling her again and again loudly reassuring himself and her. He'd half called her back. She lifted her head a few inches off the pillow, her sightless attention given him as if she were trying not to see him but be aware of him, her mouth silently reasoning, face suspended in a cross-current struggling to get to him while he asked again and again if she could hear him. She held her head poised and turned to him for seconds while he clamoured, then he saw she was waiting to be released and stopped suddenly in the middle of it drawing back, bearing down on the crying and looking for help to his father who was standing on the other side of the bed, his tears silently streaming down his face. His expression not directed at him had gratitude in it as if all this had been wanting, this sudden testimony to her life and energy and on his own he hadn't been able to do it.

Confused, angry, resentful, abject, helpless pity clamouring for release, fear and horror strangling his understanding he left the room but turned at the door. "You must get out" he said fiercely to the old man "and give her some rest." Dazed and submissive his father followed him out.

It wasn't over as fast as the doctor assumed. The two men convinced themselves, in spite of his groping statements, that the lingering was a good sign and that time was what she needed. Mark was back with his family when his mother died a week later.

7

Now Joan was at work all she could do for the first few weeks was keep abreast of the timetable. Moved from one comparatively impersonal situation to another, from lectures to tutorials to departmental meetings she began to feel hounded and, as in the past, needed to retire from contact with others as much as possible. For the first time she was consciously dissatisfied with both the hounding and the retirement - the pattern seemed to have been robbed of inevitability.

Her customary way of life wasn't good enough. Its rewards in terms of privacy and the scope it gave for living in a world of organised abstracts was in some ways more frightening than the rough handling she got from close contacts which it had once seemed so necessary to avoid. Here the larger more impersonal society had an almost total grip on its members, not just on their time and energy but the way they thought. Professionalism dictated even the moral code. A thorough loathing of a colleague as a man coupled with an equally thorough respect for the way he handled himself in the ring led to the most devious and complicated expressions of frustration and malice, reactions cramped and contorted at birth to the extent of one's susceptibility to an idea of professional behaviour.

She was taken by surprise. She hadn't expected to plunge headlong into the business of teaching as readily as she had nor to emerge from it with a bad taste in her mouth. She found herself seeing the things she needed from the standpoint of an alien. For a while the whole business was difficult to take seriously. It felt like a game the rules of which endorsed certain fouls against the human being so long as the rules of the profession weren't breached. It was a cold-blooded mockery of a living situation bred out of the pursuit of infallibility, which was the basic foul from which the others naturally emerged. It was easy to describe the pursuit to oneself in professional terms as a passion for accuracy, excellence and intellectual tolerance but the nervous individual underneath spent its life on guard against being made to look a fool - the human response to an inhuman objective.

The tension had to be let out somewhere and departmental meetings with their policy fights were the obvious places for it. It was here during the workouts between inflated egos and thin skins that Joan began to feel the stifling oppression that was turning work into a confinement rather than an escape. The actions, the obsessive attacks and recriminations - the time it took, the heat generated affected her physically and she found herself cutting them on the grounds of ill health. Things she'd accepted before were becoming intolerable. She'd long understood that personal display was important in this profession, as in any other, and here there was more than average need for the outstanding solo performer. What benefited the institution most was the fame of its individual members - it pulled in the best students and the biggest donations. For this the oiling and massaging of the ego was an important part of daily routine, and quarrels based on personal affront shored up and kept going because the protagonists saw nothing but principle involved, concealed all the vindictiveness of confined animals - the automatic and unconscious savagery that could go on for years in print and out of it until one or both died.

The most earnestly committed to their work - whether they saw this as research, the writing of books or the face to face teaching of students - could be some of the worst in this respect. But even the mildest felt the strain of constant competition and tended to push aside the complexities of a varied private life. She understood this was one of the reasons for the high divorce rate among her colleagues and one of the reasons for her own. Similar principles of suppression and right-mindedness were put into operation at home - you couldn't switch off - and there was always justified escape into a text or a laboratory. After all the quality of life of the individual members wasn't obviously socially valuable and a slowly killing process had narcotic rewards for those who wholeheartedly took part. You were socially rewarded for shirking the exacting business of maturing emotionally - a process requiring you to expose your ego to shocks it could never fully recover from. Under the guise of working hard at the professional level you could be bone idle where it mattered. She herself hadn't been bothered to think about the details of the discord between herself and her husband, on the grounds it caused too much pain and was of too little use.

She felt inclined to excuse that. What now caused such shame was the memory of the outrage she'd felt. What had been so incomprehensible and unforgivable had been his treachery. She'd seen herself as having 'played fair' and told herself she couldn't organise a life round so much insecurity. At the time belonging to a group and being imprisoned by its thinking and its tensions had offered a depressed security. To be shaped, to have one's thoughts entirely conditioned by secondary rather than primary human needs - to be milked of a social commodity because she was totally untrained for and terrified of life and because it had seemed that life had little meaning outside its wider social context, came as a depressing speculation about herself. It put her so far out of context she found herself moving quite naturally in the world she'd been trained for while being emptied and frustrated by it. The social contacts available were of the trained variety. The sounds, smiles, responses in her contacts with students and colleagues were unpleasantly predictable even when they appeared to take her by surprise. Her work that had appeared to be offering all life on a small scale, like the drug it was, had induced an illusion, and a lifetime of drug-taking ended with retirement declaring you bankrupt of the currency needed to get more. Just the same, ill at ease as she was, she was a long way from feeling the need to cut loose. The disenchantment made her look for a better way in rather than out and determine that a drug that cheated the user of reality, interest and participation except at an agreed level should be treated with suspicion and taken with care.

A new and more conscious dissociation but full of curiosity began to emerge in her relationships with others. She was less fearful and in one sense more excitedly involved than before, though she thought for the moment at least it amounted to little more than an appraisive but more sympathetic identification with others and more affectionate if bitter observations of her colleagues as well as herself. She started noticing rather than subconsciously reacting against the arrangement of bodies in chairs or bent in haste along corridors and saw in their exaggerations or nervous self-displays the manufacture of a stimulus to keep themselves and her - the group in fact - constantly conscious of group activity. Her sense of their individual differences and that they were on the whole an unusually interesting and varied bunch kept disappearing and being replaced by a sense of fine timing. In the past she'd shared with them a feeling of being special both in endowment and function in society. Now she saw this as something generated among themselves out of a variety of needs and as a source of mutual recognition. It was similar to an animal scent or birdcall keeping like souls together and warding off others at the same time as keeping life excitement going full-pelt in a small compass. The head down, its energetic purposive thrust forward, would be interpreted now unemotionally as a preoccupation with exam marks; a colleague's inward and obsessive look as he made for the periodicals in the library as mounting anxiety at finding something that outdated the article he was preparing. To the students, until they knew better, and often to each other, ambiguous signals of this sort could create a force-field that both defended and threatened but that above all kept going an illusion of life and energy that was hard come by, since the success of the system represented the sacrifice of so much of both. In general most of them seemed to assess themselves as their society assessed them and felt they must be seen to be what they had been trained to think they were. This way the act became more important than the reality. The successful act of showmanship became the criterion by which they judged themselves. That word 'professional' that carried the germ of death to the gaucheries of real involvement was the one by which they measured their achievement, and it was done in the name of several other socially acceptable abstracts like humility, working-with-a-team, and doing a good job within the limitations of the organisation and its aims. So here were the humble beginnings of a universal outrage. The outrage of the smile that looked as if the face were mechanised for it - jawline and eye-creases in synchronised automation, signals of obedience and complacency. Tones not words, sounds not sense, a buttery confection chewed by her head of department who took more delight in the flavour and smell than the food value and stretched his soul daily in a sun of self-satisfaction.

There was an up and coming would-be second in command, Saul Berry, a younger man with a useful head of hair whose forelock responded to a toss of the head. She worked with him often and watched him now with a new sympathy and new rejection - master of light facetiousness and confident 'lateral thinking' that united one observation with another not as a means of exploration and only secondarily as an argument but with the same prime purpose as prompted the endless quest for new witticisms - for that anything, personal or impersonal, was raw material. Out of it he wove his own fabric of interrelated superficialities, which got him noticed by attracting the attention of the like-minded who were after snatching the odd loose end for themselves. But there was a warped exuberance in all this nervous titillation, as she saw even more clearly one afternoon when the term was well under way.

She was avoiding a colleague in the corridor for no special reason - the habit of privacy still tricked her into retreats - and popped into an empty lecture theatre. Finding a low stool just inside the entrance and behind the wooden panelling that fenced off the seats, she sat for a moment and opened a book she'd got with her to give an appearance of purpose if she were discovered. Within seconds a group of noisy and excited students burst in without noticing her and found places at the front of the theatre. She heard Saul's name mentioned and half stood to go when another larger bunch came in and moved down to the others. She kept her seat in case more came and heard the last group talking about him. Greedy for student assessment she stayed too long and Saul came in through the doors downstairs. She stood up and sat back frightened he'd see her watching through one of the gaps in the panels - when he turned his back she'd go. The situation had already made her secretive and alert and now it was being fed by what she saw through the panels - a mime with a cigarette showing tension, excitement, dominance, all of them aspects of the transformation from vulnerability to threat - the threat of quick wits and superior information - but there was something else as well that she couldn't make out.

He was holding a brief conversation with a girl who'd come up with an essay and leaning against the table, legs stretched, thighs impressively displayed by the edge, he tossed his hair staring into her face in the manner of a man used to a great deal of sexual attention. Now his interest went to a bigger group - the front row and all girls. He spoke low, just loud enough for them, humorous. Open gestures accompanied it but they conflicted with the tension in his twisting back, indicating nothing was open. This was a closed circuit and only those who had the same motivations could effectively join in.

Apparently he'd started teaching. Names so well known to her that she could recognise them through a general mutter came up to her - Fielding, Jane Austen, Wordsworth - a backcloth to the relationship between tutor and students - and she saw it as if it were a revelation. The minutiae of changing response as intoxicating and transient as light on water - this was what mattered, the rest was secondary.

By twisting herself and flattening her nose she saw that

some young men at the back of the group were still filing down the space between bench and shelf - they must have just come in. Presumably he hadn't started. One in over-tight faded jeans pretended to fall across a girl's lap. She was already sitting, books and papers in front of her, and hit out viciously.

"Oi - oi - oi - temper, temper!" He picked himself up passing it off, blushing. "Naughty naughty!" He tipped her chin with one finger. She screwed up her face and hit out again but he sat next to her gently as if she'd been flirting.

Noise was erratic but on the increase. Silences followed by spurts of laughter and dropped books. Saul picked up his cigarette and drew on it with a prolonged and thoughtful gesture. The raised baton silenced the tuning up. He announced the opening bars:

"I thought" - voice directed outwards so she heard every word - "We'd do a survey through the next couple of seminars of the climate of thought in which the novelists wrote". He drew a chair away from the table and sitting crossed his legs. "I'd like to consider the relationship of novels to the society that produces them."

Joan was fidgeting and looking for a chance to leave when his voice subsided, not carrying for more than the occasional sentence. It released her and she went on looking. It was clear that there were two favourite girls in the front. Saul quoted a piece she recognised, raising his voice and giving it an intimacy it was innocent of. A boy with glasses, in the front with the girls, was watching him attentively. The girls were rapt, the males were waiting.

Saul's manner changed as he reached behind him for a book on the table and he named the attentive male. He asked without looking at him what he thought of Sharpe's criticism of Jane Austen's limited social focus. The lad hadn't read it.

"Fair comment, old chap. I wish I'd had your sense!" A titter from one of his girls. In moving she knocked a sheaf of papers off her shelf and he watched them flutter to his feet as a tribute. Joan left while he was picking them up.

Half amused, half depressed, oddly refreshed but restless, she thought: "Alright, but it's not enough." Perhaps there hadn't been enough of that side of it for her - that was her fault. She didn't know if she wanted or needed it but it set her looking for something closer to home, someone who seemed to combine satisfaction of the needs she knew she had with a livelier interest in things unrelated to them.

Matthew Roach was a lot more excitable than herself but appeared until you knew him to be a slow boiler. He was a man who listened and tried to see all sides of all arguments while managing to get into a succession of violent rows with other members of his and other departments. On one occasion, submitting to a lengthy departmental meeting without saying a word, he erupted over the telephone to the chairman at quarter to twelve the same night. He was liked in spite of it and in spite of a fervour of commitment to the business of teaching that in its passionately held rules crossed the paths of most of them at some time or other.

She looked out for him in the common room this afternoon and found him sitting at a table drinking coffee with two others. He was leaning stiffly and listening as if half fearful of the possibility of disliking what was said, and turned away with the speed of relief when he heard the laughter of one of the women collecting cups. A flash of enjoyment as she ducked away from the Ph.D student trying to grab something out of her pocket. Joan liked it, liked him, his quickness, patience, obstinacy, cock-sureness - an odd mixture, contradictions all giving out the same heat that she'd instantly understood and enjoyed, accrediting him his right as a human being to be anything he liked when with others she found it difficult. He was short and his black hair and greying sideboards framed a mixture of interesting features in which a poorly mended broken nose and a rugger scar failed to take attention away from his eyes for more than a moment.

Joan sat near to listen but wouldn't join his group. His attention was back with the others but now she noticed a peculiar hugging of his loosely closed fists against his middle - a gesture she remembered seeing before and that was concealed from the others by the table. It didn't suggest aggression or tension so much as a maiming and it looked habitual. He chopped his hands off when he paid attention.

One of the others was anxious - leaning forward making his point which seemed to be putting a strain on Matthew's silence:

"I find it unnerving, unsettling. I thought it a lousy idea from the start. I can't feel at ease when my group is off for a whole month with someone else and I still have to fit everything into the time left." The speaker, thin and middle-aged, was from the French department but the man answering was Michael Williams, another of Joan's colleagues:

"You mustn't pack into what's left everything you'd originally planned" - he raised his hand cheerily - "You're making too much work for yourself. It won't work."

"Exactly, it won't, that's my point. I've no grandiose ideas about my own particular teaching ability but I lose the students' sensibilities. There's nothing consecutive. It's all in bits. Anyway I'm responsible for this part of the course and it ruins my plans. Other people have other slants."

"That's the point surely."

"I know for a fact," the French man went on but to Matthew now, "two of them'll spend the whole time on relatively unimportant aspects because they happen to feed their current manias - the important stuff'll be skimmed and when I get my students back it'll be like starting with a fresh group at the beginning of a new term."

"Well, why not?" Michael persisted. "They might come back more responsive! I can't see why you need to hold on to their sensibilities, it's not part of the job. Aren't we here to help them reach a wide enough selection of ideas to increase their own sensibilities? If you're worried about one or two things not being covered you can deal with those and leave out the stuff that's been done." He was pushing his chair back ready to leave when Matthew butted in, subdued at first:

"But if they go, all the work you've put into a special teaching approach is wasted. If you're trying to get rid of the trained reaction to the trained question and know you can't begin the real job of exploring a text until you've done it, then you spend the first few weeks trying to change their attitudes not just to their study but to teaching and scholarship. I don't want them waiting on me for clues to what to think, I want them to do the job for themselves uncoaxed and uninfluenced. I'm not interested in their giving me what they think I want - that way I'm bored and they never think from first principles. Underneath they'll always be barbarians like most of us. If I've been debriefing them and they go off to someone else where the brief still operates I've been wasting my time. They'll come back with the idea, whatever else we pretend, that the highest priority is given to reference to the authorities, much higher than to the informed personal response I'm looking for. They'll see that a subtle synthesis of the obvious with the acceptable commands the most respect. We don't do it consciously I know, being victims of our own training, but we do it. Most of us get a sense of personal contribution by enthusiastically replacing the old dynasty of opinion with the new one. I'm not going to let this happen to my group if I can help it. I'm only interested in the unlimited potential of the untrained mind. If they go away my students come back slotted. Weeks of work down the pan."

There was a note of friendly conciliation in Michael's reply: "Aren't you setting too much store by a special teaching method and too little by what's taught? If it's worth teaching at all it'll have some of the expanding influence you're looking for."

Matthew looked curiously at him "Exactly - that's why our own function is to develop our skill as teachers and nothing else. We've got to find the best way" - he was looking desperately for words to give them agreement - "It's undesirable, even dangerous to put forward opinions and values to students but we do it unconsciously every day through our technique, however broad-minded we are. If we don't think carefully about it we can have a worse effect than ignorance. At least if they're ignorant they may be less likely to think they know all the answers and that'd be something. I don't mean we should only be providers of assorted opinionless information. The kind of discursive help that peels away rather than adds is the contribution I aim at so that the student can get to his or her responses and work things out from there."

"I wonder what these responses are that haven't in some way or other been trained? But putting that aside you've only told me the best way for you, not the only way that works. I'd think it more dangerous to assume mine was the best or that there was such a thing. Even a good way shouldn't be so inflexible as to find others a threat. The tutor-student relationship you're dismissing has produced some fine results - you for instance. I for one wouldn't want your negatived approach - no excitement in it. Your method seems to lead to little groups of the elite creating little groups of the elite to follow them."

"Rubbish, I'm asking for the destruction of elitism!"

"By elite methods? The ambitions of the old tutor-student relationship are a lot humbler than yours. You can't really help an individual think except by interesting and exciting his curiosity. If you do that you're teaching in every sense of the word, whatever method you use. Your kind of coaxing opinionlessness might be counter-productive. If there's nothing to strike out against or go along with how do you define what you think?"

"You answer questions you yourself put forward. Under the other conditions you're more likely to want to impress by 'getting it right' so as to be a powerful member of the group. That means being quick on the uptake as far as required attitudes are concerned."

"That could happen with your method too. In any case the effects of a method wear off. What remains later is what will've been valuable."

"But valuable for what? You've got more faith than me - I know dozens of middle-aged people carrying round crippling loads of rubbish they seem to feel is valuable."

Michael's manner became strained. "Ah well, we can't all be gurus. Some of us have to make do with less than constant attention to the eternal principles of life."

"Some of us make do with less than a life!"

Michael stood up but before leaving rested his hand lightly on Matthew's shoulder, friendlily dismissive.

Joan waited to see if there would be any more from the

remaining two but the French tutor looked at his watch and stood up, leaving Matthew with a nod and a smile. Now he was on his own she thought of joining him but decided against it.

The incident had the effect of refocussing her general attention - this time on to the one man. As the only woman in the department she'd grown used to mixed feelings of defensiveness and excitement at her position. Matthew she'd felt close to almost immediately. She didn't always agree with him but liked his presence and realised that either he was as much an outsider as herself or that unconsciously he made room for her. She found herself taking more part in conversations when he was present, fired by him if not his arguments - siding with others while moving closer to him. She felt involved in her work more personally than before through an increasing friendship that never lost, openly at least, its purely business nature. Much later she had to face the fact she was physically attracted to him - sometimes so strongly she was reluctant to use all the opportunities for contact that arose for fear he might detect the surcharge in an ordinary conversation and be put off by it. Unsure of herself, fearing involvement as much as she suspected he did, her behaviour was crippled further by her conviction that she wasn't attractive. She saw herself as too defensive and not sensual enough in the ways that made men forget their own defences - certainly not lively enough to draw them closer unawares. She bit down her responses and worried about them, half-hankering to go back to the less complicated dearth she'd grown used to but sustaining with a steady drop of fuel (appreciation of his movements, his silences, his withdrawal as well as involvement) a low-burning fire to be warmed and probably burnt by, and she was as defensive of its life as she was afraid of letting it be seen.

Her increased sense of involvement in what was going on was sheer profit. It opened her up in a way that doubled her expectations. She felt ashamed of her old disengagement and began to be deeply impressed by the vigour, variety and pace of life under what still seemed such unpromising conditions. For him she could now become a friendly member of other groups and he seemed the more solitary of the two. It was safe to join in arguments occasionally - at first not saying much but later taking as much part as he, incapacitated as he was by his hair-trigger temperament, inhibitions about over-participation and his personal rules of patient observation. His manner when only he and another were chatting often seemed strained - not unpleasantly perhaps but strained and she didn't want to be exposed to it or increase it by her own tensions. He sometimes conducted these conversations in a near whisper and the bright-eyed look could turn into a beatific mask of would-be involvement, but she put it down to a good-natured over-effort, explaining it away as the result of passionate private responses, overcharged and changing by the second, that wouldn't allow themselves any but a sociable outlet. His head closing towards the speaker consumed the conversation even when rejecting the conversationalist and it reminded her of Mark.

One afternoon over coffee he was especially involved in a discussion with a largish group on magic and ancient religious rites. Someone had mentioned Frazer's Golden Bough and someone else thought he recalled that Wittgenstein had said something to the effect that in it the magicians were treated as if they were modern Englishmen of inferior intelligence. Bates was in the group. Joan had unconsciously avoided him so far while feeling she ought to get to know him better if they were to be thrown together in the summer.

"It's so silly," Matthew was saying. "It's amazing how easy it is for a writer to get a superior tone in his argument when it's about something in the past - as if we're all so happy with the state of our own knowledge and beliefs. I suppose when something took place so long ago that even a primitive understanding of what it must have been like gets lost, 'now' is bound to seem more sophisticated. But it's only because we're still operating the ways of thinking that've given rise to current beliefs and know how subtly they can be trained on intellectual or emotional objectives. They'd be useless to us otherwise. But the same must have applied then. The change may or may not be progress, depending on how you use it. Our beliefs can be just as benighted, just as enlightened or no more than a new way of looking at old mysteries. The larger the group we feel we belong to and the more we manipulate our physical surroundings the more likely a sociological view of life should be the one to take over. But any belief can be reduced to absurdity - what could be more absurd than the Christian scheme of rewards and punishments seen from an equally superficial standpoint? Pat on the head for good boys - kick up the pants for bad! It's what people make of it when it's the current shape of understanding that matters. A belief in magic could be just as subtle. It's not the superficial structure that matters and that's all we've got left."

Entry and exit in discussion was flexible and mood-driven - it was keeping the ball in the air that mattered and now someone else gave it a smack:

"But don't you think the system of having one God is a real moral and social advance on the idea of several? If you see the ideas behind one religion as having a primarily social function such as, 'Don't worship money, property or power but the principles of getting on with each other' - that's a pretty fair advance surely." Dick Somers flung his arm over the back of his chair to show he'd finished.

He was one of her colleagues Joan found depressing without finding good reason for it. For one thing she was conscious of him separately from what he did and said, as if there were always a dialogue - sometimes an argument. Dark bags under anxious eyes over a fleshy nose. A brief attempt to get easy in the new position but the flung arm and crossed legs had been done too recklessly. Long wavy greying hair hung round the neck of a dirty tee-shirt that rode up and showed them his thin brown belly. An ignored, insulted, depleted body flaunting a carelessness that only emphasized its carewornness filled her with compassion and anger. He abused humanity in the shape of himself.

"I don't agree," Matthew answered, "several gods could be better. It gives other things a chance."

"D.H.L. rides again!" Bates's mouth was pursed after he'd said it.

"I'll grant the one God idea has its primitive undertones" - Dick had ignored him - "I can't imagine, for example, how being all-knowing he could possibly be a 'jealous' one."

"Ah, then you're missing the point," Matthew said, "that's only a symbol of commitment to the principles of life. The understanding is that if you backslide or side-step chaos rules."

"It rules if you don't! And who gets the job of isolating the principles of life?"

Joan froze. She hated agreeing with Bates and the shock of it made her speak: "So D.H.L. was making a few points after all?"

"Why not?" Bates turned to her, pleased at the

antagonism that established his place. "In something as arrogant and baggy as novel-writing it's hard luck on us if some interesting ground doesn't get covered! The trouble with Lawrence is he appeals for a fuller life and greater flexibility of response while laying down the law on how to get it. I think the thinking goes with the art form, as you know. I'll have you all converted yet," he smiled round the table, "and with reinforcement coming next week, who knows?" One or two looked puzzled. "Wilcher's lecture! We'll all be there, won't we? Can't have the poor sod lecturing to an empty room. I don't think his slant will pull in many students."

"I'll be going," Matthew said, "but out of interest." Feeling it came out a bit piously he added:" No need to work on me, I'm a dyed-in-the-wool poetry and drama man. Never liked novels. It's the would-be realism that gets me and marks it inferior."

"Why inferior?" Joan was shocked at her own voice responding on its own to a further twist to her feelings.

"It's not the highest form of art," he said, shamefaced.

"Like what for instance?"

"Drama and poetry."

She looked at him so incredulously he was for the first time thoroughly disturbed by her disagreement. "You can't praise and dispose of whole genres!" Her tone was expressing injury or betrayal and his confusion made him conciliatory:

"Novels mix themselves with philosophy and history," he said. "It isn't a pure art form."

"Thank God for that - I can't think of a worse waste of time than pure Art." She bit back something else but let herself speak a moment later and found it came out bitter and intense: "Is it just the forms you admire or does content count?" When she saw him blush she backed off. "Give me an example of what you think is high art," she said, imagining he wouldn't go that far.

He thought a moment. "The first thing that comes into my head is Beatrice's entrance into paradise or," appeasingly, "if you want the novel" - he reddened - "and sometimes it can achieve remarkable things in short spurts - the first third of *Madame Bovary*." He looked at her now as if both appealing for understanding and begging forgiveness and moved his hand on to the table towards her.

"What a good thing you don't believe in influencing your students." The gesture had brought a gentler note into her voice. "You'd be a menace! Don't you see that kind of selectivism makes nonsense of literature? Either it takes part in a living situation or it has no value. Your whole attitude's irrelevant. All writers can do is succeed or fail to take part successfully. That's where discrimination comes in - clearing the path so what isn't fake can get through. If I were your pupil and had to answer you in your terms I'd call both your selections inferior on the grounds of limited range and purpose and therefore limited achievement. I've never heard of anything more arrogant than looking for perfect moments. God help us if you're the judge of them." She paused. Seeing nothing but hurt in his eyes she wanted to backtrack but didn't see how. "Do you think there can be 'exquisite' observation outside its context? You make me use the word exquisite - it's what I feel you're being. We only give attention out of interest and the greater the writer's skill the sharper, intenser the interest. There are no rules but success. If art obeys rules it becomes a game - some kind of performance to entertain you and satisfy the author's vanity. Both parties'd be better off with cricket where unchangeable structure can highlight skill and your patronising streak can get a proper airing. After all it's 'Well shot sir!' the players want and making a score is what it's all about."

He withdrew his hand. It had gone beyond hurt. Her anger had established an intimacy he didn't know how to deal with.

"It's like saying that songs and opera are the highest form of music," she said and suddenly stopped. Disappointment, a burning sense of having been hurt and showing it made her turn away. She saw Dick's mouth was moving but heard nothing. No point in arguing. The world finally understood both academics and the art in question. She was just as guilty as him - not of seeking refuge in the exquisite in art but in other forms of it, in taste, in moral or behavioural judgment, in one set of rules or another. But the healthier animal never got completely diverted or suppressed, in him or anyone else. Fear of life, of exposure, of contacts, of intrusions on the ego and of intruding on others - it was what she'd been like herself and what gave Matthew the amputated look she decided she hated. The passion had to go somewhere and it fled to one form or other of the exquisite or the pure - or what glamourisation brought about by need turned into the pure - where a sense of the fineness and meticulousness of our participation contributed its own frisson and where the passion could be predictably structured and do no harm.

"Can you defend it?" she said. Her question cut through something Bates was saying. They turned to her, uncomfortable, faintly irritated. Matthew looked puzzled. "Tell me why you need those separate schools, I really want to know. Why do you only believe in them as poetry, drama and philosophy? Isn't structural simplification worse than silly when what they all have in common at their best is a passionate exploration of life?"

Matthew was caught by the need in her voice and missed a comment from Bates that was raising a laugh.

"Anyway I don't understand your criticism. What could be more would-be realistic than dressing up and acting out events in drama as if they were true - or more full of half-truths and in constant need of qualification than philosophy? Writers go on using those forms because over the years they've built a short cut into their own and others' sensibilities. They're the oldest with the most primitive roots. Song, mime, ritualistic acting out of important events and beliefs still carry their weight you see, but you want to fix limitations to their usefulness. Of the three schools you're keen on, philosophy comes off worst, it has to explore important issues from outside a representative living context and in being expected to come up with a refutation or conclusion is doomed. Thinking's too valuable to be thrown away on conclusions, but the form demands it. If the other two have to stay as primitive as you'd like there's no hope for philosophy. There writers are forced back to the linear - to arguments that touch reality only at the points they pass through. When a line of thought has been followed to the end, clarified and made distinct and accessible it's been hardened and narrowed by a form of logical reasoning exclusive to its own train of perceptions and too much has been left out." She paused, looking at him without really seeing him, waiting for him to say something but with a preoccupied look that made it impossible. "It's only because novels are the newest form you think of them as heresy or bastard art but they've come into being for the very reason they can and do combine all three and more. The idea of dissociating thought however well intentioned and sensitively monitored from some living context by which it can be seen to be distorted and qualified is just as dangerous as the idea you cling to of compartments - logical thought in one, feeling and states of mind in another when in fact they're never exclusive. Art gives the only opportunity there is to make an objective study of the changes and complexities that are the only constants you can rely on. If the artist is someone who looks to life to shape his thinking rather than to the forms and procedures already laid out then he's constantly breaking open and extending those forms."

Bates was sitting back with an air of amazement and amusement. There was contempt in it but not so much at what she was saying as at what he was watching. She grew aware of the general silence but had gone too far to stop. Matthew was attentive. Her beliefs were set out against his face to face. Challenged, moved, fully alive to her and what she was saying he was only interested in that, the others didn't exist and he forgot to be alarmed at both the intensity and privacy of the circuit she'd created.

"If we trust certain forms and lines of enquiry perhaps it's because they make things possible for us," he said. "When we separate one thing from another is the only time we can pursue anything - the only time achievement's possible."

"The trouble is we get carried away. You got carried away with your 'high' and 'low' art forms. Pursuit is right, reliance on the conclusion isn't. It's the belief in ideas that makes people behave worse than animals. It's responsible for the only unnaturalness. Ideas harden, separate, intensify and justify. Being separated they've an emotional world of their own they carry with them. Under the protection of feelings born of ideas like justice, right and purity the opposite runs riot. War is a form of purism licensed by ideas. It's fear or greed pursued purely. The natural balance where fear and need are controlled by the instinct for self-preservation gets destroyed, the elements are separated and the spurious emotional undertow of each drags us into a millrace of fear and greed that belongs only to the world of ideas not the world of life. It's without natural controls as a result. Only the process of separation can produce the intensification needed to pursue an idea to the death. Ideas should be monitored more closely than scientific experiments - they're the means by which we're made irrational. We don't dare stop exploring, changing and adapting them - seeing them in new forms and contexts helps. We like looking for the quintessence of things as if we're looking for answers or roads to a mythical centre. It means we're hungry for discovery and growth but also for simplicity. In the very chase we're escaping - running away from shifting views of a shifting universe towards dangerous securities. Ideas are potentially dangerous concentrates, artificial fertilisers killing off in unexpected ways the life they're meant to feed. The deadliest factor is that the processing is done by us. Each of us defines the mixture of ingredients and how to apply them and we use them as we like with the complacency of trust and ignorance. As far as Art's concerned tackling things that appear to you to be tackleable, producing something exquisitely formed, serviceable to the soul and knowing its place meets an idea-induced prerequisite for gaining your personal attention. The ideas behind it probably include your personal interpretation of sensitivity or humility or both. But it means you're worshipping your own tools for life and not necessarily those that will always be of the most use to you. You're certainly limiting the machinery for making more and subtler ones. You mention the arrogance of authors but your selectivity is more so. I'm against your apartheid in art. You want things kept simple, pure, in their categories - I'm all for mixing them up and the more thorough-going the attempt at realism the less chance there is for what you want. One can't have things too simplified in the best realism - which certainly doesn't lie in the illusion of historical fact but in a complexity of observed and likely situations and their undertows, reflecting variations of response and meaning, changing or being changed by events. A small invention of a real world where there are too many factors interacting to invite judgment, where our curiosity is fed without the illusion of satisfaction, where we're not wholly subject to events, ideas or feelings but made to experience all together at once as we do in life but objectively as we can't in life. I can't think of a more useful piece of machinery than a good novel."

Matthew, leaning across the table towards her, looking at her as if he were discovering a new self or as if this were a close friend incognito, waited to see if there was any more to come, then: "There's so much I want to agree and disagree with I don't know where to begin."

The two had closed together and the others had begun to leave. When Matthew looked round no-one else was there. Still he couldn't bring himself to move. Staring at her, interested and excited he didn't want to let it finish.

"But what an admission," he said, picking up the last statement. "Machinery's the word. They're so cumbersome and take themselves so seriously. I don't like the pretence that life can be handled on so large a scale."

"It can't be touched on a small one." Joan too was beginning to notice their situation and started to feel anxious and uncomfortable. Matthew catching it, remembered students he had to meet and stood up.

"I'll see you later" - he was trembling, wondering whether to make a definite arrangement but finding himself addressing the top of her head, left, saying "Soon".

Joan went to Wilcher's lecture the following week. The pressures of end-of-year examinations, especially finals, were building up and routine took over. The new intimacy advanced no further than that intermittently they were both vividly and secretly aware of each other's presence. The interest was sustained at a level that allowed them for the moment not to take much notice of it but for Joan the lecture was another turning point in her feelings. Coming near the end of term it turned her back to what she now felt she missed. The long vacation and the commune were taking precedence over everything.

In the lecture room, from several rows behind, she watched the strange ducking of Matthew's head towards the pale young man sitting next to him and tried to decide whether he was really making excited conversation or letting his head do it for him. He was full of symbolic gestures as interesting or more so than the conversation he had with others and that she still did her best to overhear. Deciding it symbolised the participation he wished he felt, she found she'd missed the entry of the speaker. Dick Somers was up front clearing his throat. He flattered the newcomer unspecifically, reminding us of his fame and our good fortune. The visitor came forward, stout, bald, middle-aged and from a flushed face surveyed his intimate audience. He seemed to get confidence from it. Contact established he cleared his throat:

"I've decided to put the cat among the pigeons properly today!" His voice was high and gleeful at the start but changed to a sonorous low for the last two words. Instantly alerted the audience prepared to be amused. "I propose to outline the grosser nature of the novel and contend that it's an inferior art form, and I propose to do this to an audience probably composed of novel addicts to a man and especially a woman." Someone threw a snort of laughter like a rose to a primadonna. "I simply cannot condone serious novel writing or reading." He paused. "A novel is not reliably informative, nor capable of close relativity nor, because of its hideous length, memorable - so at long last after endless bulletins as to the state of its health let's show compassion and give it the coup de grace."

Joan looked around her. He was well known both as an academic and editor of a flourishing literary journal so the audience was slightly larger and more willing than usual. For some his vanity stimulated theirs, they were already excited. With one or two students he seemed to touch a raw nerve. They were stung but couldn't square their discomfort with his playfulness. His method, designed to amuse while forcing them to defend themselves was a ploy they were used to but never prepared for.

A wide grin was given to the audience at this point, displayed to one side then the other then withdrawn.

"It's a form hopelessly vitiated by structural weakness. At best we can retain only a vague outline of the whole. It can never achieve the final beauty of form accessible to a poem or a play." He lowered his voice to a menace. "It is the play of personality masquerading as thought - it is an interest in gossip masquerading as social conscience - it is fiction masquerading as fact!"

He had to stop here. The audience couldn't control the taut-wire vibration of laughter. He waited for the resonance from the last three chords to die before continuing.

"In our long nineteenth century novel centering on life at Mudacre Manor we are told that the west wing windows were of Gothic design - an affectation introduced by the architect employed by the hero's grandfather when enlarging the house. We're there in a sentence. Mudacre Manor exists with a present reality and a past history. But let us stop for a moment before gobbling up the rest. We must ask ourselves two obvious boring questions: Does the manor really exist?" - he paused, chin raised - "No, of course it doesn't" - and lowered it - "Do we care?" - a similar pause - "Of course we don't!" He shook his head with exaggerated regularity stopping only when the close-lipped smile accompanying it had been read on all sides. It was oratorical punctuation, commentary and apology. "But -" on the sound like a cuff round the ear he paused again - "Don't you think perhaps we should?" Solicitous silence won us back.

"I've seen paintings from the realistic schools that have created the semblance of reality so well that the fly in the milk on the corner of the table in the kitchen made one itch to pick it out." A pause. "The struggle to portray a real-looking fly in real-looking milk had been effective but not so provocative of interesting responses as a real fly in drinkable milk. In what way has the painter succeeded then? In achieving what is for him perhaps a therapeutic solidification of a complex living reality. The results benefit no-one so much as the painter and I venture to suggest he could have gained as much from any activity requiring patience and application. But perhaps I'm wrong. Perhaps the special nature of his activity is more closely linked with the tasks given our more unfortunate brethren in institutions where they're encouraged to regain sanity and contact with life."

He paused to give a grateful grin to the more persistent gigglers. Some of his audience was defecting. He noted it but had some more jokes up his sleeve and a hard-pressed note came into them while he obstinately held his wits for auction to the loudest laugh.

One or two faces looked questioning or distant. There was a demand for substance. He filled a glass, drank and returned with the required material: "Let us take some of our great figures in the novel." From this point the entertainment was over but some of the audience finding themselves refreshed stayed with him to the end. He skirted round the figures he promised, using the weaker authors to back untenable generalities. By now few people minded. The lecture was seen for what it was, an amusing gesture.

The points he made about structure and memorability and the pure art forms that Matthew believed in were challenged amusingly afterwards during question time when Joan watched her colleagues confidently at work in the arena. The pale young man next to Matthew stood up, bending forwards slightly and addressing most of his remarks to the lecturer's table:

"I can't see why you insist on memorability. How much of the Prelude do you know off by heart? Can you intellectually retain more than a line or two at a time? The longer literary products cough up with the greatest number of memorable expressions. Didn't some recent statistical survey come up with the conclusion that the most commonly known and used quotations came from Dickens, Shakespeare and the Bible? And why do you assume the reader's nonplussed as to what set of standards to use? A novel-reader's no more likely to be sucked in by false ethic or false fact than the reader of a poem, a play or a history book. You're more exposed to an incompetent job in the latter I'd have thought, which stakes its all on being factually accurate. The essence of a novel's appeal is the liberty of response allowed us and that depends on certain knowledge that factually accurate it isn't but representatively accurate it may be."

He sat down. The speaker smiled and sipped water. Joan watched him. With a stance like his you couldn't lose. One thing academics did well was cover their tracks. When the pause seemed over-long and the chairman certain of no answer he called on a dainty postgraduate who'd raised her arm in a graceful curve. She stood.

"I agree with you Professor Wilcher about the inferiority of realism. The attempt at it bothers me in the way I was bothered in my last trip to Australia by what was happening to the dances of the Aborigines. They have two kinds of dance, the mimetic and symbolic. I saw little of the symbolic that I was hoping for - instead they were zooming around pretending to be aeroplanes. I felt guilty. I saw mimesis as a kind of cultural disenfranchisement."

"I think you're right," Wilcher said between sips.

"Disenfranchisement, as you call it, is a positive development - you needn't feel guilty." Saul Berry had leapt to his feet and turned towards her like a beagle on the scent. "They're on their way to assimilating an alien culture. Give it time, the simple mimesis will become part of a complex structure you'll recognise as symbolic."

He sat and a student stood up who took her time, faced Saul first and with a controlled gesture moved a strand of her long hair from her face, then turned to Wilcher: "You mention the clarity and potential of symbols in your argument on behalf of poetry and plays but why do you understand symbols only at such a simple level?" She was blushing and all out for defiance - very conscious of Saul's eyes on her back. "Good so-called realism is full of the most complex and subtle symbolism. The characters in a novel, for example, are 'people' symbols and their interplay leads to endless permutations of meaning - not one or two. You seem to prefer your symbols tied up and disposable. Perhaps it's a case of the simpler the better? If so, the symbolic gesture of the first two fingers of the right hand is one of the highest forms of art."

Joan laughed and was annoyed to find herself alone. Her irritation was partly with them, partly with herself. She'd thought herself reasonably at one with the rest of the department and with the business of lecturing but the only time she'd betrayed a sense of humour was now. She found the laugh liberated thoughts and feelings she'd been suppressing. Her earlier responses were still with her, overlain but active. Excitement at going back to the commune was pushing aside recent developments. Her failure to understand Matthew's attitude was one of the things underlying the irritation and it brought back the whole issue of an academic mentality. Perhaps a high degree of training actually limited vision. The expertise only worked when we used the methods and tools we were trained by and they could only be applied successfully to the aspects of our work that made themselves amenable. To thought outside it it was like having four thumbs. Wilcher's preoccupation with form and structure gave him away. What was or could be thoroughly known had for him the right structure. It also kept art in its place and subservient to the ego.

She remembered an argument with an acquaintance a year or so ago who'd been claiming Haydn was a greater composer than Mahler and couldn't get off the subject of "the baggy overblown form of Mahler's symphonies". He'd backed it with untenable prejudices about emotional content which came under the general heading of "vulgar" but which really grew out of a disappointed sense of form.

Emotionality, repetition, apparent simplicity were highly praised in styles he knew. If he couldn't immediately lay mental hold on the structure it hadn't got one and once he was insecure he was rejective. After the concert he said "Who can take seriously a man who uses ten French horns?" She irritably replied "Who can take seriously a man who uses two?" Playing down a powerful and original mind because the work toppled the balance you'd been trained to admire or an idea of emotional integrity that went with it was second nature to those who felt competent to judge because trained to it. This man's responses ran counter to the nature and purpose of the composer, that was all. He was careful to disguise it in the following day's review of the concert because Mahler had a place in the ears of the general public, and his prejudice came out in confining himself to praising the exquisiteness and subtlety of the performance. The conductor was an irreproachable one in most people's eyes who, she'd felt, had been distorting and draining the work to suit prejudices similar to his own.

She'd followed Matthew out of the hall and he'd joined Wilcher and Bates at the bar. Seeing them easy and in touch alarmed her further. The only difference between Matthew and the other two was that his feelings drove him harder, but at least that put him on guard against things they ignored. The struggle to get away from his training wasn't very successful and had turned him into a different kind of pedant. It was a nicer kind. She affectionately remembered his phrase, "the unlimited potential of the untrained". Sanctions and safeguards were still necessary though and outside them he was suspicious. How could he trust first-hand experience of life when as a result of his life-style there'd been so little - or untrained thinking when there'd been even less. No wonder in art he valued the manageable.

Novelists who made judgments on life while usurping the reader's identity must scare him especially, if they were good at their job. To be emotionally crowded by a form in which length, movement and variety made it inviting temporarily to give up the different responses he might have if he weren't hustled must seem like a violation.

She watched his face over his glass - talking with the man he agreed with. He wasn't like them. Each one looked excited but only he with the company. If he could only have faith either in life or his own elasticity. It was something she'd felt she couldn't manage herself but looking at him now, most at ease with the least accessible, she began to feel she wasn't doing a bad job. At least the intrusion of another ego, the 'arrogance' he feared, didn't worry her. For her it was a product of exuberance and attractive if the nature behind it were. In releasing creative energy at all you released the fearful 'arrogance'. It came out clearly enough in his own case. She'd already discovered from his students he was an exciting and rewarding tutor - creative, dedicated and thoroughly unhumble. The unconscious hypocrisy shouldn't worry her either if the alternative were Bates and his sceptical preoccupation with immediate needs. He half enjoyed and wholly dismissed everything, even his pleasures, and wore his tastes and preferences like clothes to set him off, devil's advocate or purist as the mood took him, icy when heated, anarchic when committed - his only aim to put life down and himself up. Attitudes and feelings for him were social currency for fools to idealise and the clever to use. Watching him sent her back like a boomerang to Matthew whose passion, commitment - even hypocrisy - was an attempt to escape the self into something more rewarding.

8

At the end of term the strength of Joan's urge to get back to the commune took her by surprise and brought her cooler self to the forefront. She mistrusted compulsions and cautiously decided to stay for a few days at the hotel in Corfax where she'd holidayed as a child with her father.

The journey down became a pleasure for its own sake. She liked the thought of looking the town over uninvolved with the others, perhaps taking a look at Mark's place from the outside - seeing it in perspective before being swallowed up. The intention to delay increased her excitement which drained into the totally private world of her past with her father that had made her childhood impressions of the area indelible. The erotic content of that experience had left its mark on the town as well as the countryside around it where the long walks the two of them had taken, tiring and frustrating to her child's sense of fun and purpose, had nevertheless been exciting to her imagination. All her energy had gone into sharing experiences that were relatively colourless in themselves but vivid as meeting places for their mutual need for affection and sympathetic understanding. Observation of this and that, often boring at first but condoned because of the playful tenderness behind it had been intensified to a passion. It became the key to adult experience: if you noticed enough, shared enough, you achieved the intimacy of identification. They'd evolved a relationship so close that the sudden eruption of hills or the unexpected smell of cattle or appearance of the sea at the end of a long climb taken at her father's pace, his hand either holding her back or hauling her up, had left the memory of an impact that filled her even now with aspiration and an uncontrollable energy hunting for involvement.

On reaching Corfax the nostalgia died and her attention focussed entirely on the transformed town. It was hot. The place was airless and crowded with people and traffic. She screwed her face up against glaring sunlight. In the hill-confined streets car noises were intensified and dung and traffic fumes trapped. She crossed the square to the hotel, groped her way through beery darkness to the counter and waited. A fat young man came out of the shadows and smiled. He checked her booking and gave her a key and directions to her room. The room was attractive. Small latticed windows set in thick cool limestone overlooked the square and at an angle she could see the castle.

She dropped her case and went out to look for a short cut she remembered to the top of the ridge of hills that stretched to the sea and backed Mark's farm. It was still in use but climbing the narrow gorse-walled tracks was confinement not excitement. The slope was hotter than the town and the change from Spring shocked her. She remembered seeing it lit with fierce yellow gorse, and the puffs of colour taking its place as the tracks opened up were a keen disappointment. Ragwort mostly, knee-level distractions, multi-headed, small, softened, ragged-leaved. First the town now this. She climbed faster but the heat and dung smells held her back.

Where the ragwort thinned out the slope had been colonised by a welter of flowers, harebells, scabious, pimpernels and over them pairing butterflies in droves bunching and moving apart. Insect activity criss-crossed under her nose, their thin intense fizzing broken by trumpet calls from cattle lower down. Fields and slope blended and surged in the heat, standing clear again when she reached the top and could see the cows strung across the field under her, brown against green, cropping. Further off they were shadowy - bunched in idle masses under trees and on the horizon scattered and spaced like seeds.

Twitching her armpits free of her dress she walked along the top watching her feet, her skirt moving out in a warm wind. The soft mild air left her energyless. She sniffed for gusts from the sea without success. In a field below a group of riders were opening a gate. A pony trek. Their slow disorganised crossing focussed the beginnings of exhaustion - theirs, her own, the countryside's. She turned to the castle hill standing on its own above the town. It was smaller than the rest and the arena-shaped ruin spread itself over the top in the sunlight, its relaxed tumblings of stone inviting the clambering they got while claiming attention of a different kind - but for that attention they offered no return. All suggestions were lost in the life teeming over them.

A thin chalky path led up a quarry just beyond but her hunting for cool shapes and clear space was distracted by the morse of bright cars on the road into town which her eyes followed through the suburbs past the square and out through the yellowing verges. The smell of dung rose in waves. She'd climbed for refreshment and now came down for it, picking her way through the gorse to a new path. This was alive with grasshoppers. They flew up like dust when she put her foot down and perched on needle-thin leaves, every footfall raised another cloud and the chirruping encircled her till she reached the lane at the bottom. Here the high hedges and an attractive overpowering smell that was sweet and polleny excited and drew her to the white sprays of hedge flowers producing it which in turn were covered with white butterflies that lifted and resettled every few seconds breaking shape unexpectedly. Streams of response crossing, cancelling and being reborn brought on a mood of dependence or openness that stayed for most of the next few days.

This was in spite of the fact that the first night she had no sleep. Lorries ran non-stop on the road outside. She managed better the following night by accommodating the noise in her head, giving them passage through the bedroom - a state of desperate passivity that paid off better still the night after when she incorporated them in her dreams. She thought of giving up and going to Mark's place but found she wasn't ready yet and looked for human interest in the hotel.

The man she'd met the first evening was the hotel owner's son, or so she thought. She'd pieced together information gathered accidentally (when she forgot her key one evening) and otherwise hard to come by as both he and his father tried to run the place invisibly. She saw the father only once on his own, sitting on the wall outside looking like one of his lodgers with his shirt gaping over a pink paunch. He had the same vague unseeing look as his son had when she saw him at six o'clock one morning coming over the road with six packs of sausages. An intense private world existed in the background though. When she locked herself out of her room there was no one around and she knocked on a door marked Private, eventually opening it in desperation because she couldn't get an answer. The room was dully lit and for several seconds kept its secret - a large family sitting round the table playing cards. The look of violation was neither vague nor secretive. In that role she existed vividly as a thorn in their flesh. She explained herself and was told to wait for the barman.

In spite of this in the mornings - via the waitress - the idea of service was artfully put forward. She gave a hybrid version of the owner's attitudes - commitment to cash and irritable dissociation from the source. Everyone seemed confused on some points. The guests who, noisy and sweaty, filled the bars each night came to breakfast washed, hushed and cautious. On both sides the cash and pleasure principles were booby-trapped. The guests behaved as if indifferent to money - which was sometimes a pretence that cost them dear emotionally as well as financially because the pose was instantly exploited and the waitress, her eye on the tip, served the meals with a self-conscious twist of the wrist and smiling back-step that managed to be subservient, contemptuous and greedy.

After a while the spurious tensions of living there made Joan feel the delay was becoming counter-productive and that after one more trip she'd be ready to go. This was to see Mark's place on her own before she became involved - an urge that wouldn't be denied and seemed to be powered by opposing forces, romantic and evaluative. She felt it would help 'place' everything.

She hired a bike and cycled to a vantage point. From the road the house looked disappointingly ordinary and impersonal and there was no way to get closer without spoiling perspective. Unfortunately she'd seen too many gabled bedroom windows and slate roofs over the last few days and couldn't see more than that from here because of the trees - Mark's copse blocked the view. On the ridge of hills backing it there were patches of bare chalk that made the browning grass look like a melting pelt, in fact nothing looked as she'd hoped it would. Everything was distinct in the brilliant sunlight - houses, trees, cars and cows - and made similar impacts. A vividly clear surface texture detracted from individuality and all other objects were equally important or unimportant. With no shading and highlighting, animate and inanimate demanded and deadened in the same way. Everything blazed itself without blending. The field in front of her was easier to look at than the distance, the items on it offering themselves for cataloguing - thistles, grass, a cow and a sheep. The cow and sheep were eating the same clump of grass nose to nose but hardly competed for attention with the thistles that were tall and ferociously independent.

She gave up. The only things that caught her imagination were sounds - cattle noises carried in snatches by the light wind, a helicopter moving in from the sea and the vicious buzzing of flies bombarding the ragwort where she stood. One of the background noises slowly intensified and identified itself as a tractor. It moved on to the road behind her and she turned to watch the man driving it. Fair haired, rosy, gleaming with health, the landscape exploded into life behind him, giving meaning to the rest. When he waved in answer to her smile with a relaxed and sun-drenched curve of his arm she got on her bike without thinking and followed him.

The next day Mark came to meet her with open arms. She stood in the shadowy hallway, cases at her feet, explaining why she'd let them know only the night before and blushingly confessing to the few days she'd spent on her own. The children came to see who it was, waited for their sense of something new to be fulfilled, were ignored, got bored and moved off. Sheila popped out of the kitchen with floury hands to give a loud-voiced welcome in a tone Joan recognised and obeyed. The pleasure in her voice was genuine but perhaps for a recruit more than a person.

Single-minded passionate involvement with the running of her chosen world snatched Joan after her and in the kitchen with the windows wide open and the light softened from the closeness of the hedges but penetrating to every corner Joan felt suddenly refreshed and at home. This room especially seemed to stand for the central and business-like involvement she longed for. Mark, carrying her cases, followed after, urging her back to the sitting-room where he said they were all coming to meet her - he'd sent Peter to fetch them.

Bess and Tom were first, smiling and so brown they looked changed. They were followed closely by two youngsters introduced as their daughter and her boyfriend. Joan hadn't thought of the Blakes as having a child. She'd not heard about her. The new dimension and their changed appearance made her feel that with them she was starting all over again. They clearly belonged together and formed a small group of their own. The girl looked rather like her father but with her mother's colouring and was pretty, rosy and gave her an amiable smile. The young man, thin and tee shirted, had nervous emotionality written in his eyes, and his big nose added to their outgoing expression a look of vulnerability.

Mark said Bates was already there and would be in to see her in a minute, and "Beatrice is coming for a short stay". He put his arm round her happily and Joan, equally happy, let herself be led upstairs to her old room. The immediate involvement was wonderful, it frightened, distracted and captured her so completely she felt shame at her usual self and its nervous cautiousness and suddenly inferior to the vigorous individuals she'd given herself up to.

She didn't see Bates until lunch time when he smiled at her with that distant curiosity she was used to. His answer to Mark's rebuke about not coming in earlier was, "I lose all sense of time picking peas!" If she hadn't already found her feet he'd have made it difficult - he gave the impression she was an odd addition. She found his presence equally incongruous. He'd gone pink, showing the first signs of days in the sun and was dressed in khaki trousers and white shirt with sleeves rolled, obviously making a concession. She was surprised to find the pink neck and arms made her more humanly aware of him than before - something his manner soon corrected. He was looking round the table with the objectivity of a gull, dissociation and alertness on the make, but this time she had a comforting sense he was matched or overmatched. He'd find it hard to disrupt, harder still to destroy - the best he could do would be scavenge.

In the afternoon Joan stayed close to Sheila. She did the jobs she suggested while taking in the sights and smells that would leap the final barriers of strangeness. There was a strong smell of peaches when Sheila added yeast to brown sugar and warm water for the bread and when she was kneading the dough Joan was allowed to feel the texture at two different stages to judge its progress to the silkiness required.

For a while Sheila silently convinced her that what happened here was the culmination and justification of the whole project. There was persuasion in the way she moved. Confidence, ease, a brightened look that came from doing several things in overlapping stages - all needing concentration and a sensitive responsiveness - left her smile to do the work of filling out brief monosyllabic answers to curious questions. Her preoccupation was being fed by more than the need for efficiency. All this was a dream world, not one to offset the boredom of activities but created by them. The exclusiveness and remoteness in her behaviour didn't look like an evasion of reality - more a way of reducing it to manageable symbolism.

Joan stayed close to her for the first few days and saw comparatively little of the others as a result because Sheila was happiest when she was in the kitchen or fields and more or less on her own. Tiredness that came as a result of the work was acceptable, she resented the other sources of it. It upset her that the others spent so much of their time discussing or "arguing" as she saw it. She told Joan if they had that much energy left over there were always jobs to be done and the "nastiness" could be avoided. She felt discussion worried and exaggerated responses that were marginal and made difficulties where none existed.

Joan eventually separated from her because she enjoyed the times she spent with the others more. She found she was easier with the demands they made on each other than in the Spring and was beginning to think the success of the commune would lie in encouraging the differences between them rather than suppressing them. They needed the crossfire to define the new rules being evolved, their life together wouldn't last without it perhaps. Each of them stood out vividly as an individual because the circumstances demanded it. The formation of a new community - one as small and independent as this - needed the special gifts of each and must be based on the needs of each. Complete co-operation was its only hope. In discussion not one of them, except paradoxically Sheila the commune's most fanatic supporter, seemed ever to have been at ease with the comprehensive rules of the massive society. Stripped of their dependence on it they'd become more conscious of their need of others and what this meant in terms of give and take and most of all what was worth the effort of assertion. She wanted the scheme to work, she liked the people and the life-style, it must be given room. It was the honeymoon period of Joan's marriage to the forces that had got it underway.

For the next couple of weeks the pleasure of having no resistance and boundless curious goodwill altered the resonance of every incident. The potentially alarming could become exciting, the worrying a source of challenge - the challenge, for instance, of not recognising the flare of suppressed excitement in Mark's eyes when he was squashed up against Bess on the sofa as the fuse that if lit would blow up the whole thing about their heads. Instead she was amazed at the trust all this freedom and closeness had bred and sure the group could both inspire and accommodate strong feeling. Given the natures of both it was hardly possible for them not to feel as they did but equally impossible for them to do anything about it. Intense feelings would be inhibited by stronger ones. The strain no more than of being fully alive.

The heat and brilliance of these weeks was distracting. The hard physical work lost its strain once the sun depleted her nervous energy. In general she lost the detail in a blaze of light and heat and relaxed into the group. When she surfaced again she found she was paying most attention to the Blakes whose new sub-group intrigued her. There was a different feel about their contribution to commune life that blended and commented on the Lewises'. With the Blakes she felt a confidence and assurance that was as good, perhaps better than safety. Sometimes everything seemed at risk - Bess was a dangerously volatile ingredient - and at first Tom seemed the one holding them stable, his liveliness increasing with the challenge. The Lewises on the other hand had definable aims which made their day-to-day behaviour more accessible but less spontaneous and rewarding. The Blakes' group was close-knit but eager outside itself. When variety of interest seemed hard to come by in the larger group they turned to each other for it - horseplay, fights - constantly on the lookout for fun. When John horsed around with Mary, Bess sometimes joined in. He had a temperament similar to her own - loads of energy and affection and a passion for involvement in spite of risk.

He came downstairs to breakfast one morning excited. His group, dozy but accessible, listened. He'd been locked in the bathroom with a wasp: "Bloody thing tried to get out through me ear'ole!" He was throwing his leg over the bench and pulling a bowl towards him. Mary grinned and pushed over the muesli. He shovelled it into his dish still looking round to hold their attention.

"Blooming sharp they are! I knocked him towards the window with a towel. He flattened himself on it vibrating up and down like a mad thing. Soon as I opened the flap he was off like a shot. Intelligent things, wasps! Not like stupid flies - you can chase them round the room for 'alf hour and they can't find the way out. On second thoughts they're not so stupid - they don't want to. Rather paddle their feet in your butter. Makes a change from shit."

Mary was wide awake. Pause while he ate. He saw a nut he fancied in Bess's bowl and took it. She was passing the milk and spotted it out of the corner of her eye, grabbed his hand with her free one and spilt milk over Tom's toast. Tom took the jug while she wrestled to get the spoon or the nut out of it. Bates leaned back watching the pantomime. Mark's amusement turned to irritation. Tom consciously ignored them, broke off the wet toast and made a mime of long sufferance.

He got on well with the newcomer and felt he had the key to his nature through Bess. He could enjoy almost any addition that seemed able, sometimes at least, to transform Mary's moods. She was, as he'd been as a teenager, moody and intellectual but shyness made it difficult for a powerful nature that thought pretty well of itself to find sufficient expression. The resultant 'black' periods could be a nightmare. Like himself an interest in food and sex could break her out of it and for each of them the nervous liveliness of their partners let them escape minute by minute a potentially miserable self-confinement. It was difficult for strangers to guess at Mary's nature. The Lewises still treated her like a sweet child. She hid behind coy smiles and her rosy milkmaid appearance. Taciturnity finished the job and left the uninformed with the opinion that she was docile and self-effacing. She'd not been here long enough to give even glimpses of the fury of rejection she could go in for when the social facade that timorousness and confused responses imposed on her had gone on for too long. Her physical appearance fitted her into a stereotype that had already enabled her to run through thirty boy friends with increasing appetite and diminishing ability to tolerate those who scared easily or tried to dominate the features of her growing mind and personality. John was the first not to have bored and irritated her in the last couple of years - he seemed to thrive on, without always liking, the challenge of her moods and she on the unsombre quick-changing succession of his.

As Joan watched the family and Tom's responses to Bess's foolery she felt, guided by him, that Bess's general responsiveness meant nothing more than that she felt both free and secure enough to have it. Quite possibly her daughter carried a similar immunity. She knew how to 'play' Bates's self-loving interest in her as skilfully as a mature woman. Joan noticed he was often to be found working near her without being too close and was untypically friendly and attentive to John's conversational interests. Her first cold dislike of a predictably cold tracking of an apparently defenceless prey was beginning to change. She had flashes of insight that suggested if he meant business, rather than vanity, he'd bitten off more than he could chew. Mary and John were absorbed with each other but she took time off to throw Bates a glance when she felt like a bonus. Her years made her as emotionally undeveloped as Bates but they also made shocks to the ego a commonplace and not as damaging as to him.

This was a family whose very strength lay in its apparent vulnerability. Joan came over the weeks to regard this feeling quite unjustifiably as a source of great assurance. The bond between Bess and her daughter for instance was frequently tense but very strong. Joan often picked up remnants of fights and reconciliations and once overheard them screaming and swearing at each other at the far end of a field where they thought themselves alone. That same afternoon they were wandering around the house with their arms round each other. It looked like an established way of life. Assurances seemed to be re-affirmed easily along those lines. They were a cuddling and hand-holding family and all four of them in a chain on the sofa in the evenings watching the new television were a warming and touching sight. It signalled closeness or the need for it, but not unbreakable closeness.

When she turned her attention back to the Lewises she felt that here she had to ask questions and get answers rather than watch. She asked Mark about Selby and his replies suggested less tension than in the Spring. He even told her quite readily and in front of Sheila the outcome, as he saw it, of the late night digging. The potato crop in the field next to the coppice had been ruined because the field was waterlogged. Selby had sabotaged the drainage. Mark had found the ditches he'd cleared earlier full of rubbish and one drain blocked with rubble.

During the course of the conversation it was clear his reactions had taken a new turn. He gave the impression he was hot foot on the track of freedom. Selby had been making demands for improvements on his side of the house, he said, and he'd countered by telling him he'd put up the rent. Apparently he was entitled to put it up by 12.5 per cent of the total cost. He'd reminded Selby there were things a tenant was legally obliged to keep in good repair and that he might be forced to pay for. His suddenly pursed mouth expressed this was all legally proper and that it was an exciting phase of the battle - even so she felt he was giving only half the story. There must be something more positive behind the change but she was pleased at the hangfire whatever the cause.

Sheila on the same subject was calm, deliberate and still flying the flag of tolerance at all costs. She didn't seem to be aware of new or positive turns of events. A few days later she had one of her old show-downs with Mark in which the only difference was the openness of his rejection of both her attitude and herself.

There'd been some kind of child's initiation ceremony instigated by David and some of Simon's front hair had been burnt. Mark remembering David's history was filled with terror that became anger against Claude who'd been present and allowed it to happen. Claude's sense of the injustice of it made him sullen and defiant giving the impression he'd approved the whole thing. He was miserable at the intensity of Mark's rejection and had gone to his mother for comfort. He told her that he'd undergone a similar bravery test and was proud of it.

"It's no good carrying on like that," she said to Mark when she'd managed to reassure Claude and get him out of earshot. "What you should do is make him see the danger of testing himself and others in this way!"

"It's the danger he's after, you fool."

She ignored it and pursued reasonableness. "David's got an odd code of ethics. He takes pride in standing up to pain or terror. Naturally his friends have got to be as good as he is. Claude felt that he'd qualified. All anyone can do is make him see why it's wrong."

Mark stared at her incredulously. "What code of ethics? Simon's a baby, Claude knows that. You and your schoolgirl mentality! David's a vicious lunatic and Claude, for reasons of his own, was an accomplice. It must never happen again. Why didn't he tell us about it in the first place?"

"Too scared." Her tone was oppressive. She moved away. "You say yourself they can't be protected from everything and that they must be allowed to find things out for themselves. It's clear to Claude now that it's serious. The worst - the most dangerous part of the whole experience was the sight of your face."

For the rest of the day she fought him without words - chatting to the older boys, giving them little jobs to do, wafting through his concentration on them with breezy distractions. She dissipated the effect like an open window in a room being heated to sweat out disease. Joan understood but was bewildered by them both.

A few days later she went with them on a visit to some

friends in Kinemouth and came up against a similar, partially deliberate restriction of view on both sides that enabled them to fight. Sheila had been especially enthusiastic about this family, "brilliant, all of them" - which had prompted questions from Joan and ended in her being invited to go with them. She found out too late to back out that only the three of them would be going and began to find Mark's silence on the subject ominous. She prepared to move into Sheila's camp.

The need to align herself with Sheila while the bulk of her affection went to Mark puzzled her. Sheila didn't need her support, she wasn't an underdog, she made her own points in her own way, worked harder than anyone and was absolutely central to the whole project here, yet Joan felt that though everything circled round her nothing much came to her. She was friendly with everyone and everyone with her but there was something lacking in both the intimacy and the ease with which it was established. Her enthusiasm made her bright-eyed when she spoke of her plans, children or friends but seemed regularly to circle or miss the objects of it. She more than anyone seemed to live for the substance and reality of a working commune, not for ideas of what it might be, and the success of it was hinged on her practicality and fairness but she, totally dedicated to the realities of living together seemed the most totally excluded by them. Sometimes Joan thought Sheila had missed the point of what was going on, only to discover later from her or by accident that she'd seen and dealt with it in a way that unintentionally separated rather than involved her. Watching her without knowing her you'd say she spent her days in a whirl of involvement and that it was only by means of a bewildered innocence she escaped constant collision. But it was beginning to feel as if it were the gust of activity she wanted - something to whirl her and keep her in action. When it stopped she fluttered to rest as if she'd never really been part of it, as if her activity were proof of its existence not part of its course. Joan knew the view was unrealistic - that what Sheila was and did were central factors in everything that happened but it helped express a compassionate concern she couldn't get over. She was going on this trip so as not to let Sheila down. She didn't want to be part of a silent or open row and didn't want to see strangers especially since they'd been described in Sheila's object-missing terms.

"They're a wonderful family," Sheila encouraged her. Mark, driving, nodded his head. "He's an architect. Sarah's a very talented woman, very! She made their furniture - even the bed - and Martin built the house round some old squash courts, so the main room is vast. They have terrific parties in it - get 80 people in easily. Their children are brilliant. Michael's just got a First in computer science, that's the oldest boy, and James is reading law. He's in his third year. He's already had two Firsts in a row so he'll probably get one in Finals." She grinned.

"Excellent," Joan said.

"The girl's an oddity in a sense. She took up English" - nodding at Joan inclusively - "but she's only just started. She's hardly ever at home. At the moment she's holidaying abroad with some friends - Greece or somewhere exotic - can you remember, Mark?"

"Yes, Greece."

"You'll be impressed with the house! Martin's a first-rate architect - could have been earning God knows what in London but had too much sense to stick it out there."

They arrived at a large house next to the golf course. The front gave nothing away but the approach was pleasantly winding and the sea was close. They had a warm reception from the wife, a tall big-boned woman who hustled them into the main room. They avoided sitting so as not to lose sight of each other and spent most of the evening either in the kitchen or standing about following her, chatting on and off. They watched her cooking. She threw spaghetti at the saucepan, missed, watched dispassionately while it rolled on the floor, picked it up and put it in the sink tidy. She threw another handful that hit the mark except for bits that stuck out like stubble from the cooker ring. She was tense and distracted from the cooking by them and from them by the cooking. Conversation got lost in the cross-current.

In a few free moments she showed them round the house which was a barn of a place and cold. The bedrooms like all the other rooms were too large and sparsely furnished. In the main room all the windows were open. The ex-squash court feel had been domesticated by a couple of rugs and a little more furniture than usual which when you sat turned out to be more inhospitable than the room. The metal-armed chairs had first a soggy then a resistant response. Insufficient padding gave suddenly on to a hard base so that Joan felt chastised for her expectations.

The man who was in the background most of the time turned out to be the husband and was introduced just before they ate. Joan warmed most to him - he had a firm emphatic handshake and a brilliant smile - but apart from the formalities was silent the whole evening and stopped smoking only to eat. The two sons were the talkers and offered non-stop observations on the financial and social possibilities of their subjects. Sheila listened with the excitement of someone who aimed at the same things - their faces were shiny and innocent with materialism, hers with admiration. It came to Joan that perhaps it was the way they talked rather than what they talked about that excited her. They were articulate and acquitted themselves well on their skating rink of frozen responses - there was, after all, nothing left for them to do but improve the choreography.

At 10 o'clock Sarah shepherded them to the main room and went back to clean the oven. Dispersed and left behind the guests waited for the right moment to suggest going home. The sons knew it was all over and facing inwards at either end of the sofa played at talking to each other.

On the way home when asked Joan said she'd enjoyed herself but there was something in her tone that made Sheila unexpectedly give information that seemed to be an attempt either to answer or correct it. She said the husband two years earlier had tried to commit suicide and followed up with a eulogy on his ability not just as an architect but a scholar. He'd taken three degrees in his spare time through the Open University. Her verdict was brilliance bordering on insanity.

Joan looked to Mark for help but he was hunched to the wheel staring down dark lanes with a manic delight that made her feel they might never reach home. Sheila's face was safer even though full of the reflected glamour she'd found in what she'd told her.

The bewilderment and anxiety Joan felt with the Lewises on occasions was felt equally but handled differently by the Blakes and in their case it often arose from a failure of well-meaning intentions on both sides, especially between the two women. They tried to understand each other and the failure wasn't based solely on Bess's interest in Mark. Bess tended to rely on sessions of rapid identification and came up with little, Sheila on sessions of working together and came up with less.

Bess had been upset over the hair-burning incident and running her fingers through Simon's burnt curls had glanced angrily sideways at Sheila's closed face. The result was that later in the week this anger touched off by others, especially against Mark who'd just given her a public but overlong cuddle for doing a job, exploded in argument. They'd been watching a television programme on London tramps which had left Sheila in tears of compassion. Bess looked at her, looked away and looking back saw her tearful eyes turned towards her showing her the way. It was too much.

"What's the matter with you, Sheila? You shovel all your emotionality on to general issues and keep stone cold at home." She felt stranded. The suddenness and unjustifiability of the attack looked indefensible. It was too late to retreat, and comment would look like spite. "You didn't champion David and his father because they needed your help but because you needed theirs - bugger poor little Simon. All it meant to you was a chance to attack Mark's disorderly responses." She was going from bad to worse - now that needed explaining. "His reactions are a bigger threat to you than the Selbys" - she thought a moment - "not even to you personally, just to the world you wish we lived in." There was hardly a pause, she needed to finish before the others could get to her. "It's O.K. to let go on things in categories - you feel on safe ground there. You've got the tramps categorised as unfortunates who can't cope but they can cope you off the face of the earth" - a pause - "why weren't you angry at Simon's being burnt?"

"I was!" Sheila was blushing, angry, wrestling with the shock. Others looked angrily at Bess or avoided looking as their sense of danger took them.

Tom banged her roughly on the thigh: "What's wrong

with you?"

She went on, taking no notice: "You think the tramps' response is a controlled one but do you know who's doing the controlling? They are. Does that make them helpless? Cry about some of the things you're personally involved in and stand more chance of understanding. You permit yourself too little and pretend to too much."

The chorus of refutation made her back down. The two youngsters, both sitting in the same armchair, were pale and looked desperate to get out but afraid to get up - as if any action might be precipitous.

"Alright then, not pretend - aspire - redirect - avoid anyway. David and his father are what they are and no one thing made them that way. There's nothing you can do by condoning any more than Mark can be being outraged, but at least a certain amount of outrage puts you properly on your guard. Crusades are only useful to others if you aren't sucked in by them yourself."

Mark's face twisted with fear and anger. She felt he was going to speak, felt his hatred and feared his need to support his wife and champion hard where he couldn't love hard. She cut him out, turning in appeal to Sheila: "Tramps have got a good system that cuts you out one way and brings you back another - a sort of ju-jitsu using your sense of pride and social values against you." She moved so that her back was to him. "If they can't stand normal contacts or normal responsibilities they can't join or avoid you in normal ways. They want you to feel what you do - horror and compassion - it's their way of dealing with you and with life."

"So!" Sheila exploded. "They can't cope. I should be asking what's the matter with you." She tried to cool down enough to talk. Bess had picked the arena but wasn't going to win in it. "Didn't you see them digging in bins? - did you see the last one on his knees in the mess running out of the can, he was chewing something he'd found like a dog."

"He was plump and intent. He was a nut!"

"No-one chooses a life like that, so isolated and humiliating-"

"Not to them, only to you - humiliating to you. As far as any of us chooses anything they've chosen. Nothing'll make them cope except on their terms - they want none of you."

"But it's not natural! Everyone needs to belong and needs people."

"They do belong, they've got people. Perhaps in their eyes you're the ones who can't cope - trapped in messy permutations of greed and altruism. They've slipped away from you and your view of things. They probably feel superior - I hope so - they're purists by comparison. They don't want and can't cope with the confinement of materialistic ease. Above all they reject the stress you'd make them pay for it. Why not cry for the businessman begging for ulcers and heart attacks? The reason you don't is that he doesn't want you to. He works instead on your sense of power or success which is his reward for giving up his freedom which he probably couldn't cope with anyway. Offer him help suited to his needs and he'll put a flea in your ear but I don't see that he needs it less. Why shouldn't tramps do their asking and taking with an equal sense of victory? In both cases you're reacting as they want for their reasons - not conscious reasons perhaps but those are never important. They manage and fail in different ways but give you only one way of helping- their way. You can let the tramp make you uncomfortable and pay up and take the businessman's or doctor's or teacher's opinion of himself seriously. You can't psychoanalyse us all or do anything about our genes. The world's exciting because failure one way leads to possibility another." Her anger had gone and even Mark was interested. Feeling the general appeasement she turned a little towards him - "Real compassion's too flexible to be pinned down" - and to Sheila: "If you want to cry for one section of society at a time you'll have to spend your life at it ending up with the biggest bawl of all for the maladjustments of the Prime Minister and the millionaire pop-star."

"Especially the former if you pity the rest of us!" Tom had joined her. Even Sheila was half-eased. So, Joan thought, she'd managed it. She'd done successfully what she'd accused Sheila of doing unsuccessfully - turning the personal into the impersonal.

Sheila made her next remark almost without anger: "You make it sound as if no-one can really help or really needs to - it's not true." But there was a sound of tears in the background that filled Bess with remorse.

"I didn't mean that, I didn't" - her face begged forgiveness - "I meant you can only help when they want it, the way they want it and then only in bits. Sympathy's got to go further than pity."

"I agree."

Bess frowned. "I mean, if you love people you've got to identify with more than one bit of the picture. It's no good trying to keep your world picture intact while identifying with theirs - all you'll do is minimise and patronise and they'll tell you to stuff it."

Mark, at last throwing her off, came in with a dismissiveness he no longer felt: "You want to make it too complicated and personal. Understanding and help are simpler than that."

"Only at one level - the simplest - in bits and pieces -

when and where they ask it." She was cold to him. "You can't make a crusade out of that!" She looked at him and saw the old appeal to be loved re-emerging. "We've got to be free to deviate even from our own world picture - most of all from that. In a society where everyone can afford to eat, the danger is in fobbing off progress of a different kind. Social thought starts by understanding our own needs, not ignoring them - then interpreting them on behalf of others. If we're stifling and punishing responses that don't fit our current picture we need a new picture. Once you're fed and warm you look for something to do with the energy - a well fed society has to be a growing one but not territorially - we've reached the limit there and about time - now we can grow up." She looked at his hesitant expression that was wondering where she wanted to push him. "If you cramp yourself too much you lose interest in life and lose the love you felt and wanted. You can't get love till you feel it and can't feel it till you stop being afraid of the ingredients that make it up. We've got to let go. Put peace of mind first and you'll never get it. Happiness comes in the teeth of chaos."

Bates had been watching the whole business with interest and leant across to her: "Love begins at home then, right? Now give us a definition of love so we know when we're feeling it!"

Mark was staring at Bess, locked into what she said as if Bates hadn't spoken. "Someone's got to think about the way society's developing," he said, "at whatever cost to his own salvation. Someone's got to be concerned with the success of the race as a whole. You can't rely on a system as personal as yours. You can't be sure enough people will understand enough. If people in general seem more worthwhile than yourself perhaps a general concern is all you can or should have."

"But you're part of the race, equal to the other parts - in terms of worth-whileness there aren't grades only differences. Why are you more interested in millions like yourself than one? Think of it in terms of one - yourself. If you cut down on any one part however small you change the balance of your view of the whole and your attitudes become unbalanced and dangerous to the society you want to protect."

Tom found himself irritated at the turn the discussion had taken and the shift of focus from Sheila to Mark. "You can't live openly and closely with an individual," he said - "anyone, from any social class, without realising how stupid it is either to think of him in terms of categories or imagine you can help in terms of causes. You can't enthrone a cause without relegating the members of it to the background. To crusaders individuals disappoint, only causes elate." He stopped a moment, looking across the room. "Don't look at me like that, Sheila" - he was laughing - "of course we must make sure there isn't too much oppression or injustice but that can't be enough. We can't imagine we're satisfying the highest claim to our energies in doing it, it's too dangerous. Bess is right. The ignorance, callousness, dreaminess, obtuseness you take to your own life appears in the handling of these other issues and on a much more appalling scale. You can't convert failure in this particular field to success in another."

"You two are so blasted sure of yourselves!" Sheila snapped at him.

"No more than you," he smiled. "It doesn't matter."

"It matters," Sheila said.

Bess got up and pulled Mary out of the chair by one hand with John still attached by the other and the group broke up.

A few nights later the Blakes and Lewises were in close accord on a trip to the local church to hear Sheila sing. She'd joined a choir and this was her first appearance with them in public. Mary and John stayed behind thinking they'd be bored and Bates stayed with them saying he didn't like amateur performances. Sheila appointed them all babysitters.

The youngsters went for a walk in the early evening, exhausted themselves and came back bickering. Bates, putting aside his book made them coffee. In a tired way Mary wondered why he put himself out. He took his drink, sat next to her on the sofa and got her to talk, monosyllabically at first, about the work. Bit by bit she opened up, fed up with John and glad at an opportunity to grouse about things in general if not him in particular. Her general tone of self- and life-depreciation seemed to appeal to him and his excitement became obvious. She sat flushed, suddenly wide awake, and lapsed into inarticulateness and smiles. He leant back cross-legged, his motor idling - only suggestive of action, not threatening it. John, hurt and irritated, went out for more coffee, muttering "Old fool!" to himself. When he came back Bates had improved his position - his arm was along the back of the sofa behind her.

In the church the choir and orchestra were flooded with light and the evening sun streamed through the stained glass windows on the roses round the pulpit, double-dyeing them. For a while Joan couldn't take her eyes off them. When she did she found the place airy, full of people, sumptuous with colour and alive with excitement. Sheila radiated it. She was taller than the other women in the choir and her eyes were fixed on the orchestra. There was a hush and it started up with excerpts from Handel's Water Music. Lionel was in it. Joan spotted him by following Sheila's eyes.

His chin was pressed in a grappling position on the violin while his left hand grabbed it from the rear, wrestling it to a standstill.

The conductor got ready for the next piece. Joan's eyes wandered to the first violin. She was thin and kept an anxious glance on her instrument, especially through the lively passages - placating it and tending it till it passed the climax, only then looking at the conductor in relief. Joan looked at Tom to see if he'd noticed and he smiled, but at the whole performance. They were packed together in the front pew, Mark, Bess, Tom and Joan - at various times all of them trying to catch Sheila's eye and beam encouragement - the Haydn Nelson Mass was about to begin.

From the moment it started Sheila was inaccessible, giving every glance to the conductor, every muscle to the business of singing and her whole soul to the rough, beautiful, uneven volume of sound.

After a while listening was tiring and in Bess and Mark was replaced by a sudden awareness that their thighs were touching. Mark, staring ahead, moved his hand down between them. Bess lowered hers and the joy and energy released burnt up the sights and sounds like fuel and blazed in her face.

Sheila's face, rapt, was lifted again and again to the conductor - hungry for the smallest signal and glowing attention and abandonment.

9

For Mark the next few days were exciting - nothing was missing and everything in balance. The work was light, the weather good, the group in harmony and Bess a joy. Occasionally the open statement of their holding hands produced a frown but was mostly remembered with delight and he thought of these days as he would an unexpected period of superbly good health - something to be enjoyed to the full and extended for as long as possible. He started to work hard and realised it wasn't the lightness of work but of his responses that gave anxiety no foothold even when he was tired. What had taken place meant nothing more than the pleasure it gave because he meant nothing more by it. He didn't wonder what Bess might expect as a result or if he should counter expectation, it was a subject for gratitude not thought.

When at last he was coming out of it he noticed a certain stiffness in Bess's behaviour with him. She kept close to Tom, he never saw her alone or met her by accident and his sudden anger and disappointment started a reversal. He'd not taken the episode seriously but now he dismissed it, scoffing at himself for his romanticism. The recoil left a hunger. When he was walking past a patch of long grass by the barn where it was quiet and screened from the house he thought it looked as if it had been pressed flat in the centre. A couple had been sprawling there. Confused, roused, he remembered with a sudden rush of pity and guilt the girl he'd broken with two years ago. He hadn't even answered Joyce's letters. How could he have been so cruel? If he couldn't stop forming attachments he could do something about his conduct in finishing them. Perhaps even now it wasn't too late to offer a new footing to a relationship whose only sin had been that it was too close.

When he thought about Bess again it was as if the experience had found its place. It was another battle in the war against himself. A personal problem. One of the hazards of his quest for more. Nothing was ever enough. More in terms of many was easy to get and to deal with, in terms of one it was a menace. There was only one expression of total intimacy and he couldn't afford it - mental and emotional balance lay elsewhere. Only the commune mattered. But the obsession for love came from the same source. If he could be so close to someone that understanding was as natural as breathing - that he couldn't hurt without being hurt - the harmony and peace of it would carry into all his contacts. There'd be less need to fear. He could let go. Bess was right then? The drive towards it was the major source of his energy and pleasure, and a threat to both. This was his problem and whatever the misery the perspective offered it had one advantage - that of leaving Bess out.

The immediate result was an anxiety-ridden mood but with the outcome in his hands not somebody else's. What he needed was to be completely in touch with the commune, not any one member of it, and he might be losing that under her influence or through misreading signs of failure. He planned a day off for all of them to satisfy his nervousness, one to be enjoyed together not in ones and twos, and leapt at Tom's vague suggestion that they visit the birthplace of a famous local writer. Bess and Tom were going to London at the end of the week to sort things out with their publisher and the book was uppermost in his mind. For Mark it was a good choice because it united them in yet another field.

The day was hot and windy. They took two cars, Bates's and the Landrover, and under Mark's direction took the road across the heath where the flat land dissociated itself from the road, making no encroachment and offering unbroken views of heather. The heather made its own world, dark and light mauves tossed by the wind and islanded with gorse, the occasional extended growth of gorse, rarely at the roadside, destroying any unconscious attempt to see the scene as organised around their progress.

Mark in the leading car with Joan sitting next to him remembered the last time they'd crossed the heath and how much she had responded to it. He waved Bates down, drawing up at a place where great areas of soil had been stripped down to the shale. They crossed the road to see the heath from a ridge on the other side where the slope was already green in patches and the ground not so recently worked. Mark put his arm round Joan's shoulders, climbing with her and apologising for not having stopped at a better place.

The desert of yellow chippings on the other side of the ridge had an oasis. Joan couldn't take her eyes off it. A hole that had been filled with water had a bank halfway round it full of delicate silver birch saplings, ragwort, heather and gorse as high as the trees, but the blaze of colour came from montbretia scattered at mid-height through the rest and completely colonising the nearest edge. Mark felt through her shoulder the tension of surprise and pleasure and catching it interpreted it after his fashion. She was a loner as he partly was himself and life focused on its own resources and blazing in a desert exhilarated her. He looked at the horizon where a plantation of fir trees emphasised the darkness and flatness of the land in front of it while being in its own way separate and uninviting. The trees speared into the right corner of the heath at a geometrically neat angle made by the two flanks of the forest.

In an instant he was restless. He got back into the car as some of the slower members were getting out and waited impatiently with his hand on the wheel while they stretched their legs.

Within a couple of miles the land was completely wooded - thinly at first then with planted firs on one side and natural woods on the other. The mixture in the natural woods held his attention for a long while - differing greens, densities and heights letting the sunlight penetrate unexpectedly, mature trees next to saplings, bushes filling gaps, some already fruited, cycles and stages overlapping and giving the diversity he loved - but it was the other side that gave relief. The grey-green conifers towered over the car like an arrested sea and the uniformity gave his imagination a chance. He slowed down and waved Bates ahead so that he could look at the brown pine-needle floor. He remembered the startling quiet and softness of walking on it and stopped altogether. As soon as he'd done it the straight and close-packed trunks took precedence. Concentrations of brown and smoke-green made the dusk in there exciting and matted branches hanging over cool shadows suggested secrecy. As an animal he came alive while his mind was still sheltering in cathedral responses.

In another mile the road came into the open and he overtook Bates's dawdling car to show them the way. There was a National Trust carpark when they arrived that was scooped out of a shallow wood next to the birth-place.

Mark watched his group climb out of the cars with hot faces and legs at odd angles. He moved from one to the other snatching contact rather than helping - his face gleaming with an impersonal and undirected delight that Bess mistrusted. Sheila caught part of his mood and joined him. They moved as a pack into the wood with those two slightly in front and Sheila holding a pamphlet she'd picked up that marked out a nature trail. When the track narrowed they couldn't keep together and as they broke into twos and threes Mark noticed Bates and Tom were a long way behind and deep in conversation. They must have started it in the car. He hung back to gather them in.

Tom was well into his stride, shoving leaves aside or walking into them according to his presence of mind but instantly responsive to Mark's arrival as if he too must be in need of something to interest him.

"I'm talking about our book and the authors I'm finding it difficult to write about", he said, not noticing Mark's expression clenching. "There are different reasons each time of course but both Bess and I find it toughest to get on with the ones the journalists call committed. You know the sort of thing - not a good parable and certainly not a good novel. If they want it to be more novel than parable there's a struggle to do justice to ordinary life as they see it and the common man as they see him. A lot of painstaking detail goes into their version of an average mentality, thinking it's not their own. Worse than anything is when they try poetically 'freezing' common acts or common thoughts by highlighting them in the context. I hate it! The condescension of it! I hate their wanting stupidity and arrogance to be seen as compassion - for me the book's doomed from the start. The author's sense of what's likely makes him minimise and his need to be instantly believed makes him concentrate on the surface and squeeze every drop of it for the typical and representative. He wants the reader's surface emotions - easy compassion, easier shock. At that level the real thing doesn't exist."

Mark looked puzzled and irritated. Neither subject nor attitude were right for his mood.

Tom felt he was on tricky ground. "It's not always a political commitment" - he got that out of the way - "sometimes it's just one or two issues that bug him but these issues are seen as 'real' ones as if all thought outside them were wasted. There's another kind of 'real'-ism too - that of writing about everyday life as if preparing a documentary - looking at it from the outside but with sensitive insights thrown in. With those novels you sometimes feel the attempt to keep in touch is the only real thing about them! The purpose of communication is to promote response but the documentary style is the least honest about it, never admitting to the selection of detail that goes into making a coherent picture and which turns it from an objective portrait into a dishonest argument. What appears to be sensitive awareness manipulates and promotes as effectively as anything else and under those circumstances an attempt to be objective can't be given any more credit than no attempt at all. What you see depends on what your nature lets you see. The only thing that matters is the result and a writer who's hung up in this way is especially at risk because he's playing for safety. A need for agreement leads to so many permutations of the safe and obvious it ends up destroying response rather than promoting it. The simplifications and falsifications you go in for to offer your readers a world they'll instantly agree they live in can only be done at the expense of the complexities that writers know, just by being alive, lie in the simplest responses. Preoccupation with a norm you can agree on, or with a consensus view of 'common' man, or with 'reality' is a waste of time when there are no such things. The 'real' business of life is ninety per cent unreal and the simplest man's too complex for such writing. All any author can do successfully is communicate passionate interest - that's what involvement is - and that can take any form but is perhaps least likely to take the commonly accepted 'good' and sensitive routes which are paved with lethargy. Commitment that wants to show itself too obviously is the product of fear not love. It makes me prefer writers who are arguably perhaps not such nice people and love as best they can."

Mark turned to him with a look that told him he was being perverse.

"I feel on safer ground," Tom explained. "A writer like that's more interested, benightedly and limitedly like the rest of us, in his view of the object than in his view of himself. A response that's more wholehearted can go further than just shock or concern but is likely to introduce elements that can't readily be seen as highly moral or even warm-hearted. I can enjoy this because the writer's up to his armpits in the business of living and communicates from that position with all the sins of a difficult responsiveness intact. Take the satirists and depressives. We all withdraw or hit out when hurt, which makes what they say valid for the rest of us, but only if it's being understood and worked with, not struggled against. Until the writer's open about the whole of his response his intelligence can't possibly come into play. Once everything's admitted the very least it can offer is evidence that life's got to him, at which point the way he deals with it can become interesting. At the best a negative response can have positive results, depending on its honesty or thoroughness - Swift and Beckett manage it. But most of all I like writers who see individuals not masses, the ones for whom social class or physical circumstances are only part of the picture. Any individual in any circumstance can make mincemeat of mass judgements, so why do most of us make them? To make mincemeat of individuals."

In the pause Mark let out a bewildered anger: "So what's left then? A chaos of not very reasonable or very generous independent assessments and finally everyone for himself? We can all find justification for what we do and think - there has to be something else."

"Yes, but the something else has to be based on a complex understanding or it's useless. It's no use trying to write off large chunks of ourselves as if they don't exist. First we've got to see ourselves and others as we really are and for that we can't have directives shaping the enquiry. That was the point of Bess's argument with Sheila over the tramps. Like her I get afraid of the people who make a virtue of not thinking."

"So you'd be prepared to dismiss the social effectiveness of a writer like Dickens, would you?" - Bates had been itching to break in. "His concern for the masses and his clamouring for social reform were wasted, or worse still aimed at destroying individuality?"

"Of course not!" Tom turned, excited. "But that's because in him there are two kinds of social effectiveness and the one you're talking about isn't effective without the other. As far as the immediate social reform was concerned he simply helped bring to a head the guilt and sense of danger society was ready to face. Identifying with characters, recognising events in his stories helped bring feelings into the open and for some this would be the easiest, even the only way of being reached because the stories kept them free of ambivalent living response long enough to let them feel the outrage necessary to make them act. He helped them accomplish the necessary identification impersonally while enjoying a deep sense of personal involvement. He knew, used, encouraged it at the same time as pointing out its limitations in characters like Mrs Jellybee and Pardiggle. What he's doing works because of the presence of the other social effectiveness which tackles injustice and cruelty at the roots and this turns up where no obvious social outcome is apparent. It's part of his personal responsiveness unrelated to a cause, and when the prisons have to a certain extent been reformed and the slums to a certain extent cleared, it's this that stays alive driving new generations to face similar problems and it's aimed at society as a mass of individuals judging for themselves. This kind of involvement takes different shapes and includes an awareness that one might be expressing a diminished human involvement while accomplishing important social changes, so it blurs the guidelines of the kind of socially committed writer I'm talking about and goes on blurring even while most about their business. It's a matter of one individual with the variables and fallibilities of his nature on show communicating with another. It's successful because where we might be bored or made suspicious of causes we're all curious about other people and ready to share thoughts and feelings. A writer's got to prove himself more than a committed man. The word means nothing - it and other dirtied words reviewers are always using like 'original' and 'professional' are becoming new excuses for old deadly sins. The writer whose writing is based on political or stable emotional concepts about man is one who in spite of all appearances is locked in himself and in his image of life and wishes to be seen in the light of that image to the exclusion of everything else."

Tom found himself talking to Mark in spite of the fact that he was countering Bates. He'd been turning to him, looking for agreement or just a willingness to see his point and now momentarily rested his hand on his arm. "What are you left with otherwise?" he said. "You bog down the prose with selected practicalities - sitting, drinking, smoking, chit-chat - to impress us with reality, but reality doesn't live there - life doesn't live there! It's a puppet show where we let the writer operate his wooden responses and opinions. It's distraction but nothing else. For me a character can be faceless so long as he develops one in my mind and stands free of the author even while he's reflecting the writer's confused experience and understanding."

"It won't do!" Mark snatched his arm away, disguising the aggression by reaching up for leaves. "Ideals are useless to you! - you don't want social or political guidelines or well-intentioned novels - what the hell do you want? What else is there? If I were a political man, which I'm not, what you've been saying would sound suspiciously like a cover-up for right-wing attitudes!"

"Right wing, left wing - oh, for Christ's sake, Mark!" Tom was angry. "Why've you got to call it something that gives you automatic reaction? What I'm saying's got nothing to do with politics."

"Hasn't it? Aren't you in effect saying material changes aren't fundamental enough? Doesn't that mean there's no real need to disturb the current shape of things?"

"I don't believe this! What I'm saying is that disturbing the current shape of things is the only thing that matters!"

"Well, if it's not politics it must be religion you're banking on. If neither, there's only anarchy left - your own patch of life and relationships and bugger the rest!" He paused for breath. "Your kind of scrupulousness prevents large-scale change."

"There aren't any large-scale changes except by small degrees. Revolutions might think they've done it but when it comes down to it -"

Mark wasn't listening. "There's got to be some order, some consensus of agreement or we can't co-operate, if we can't co-operate nothing's achieved. There's got to be a moral and social system that liberates the maximum of life in all of us not just some of us! Because a system can't be perfect doesn't mean we shouldn't be working towards that end. That's the objective."

"You're not listening," Tom said. "We're in agreement about objectives - all we're arguing about is the means. Politics is the last thing to trust. All this left and right business is rubbish. Both boil down to the same thing - group interest. The best party is the one that serves the welfare of most people but to keep it fair there has to be more than one party. If you want an example of how mixed up even the concept of 'welfare' is take a look at our publisher. He cares about little but success - it means money for his firm to go on functioning and he quite naturally brings his moral attitudes into line with it. As a result his large income becomes a mark of social approval. After all, being a successful publisher is the result of insight, skill and broadmindedness, so cash is the symbol of a semi-moral achievement. In such a system commercial success means 'right'. It's when you find out he's passionately Labour in his politics that things start to get confused. You start reading his intentions as 'good' - not wholly selfish - and make allowances for the Conservative ethic behind everything he does. With his authors his attitudes are the same. He sees himself operating in a literary democracy where everything that will sell gets a place and where he's the judge of what will sell. Being a good man he aims at being above board and realistic with us all: 'It's of no use to me how a book does after the first six months with inflation as it is - unless it's a bestseller.' And as a mark of courtesy he takes us out for a drink when we meet to talk things over, but to places where we can feel we're on to big things in working for him - and for him that means the Café Royal or the Ritz. It was at the Ritz he suddenly leaned over the table, relieved to find common ground with us at last, and told us about his lifelong commitment to the Labour Party. Politics are a joke!"

"A joke?" Mark grimaced at the leaves he still had in his hand. "There has to be a central organising body. It needs challenge, as you say - parties to keep it on its toes."

"Much more than that. More radical challenge. Since it's no more than a central organising body it's ridiculous to give any of the parties strong moral overtones. They depend for their survival on the basest self-interest of us voters."

"Nevertheless," Mark said quietly, "people do associate the parties in their minds with different moralities and I'm interested in all of them, in any of the systems for improving our way of life. The fact that systems are clumsy and hypocritical can't stop us applying them. Unfairnesses have to be dealt with as we go along. The alternative to thinking about society in an organised way is the law of the jungle."

Tom stopped walking. "How do you deal with them as you go along, Mark, unless you look at them from a standpoint that's completely unrelated to party procedure? You've got to be free to see round or beyond if you want to improve it. If all you're interested in is manipulating the system towards good objectives you're already being manipulated by it. If on the other hand you keep your independent voice and only go along with the broadest features of government - never with the ethics evolved from inside this order-for-convenience for its self-preservation - then you stand a chance. Otherwise all you can do is manipulate and be manipulated and you're killing the very principle of growth you've set the system up for."

They moved on to catch the others up. There was no radical disagreement but Tom still felt tension and irritability coming from him and was sorry he'd produced it. Anxiety about the London trip was making him edgy and he turned to Mark again smiling apologetically: "This is a lovely wood. I'm glad we've come."

Mark was relieved. There was something else as well. In some way the discussion had released him. It seemed he wanted Tom and Bess to stay more than ever - they were different and fascinating - but at the same time the difference freed him from trying too hard to identify. The exhilaration that followed the thought amazed him. He caught sight of Bess's dark hair and beyond it along a corridor of trees the line of adults and children that he felt belonged to him.

He moved ahead, catching up and passing Sheila and grinning at what she was doing. She'd got a stick insect on its back in her open palm and Claude was holding her hand down to eye level while flexing its legs backwards and forwards. Sheila told him to watch its joints. Peter and Simon, no longer under supervision, wandered ahead and, as they passed Joan and Bess, Mark caught them up, telling them to stay close. He fell into step with the women, who stopped talking and kept company in silence. Within a few paces the track narrowed and Joan on the outside dropped back.

Bess and Mark unconsciously increased their pace and started talking. Mark told her about the conversation with Tom and commented on Tom's anxiety over the London trip, saying how pleased he was himself not to have any more professional aggro. Bess responded to the manner, which was designed to draw her closer, but stood back from the remarks that were faintly irritable. She said she was like Tom and needed her work. Mark nodded. The sifting and piecing together was important to her, she told him, and thinking about literature seemed to help her personally.

They wandered off the marked track. The new track led to a field at the edge of the wood. By the time they reached it Mark was totally attentive but barely listening and helped her tenderly across the stile holding her hand and leaning into her as she stepped down. The closing in was momentary and rapt, body and head seemed focussed by his mouth which moved to within a few inches of hers, but he moved on, swerving outwards in a continuing movement skirting the conflagration. She, scorched, lagged behind waiting for normal consciousness. When it came she heard movements behind her in the trees the way they'd come but looking back couldn't see anyone. They'd lost the others and she shouted it to Mark who wondered how it had happened.

On the way back the part of him that was genuinely bewildered assumed complete control. It was responsible for the disarming schoolboy grin with which he swept Simon off his feet and perched him on his shoulders.

"Sorry - we got lost," he said to Sheila. "More looking, less gassing from now on!"

Sheila and Joan had watched them branch off and it had produced a matter-of-fact "They've gone the wrong way" from Sheila but had driven Joan after them. She stopped only when she fully realised why she was following. She'd seen the dumb show and the stranded silence in the field and full of remembered terrors stumbled sideways through the brambles to get off their path. She needed a pause to collect herself. While she waited she stared at the sheep coming up to her edge of the field. They raised their heads when she moved - a sudden arched tension in their necks and nostrils, open black pits gleaming dry in the heat, foreign as rubber and expanding with the disturbing sensuality of flesh. The wood was stifling. She looked downfield panicking. A horse, oblivious of the sheep, worked his jaw mechanically - bunching, knotting, protruding the muscles from a skinny face like portable millstones. Refusing to let it make her feel worse she put her hand on a trunk to brace against it but recoiled at the unexpected touch - networks of unleafed ivy glistened over it like swollen veins. The violence of the shock brought her to and she rejoined the others.

Bates and Tom were still last and still talking. She didn't listen but stayed close, watching and absorbing from Tom's face and manner the reassurance she needed. It wasn't enough and moving further into the group, avoiding Mark and Bess, she came up to John and Mary. They looked as if they were flagging from heat and boredom but perked up as she joined them, expecting conversation.

John spoke first: "Enjoying the walk?"

"Not much" came out without thinking. "I'm probably not looking for the right things" was an afterthought and offered with an apologetic smile.

In spite of Mary's bored disapproval John never turned down an opportunity to talk about his subject and took this as an invitation. He gave Joan a few facts about the trees - how many gallons of water a day they drank and how their growth reacted to different kinds of deficiency. She was interested but conscious of Mary's falling behind and looked round to see Bates moving up in a motivated amble.

"Litter everywhere! Slum of a place," he said when he reached her. Mary nodded. He'd picked up her mood.

Over his shoulder Joan noticed that Bess had fallen back and taken Tom's arm. She turned back to John and gave him her full attention.

Finding himself partnerless Mark tried chatting to both the Blakes but grew cross at Bess's silence. What was she up to now, hugging Tom's arm and easy with him as if she'd never defected? Their closeness became a threat and the growing need to make her notice him gave an angry frustrated edge to his voice that made her draw closer to Tom - she reached up to kiss him when she thought Mark wouldn't notice. He noticed and turned to them baring his teeth in compliance and approval. It was his vicious kick to a piece of dead wood that finally brought her round but almost simultaneously a light, warm breeze penetrated the wood and Bess looking up saw sky for the first time through the parting branches and in front of her two straight-trunked beeches mounting to the light in an exhilaration of leaves.

She burst into life. Sex was everywhere and in everything - there was nothing else. Energy streamed outwards - plants, animals, it made no difference - inviting, enticing anything it could reach. Wind, water, insects, us - everything was an aid to sexual fulfilment. If it was alive it was sex-obsessed. Wild flowers ablaze in light-soaked patches. Colour, perfume, deceptive designs for sex-hungry moths, landing strips for nectar appetites - nothing but appetite and the appetite was sexual. Self was never enough. Food for the individual fed the race. Only unimaginable possibility drove us to so subtle a responsiveness it amounted to curiosity and a salvation so dangerous it demanded total exposure. Knowledge, interest, passion, beauty streamed from the source that linked and explained them. She felt her arm, lying over Tom's, in a pool of sweat that softened the friction and in front of her Mark's back moved under its shirt with a suppleness and life that made her giddy. Challenge and increase were the same.

Mark intercepted her radiant gaze as it moved from Tom to himself and interpreting it wrongly went off in a burst of anger.

Just ahead Bates was pushing branches from Mary's path like a following breeze. His smiles and the rhythmic ducking of his head orchestrated a conversation just distracting enough to leave her real attention free. The very careful responsiveness under carefree attentions and the exclusive concentration fired her. She grew stiff and acted up to it. By the time John had missed her and dropped back to join them she was entirely focused elsewhere and dismissed him with an uncharacteristic sweetness of interest in his bits of news.

He saw what was happening and who it was really for and fell silent. Bates was outrageous. Flattering her vanity in a way that should have made everything clear. Couldn't she see the cold-blooded whoring? How could she stomach the poncing around? He watched him closer. Essentially unreachable, 'high' on himself, she was no more than a catalyst to his enjoyment. John tried to catch her eye but when he did he wished he hadn't. She looked like Bates.

Dropping back he let Mark pass. Bess's voice reached him and he waited. Bess saw the strained unhappy mouth and glancing ahead guessed the reason. He walked doggedly silent at her side and she dropped Tom's arm and took his hand, asking questions in roughly the way Joan had earlier - the difference lay in the probing, curious, compassionate exuberance looking for a new place to go now its happiness was disturbed. In time it worked - for him as well as herself. He became excited and garrulous - relieved at the new rush of energy that took the incident with it and stranded it out of reach. By the time they'd reached the cottage he was explaining photosynthesis and drawing cell diagrams in the air with his fingers.

They'd outstripped the others and talked themselves into an excitement that seemed to threaten the woman selling tickets at the door. They were standing about the entrance, noisy, disruptive of her view of a pre-entry frame of mind and it was only their seeming to belong to the more formal group approaching that prevented her from telling them so.

Inside Bess was on her own and found her restless excitement harder to find a place for. People moving from room to room and crossing each other's paths with controlled purposiveness set the tone. She identified more with the ones whose vague or bored expressions suggested they'd only gone to be sociable or because they were too young to have a vote, but finding a place with them freed her for enjoyment.

She went through the small sitting-room without looking and came to a tiny adjoining office. It was like a cell with no windows but a small open pay-hatch which was head-high and had a rounded top. According to the notice the author's father had been a builder. He'd paid his men off cautiously from here. Images of friendly formal interchanges between hands and faces pleased her. Just outside trees and bushes pressing close insisted on single file. It felt orderly. A passage off the cell contained some narrow stairs that led to three small bedrooms and the largest had a board propped up giving sparse information about the author's unpromising birth and defiant departure 88 years later. Her group's interest perked up here and Bess went looking in corners and touching things. She found a black wooden cupboard set unusually low in the wall and pulled it open.

A middle-aged woman moved in from the passage: "That's a private cupboard!"

Bess blushing and apologising told her it was empty. From that point she lost interest. The place irritated her and she stared out of the window with an unforgiving expression. Some Americans in the garden were excited. She heard their voices floating up and liked them and moving out came to a ladder that led down to the kitchen. She found Sheila in it peering into around brick bread oven set in the wall. Her face brought the kitchen to life.

"I want an oven like that," she said as soon as she saw Bess, "you pack it with gorse, burn it till it's red hot then rake it out. You cook bread on the ashes and it stays hot for 24 hours." Bess, pleased, wandered into the garden with her. "Do you think Mark would build me one?"

Mark was already there and heard his name. He came over. He'd been standing about earlier with a clumsy disengagement that made Joan decide he was too big for the rooms. He felt he didn't fit. The only thing he really noticed was Bess's indifference, as he saw it, not just to himself but the place too, and he'd been nursing the grievance. It wasn't that she was cool but indiscriminately hot! She went off one thing or person and on to another too easily, as if things were equally enjoyable, and took an intensity of expectation to it that left out relative values.

"I heard you call?" he said flippantly as he approached them but they were already moving off. He watched Bess's back and her head tilted towards Sheila's talk. She was right, he supposed, but what was the use morally approving when he hated her for it? As they started back he made a point of ignoring her.

He asked Tom how he'd enjoyed the visit.

"O.K." Tom said.

What did he mean, 'O.K.', it had been his idea to go there. His irritability got stronger now there was a comfortable place to put it. "Disappointed were you?"

"Not really. I got the feel of the place." There was a pause while Tom tried to understand the tone, then he explained himself: "I'm not keen on the author, you see, just curious."

He'd made things worse. Mark, looking round for a safe target, made for the general: "It's all the stupid adulation gets me down. Why do people do it?"

Tom took a second or two to clue in, then laughed. "It's not real. They want a good time and to get their money's worth."

Mark looked sideways at him. Bess, seeing the two together came up flushed with the plan of squeezing between them and taking their arms. As she got there she heard Mark telling Tom he wasn't interested in the world of the Arts any more, only in first-hand experience. This might have been encouraging if he hadn't added, "Except for music - that's so abstract it can't taint!"

He stiffened as she pushed between them. Feeling insufficiently abstract she had an obstinate urge to carry out her plan - partly defiant, partly to bring him closer. The moment she took his arm he snatched it away. Hurt and furious she attacked: "Fat lot you know! You wouldn't recognise the first-hand if it bit you!"

Tom, puzzled for the second time, wondered what it was about the house that had rattled them. He took Bess's hand and she let it stay before freeing herself.

"Anything's capable of being first-hand, including reacting to other people's experience. Why else would people write or even talk!" Her voice was calmer now and her glance when she looked at Mark was removed. "I wouldn't rely on your new world for anything different if I were you. It'll be full of soiled responses and preconditioned reactions and not even of a different kind. The real world's as full of them as art. Music too or you're not really listening."

The attack pleased him. It meant she was accessible in spite of her manner and it gave him a chance. He homed in: "The art world doesn't cover what I'm looking for, nor does the way most of us live. I'm after something different - a new way of thinking and feeling where the two are one act."

"That's an old way. All animals do it!"

"Not quite. I mean something inseparable but conscious as well as unconscious, in which we feel as fully as we understand our dependence on each other and feel it to the point where it becomes emotionally impossible to react except constructively. Personal satisfaction at the expense of the group becomes impossible. I'm after a dolphin-like combination of freedom and oneness with others."

"Dolphins!" Bess's face shut completely.

In the silence Tom had a chance to see Mark in a different light. "Art's not going to give you a new religion, if that's what you're looking for," he said.

Mark's flash of irritation got lost in the pursuit of Bess's understanding. His face almost begged. "They're so intelligent and radiate joy and curiosity. They associate easily with each other and with other species. They're defensive without being aggressive - playful and curious without fear or shame and so full of life it can only come from a freedom to be themselves. To me this means basic understanding has risen to the level of a need that like any other has developed the emotions necessary to its satisfaction. For me they represent the maturity we long for and have to find."

Bates had passed John and Mary, now glum in silent battle, and spotting from the distance action of a different sort he made for it. He heard the last remarks.

"We had it once they say." Bess jumped as he spoke over her shoulder. Mark didn't understand. "The Garden of Eden and all that! We were supposed to be more honestly animal."

The dismay in Mark's face came out in his words: "It's not what I meant. I meant something that needs understanding and objectivity to develop. Animals won't have it unless they've developed far enough. We're only born with a capacity, not the finished product. I'm not interested in the non-conscious life but a form of consciousness we've never had."

"Well, if it's like the dolphins it's simpler and we can't go backwards." Bates was pleased with the way things were going.

"What makes you think that? More likely the boot's on the other foot."

"You're not serious? They've no music, no literature or science that isn't oral, and no artefacts. There's no moving on without those. Everything has to be learnt afresh, which must limit their potential, to say the least."

"They're not learning the same things. Only the whole body can really learn and the head's useless unless it's a tool to that end. Ours is the plodding understanding - fact by misunderstood fact - theirs the swift analysis. Science and artefacts, even the art you talk about, hold us back."

"So you're ready to dismiss without a backward glance all the products of a complex intelligence like ours? You must see it's hopeless. You're sentimentalising - like it or not you're hankering for Eden. No life-style's easy and I can't imagine you swapping lives with a dolphin given the chance - you less than most! Given the choice between total exposure where you're at the mercy of hunger, disease and sudden death, not just occasionally but all the time - and getting a merely mental sense of unity with the forces of life, the decision's obvious and we've all made it. We developed ourselves to deal with the hazards and not go under, and to a point where we could see we'd made the choice."

Bess stepped back, waving Bates forward. Mark could deal with it.

Suddenly losing her he looked tense but stayed put, unable to let the subject drop. "I'm not dismissing anything, just looking for something better than we've got. Can't you see it's possible the way they live is the result of a more complex as well as subtler intelligence? As a 'facts' man you'll appreciate the physical evidence - a brain larger than ours and just as coruscated. What you're listing as our assets are evidence of simplicity. We function along set lines and with only part of ourselves at a time. We use our heads almost entirely as filing cabinets and if that doesn't limit our potential I don't know what would! As a result we learn very slowly - fact by obsolete fact - putting confidence in knowledge proved wrong in a generation! We need to use all our resources to survive. It's the imbalance that'll wipe us out. If we and the dolphins are twin peaks of different kinds of intelligence then they're the Greeks and we're the Romans. We're the possessors of aggressive practical deductive intelligence that attempts in its crudity to shape the world to itself, using its tools to hack the impossible to suit the limited and succeeding in building only a prison and a grave. Dolphins have adapted themselves - don't you understand, themselves - not their environment. It's no use talking about music and literature or religion for that matter when they're there to compensate for what we haven't got. They integrate and encourage and we value them as far as they adjust the balance with the filing cabinet. They give us a chance for self and social discovery and at their best for hope - even something to live for. At the very least they offer escape. What use has all that to any but our kind of intelligence, living in our kind of society where all the hammering we've done on the outside, all the security we've built up round us has sealed us away from what we did it for in the first place - more life. We wouldn't need something to release us into a 'whole' world or a vision of balance if we could get it all the time. Suppose for example communication between us were free-flowing and associative all the time and at all levels. If it were we'd understand our potential and limitations in relation to each other and to everything else and value difference as increase. Understanding our limitations would feed our potential. We'd have to draw on all not some of our resources in order to profit from the pool and in pooling become one whole body in which the uniqueness of each part was essential. Our assets are life-draining because they separate one part of the body from another, one individual from another. We're victims of the filing cabinet that has indexed art and science under 'Self'."

Bess hadn't managed to persuade herself to fall back far enough to be out of earshot. His last remarks loosened her tongue: "Science, writing, music, talking - it's all the same - it's communication and discovery exactly like the dolphins - why should theirs be better? It means the same too that we're coming to terms with things for ourselves in a way related entirely to others. The rest of us spend our lives expressing the need you seem to have just discovered!"

He grinned at her: "No we don't."

"As best we understand it."

"We don't understand it."

"Nor do they."

"At least they know that the only information of any value is immediate. Things are changing while you express them. They also know the only knowledge worth passing on is genetic."

"You're hopeless!" - but she was touched by his mania - helped to it by his pleasure at her coming back into the conversation. "It's because you're doing it all the time that you hate it - it's your deductive panic that seals out possibility. The worst hazards of the kind of thinking you're frightened of are the ones you're putting faith in - purism and prejudice."

"That's not fair. What can I do but try to see what's missing? That's how we work at this stage. Are *you* satisfied with things as they are?"

"I didn't say that."

"Well then, what've we got that compensates for their endless play and discovery? We're limited by our products. They're freed by having none. We're closer in understanding to Bates' 'animal' ancestors than to them. How can we adapt to get more life when we adapt the world to our fears?"

"Poor old Mark!" - Bates came in with a smile. "You dislike people so much you worship something you can't understand. But it's an important part of the regression, I suppose, and in keeping with the rest. Most primitive societies do it."

Mark looked angry for the first time but it was Bess who

looked at Bates with hatred. It only goaded him on:

"Tell me why our deductive intelligence and its permanent records shouldn't speed up change - genetic change I mean. If you knew all there was to know about dolphins or could become a human replica you'd find as many disadvantages - not the least of which would be that we as deductive humans could decimate you if we wanted and you as associative fish would let us."

"Doesn't that example tell you something else? Why do you both assume I'm against the human race?"

"Aren't you?" Bates was amused at his persistence.

"If I was I wouldn't care! I don't want us to be something we're not, I want us to be more than we are - in fact we've got to be. Nothing lost, something gained. Develop along their lines and we'd know more, not less, about ourselves and everything else."

"Well then, dolphins aren't a good model. You can train them to stick mines on ships. Their ability to know what's what is limited. You're dreaming, Mark, you must know it! We're on the only tack we know that leads anywhere. Only we have the power to shape our future."

"But to what and for what?" He began to look desperate. "How do we make the shaping an increase not a disaster? It's that very power we should be most afraid of. We're so limited and limit ourselves further in using only part of our equipment. I need something more rounded and balanced, more varied and imaginative than me to shape my future. Chaos is better - I'd trust it to be more flexible and generous. As we are, everything we do gets turned against us, indirectly through the environment or directly, person to person. We'll happily get rid of each other to achieve an objective. To the deductive as opposed to the associative ego, everything else is 'other' and expendable. We may be a constant menace the dolphins can't do anything about, but we're a bigger one to ourselves. Totality of disaster is something only we can accomplish - is that proof of intelligence? It's simple-mindedness that doesn't know its limitations. The solution lies in a different direction. Theirs is the direction we must move in."

"Count me in - more play and fore-play. Yes please!" Bess put her hand on his shoulder. Without shrugging it off he moved closer to Bates.

"We'll disappear as a breed if we don't. We've overdone it in one direction. Our advantage as humans that made us such successful survivors and gave us our paralysing hold on the world's resources will wipe us out. It's helped us out of one set of difficulties into another and if we can't adapt to those we're done for. It's not easy because over-development in one field unfits you in others - if we don't, though, we're the next dinosaurs. It's time to give our best blood to other faculties. All the attention we've given the old one developed it too fast for changes to take place in us that might compensate or adapt it. You say why shouldn't our kind of reasoning speed up genetic change - I'll tell you why I think it's unlikely. The ability we over-developed made it easier to change our surroundings than ourselves. Inner change is much more exacting and is motivated, initially at least, by the sense of being victims of things over which we've no control. That's something that runs counter to the very motor force of deductive effort. It could be that slowing down is all we've achieved. We certainly can't change fast enough genetically to be able to live in the environment we're making. There's no way we can know, in the kind of detail required for safety, what we're doing when we change the upper atmosphere or the balance of nature or tamper with our food or the air we breathe or the temperature of the world. There's too much to know. Everything's linked to everything else and the crudity of our mental equipment makes discovery - even suspicion - of all the links impossible. If we spent every minute of our lives for the next million years studying the complexity of the balance, some unpredictable movement - some unsuspected sub-atomic particle - would blast a hole in the deductive fabric the size of Etna. There are other areas of ability in us to develop. Conditions aren't constant and can never be fully known. Something alive has to be constantly responding and minutely changing in order to stay that way. Nothing is sacrosanct but change. It's true for living and non-living alike. Endless reshaping, re-combining - the universal adaptation to chaos and accident - that's what fulfils our destiny. What we now value most is least useful to us under such conditions. Why, for example, do we bother to find things out when we can't actually learn from them? For centuries we've been glimpsing the chemical, bacterial, viral empire our bodies are, for instance - worlds within worlds, universes of related and totally interdependent life activities and yet the insight you'd think we'd have as a result is still missing. The faculty that helped us to the information keeps us from using it. We haven't developed the rest of ourselves sufficiently to be able to assimilate our findings into everyday response where it matters. When nothing works as well as the part of us we've cherished we naturally hand everything over to it. Very little life-information is suited to its processes and the rest gets filed away. Once catalogued the information's dead. The rest of our equipment is too crude to see the danger - under-used, undernourished, the result of centuries of neglect. We draw comfort from limitation and confidence from stupidity. From the ferment that life is we skim a 'will' and for some reason, best understood as insanity, use it to direct our lives. A will that neither understands nor controls the factors that bring it into being, nor knows what will happen as a result of any decision it makes, nor knows what's best for it in making one. My God, I don't believe in our ability to shape our minutes, much less our lives! Perhaps the primitive societies were closer to the truth; Bates, in feeling an awe amounting to religious respect for what they didn't understand. Take a look around you. What do either of us know, or what could we ever know, about the vegetable world we're walking in? Protein patterns similar to ours - alive, responsive, adaptive, therefore intelligent, but the sensitivity and curiosity, above all the chemical communications, are a mystery to us. At our best we feel an association but ignore it. Generally we just feel it's good for us. We find it impossible to operate as if we're part of the same process. Without our sense of difference (and sense of superiority that makes it bearable) we'd start to question our arch-faculty. But suppose we relegate it to the helpful but inferior position it's equipped to take? We could achieve a freedom and purpose - a fulfilment we've never known. If we don't we'll have failed in the very field we're so proud of, our intelligence, and be ousted by a cabbage."

Bates, silenced through all this, turned to him suddenly and stopped the progress of the group. A little knot had gathered. Joan had moved up to Bess's side and was listening. Sheila, suspicious and uneasy at Mark's look, had pushed by with the children and gone ahead. Tom, coming up a few moments after Joan, stopped on the outside of the group, attentive.

"And all this so passionately advocated", Bates said quietly, "has been achieved by the use of your deductive intelligence. You're really saying that our salvation lies in a more extensive use of it and there I think I might agree with you. I'm not sure about the direction you suggest, that feels like the product of your personal discomfort and dissatisfaction. Mine, if I were asked, might be, would be, different and it'd be no use asking me what lines it would take because, as I understand it, discontent supports no organisation of it. The big difference between us is that you're a religious malcontent, I'm not. I don't need to be imaginatively backed in my actions."

"Of course you do!" Bess, rushing to Mark's defence, doused a spark of agreement. "You're backed by feeling superior to it. People don't act in a vacuum. Mark's just as clear about the general chaos as you are - he's just said that's where life is -"

"And I'd be the first to agree," Bates insisted.

"- But knowing it gives him another knowledge that seems to run counter to it - the making, unmaking and remaking of patterns of association that has a rhythm so unexpected we can't discover it except at the level he's suggesting - and it requires a new willingness to co-operate."

So now they'd all explained themselves, Joan thought, according to their natures. She dropped back. Bess was as vigorous a native of chaos as Bates, with her "willingness to co-operate", and perhaps as dangerous. She stared at them, at Mark and Bess. They'd moved together again, watchfully close. She turned away. When Joan had dropped back Tom was forced to and she turned and smiled at him. He was looking at Bess, rapt and approving. The pain and sense of helplessness she felt made her step aside and let him pass. What made Bess do it? Ready to plunge into anything, knowing she couldn't know the outcome and not caring. Amazing confidence in herself and others and the effects of her actions. It attracted and repelled Joan. If the difference in attitudes of Bess and Bates were radical, the effect on the rest of us was likely to be the same! Bates preyed on chaos, Bess prayed to it.

In the car-park she still hung back. Tom had gone into the front of the Landrover with Mark and loosened his tongue. He was asking him what he'd missed. Sheila and the children, John and Mary were bouncing about in the back getting themselves organised, which caused a scuffle between the children. Claude was separated and Joan found herself with the other two and Bess in Bates's car on the journey back.

Simon and Peter were quiet. They were tired and fed up, stuck in the back with her, and she left them to it and looked out of the window. They were going back a different way and through Tachester. The main road went downhill through the centre and for a while the town was spread out on either side of it. When the buildings swallowed up the view she stared at those instead. The shops were three or four storeys, old, dark-bricked and with small windows and small displays. What displays there were looked interesting as a result. Even the supermarkets had tiny shop-fronts lost under the brickwork. The town's real tourist attraction was advertised everywhere. Tea and bookshops named after the famous writer and his characters were given support by the town's concentration on middle-class intelligentsia tastes and Joan was interested to see most of the dress shops displaying the sort of dresses Sheila favoured on special occasions - long skirts in browns and oranges, leather, scarves in ochre and green. Every sixth or seventh shop was a crafts, books or antiques place. Just as she was beginning to wish she could get out and look the car put on some speed. The Landrover was out of sight and Bates wanted to catch it up.

He was deep in conversation with Bess who appeared to be getting on well with him. Joan heard him mention Tom and became interested. He was in the middle of a story given him apparently by an ex-student who had at one time been Tom's. It seemed a charming pointless one hardly worth telling, about the girl's responses to the two universities but it was interlaced with anecdotes Bess might find interesting. At the moment he was telling of the girl's waiting in Tom's study one afternoon on her own. The door was shut and when someone rapped on it she refused, out of nervousness, to answer or open up. In the silence following a second rapping she heard the women outside talking. One had an Irish accent and sang Tom's praises - "I'd do anythin' for 'im" - and for Bates the point seemed to lie in the cliché that followed: "He's a darlin' man, a darlin' man!"

Ignoring his tone Joan smiled at the story and was surprised to learn he'd even heard of Tom before this summer. Bess too was amused and Bates elaborated.

"The girls found him sexy and fair-minded and generous." She smiled again. "To them anyway - not always to the works they were studying."

Bess was very pleased. "I know he's popular with his students - I wish he were with his colleagues. He gets fed up too easily and he's obstinate about what he wants to do. He hates meetings - either he doesn't go or doesn't take part. He came out in a rash when he was trapped three hours in one. He was very pleased when an ex-student met him in the street and said she'd never forget him because he'd opened up a whole new world for her."

"Soft touch for the ladies, like the rest of us."

"He likes them best, of course - as I do men."

Bates was watching the road, then turned to her with an open-mouthed smile: "You forgive his peccadilloes."

Bess shrugged.

"Gives you room for your own?"

Joan's stomach knotted while Bess's face flared with pain and discomfiture. In the following silence Joan panicked. Was he punishing Bess for her antagonism earlier or just putting her in her place - for him a reflex natural as breathing - fragmenting egos, especially women's, was always a good idea, the bits couldn't be so obstructive, might even come in useful. He wasn't finished:

"I'd assumed yours was a modern marriage but I'd like to know how you get it to work. Not that I'm planning to risk my own freedom. It's just that the compromise of making a compact then breaking it when you feel like it has always seemed worse than illogical - positively inviting a sort of mutual destruction."

The manner of innocent mental venturing left Bess dumbly looking in her lap trying to put her world together.

That evening, though, Joan found her unusually elated. She was dressed up - not in her usual style, more as if she'd taken unconscious notice of the shop-windows. A long skirt and a necklace made of seeds, for her extravagant, gave the impression she was going out. The skirt was a striking orange with rough flecks and the ends of the necklace, knotted halfway down, fell over the top of it so the effect was like pips on a hessian tablecloth. Unusual for Bess but very much in the style of the Lewises and it claimed Mark's attention instantly. She wasn't interested. Dressed in Mark's idiom she spent the evening with Tom talking almost exclusively to him and when he spoke to others looking as if her soul was in his mouth.

The effect on Mark grew worse as the evening went on.

Less and less able to divide his attention, watching her became an obsession by the end of it. She seemed unaware.

He spoke to her at last, when she was going upstairs to bed: "Strange!" - yanking the necklace so hard it hurt the back of her neck - "when it was the fashion I was given one exactly like it." He fingered the pips. "A friend gave it me. She was enthusiastic about male jewellery. I might wear it some time."

Long after they'd gone to bed he was still finding jobs to do downstairs, partly to dissipate his fury, partly to re-establish contact with normality. Familiar actions and routine attitudes were linked together and under those his deeper interests lay. Finally giving up hope of reaching them he went for a walk round his land. The night was warm and expansive, he could smell the stable and hear his horse snuffling and his jealousy and anger softened. They took on a new role as part of the new wave of feelings and became testimony to the fullness of his new way of life - even a validation of it. Only here was his world so structured that failure to contain them was impossible. Loving Bess wouldn't make him swerve but keep him on course. Here challenge was a stimulus not a burden. With everything at stake circumstances made decisions for you which were not the property of the head nor made in a moral vacuum. Decisions were made before they were recognised as such and when something was removed something else took its place. All he needed was a bigger commune, more variety, more contacts and diversity of interests to guarantee that nothing narrow - nothing wholly egocentric - could survive or even needed to. This was already the extended family he'd hoped for, already subversion was being controlled by need and offered alternatives.

The sense of loss he couldn't help feeling attached itself

to the memory of Joyce. She was just the addition the group could have done with - loving, intelligent, curious but unexacting - so unexacting Sheila had even found her cold. Again he felt shame at the cruelty of the break, but then he'd not had the assurances - only the tenacity to reject. When he got back to the house he wrote her a letter, brief but friendly with an intimacy so natural it gave the impression there had been no two-year gap. He asked her to come for a weekend or a week, or as long as she wished, and talked of nothing but his work. As a postscript he suggested she might like to write - he'd love to hear news - and it came to him and he put it to her, that whereas a visit would be a "fait accompli" and self-explanatory, writing might seem insidious to Sheila and make things trickier. He reminded her of the unfortunate scene at their last meeting. It might after all be best to write to him care of a friend in Kinemouth and let him find the right time to introduce her to the group. He didn't alter the first part of the letter because for him the tone and open invitation represented the innocence he felt but he did make a point of adding to the postscript mention of his great desire for Sheila and her to be friends. As he sealed the envelope the image of Sheila's mouth, twisted in pain and hatred at even the mention of her name, made him realise the job wouldn't be an easy one.

The following day he took his eggs to Kinemouth and arranged to pick up his letters. His most regular customer was a shop-owner who'd become more of a friend. They had a business-based respect for each other as competent, practical men who were necessarily emotionally objective and it brought out in each the role that set women at a distance. Once or twice in the past they'd exchanged playful commonplaces of antagonism to the sex and Mark thought it likely anything that smacked of male independence wouldn't raise an eyebrow. He was right. The man acceded without curiosity and was offered no explanation.

Now the letter was written and sent it gave a new dimension to Mark's feelings. As the mood took him the thought of Joyce could become a balancing pole or a weapon and its presence in the background helped him put a little distance between himself and the others. Bess was right. Complex needs needed complex satisfaction. Where danger seemed to be lurking new life was hidden, ready.

The rest of the week went well. He took an artist's delight in watching Bess doubled over the heat weeding carrots with trickles of sweat running down the sides of her nose - the only thing that spoilt it was wondering why she was persistently irritable with him. He'd wander from her to his work and find himself staring at Sheila picking beans in her large frayed straw hat. He even noticed the men - especially the short spurts of dangerously active enthusiasm John put into hoeing the beetroot. If he was watched it got worse - he chopped with a nervous exhilaration that sent Mark off, fearing for their lives. This was a rich month for harvesting and this year for the first time he could enjoy it. When he pushed his marrow leaves aside a warm smell wafted up both exciting and easing and after he'd cut the bristling umbilical cord and lifted out a heavy-bodied vegetable he found himself elated and proud far beyond his share in its growth and found he couldn't stop handling it. The skin, warm and cool at once, fascinated him and tapping it with his finger he heard a juicy resonance he couldn't keep to himself and demonstrated to each member of the group in turn.

It all led to making further plans. One of them was to

improve the gourd crop by enlarging the greenhouse and he was tempted to do that straight away but it meant using some of the glass that had arrived a week or two ago for a prior passion - the building of a thermal wall. The wall moved to the top of the list and he took the men off all other chores to help him. They set about painting the southern wall of the house black. The women's complaints at the loss of a beautiful stone wall part-covered with ivy had already fallen before scientific adventure and future economy - opposition had even helped the scheme achieve symbolic status. What could be more appealing than a co-operative and undestructive adaptation of a natural resource? In any case it had to be done - the glass had cost a small fortune and must now pay off by giving free heat.

The plan was to mount it as a glass wall about six inches outside the painted one. The gap between would be sealed at the sides and a shutter built at the top to control the input and output of sun-heated air which would be circulated round the house at night through long slits in the wall. It seemed a good scheme and the men were excited. The women saw it as scientific game-playing and the boyish enthusiasm as concealing the knowledge that it was a costly experiment, visually and financially, to go wrong. Every evening for the next few days the men discussed new problems, went over old ones and made conjectures about the degree of efficiency they could expect in this climate. Mark put confidence in the percentage given for walls like this built in northern France and wouldn't have the women forget that the system worked two ways, they could not only get a third of their heating from the sun but have summer air-conditioning into the bargain if they put flaps over the slits. He explained that by closing the top ones and opening the outside shutter the hot air could escape the reverse way so long as you left open the bottom ones and a north window or door. Hot air in the glass space would rise, be sucked in from the adjacent rooms and be replaced by cooler drawn in from the open window.

Sheila ended up captured by the plausibility though still worried about the cost. The other women voiced their doubts. Bess hated it:

"Suppose it roasts us on hot days and does nothing much when it's cold?" Mark didn't answer - as far as he was concerned the comment was ignorant - but Bess wouldn't let it alone: "Suppose all the air-conditioning does is bring the temperature down to what it might have been if you hadn't stuck all that ugly glass outside? What cooling air's going to get sucked in from any window when the temperature's 80 in the shade?"

It was a minor rift and the two sexes didn't bother to mend it. The women, excluded from the main event, drew together in the evenings and took stock of the day's more relevant ones.

One of these got Mark's attention but he didn't follow it up. They were talking about an incident he hadn't forgotten but pushed aside. Selby's dog had nipped Simon's ankle and drawn blood. He'd downed tools and been ready for a confrontation but Sheila had stopped him:

"The children bait the dog, Mark. When it's chained up they shout and dance up and down in front of it. They nearly drive it barmy."

"What d'you expect? - it scares the life out of 'em - it's their chance to get even."

"It's got a job to do."

"Selby's job. It's him it's scared of. It scuttles if he suddenly turns his head."

"Well, then,"

The crisis had passed because Mark wasn't ready for it but when the women were talking he heard Bess corroborate his view. She was telling another story to Sheila in the hope of making her extra careful. She'd seen Selby take a swipe at David with the back of his hand and knock him into the bushes and while he was down the dog went for him. Selby grabbed its collar to let the boy get up and booted it into the house.

Mark wasn't the only one interested. Joan with a surge of compassion she hadn't felt before, kept an eye open for David the following day. She was working the salad patch next to their fence and Bess was with her. Sounds of excitement coming from Selby's greenhouse told her where he was and she saw heads bobbing behind the boxes of seedlings. Claude was with him. He had Simon in tow when he came out - they left David intent over the lock.

David looked up and saw her watching. Shock followed by an emotionless blank, followed by a selected social imprint came on his face in quick succession - she was beginning to get used to him, even to feel something like affection. The imprint was a smile.

"We were about to have a competition," he said, ignoring Bess. "You can judge if you like."

Joan rested her bowl of radishes on a fence post. "What competition?"

"We're pop stars. He can go first." He jerked his head towards Claude who had come over with Simon. Claude shook his head.

Bess opened the gate and let them through. David followed.

"What'cha waiting for?"

When Bess bent to pick up Simon, Claude felt exposed and bullied and sang a snatch or two or a song they barely recognised. He jerked round unrhythmically and stopped without warning.

"O.K. - my turn!" David started up as suddenly as Claude had finished. Out of his mouth came an adult voice and tone that shocked them both - Bess felt she was listening to an invisible ventriloquist. Tortured, onanistic, violent - expression and movement so perfect an imitation of the real thing Bess searched anxiously for a child under it but found no excitement or release or childish sense of glamour to flaw the copy. When it came to an end there was a pause.

Joan mumbled something like "nice" and moved off. The uneasiness Bess felt lasted the rest of the day. By the end of it she was in a passion to get away, feeling suddenly confined - caged by her own exaggerated responses. Life here was in too small a compass. The trip to London became a need more than an adventure - an escape into the world.

On the train down Tom caught her excitement. They were trying to make a list-minute line up of points they wanted to discuss with Macfaddien but couldn't give it their attention. Scalding coffee in paper cups, the wall-eyed expression of the man opposite or the dreaming fat woman on the other side of the gangway now wiping her little girl's chocolatey mouth with the back of her hand were all more interesting. Her husband, seeing Bess watching, smiled. He was tired, in his eyes the interest and exposure were warming but his mouth, tentative over a quick flash of teeth, made her turn away and leave him in peace. She was launched. The carriage clamoured with life - people open, defensive, vivid, removed, intimate, insulated took her over and there was no room for anything else. Tom made notes on his own.

In the city they went straight to the park by the Embankment to eat their sandwiches and found several others doing the same, sitting on a wall in the sun, two tramps, an uncomfortable-looking woman on her own, a middle-aged couple eating from the same bag and, just in front, a student on his back on the grass, legs stuck out but occasionally propping himself up for a bite, with his face turned up to the sun. It was the band that had drawn them here. Bess had a passion for brawny arms manipulating gleaming trumpets and when they started up after a rest she took off with the brass. Lilting, seductively simple and confident tunes streamed in the sunlight. The men, sleeves rolled and faces wet with sweat, set an energetic waltz-like pace through one tune after another and she'd have stayed to the end if Tom hadn't moved her off in a daze. He was guiding her by the elbow up a busy narrow street to the Strand.

The meeting was half an hour away but the walk to the publishers along a route he'd worked out from his map was to give them time to get into the right frame of mind. It didn't work because the generalised hunger for life was still dominant and slowed them down for Bess to peer through office windows and privately interpret the life of coats and pegs or feed off faces in the street and half-heard conversations.

As they got closer and more nervous they managed to focus on the meeting. Tom had several points he wanted to be sure to get across. One was that he wouldn't budge from their overall concept of the book. If they changed it along the lines the publisher wanted there'd be no excitement in writing it and they might as well stop now. Bess was in agreement but wanted to keep the tone friendly - she liked Macfaddien, they both did. It made Tom worry they might in their present mood make things over-easy. He didn't want to make meaningless agreements through an excess of good will and he had to fight Bess on this or they'd come away with things as they were.

This time preparation was useless because the tensions changed as soon as they got there - the publishing house produced its own complicating responses. Doors and floors made suggestions and mirrors wrested a confusing sense of space from an entrance hall not much bigger than a larder. A woman who seemed awake to them as individuals showed them up a flight of stairs that got broader. Bess asked for the lavatory. She was directed to a room so small one step took her from the lavatory to its door and another to the washbasins. Mirrors, green tiles over ceiling and walls and lavish provision of soap and hot-air were distracting and reassuring. Scallop-shaped sinks under a high window and cushioned carpet under foot, thick and soundless, helped to give the impression of imprisoned luxury yearning towards the light and kept her poised to receive the counter suggestion that she was weightless and therefore more than usually free.

When they reached the main office by contrast it seemed enormous. Four or five large polished desks reflected the light from a wall of windows that overlooked the street from which surprisingly little sound got through. People in here looked, moved and talked more freely than those outside and with a suggestion of questing curiosity. Bess was captured. It was offering itself as a haven but of well-organised purposive intelligence. Here only unselfconscious affluence was allowed to suggest that success liberated. She looked more closely at the people. Lively eyes and faces confirmed the reading. Everything was geared to the machinery of contact - the resulting liveliness made the other objectives plausible.

When Macfaddien came in, large, amiable and pig-headed, he brought yet another world - one they had met already in previous interviews - geared to the moulding of new authors. It was built privately out of reminiscence, personal contact with the famous and the quirks of his own taste that had been rubber-stamped by success. His manner suggested, and he did in fact have, a worldly acumen they could not hope to come by and that instantly set him aside or above and put him in control. It was disarming because far from being cold it suggested a rich private life that he'd managed to lock intelligently and successfully into the world at large.

As soon as they'd shaken hands he wondered if they'd like to go out.

They followed him downstairs and, as before, to the Ritz but too early for afternoon tea. They talked in an empty restaurant round a marble-topped table set among pink plaster statues and plastic ferns. It reflected his state of mind and didn't affect either of them badly - it was part of the machinery and could represent whatever he wanted, after all it belonged to a world that never existed except in the minds of its visitors and identified perfectly with his memories and objectives which were all the time being excitedly eclipsed by the here-and-now - the new interview or the new possibility. Innocence and worldliness made him unassailable. The more aware of his position he became the more his presence dominated. Energy, confidence, health, a voice and body attractive and at 65 impressively fit for life began to be the forces to be reckoned with. It was clear that with the best will in the world they'd never understand each other. For Bess watching him at work became so absorbing she lost all sense of why she was there.

He ordered a pot of coffee and some biscuits. Stretching his arm out to reach the coffee-pot he told them he didn't want to push his authors. He'd leave them free because nothing exciting could come of a work too confined by the requirements of a series. Bess watched the neat shiny cuff recede into the sleeve and leave enough of itself behind to draw attention to the suit which was attentive to his every move. Tom, finding the carpet pulled from under him, looked to Bess. She smiled, obsessed with costume, set and actor. Tom missed the point at which he could have added his comments and found himself listening to Macfaddien's enthusiastic exploitation of the series' intellectual objectives.

Bess felt mean at not having given them a proper hearing before. The artless sophisticate disappeared and a new boy took his place - a warm and loyal one appealing for special mentions for his friends, writers who needed and deserved the recognition of being included in a book of this kind and he hadn't noticed them on their list.

He shared a joke about one of them illustrating the delicacy of her sense of humour and mentioned a "poignant" and "hilarious" episode from one of her novels to back it. From the title the Blakes had certainly read it but were convinced they must have missed the scene or he'd got the title wrong. Seeing them vague he went into detail. The piece emerged slowly in Bess's memory - arch, wry and sentimental - and she gave a smile of relief that they were in fact talking about the same book. Interpreting it as spontaneous agreement he reinforced his point about including her.

Tom agreed to accommodate some of these authors but only a personal selection. Macfaddien found that reasonable. Tom held out against the inclusion of detective fiction because he felt neither he nor Bess had anything to say. Macfaddien went along with that. Bess was grateful for the way Tom was handling it and this quickly became part of the interest. It was amazing that while their understanding drew further apart their natures came closer together. Useless herself she accepted Macfaddien - his personality, his world - as she did his clothes and watched his face shining out of them.

As they were leaving the publisher stretched out his hand unreservedly - one human being to another - and she pressed it affectionately so that for a moment he looked puzzled, even alarmed. He was rushing off. He was meeting his son who had just come back from Paris. At the mention of his son there was a new expression - exposure. Like wiping a slate it removed the previous information except for keenness which was now riddled with uncertainty. When he walked away there were only traces of the former self left over in dress and bearing - just enough to wrap him from the crowd.

Tom was tired afterwards and depressed. He understood what had happened but had missed her co-operation. It wasn't the additional authors, he said, that bothered him:

"A few sentences'll cover them and make little difference to the layout or, more to the point, the attitudes behind it, but these are what Macfaddien really doesn't like. Did you notice the bit about Leavis?"

She shook her head.

"He said pointedly, 'I wouldn't let Leavis write a book for me'." He watched her expression.

"He should be so lucky!" came out angrily but her mood changed back again. "The book'll be so interesting he'll have to like it."

The confidence and question in the gaze did its usual work. He took her hand and as her excitement re-emerged caught it himself. The situation was, whatever else, a challenge and adventure.

They'd booked for a play in the evening - a well-reviewed production of a dramatisation by a popular contemporary playwright of a nineteenth century Viennese short story. Bess had achieved her ambition for all theatre and concert performances - a seat in the front row. She wanted to take part in the game and see everything, including what she wasn't supposed to see. The fun was in illusion broken by actuality. The illusion, even when good, was a limitation but the actuality was an animal activity - something to be wholehearted about. She enjoyed the smell of the make-up and the dust rising from a foot stamped a yard away and this new theatre had given enormous floor-space to the stage which at the front was only two or three feet off the ground and allowed you to become part of the production. Turning round she saw the massive audience sloping away from it gently - not towering but intimate, both arena and drawing room.

The lead actress, middle-aged and heavily made up, was acting the 'grande dame' but this set off the leading actor's performance. His was the only real character study and all the others had a tough time - even the plot stood round him stiffly watching. In the nature and bearing of this character there was just enough resemblance to Mark to sharpen Bess's interest and she began to take more pleasure in the patterns of behaviour built up round him, but when they lost their hold she watched the set.

It had the right mixture - realistic and unrealistic in equal proportions. The separate bits were blended through diaphanous curtains - mauves and greens beautifully draped between solid wrought-iron gates and cardboard vista. A thin cloth wall and window had a real bush tubbed in front of it. Reality and unreality on stage and in the play were almost indistinguishable and hardly different in proportion from anywhere else. Unreality was the conduit for reality and vice versa.

On the way back Bess's memories of the play came over with almost as much relish as of the afternoon meeting. Tom, tireder than her, hadn't watched with the same enjoyment. Halfway through he'd been fidgeted again by the afternoon's events and spent the journey back planning and replanning a follow-up letter to the publisher.

10

Sheila's drawn face when she met them at the station announced trouble and Bess, questioning her on the way back, was told some of the glass for the wall had been broken and they didn't know how. Obviously she was worried about the expense, she said. To Bess it didn't seem reason enough for the hesitations and sudden switches of direction her anxiety took and she went on questioning.

Suddenly, relieved, Sheila gave in: "It's Mark, he's behaving like a lunatic." There was a pause while she felt better. "I can't prise him off the idea the Selbys did it." Bess looked grim and Sheila was encouraged. "He keeps thinking up schemes for revenge - he's been taking it out on the children because he doesn't know how far they're involved - and can't stand the sight of me."

"Why wouldn't it be an accident?" Tom asked.

"Precisely! He's got this fixed idea that because the older boy was standing at the fence when he made the discovery he must know something, especially as he was white and quaky when he looked at him."

"He does that all the time," Bess said. Sheila raised her hands momentarily from the wheel and ducked her head in acknowledgement. "It'd be enough for him," Bess added, "that he was there at the wrong moment."

"I said it wouldn't be him unless it was an accident." Sheila momentarily concentrated on the road in silence.

"Mark thinks his simpleness gives the game away - that he was standing there because he knew something and was waiting to see what would happen."

"If he knew anything he'd get as far away as he could at the dangerous moment."

"You convince him then!"

When they got back Mark had gone to bed and Bess didn't see him till the following morning when he passed her in the garden.

"You're back then!" snapped out of him as if she'd been party to it all. The tone was so personal and intense she wondered if she'd done something else wrong but noticed the spite in his face recoiling instantly on himself. She'd had no time yet to talk to her daughter and seeing her she ran to put her arms round her and feel at ease. For the rest of the day she relived the London trip and no-one outside the family existed.

The Blakes closed ranks and managed to keep themselves to themselves by working in the boxed garden. The hedges were tall enough to make a sun-trap and capture perfume from the roses, which heightened their responses to everything inside and sealed out everything else. Whenever fresh soil appeared birds took it - frightened and excited. Bess caught their feelings, watching furious heavy-bodied jabs from single blackbirds while the starlings waited for distance and numbers. When she moved off they moved in - gleaming, green-shot, keeping an awkward but accurate balance of spear-beaks over stiff legs and her tensions eased as they blended with theirs. It was this she needed. In the scuffling retreats and nervous spurts of warning chattered out from all directions, in the relentless progress over the soil was the passion of reality that nothing could resist. By the end of the day she felt happy.

Nevertheless, she stayed in her group and a continuing manner of unconscious self-sufficiency made Mark draw closer to Joan.

He liked talking to Joan and valued her opinion. For one thing she listened to his fears without resisting or increasing them and her comments sometimes made him see them in a new light. He felt freed in her company and began to think if he needed a close relationship then this was the woman to have it with and enjoy the pleasures of a shared responsiveness without its threats. On this occasion it released him to act in a considered way - gave air to the suffocation preventing him from acting at all - and a decision emerged to try the legal action he'd had at the back of his mind for months. He made an appointment with Lionel and when the time came asked Joan to go with him.

They stopped on the way because Mark wanted her to look at the river that ran through Warford before they reached the town. It changed its appearance dramatically, he said, in different contexts - "Here", leaning over a bridge with her, "it feels more like a stream." They stared for a few moments side by side and Joan waited for something more but nothing came. She felt he was moving closer emotionally but through a form of pressurised intimacy directed at other things. It was flattering but made her uncomfortable and she turned her attention to the water which was clear. It looked shallow but the current was evident in the streamers of weed yanked from under them, anchored and tugging - one tress was teased out at least twelve feet while those round it coiled and undulated under different pressures. When he spoke again it was to tell her this was a treacherous stretch and cast an anxious eye at the boys who'd come down to fish.

He was right about the change. The car park, when they

reached town, was next to the river. At this point with boats moored along the bank it had lost its independence and, though wider and deeper, its threat. It was the park that claimed attention, packed with even more people than cars. Some of them sat inside with the doors flung wide, eating their lunch, but most were lolling on the grass looking for distraction in a half-aimless holiday mood that wouldn't join it if it found it. Ease was the thing and it resulted in what looked like the almost insolent indifference of one group to another. The members of each might behave as if more at home than at home, but from inside invisible walls outside awareness was sharper. It produced a strange but exciting tension underlying the prime objective. Parents, denying everything in prone bodies and shut eyes, left the children to express it and they wandered from group to group making tentative action. Some who weren't up to it sucked their thumbs. Over all the atmosphere was so intimate that passers-by leant over the bridge, ignoring the river, to watch the park, and through all this Mark cut his way like an alien. Joan wasn't ready to move and hung back watching the tension in his wide shoulders with a mixture of attraction and rejection. Distinctive in looks and movement it was finally neither of these that shifted her but sympathetic identification with the isolation. She stood outside with him for a few moments while he gave her instructions for meeting in the late afternoon and they separated.

Mark on his own was suddenly excited and made for the older part of town where Lionel had his office over a dress shop. His window was filled with the advert in white paint, 'Lionel Tench, Solicitor'. At street level there was a plaque by a narrow flight of stairs. At the top of these, he met familiar obstruction from the door which was panelled and heavy and only opened in response to a push while focusing on a shiny brass doorknob that slipped in the grip. His entrance as usual was sudden and distracted and confused further by Lionel's walls. These demanded attention unrelated to the job in hand and equally unrelated it seemed to the businesslike figure behind the desk that raised its bottom an inch in welcome. The walls were festooned with lutes, mandolins and gourd-shaped instruments echoing the colour of his walnut desk and finally leading you to the man behind it who on second glance looked ready to play. At his back was a large painting of a ship on a choppy sea - to one side a nude that periodically took his attention.

"Nice to see you, Mark," he said. "Sit down, you're making me nervous." Mark sat. "You're not going to like my news" - he glanced at the nude - "but it's not all bad" - and brought his mouth to order. "You could bring Frank Selby to court over the original contract but I'm afraid you'd probably lose." Pause. "There are too many loopholes -" pause - "in fact I'm sorry I started you on that tack. Your case isn't a straightforward one." He shifted position to put his hands on the desk. "The joint tenancy contract ran out when the other tenant left and the previous landlord sold up but a new one would have to take Selby's wishes into account and that's the problem. There's only one certainty. You can raise the rent" - his hands opened towards Mark - "but that'll be governed by rent regulation and you must make the improvements he's been asking for" - and they folded.

Mark suddenly remembered why it had taken him so long to make this visit. It would never have happened if he hadn't been desperate and now the despair coming in a flood brought an undertow of anger against the man who in a couple of easy gestures had dammed the only outlet.

Eventually Mark's fixed attention on his hands made Lionel nervous and he put them in his lap. "He's been asking all year," he said resentfully - and surprised at his own tone made amends: "You could make a small but steady profit by doing what he wants - 12.5 per cent of the total cost on each year's rent." In the long pause that followed he decided to get it all over in one go: "And as far as the glass is concerned you've no proof. Without it you don't stand a chance. Make money out of him!"

A complete misunderstanding of his needs and their seriousness, coupled with the uneasy jostling of rebuke and conciliation made Mark angrier.

Lionel tried reasoning: "You must forget about getting rid of him for the time being. There's no indication he's ready to leave voluntarily. There's one thing you can bite on though, if you're desperate - if you claim you need a full-time employee and want Selby's place for him, the picture changes."

"I can get rid of him?" Mark looked at him properly for the first time.

"Maybe."

It wasn't enough and Mark slipped back but not so far that he couldn't comment, "We barely make ends meet now - I couldn't afford one." His face tightened. "I'm starting a commune not a business." Lionel didn't answer. "The verbal agreement to leave - anything you can do there?"

"Shakey. You've only the estate agent's word for it and Selby's ready to prove he had long-term business projects in the area when you bought the place." He paused. "Have you ever thought the estate agent might have been leading you on or exaggerating to make you more interested? He may have squeezed some meaningless comment out of Selby to use in a sale."

"Nobody squeezes anything out of Selby." After a pause: "And the malicious damage?"

"You've no proof, Mark. Blocked drains and broken glass aren't evidence. Put forward those suspicions in court and they'd work against you." There was a long silence that neither of them seemed able to break. Finally Lionel brought the interview to an end: "We're meeting up in a fortnight, aren't we? I'll see what else I can rake up by then - no promises, mind."

Mark stood up and shook the offered hand.

Lionel breathed freely the moment the door was closed, but dismissing Mark completely took a bit longer. He paused on the way back to his desk to finger a lute and it relaxed him. Rolling up his eyes he pouted and puffed out the residue.

Outside the heat struck Mark with unexpected violence. Lionel's office had been cooler and with little light coming in. In the street it was suffocating and the light glaring. He headed away from town for the river where there were trees. The water swift and cool helped him go fast and when the trees became a wood leading the path away he felt uneasy till it returned. Here the water in patches was smooth as oil. The track became difficult and through the bushes he saw the water now turbulent and throwing up foam, making a vortex under the roots. A few yards further on it was smooth again. Rather than slow down or lose sight of it he put up with the occasional slashing from shoulder-high thorn bushes until he was clear, but the path was thickening ahead and over the bushes he thought he saw someone - more a movement than a shape - and the river was changing again, the water's edge reedy, with a weed-locked progress in midstream. He turned a corner and collided.

The shock stopped him dead. He was about to apologise when he recognised who it was. Incredulous, then dismayed and angry, he was suddenly filled with the thought that as Selby was here he'd been to Lionel's before him. That's why Lionel had his comments off pat, that's why he'd behaved like a stranger - he'd known it was hopeless. A riot of cancelled impulses kept him standing there while Selby taking stock of the situation mastered it. He dismissed the idea of passing without speaking, saw this was a confrontation but a blind one and seeing the paralysis of confusion snatched his victory. The exhilaration came over in his voice: "Been busy in town?"

Mark reddened and making a dismissive grunt moved to pass him. Selby stayed put. He moved again, hearing Selby speaking but not understanding. Long, sinewy, he couldn't get past. A couple of words got through - "market" and "repairs" - the last one took fire, burnt out and left his nails dug in his palms. He moved again but now Selby seemed to be blocking him deliberately - his arm thrown out in a gesture describing something. Mark studied his mouth, focusing on the sound: "Don't want to lose the lot and glass is expensive." His fists exploded. Selby drew back, brought his arm across to protect his face and down on to Mark's neck. Mark fell through the bushes into the water. Selby, standing over, watched until Mark was upright and grabbing a root clutching for the bank, then made to go but not before Mark had seen the fear and anger in his pale face become translucent hate.

Mark panicked as his feet with every movement were sucked deeper into the mud. He groped for a better grip in the bush and wrenched one free, finding a foothold in the roots. When he heaved again he found his body-weight had doubled and hauling it high enough to free the other foot took so much energy that he fell through the bushes on to the path and lay there resting with his chest on it and his legs still hanging through them. Though the earth, warmer than flesh, transmitted perfect stillness he moved to put his hand in sunlight and when he came round found he was shivering and his teeth chattering. He got up. A body-memory of his own dead weight made the shivering worse and he stumbled up and down the path quickening pace as his body loosened and forgot its co-operation in its own destruction. Eventually he took his clothes off to dry in the sun and dried himself with his hands, than ran again and was amazed at his lightness that had a freedom and flexibility in it he remembered from childhood.

When he met Joan later he had the fresh damp look of a schoolboy who'd been swimming and in his eyes an openness, an unquestioning availability, a responsiveness to whatever happened that she'd never seen in him before and that within minutes she was finding irresistible. He'd patted a horse, he said, and it had kicked him into the river. The touch of alarm she showed filled his eyes with affection. On the way back she found herself leaning towards him, listening, smelling the river in his hair and clothes and getting excited at the way they clung to him emphasizing his movements.

Mark told no-one the truth. He was ashamed but released and felt a subdued exhilaration that he managed to keep going for several days by ignoring small signals of returning anxiety. When the change came it seemed like an accident and unmanageably abrupt.

Tom came into the sitting-room one afternoon after lunch waving a letter. They were all there because it was raining. He shouted, "He's at it again!" to Bess but included Mark in his glance. Mark had been engrossed in his newspaper and looked up. There was something in his expression that made Tom feel intrusive but he wouldn't be stopped and it made him more emphatic: "That bloody word professional - he's used it again." He sat next to Bess and feeling Mark's irritation kept his voice up. "He wants a professional job, he says, covering the prescribed area - we're not to worry about detail, it's coverage that counts."

Bess looked angry but it was Mark who spoke: "He's got a case, don't you think?" He stopped suddenly because he hadn't wanted to sound dismissive. He folded his paper and took breath. "I can sympathise with what he's up against," he said, feeling his way - "however fair he'd like to be he's got to keep his own interest alive" - another pause - "we all have different ways of doing that." He realised he couldn't leave it there. "When I was teaching, for instance, I was a different person at the end from the beginning. Books I'd loved were offering less and less. They only became exciting again as building bricks. I wanted my own adventure, you see, which was in my theories and when the books co-operated with these my interest returned. Your publisher's interest lies in commercial success and he won't respond much outside it. It's perfectly natural. We've got to keep our creativity alive or stop working." His tone sounded all right but the content was for him too antagonistic, so he turned it against himself: "I found myself getting really sick of the academic game when others did it better than me. I've forgotten the name of the Cambridge don who had a big effect on me. He had a reputation at the time but it's fading now. I remember that in his case it was such an obvious ego-trip even I couldn't stomach it. The skipping from one book to another, one idea to another worked like a conspiracy against the works in hand in case they stole attention." He clicked his fingers impatiently. "Sylkin, Gregory Sylkin."

Tom's face twisted in disgust. "I started to read his book on Lawrence but couldn't recognise the subject! For him no reference is too small or too far away. It would be nice to think it was nervousness but that's not what comes over. We're expected to watch his grandstand go up brick by brick and applaud not the industry but the brilliance of humping around more references than the rest of us care to." He paused to redirect his irritability. "He'd got as much understanding of Lawrence as a flea of its host."

Bates moved to the sofa partly to get into the fight, partly to fill the place next to Mary now John was leaving the room. It broke the flow. Both Tom and Mark found the intrusion disturbing and Bates spread his legs and made himself comfortable, not wanting to be watched. In position he kicked the ball into play:

"He'd know one thing" - turning his profile to Mary - "the flavour and food value of the blood!" It lay there long enough for him to get the attention he wanted, then he eased himself into the social position to getting it moving again - "We can't hope for more, we contribute what we can" - and smiled.

Tom's face changed. Mark's antagonism made him obstinate, Bates's egotism made him angry. Giving a reflex kick aimed at the intruder, "Fleas," he said, "only know what excites them." He looked past him at Mary to help him manage his temper. "Too busy getting drunk for an accurate analysis," he told her and she laughed.

Mark was excited in spite of himself but stared at the floor between them as if he wanted no part in it.

Bates now lolled his arm on the sofa back behind Mary and asked Tom if he found all reference outside the text irrelevant. If he didn't, where did he draw the line? "If you read a lot and think about it the results can be interesting - even illuminating. You say nothing's too small or too far away, but it's all related."

"Related? Ah well, if we're on to that, what isn't? A beetle's related to a hawk. You could make an impressive book on the enzymes and cell structures they've got in common, even on the direct or indirect influence they might have on each other, without coming any closer to an understanding of the distinctive purposes or experience of either."

Mary began to feel uneasy and looked round to see if John was still in the room, finally leaving to look for him. It left Bates exposed and for a moment he forgot to be bland: "As far as you're concerned only an intensive approach has value, an extensive one is pedantic - am I right? Let me tell you what I think. The kind of picking and poking, discriminating and evaluating that intensive criticism goes in for is a more self-important exercise than the one you're accusing Sylkin of. For one thing it's based on under-estimating the intelligence of the average reader. The assumption is he won't have understood as much as you, not that he won't have read as much."

Mark, wanting to be politely attentive at this point, only made more obvious a suppressed involvement either with the point of view or the general anger, and it intensified their antagonism. Tom was about to speak when Bates raised his voice:

"If the author's worth his salt he can be left to himself to communicate what he wants better than you or I. The only function we've got is to point out the general context. It's from there we can pick out the odd nuance that might be missed without a wide reading experience."

"Not if academics are anything to go by." Tom's expression was openly aggressive and made him look the most violent of the three. "If we're anything to go by authors need friends and without them they might as well write in code. It's our sort who make that clear. Other readers don't open their mouths. If criticism isn't a form of shared responsiveness with the work as well as with other people it's nothing. If it isn't a way of bringing the two experiences together to see what's there it's nothing. Ninety per cent of academic articles show little or crude understanding of what's there. What they do instead is blend the ideas that interest them with their reading and replace the original synthesis with one of their own. They do it for the reasons Mark was suggesting but the result is either their own fiction or an autobiography impacted on someone else's work. It may or may not be interesting on its own account but it's of little service to the book under discussion or the readers of it."

"You think your approach better, a personal definition and personal assessment of everything read? Surely you can't flatter yourself it covers everything of interest and value."

"Ah, but at least we're on common ground!" Tom looked happier. "It's the openly personal definition that counts. In fact it's the only approach that doesn't waste the reader's time because he knows exactly where he stands. When it's someone else's view he can share it or not and that might help him define his own position - it could hardly do otherwise. What wastes the author's work and the reader's response to it is airing your knowledge and managing to lecture both reader and writer at the same time. Those techniques might just be okay in a purely historical context but to distance the actual reading experience until it becomes meaningless for you and for him is something that ultimately puts you out of a job. It's difficult to remain in business in a field with no apparent value, and its value disappears as the reader of your kind of book begins to feel he's had only the gut reaction to a book that a clever man moves beyond. We all want to be clever. His original and real response is at best made to look half-educated when in fact the boot's on the other foot. It's only along those lines he can challenge the author's responses or have his own challenged and the education he needs for that is life. If a book isn't to die at birth it has to establish a two-way process of the kind that makes great art neither didactic nor sufficiently amenable to classification to make the pedantic approach worth a candle - it survives through vulnerability as much as strength and neither has much to do with what Sylkin deals in. The only relevant fact is the personality of the writer. A different personality would respond to the same cultured circumstances a different way. A work's survival depends on the honesty and clarity of its expression of the writer's experience and if you're discussing anything else you're off the track - usually so far off you're looking at it from a distance that makes all objectives seem equal - which they're not. If individuality in literature doesn't matter literature doesn't matter, social interchange (which it's part of) doesn't matter, even the human race doesn't matter because as a species we're replaceable, it's only as individuals we're not" - he looked at Mark for support - "it can all go to hell for the sake of the false fair-mindedness of our academic machinery, the technology that's meant to support life not kill it." Turning back to Bates he leant towards him. "It's worse than just watching individual books go down, though, it's knowing the real reason for it. The kind of critic you're supporting is really afraid of anything so vulgar as a personal response. By that I mean a moral, emotional and intellectual involvement in the issues raised that puts him on a level with the average reader. For one thing he knows himself better than to risk it! What he replaces it with is vulgarity of a different sort, satisfying an urge for conspicuous consumption that publishers, like other salesmen, can rely on. Macfaddien feels so safe with it he denounces F.R. Leavis confidently as arrogant and limited and feels he's made the ultimate judgement."

"Well, hasn't he? - but don't let's get on to that," Bates added quickly.

"No, let's. It'll clear the air."

Bess had been anxious at first then more relaxed as the general animosity took predictable shape. Now that Tom was on his hobby horse she felt easy enough to leave the room. Joan was still avidly attentive.

Mark, finding he'd launched the discussion accidentally, now felt it had taken off without him and in a way that quickly replaced his excitement by a sense of threat. Other natures than his own, other passions suddenly seemed destructive not supportive of his central theory of the commune - the theory that our differences would be the source of its renewal not defeat. In a panic he felt they could be as dangerous in their ways as Selby was in his. Although Tom's argument had other overtones it was centred in a world of literary criticism that because Mark had given it up seemed dead. It seemed that his friend's most passionate thoughts were locked into it and he was never at any other time so accessible. How much room could there be in others for Mark's own obsessions? To stop a sense of isolation taking over he'd mentally taken part, first one side then the other, as if his life depended on it but his tension had increased. He couldn't accept his own responses. Having denied he wanted an orderly community of experience he found himself desperate if it wasn't evident. The unconscious recognition of mutual need he'd relied on seemed suddenly left to conscious effort and there was no way he or anyone else could keep that up. He wanted social wholeness to come out of multiplicity like an organic accident, to have his world similarly made up of separate lives inseparably united in an adapting body. From the bacteria that helped him digest to the bugs that held his skin together he was himself a walking commune, so why be afraid of his friends' differences or his impressionability? Just the same there had been a few moments while they'd been talking when their world had been a whole and valid one for himself too, and that had shaken him. They had robbed him for a while not only of his sense of independent action but of the need for it. He wanted to attack or join them and couldn't do either. The more he immobilised himself the worse the strain. Life was romping away from him on all fronts. Plans, organisation of any kind were useless. With all of us whirling in worlds of private response, picking up and dropping contact through accidents of need, the overlapping rationales only perpetuated chaos. In desperation he fixed his eyes on the one who was talking. It happened to be Bates:

"Applying similar standards is silly." Mark was glad they were on to personalities. "What's sillier still are the pompous enthusiasts he leaves in his wake." Mark grinned. "A good thriller is a good thriller and has its own standards and rights to recognition. Why should the public be cheated of a different mental and emotional exercise just because he thinks he knows what's best for them? Anyway you people aren't consistent. Your views on the value of individuality should make you keen on all types of writer, especially those who lean heavily on their personal charm. Fielding, for instance. Why should I see him as inferior because he doesn't follow the rules Leavis thinks are highest?"

"Fair enough," Tom said, "but if you're dealing in charm you must allow half of us not to respond to it. I personally react badly to an author who's got his eye on his audience more than his objective - or should I say whose objective is an audience. If he makes a point of trading in personality he must be ready to have the dubious aspects of it challenged. As for the thriller" - Tom crossed his legs - "if it's good or bad it's basic to a Leavisian approach to try to find out why - not deny its value. If it's good, though, it'll be because even though it's done on sufficiently predictable lines to be classifiable it's moving and interesting us more than we expected and if it's breaking the bounds of expectation it's breaking the boundaries of form. It's really only facile assurances in literature and life Leavis doesn't like. On the other hand his attitude won't be popular because if you're going to scrutinise a work closely you have to scrutinise your response to it just as closely or look a fool. It's safer to be catholic and well-read. The trouble is", he added sadly, "by not discussing the work on its own terms we lose what we all started out with - an understanding that a good book can open up a new world, or an old world in a new light." He looked at Bates without irritation for the first time. "When you prefer some books to others don't you sometimes wonder why?" But before Bates could answer he'd added, "Or have you exchanged challenge for patronage so completely it doesn't cross your mind?"

Bates looked back trying to gauge how innocent the new offensive was. "Now you've brought me to one of the worst problems with your approach," he said, "which I'd like to say now I mistrust more than despise, but before I get on to it I'd like to ask you a question. Do you honestly think anything I thought about a book could affect my next action?"

Tom hesitated a moment. "Not yours perhaps but for me the answer would be yes. Only in a marginal way to begin with - more as I assimilated it."

"That's interesting. But you see the soul-stripping that's compulsory for you, and the only way to read a book, is for me completely irrelevant. You need to check your responses and the author's in terms of them - I don't. Even so in mine the balance of curiosity and egotism is the same. For you it's a way of increasing your understanding of yourself and life and therefore your pleasure and sense of belonging, but my pleasure's best got without it and as far as belonging I think I know what to expect from the world and perhaps belong less effortfully. Your approach is good for you, you see, not me - but the aspect of it that's intolerable is its self-righteousness - and it's unavoidable if your own values and vision are to be the only criteria. It means if your criteria are attacked you are."

"But you're using personal criteria without stating them and I'm saying there's no reason for it unless you're afraid of attack. We ought to be able to discuss things openly (which means emotionally if we're really interested) without hating each other - and it's only difficult because we can't see or be bothered to look for the personal reasons for another's point of view. On the other hand how can we look for them if the objective's concealment?"

"Why shouldn't we be private with our feelings and objective with our thoughts?"

"Not possible. If you try it we'll only criticize what we're allowed to see of the other's objectives which will seem on the face of it unacceptably fearful and egotistical."

Bates gave a strained smile. "Don't you see that for you judgement runs riot over everything - everything is in fact made personal and judgemental."

"Everything *is* personal and judgemental and nothing you pretend will make it otherwise."

"Will you at least agree it's a disadvantage in argument to be as personally offensive as Leavis can be?"

"If the argument's a good one it won't be disadvantaged, but I agree it might be 'bad form'."

"Bad-natured I'd call it. What's worse it leads to factions and camp followers. I refuse to be a camp follower, for or against, and suspect the motives of anyone making rallying cries."

"Judgements come from the most unexpected quarters!" Tom said grinning.

Bates smiled in spite of himself. "You'll agree it's unprofessional then" - but seeing Tom's face - "all right, ungentlemanly."

"When you're very interested in your subject I'm afraid gentlemanliness sometimes gets stampeded by irritation. Surely you're only primarily interested in being a gentleman if you're primarily interested in being a gentleman. Almost any other interest will take precedence over an objective so boring and self-regarding, because real kindness comes from another source depending on genuine sympathy with another's point of view. How do we get that with no evidence anyone's there? - no conflict, no challenge, no urge to define one's position clearly, nothing but a blank wall of clever caution and complacency. You shouldn't be surprised if some of us get touchy! What's communication for? A writer's got to be interested enough to be vulnerable or he won't be interesting. Politeness for the sake of it is only concern for self masquerading as concern for others."

"Couldn't it be both?"

"Not as an objective."

Bates lifted his hand. "Enough. We'll never agree but I'm

gentleman enough to take your point."

His smile made Tom feel that putting an openly personal point of view was certainly useless in this case. The concession it offered put more distance between them than opposition had. It also earned Bates the right to turn the discussion on the pivot of his choice:

"It looks as if you'll never agree with your publisher either. Have you ever thought of leaving him?"

"Only every day."

Mark had lost his pleasure in the fight and felt relieved it was over - grateful to Bates for his distance and Tom for his adaptability.

"Ever thought about publishing it yourself?" Bates asked.

"Too costly."

"I know a small publishing concern that might help. A few thousand could buy you into it. An acquaintance started it up a few years ago and when I met him last he was thinking of extending his range."

Tom was silent but looked interested.

"It could buy you the right to have a say in what gets published in your field."

For some reason Tom's response was upsetting Mark - for a moment he himself couldn't make it out. When it finally came to him he felt depressed and ashamed. Tom would of course be interested in any suggestion that might solve his problem and what luck if he had the money to back it! There'd never been evidence that the Blakes lived hand-to-mouth but for some reason he'd assumed it. There'd never been evidence they'd be interested in backing him but it was disappointment and hurt he was dealing with now.

"Don't do anything rash!" came out of him almost belligerently.

Bess had come back to see how things were going and looked approvingly at this point. Mark blushed at the misreading. It deepened at the gentle glance that followed and he left the room.

Tom's pleasure at the whiff of fresh air Bates let in had been obvious to Mark but his response had nothing to do with the Blakes' security, only his own. No one was a more dangerous individualist than himself, bent on a personal solution to a personal problem. Tom was right - you could only act honestly as an individual. Like everyone else he'd been pretending his moves were part of a movement. It should have been obvious when he left the Ecology Party but again like everybody else he'd made associative excuses for dissociative acts. If he'd cared enough about his cherished objectives he'd have linked up with others before he bolted.

He walked over to the kitchen window to see if the rain was stopping but failed to notice, his head full of vivid memory of the Ecology Party candidate who'd visited their old home. He was a dreamer but Mark instead of suggesting another candidate had dropped out of the Party. The man had filled him with despair. As he came into the house his hair blew back and left a bald expanse that because of its featurelessness Mark's memory had latched on to as a symbol of defeat. The man wasn't stupid, just empty of the vices that made politics possible, being neither greedy nor self-righteous, just hopeful. Mark found himself looking for assurance from his assertive spectacles rather than his eyes and when he left saw his shirt tail resting on his bottom.

At the time an individual act had seemed the only way and the visit released the energy he needed to get things moving in the direction he'd taken. It was only now it was beginning to look like the logic of rejection, but it was only now his decisions were coming home to roost. He could have done with the Party's backing in the light of what he'd just read in the newspaper. The full force of it had only just reached him because of Tom's argument with Bates. It was an article proposing as one of several possible sites for a nuclear power station a place twenty miles from him. So they were still doing it! There must be a suicide streak in our race. Healthy animals weren't that stupid. But if he put all his energy into getting this site dropped the foul thing would go somewhere else. It took the zest out of the thought of lobbying. He could form a group of protesters - but they'd have to be noisy ones. He could go to prison for some minor infringement - something to reach the papers and draw attention. From that position he could make a general statement and be as impassioned as he felt. It would mean committing himself to getting political policy changed. The massive financial backing the project already had would make this a full-time if not a lifetime's work. His commune would go to the devil. If he did something or nothing now it looked as if the failure of the commune was assured. Who'd join them with a nuclear site on the doorstep? His only hope was a change of government. Perhaps he should carry on in expectation of it? He'd committed himself already and couldn't change in midstream.

He'd been a fool about action all along. A man of action needed a resilience he himself couldn't rely on. It depended on keeping a balance which in him was achieved by lurching from one stance to another in successive rejections. If he chose action in one field it became impotence in another. If he made an aggressive move he victimized himself. In one independent act he'd subjected himself to the acts of others more helplessly than when he'd identified his style of life with theirs completely. So much for Tom's individualism. A purely individual act was an act of suicide. Any act individual or otherwise murdered a thousand possibilities. Action was a drug leading to an insanity in which every determined effort to get close to the objective pushed you further away - but tying yourself hand and foot led to something worse. Frustration took on a life of its own independent of cause and automatic in expression - it had done it already so successfully it had felt like life. An insanity masquerading as sanity getting stronger as he got weaker, clear-headed when he was confused and liberating him in action that was evasive and deadly - life assertion made by an alien.

He'd wondered what it would be like to be unhinged. He'd thought it might bring relief from sanity, but it brought a cock-eyed variant. It had a logic of its own that worked itself out in subtle detail directed by lunatic laws as difficult to escape as objects from gravity once they were put into action. The fight with Selby hadn't been the first sign but the most important. Until now he'd offered petty resistance and won small victories. Good victories, moments of peace when things slipped into place and life was manageable and he felt certain he was as others seemed to him to be. They'd been won always the same way, by losing himself in an interest. But he had a problem. To achieve that degree of interest he put more in to it than others wanted. Involvement with an idea, a movement, his work, people or a person was risky - it was so easy to defeat the objective. Over-intensity destroyed his own and others' balance and he'd been pulling back all his life. It would be the damage to others that would destroy him. He needed them as they were, not as his lunacy directed. If it had its way intensity and excess would take the place of diversity every time.

He wanted more life not less - to increase his scope not

reduce theirs - and it was diversity that offered the minute by minute challenge that forced him to be unconsciously objective. Whether he achieved it or not the need was there, and the energy that made it a need. It produced a life-hunger hard to handle but which he'd seen handled successfully by someone else. Bess's nature was just as intense as his, perhaps more so, it was one of the reasons he ducked back from contact with it. If people moved at different paces in different worlds it excited without threatening her and it seemed as if she reached them as easily. Were her hungers stronger than his? There was no maiming control but it wasn't because she didn't see the dangers, just that her energy took the risk. He didn't want his battle to be a conscious one but it took place not just through a failure of nerve but of understanding and when he won it produced an artificial balance the opposite of involvement. Bess could be immoderate and refreshed by action and get away with it. In him it produced a tension that strung him out over a widening field. She invited difficulty, indulged intensity or pulled against it with equal success while keeping the security of her group. Tom and Mary supported her because they shared in the benefits. If she could be involved at random with so little damage why not him? She accepted greed as the way to be fed enough to keep resilience alive. In that case it was a balance so dangerously achieved he couldn't do it because his strongest hunger was for the balance, not the means to it. She made that objective look like a bonus. The closest he could come was a brief peace in the aftermath of indulgence. Even his involvements were really submersions. Perhaps it wasn't more life he was after but to burn himself out, in which case his strongest commitments would turn out to be rejective. His most cherished dream for the commune - a fully realised interdependence of lives - was for her a reality. His oscillations through fear or protectivity were more destructive than her spontaneity. She accepted the chaos he only recognised. But he couldn't escape the need to impose a shape. Shape? More like a path backwards and forwards offering the illusion of moving towards something while fleeing from something else.

The memory of his dying mother came vividly into his head. A helpful nurse had twisted her into a position she couldn't get out of. She put up with it, hardly noticing it because her face, dealing with the past, was blank to the present. Moist-eyed, angry and confused her lips were moving and twisting in an argument that didn't exist.

Sheila broke in on him suddenly and he was so grateful he went over to put his arms round her as she stood at the sink. Surprised and pleased and trying to enjoy it she waited for more but when nothing came broke away to get on with her jobs. He hung around silent, with his feet in the way whenever she moved. In a few minutes she felt confined and squeezed his arm when she passed as an affectionate signal of dismissal. He responded by leaving the room.

She mulled the incident over, compensating for the sudden sense of loss, and feeling now how genuine as well as unexpected it was, saw it as more than just reassuring. If they were so sure of each other that no more than this was necessary it amounted to a triumph. Spontaneity had always been there and its unpredictability transformed the drudgery of obedience to the inevitable. After all, they were such different people. His nature marked him as special - it was so complicated.

When she saw him later hard at work at his obsession (closing the gap between himself and others) she admired him. Looking at his arm hung loosely round Joan's waist, at the earnest if forced interest in Mary's gossip about university - even at the flashes of attraction and rejection between him and Bess - she found herself touched. His problems were brought on, she thought, by a nature more spiritual than sensual that had confined itself now to a world of the senses. Naturally he concentrated on the women. The opposite sex was always more accessible (she thought lovingly of Lionel and how ready he was to take her part) and with women Mark was never aggressive when challenged. She began to feel as tender towards his way of submitting to the inevitable as to her own and the compassion she felt for the complexities she shared freed her from bothering with those she didn't. The encounter seemed to have given her power as well as ease. She found herself feeling she didn't need or really want to know him better and that enjoying their differences gave each a mastery in their field, and hers was one that he needed so desperately that their success here, she was certain, depended on it.

When the rain finished she went outside where she noticed Mrs. Selby busy in her garden. It was the perfect time to tackle a job she'd been avoiding.

"I say, can I have a word with you?"

The older woman came over eagerly in spite of the unpromising note in Sheila's voice.

"It's about the dog or rather Simon's ankle" - a reproachful note crept in. "It still hasn't healed." She felt she'd more or less done what she wanted and waited for her to take up the challenge, but nothing happened. "The doctor's given him antibiotics, it's so inflamed."

"What a shame - poor little chap!" Mrs. Selby puckered her face.

"Mark's very uneasy" - and to give it a boost: "Alarmed would be a better word."

No response.

"I've noticed the dog's still loose. Do you think you could find a way of keeping him out of the children's way? They can't always be relied on to do as they're told. Best if we did something about it, I thought, rather than trouble the men."

Her instant understanding took Sheila by surprise. "If it works," she said. "Like as not it won't make any difference."

Sheila was puzzled.

"'E's trained 'im to do the job, you see, and 'e'll see 'e does it. Don't think I don't know what it's like," she added compassionately, putting her hand on Sheila's arm. "It's a burden, the worst, being saddled with a man whose next move's a mystery and likely to be nasty."

Sheila blushed. It started in shock but spread in confusion and alarm, making Mrs. Selby more tender:

"Don't worry, m'dear, I'll do what I can."

The conversation came to an end as abruptly as it started, leaving Sheila disturbed. She went indoors but couldn't settle. The thought of going out again made her cringe. Anger followed. How dare she! What had she meant? She'd taken an unpardonable liberty. The sense of violation wouldn't go.

For the next couple of days she was touchy and restless. Even Mark noticed the tension and questioned her. She said she was trying to step up supervision of the children and it made life more hectic. It was partly true. She'd heard Mrs. Selby the next day telling David not to let the children in but had seen them in the nearest greenhouse on the same afternoon. David regularly broke in - embargoes were fuel to the fire - with a passion to violate orders, one more was a bonus.

The following day the dog was sitting outside the same greenhouse, nervous but not irritable. It jumped off its bottom in quiet moments to follow a scent or investigate a noise but leapt as if shot at whenever the back door opened, and returned to its post with yelps of confusion. Sheila had chosen to weed near the trellis, partly to watch him. Her movements got on his nerves and he started barking - a rhythmical protest at first but growing raw and mounting to a frenzy. He came to the trellis and barked in her face. She didn't budge. Stepping back he took a run at it, jamming his head through one of the squares. The trellis was sturdy and he fell back squealing. It looked as if it were over. He was padding back to the glasshouse but stopped on the way and turned. Light and swift he was back, muzzle pointing, eyes witless with rage. The impact of the second explosion made her stagger and she crossed the plot to get to the path. Success drove him wild. Forcing his head through the square she heard it crack and saw his eyes bulge with the effort to bring his body through. She went indoors but the image of squirming body and hairy face tortured with frustration wouldn't go. He was going mad. Mark was right.

She punished the children a second time and so hard they were white-faced at supper. It wasn't till the following day she confided her fears to the other women and enlisted their help in keeping an eye on them. This worked and things calmed down - so much so that within a few days she decided the dog must have been ill. He'd been padding around normally since then and she was relieved, feeling she'd exaggerated her fears like Mark, but the situation changed again towards the end of the week. The weather grew hotter and humid and the children were restless. Once or twice they managed to get past the slacker vigilance but Mark, who'd been left out of it, had been unconsciously taking stock and found as the women's tensions lessened his increased.

One morning as he was crossing from the cowshed he heard a child's shriek coming from Selby's direction. The silence afterwards made him think it was a game but he moved towards it. A moment later a peal of broken screams scared him into dropping his bucket and as he ran he shifted his grip on the spade. Simon came wobbling round a bend in the path. A cracking impact on wood made him push the boy into the bushes and rounding the bend he saw the dog suspended at the waist in the trellis. At Mark's appearance he coiled back on himself, propelling outwards like a spring and dropping with a squeal of pain and triumph on to the path in front of him. Mark raised his spade and struck.

Several hours later it began to rain. Mark was sprawled in his armchair unresponsive to anything but drinking tea. It came a drop at a time but quickened into a downpour, and the sound, change of atmosphere and sweetish smells helped him relax. Going to the window to watch he found it an onslaught - perpendicular shafts gorged by the soil were rebounding from the path. Simon called him a few minutes later and when he turned to pick him up Mark's face was bright with excitement. The indomitable energy that followed lasted several days, carrying him through his dealings with Selby's ominous diplomacy after the dog died. He was aware of qualified responses coming from his group but dismissed them.

The same week he had a letter from Beatrice and from that point nothing could hold him. She wanted to stay for an indefinite time and was bringing a friend. For him it marked a new phase and his surge of energy and optimism was infectious. She was arriving on the heels of her letter so the public aspect of the group's responses to the incident died away, though Sheila was still sufficiently on the defensive to say, when she heard Joan comment that Mark seemed amazingly untouched by the whole episode: "Why not? - his conscience is clear!"

Joan, upset by the sharpness of tone, backed down and after a moment Sheila followed up with: "It wasn't nice but a very good thing." She raised her eyebrows and tipped her head. "Mark doesn't know his own strength."

"It was an accident," Bess said but the remark was too quick and Sheila turned irritably.

"I've never known anyone more careful, more responsible or more principled than him."

Bess nodded. The episode was over and forgotten but provided stimulus to Bates after dinner to tell them all a story, once both Mark and Sheila were out of the room. He delivered it without preamble, certain of his audience:

"Mark's a complicated chap. I remember he was on loan for a time to the Education Department when he worked at the university. It was a new acquisition - the result of colleges of education merging with polys and universities - and their system of each subject tutor spending only a third of his time on professional training hadn't been phased out. Mark became friendly with an interesting potter who in general liked the pot-making side of his work at the college best. I knew him myself - fiercely independent man but affectionate and the students relied on both qualities, especially when they were worried. He seemed unflappable and apparently their problems seemed to disappear if they told him about them."

Joan saw this was a parable and of special interest to Bates. For both reasons she got ready to resist. His tone was uncharacteristically leisurely and he stared musingly ahead.

"He was an interesting fellow because almost as soon as he'd got there he'd assessed the system and worked out a suitable relationship with it. If he thought it fussed he adapted it rather than himself to it and had the sense to see how it could be done without cheating his students or himself. He was determined the paraphernalia of an institution at work shouldn't rob him of the time he needed to make pots. The advantage to his students of his being a working potter more than balanced out his dismissal of departmental procedure, but word got around, especially as he seemed to enjoy life (he liked the open air and was rosy and healthy) that he was lazy and that his independence was arrogance (as in a sense it was) and that he was only interested in his pots which, for most of his colleagues, was synonymous with being only interested in himself. His objective passion for his work was in fact a self-forgetfulness that led him further and further into his colleagues' bad books while he stayed oblivious of it. Not one of them saw their own reluctant conformity as self-interest and they resented his freedom from fear of the system - it seemed to be based on the confidence his pots gave him which, incidentally, nobody seemed keen to buy when later he tried them on the open market. When Mark first met him their two kinds of enthusiasm leapt towards each other. Both seemed to need independence and to come to the essentials in a given situation, both were intolerant of the rubbing-shoulders and jogging-along styles of life and read justification of it in the inertia and life disappointment the faces of many of their colleagues showed. They became good friends." He paused and sipped coffee.

"The point of my story is this: Mark's enthusiasm for essentials was based half on the same need as the potter's and half on 'principles' - a passionately involving set of concepts about life that took the place of the potter's absorption in his craft. The potter couldn't get to close enough grips with his work and the things that fed it unless he stripped away the intrusions that had least to offer his main objectives, but Mark's life-principles were his main objectives and ideas about sympathetic identification or about duty and service to others when least convenient to the self were so emotive that the faintest suggestion of his own neglect of any part of them made him double his assiduity - not to satisfy his students but his colleagues, or perhaps I should say to satisfy what he saw as his *duty* to them, which amounted to a sort of slavery to their whims as well as their rights. Mark always got very close to his students - always had an ear for their problems and an expression of alarm or encouragement to go with it. The potter listened and whisked the anxiety away - 'made me wonder what on earth I'd been worrying about,' one of them said. With him an anxiety seemed finite and disposable." He paused again, collecting his facts.

"A group of students who were well known to Mark because he'd taught them earlier had the potter for a supervisor on a school practice. One of them was a girl who was doing well on the practice but phoned Mark up one evening on the school's behalf. She phoned Mark, you notice, not the potter who was responsible for her work at this stage. When an institution was doing the pushing she knew where to go for the 'correct' response. The potter had told her, and she knew, that she was doing well but he didn't always make the standard number of visits and the school started to fuss. It made her think perhaps she wasn't getting the right treatment from him, and she aired her worry to Mark. Once done she forgot it. The following day Mark informed everyone - the head of the potter's department, the chap who organised the school practices, in fact everyone except the potter - that a complaint had been made against him.

He did it, I think, not out of malice (he's not, as you know, a mean man) but as a result of being hustled by his principles into an unprincipled act. His ideas were outraged. His friend's behaviour had disregarded what others might think and the anxiety that this might cause. If for him sympathetic identification should have no limits then there would always be a valid moral rather than functional purpose behind any idea of duty and service, and from such a standpoint it was an easy step to join the common opinion that his friend was a man who thought too highly of himself to be bothered. All systems lean heavily for their survival on Mark's principles and it's easy for us all to identify their specific demands with what we see as a law of life. When the power and social rightness of an institution and of the principles involved in its upkeep became one there was no need for him to feel either slavish or spiteful in his reaction to official pressure. You might still think the only person to tell, friend or not, should have been the potter, that he should have been warned that a formal complaint might be lodged against him, but a passion for principle leads to morally justifiable acts of the purest self-expression. It's the real means by which it becomes powerful, not to say dangerous, to anything standing in its way - even the self. His ideal of duty is never as simple as it sounds and increases its strength and complexity by an unlimited ability to bond with other ideals. If you have 'sensitivity', 'equality' and 'humility' pitching in, the assumption that the potter needed an official boot up the arse might have been the only logical one to make. It may be that Mark sees the sharing or serving of even a slavish response as something that should be a point of honour for others, as for himself. The ethical system has ways of twisting its victims' most critical analysis of it. Anyway he found himself denouncing rather than speaking to his friend and it caused the potter a great deal of distress - not, I want to emphasise, because of the ensuing operations of the system which he understood but because of the behaviour of a friend, which he didn't. In my chat with him I got the impression he didn't dislike Mark for it but was both puzzled and depressed. He struck me as an obstinate man but very good-natured, someone who apart from those collisions of nature with fate that we're all subject to was relatively incapable of a dismissive or destructive act."

He fell silent and they wondered if there was any more to come. Joan watched him with a new curiosity - almost as if she were seeing him properly for the first time.

Bess who'd been spellbound suddenly blurted out, "That's it, the impersonality behind the personal approach", but then she hesitated. "Are you sure of your facts? There wasn't more to it than that?"

"It was a simple state of affairs, just as I've told it." Calmly assured he went on: "Vengeance, you see. We're all prone to it, especially the hidden kind, and when an idea of public good hides it you're home and dry! What made Mark's reaction suspect was the violence against another individual. He is as you say responsible and sensitive but if he's spying or supervising or denouncing he's acting out his own private situation in which every ounce of personal volition comes under the inspection or dictatorship of a code. If you hand over your personal power so that it comes not from an impressionable and variable source (yourself) but an outside and unvariable one then your destructive acts are likely to be more common and often indistinguishable from acts of spite or vengeance, vengeance against someone else's freedom or the assertion of his power because he hasn't sold out to your rules. Life is a very personal responsibility and if you hand it over, however good your intentions you'll end up murdering the rights of others, whether it's man or dog."

"Are you suggesting Mark should've let the dog kill Simon?" Bess said scornfully.

"No, just that a different man might have achieved the same end without killing the dog."

"You're mad," Bess said, "it was an accident."

"Perhaps." Bates dropped the subject but the uneasiness he'd brought to the surface only really disappeared when Beatrice arrived.

11

Beatrice was thinner and looked taller. She came this time with a man in his forties and as tall as herself. He was burly and running to fat around his belly, giving a warmer sensual dimension to an otherwise leathery skin and sociability. An Englishman who'd been teaching in Australia for the last ten years, he was decisive about never returning home and answered polite questions along those lines in an Australian accent and with a dismissiveness towards his old way of life that piqued them from the start. He was on sabbatical leave and had met Beatrice at the Bodleian - they'd been together, on and off, ever since. Nobody asked what had happened to Jack - the new consort was accepted with the same interest as the last, and attention as before focussed on or around Beatrice.

This time Mark was excited rather more by her presence than her self. He hovered around, appreciative, sometimes with a half smile of anticipation of the next move - the next subject to arouse her interest and with his own ready to pounce on whatever would be turned over by the confidence and insatiability of a well-fed curiosity always on the lookout. When he was near her, watching and catching her responses, it felt like a childish excited exposure to a world full of those exultations of interest that freed and let him be unanxiously alive while endorsing a power and confidence in himself he rarely felt. The very nature of the excitement kept him at a distance. She was important to him as a catalyst, not a person.

She noticed a difference and wasn't sure that she liked it. In fact the place felt different generally, as if something had happened or was about to happen and the facts were being withheld. If she was right and there had been a change they didn't seem aware of it. It became important to track it down but the job was made difficult by the group's having become more homogenous since her last visit. She wasn't convinced that this in itself was responsible for her feelings. There were disturbing undercurrents - of turbulence rather than discord. The reasons for them might be trivial and magnified by her feeling of not being included but looking in the obvious places for evidence of that she found none. There were no signs of resentment or frustration either with each other or the long hours in the heat doing boring jobs - in fact they seemed to be getting something out of that side of things she hadn't expected. What impressed her most was the relaxed intimacy with their physical world. They wore minimal clothing and their faces and bodies blended in a red-brown blush that threw less emphasis on expression. The result was a sensual unity she had only noticed before in the healthy blind, and it prompted, as with the blind, affection and trust unrelated to personality. Backs, arms and legs had a half mechanical generosity when moving, as if used to and pleasantly used up by the work. Individuals seemed equally content working alone or in groups and if she noted specific responses they came along with their opposites - when overheated they managed to look gratefully melted out, when sweating with effort indolence wouldn't be far under the surface and no matter how tired they were something in their expressions looked renewed.

There had to be a flourishing emotional underworld keeping so demanding a lifestyle fed and focussed. The sense of purpose coming across wasn't entirely caused by the physical pattern of their lives nor, except in the Lewises' case perhaps, by an overriding desire to make the commune work. There was something else. Mark seemed to be the one to watch since he'd put her on to it.

She was watching him more acutely than usual one afternoon because he'd come up unexpectedly into the kitchen where she was taking her time preparing vegetables and keeping out of Sheila's way. Distracted by light and heat and bared to the waist, his chest was shining with sweat, with a scrap of straw swinging in its hair. He reached up for a mug. The shoulder-blade flattened, disappeared and returned with a life of its own. His hand turned the tap and raised the cup and in spite of its eager softness and tenacity his underlip leaked water down his chest. He knew she was watching and ignored her. In the general lack of expression there was a mix of conscious and unconscious response left there for her to see. Dismissal, appeal, attack were embryonic and waiting to be shaped by circumstance. She'd seen it before but in animals and felt momentarily foreign to his species.

During the night she dreamt of him and woke up with a sexual longing that took her by storm. She'd resisted his appeal when he was selling it, only to be a customer when he wasn't. As soon as she got up she went looking for distraction.

Sheila, the obvious choice to put her in touch with reality, was so pleased to be sought out Beatrice felt guilty and appeased it with fussy attention to the chores she gave her and with affectionate questions - mostly about the children. Just the same the questions developed their own objectives and she found herself using them to get in by the back door.

She started looking for release in her work and in company and found unexpectedly she'd joined the group.

Early one evening the men were all outside except for Bates who stayed in the sitting room with the women. The windows were wide open but there was no air. The women lolled in chairs, breaking into a sweat whenever they moved. A book on the arm of Sheila's chair and a pair of torn jeans on Joan's were getting no attention. Attempts at conversation were doomed. Bates got up with a sigh and went outside and they watched him pass the window. Almost immediately there was a change of mood and Beatrice came out with:

"This place breathes sex like air!"

They stared and looked amused. A half-concurring alertness made Sheila's comment seem out of place:

"We can hardly move and you come out with that!"

Beatrice was smiling. "Since I got here I hardly think of anything else. Whatever you're growing it's aphrodisiac."

There was a laugh and the group refocussed. They were waiting on her, ready for anything.

"You know the sort of thing," she said, "usually it's occasional, here it's all the time!" No one questioned her. "For a townie like me it's no more than the fillip you get when, say, you're phoning for theatre tickets and a man's voice answers. If it's a woman's you're part of the machinery, for a man you're extending his world - instant relationship, bodiless and sex-induced!"

No response.

"Look at us. When Bates leaves the room we're suddenly changed." A chorus of derogatory noises made her add: "Not because of him, he's not very likeable, but because he's male."

"We're more relaxed," Sheila said coolly.

"But that means we were keyed up before."

"Or tenser." This time there was an irritable dismissiveness in Sheila's voice that made Beatrice appeal to the others:

"It's exciting. If I stayed here for any length of time I'd never leave. You're succeeding," to Sheila, "we're all people to people - no role-playing. If this is the feel of the new society I want it."

Sheila looked up with a smile.

"I saw my first dustwoman the other week," Beatrice told her, "it was great! When I see us driving buses, digging in parks - anything that a few years back you'd never see in a town - I feel freed. It's the same feeling here - of limitless potential." She looked round the group. "You're living proof of something I've always known - that society needs the sexual revolution even more for its non-sexual possibilities. Men benefit as much as us. We've kept our captors captive. Don't you feel this place has changed - expanded?" She was looking at Bess.

"I don't know - I'm too close to it."

"For instance, I thought you'd all be broken by work but you're not. There's a marvellous freshness about you." Sheila looked more relaxed by the minute. "It's a woman's world here just as much as a man's. You've done it."

"What?" Bess asked.

"You're living together in a way that increases individual expression instead of decreasing it. You've done it - and it's only indirectly related to your being a commune."

"We couldn't have done it without," Sheila said.

"Yes you could - by seeing it was possible. Look at the rest of us. Things have changed for us too and not just between the sexes. All our attitudes - to each other and the rest of the world - are in the melting pot. Only a while back, starving some and killing others guaranteed the survival of a few. It seemed the way for some of us to stay alive - now it's the way for none of us to stay alive. The old priorities gave us a survival kit - barely that. Laws, religion, codes were poor substitutes for understanding. But who's better fitted than us women for a life-supporting understanding? Who's got a deeper commitment to it? Our development has always had to work with the human variables that destroy simplified objectives - or ideals if you like. Men have been asked to look to the practicalities and be guided by practical ethics but security based on moral systems doesn't work - based on understanding it does. It's that kind of mutual involvement and discovery this place is full of. You've not set up a new system but a way of living. Without that any new system is the old one rehashed. I'm bowled over by what you've done because I can lose every feeling of limitation here even while being confined. If this is a taste of the future I want it!"

Sheila's smile had dimmed. "You think the men feel this?" she asked.

"Can't help it. I noticed it first in Mark. He's more given to everything - more than even he could have predicted."

"Maybe you should talk to him," Sheila said. "You may find he's not changed as much as you think."

"You mean his ideas haven't caught up yet, or his responses get stuck in a rut?" Sheila didn't answer and Beatrice sounded uncertain when she spoke again. "You can't expect miracles. If society can change as much as this in a short time individual possibilities are boundless. You're so exposed to each other here that change is happening whether you know it or not. It's the same sort of thing on a subtler scale that television's doing for society. Social and scientific discovery and events available at the instant of their occurrence along with the different interpretations of them, keep us moving all the time. It means we're beginning really to live with masses of people and their views for the first time. Even so - even though we've changed so much - our thinking hasn't caught up with our understanding - that's always miles behind. It takes a long while to get it consciously accessible. All we need is the openness you have here and growth can be limitless in a lifetime. I feel something's happened in this place that undercuts anxiety about its value."

No-one answered but Beatrice desperately needed to carry them with her. "If Mark's ideas seem the same," she said to Sheila, "it doesn't matter. Crude compartmental understanding is what he's been trained to. Men are underdeveloped in other forms of learning. It doesn't matter what he thinks - only what he's becoming."

Sheila got up suddenly and brought the monologue to an end.

The disturbance she'd been feeling carried on into the night and prevented her from sleeping. She lay like a board in the bed, turning occasionally to stare at Mark's dropped jaw and hair scuffed back to the receding hairline, showing a wider than usual expanse of intractable bone. He could have agreed with all Beatrice had said without its affecting him. Ideas were flexible. It's feelings that got stuck in the mud.

She got up for a drink and feeling so much better stayed up and prepared dough for the following day's bread. When she got back he'd taken the bed over. She shoved him aside and lay next to him, turning over irritably and dragging the sheet with her, making him move and mutter.

Looking back she saw she'd stripped him and watching his body, naked as always, settle into its new position her eyes filled with tears.

The following day she was depressed. Things about Beatrice's company that usually excited her now made her feel hopeless. When she spotted her in the kitchen garden negligently trussing tomatoes she wanted to throw them at her. She'd gathered a small group round her and Mark was one. Sheila watched the active jaw from a distance and determined to keep away from it but Mark's excited bursts of laughter were too much for her. She joined them without their noticing and found they were talking about sex. At the mention of orgasms Sheila blushed.

"No woman's are hit and miss," Beatrice was saying to him, "they're as easy for us as for you if you know what you're doing."

"What if we don't?" He was grinning.

"We find out."

A surge of anger caused by both of them broke on Mark. She had expected Beatrice to be dismissive of what gave her no problems but Mark's face, grinning like a schoolboy, choked her.

"It seems it doesn't matter that much," he said airily, "or I expect we would."

She couldn't believe it.

"Oh, come on - fun in bed can see you through a lot!"

Mark suddenly became aware of Sheila and turned. His manner changed. "Security," he said, sure of approval - "knowing where you're going - is more important!"

"Can't you have both?" Beatrice said. "Where's the security in a dissatisfied partner?"

Bess was watching Sheila's face and broke in: "Beatrice, you're being dense. If there are other problems the fun side's spoilt."

Sheila looked grateful and Mark nodded. This time the agreement with Bess made her angry.

Joan moved in closer. Beatrice and Bess, on opposite sides for the moment, were so alike, she thought. Sheila would find no ease there either. Confidence or energy took them through most things. Perhaps those qualities were the bonus of a good sex life. On the other hand how did you get such a life unless you had them in the first place? She stood next to Sheila supportively.

"Sex is a priority," Beatrice was saying, "the rest stands a chance if that's alright. Complications of the sort you're making are a kind of hang-up - I swear it. Sexual pleasure is a matter of mechanics."

"Only if you're asleep at the time," Bess said angrily.

"We don't need mental frames of reference for a physical good time!" Beatrice was obstinate.

"Yes we do!" Bess replied and Joan was muttering agreement. "Anything getting in the way of the relationship gets in the way of sex."

"Are you sure? Are you sure it isn't something you're doing to yourself? Some of us can only enjoy sex when we find a way of approving it. A personal, limited, animal pleasure just isn't on. Most of us, women I mean, are still power-shy and body-shy. It's too easy to transfer old hangups to a more liberal field."

Bess made a noise dismissing the idea.

"You might be interested in a report I read," Beatrice said. "It didn't set out to stand old values on their heads but that's what happened. It set out to prove there was no difference in effect between vaginal and clitoral orgasms. They weren't disputing quality, which is purely subjective, just comparing physiological effects. They took a cross-section of women regularly having vaginal orgasms and a similar one having clitoral and found that vagina-oriented women had a lower anxiety threshold. The word 'depersonalisation' was used in connection with such a woman's view of herself and of a good experience. They suggested she had to spiritualise - to share not just possess her own physical response. A sort of abdication of self in the most selfish and sensual of pleasures."

Bess was ready for a fight: "Low anxiety threshold, depersonalisation - they describe a viewpoint, not a condition. There's no reason to suppose there's a sturdier sensuality behind one than the other. Perhaps the more anxious you are the more pervasive the pleasure needs to be. One of your depersonalisers could be sensually greedier - not giving up but improving her sensual rights!"

Mark was watching her as she spoke. His face, alight and excited, was a copy of hers. "And if you see anxiety," he said, "as responsiveness to others and the pressures they create, the experience looks richer still." He turned, suddenly remembering Sheila, but she'd gone and his shock, reflected in the group, broke it up.

Over the next few days Mark, while behaving in a way calculated to reassure Sheila, moved closer to Bess. Neither of them cosseted the feeling but acknowledged it. Mostly it took the form of spending more time talking but one of the afternoons was very hot and while the rest of the group were laid out indoors their vitality, kept alive by the situation between them, kept them working. The heat had a loosening and dissolving effect on Bess, making hoeing difficult, especially in a patch enclosed on two sides by the orchard and outhouse. Beating back from the wall it was half seducing half repellent and she loosened her grip, letting the hoe fall. Mark had intended to collect eggs, but had got no further than watching her from the orchard. He came behind to commiserate and put his arm round her waist. She'd expected to see Tom or Mary and looked up smiling while her body, going suddenly limp, forced him to tighten his grip.

"This sun isn't good for you, you shouldn't be in it," he said gently backing her to the wall. It touched, scorched and drove her against him. She waited for him to snatch himself away but felt him lever himself off instead. He'd put his hands on the wall over her shoulders, confining her. It felt like an invitation and the ravishing smell of his sweat made her raise her hands to his back where they moved in a passion of tenderness - amazing in its power to satisfy. She looked up but his mind was out of reach. His eyes were growing more brilliant as the marks under them darkened but his smile stayed fixed in the contrivance of compassion. Her spirits dashed, her hands stopped moving. When she looked again he was poised - turgid with sensation and balancing it like a full glass. He came to in a moment and looked hurt and reproachful - then guilty. Breaking away he picked up the hoe but instead of offering it held it. When he looked at her again his expression was asking her to forget it. She walked off, leaving him standing with the hoe in his hand.

She couldn't forgive him and avoided him all evening. It wasn't difficult because he kept his distance with the hang-dog look of someone who'd done wrong. Even that was dishonest - the full glass had been for him to drink fearfully and in secret. Just the same, the memory of it tormented her and by the end of the evening she wanted him more not less. What should warn her off inflamed a compassionate identification deepening the obsession.

For the few days following they were uneasy with each

other, and Sheila, when not blocking them out with work, noticed and wondered about it. Bess was aware of her attention but couldn't keep her mind on acting a part for her sake. Extremes of feeling were wearing her out. Her own guilt, mostly towards Tom but towards Mark as well, drove her into a rage of self-disgust, since essentially she seemed to agree with Mark's view of their situation and had no right to be angry at his accepting it. Alternating guilt and desire filled up the spare time left over from the hand-to-hand fight and surrender of constant contact. Personal decisions were so various they were meaningless. Unhappiness when Mark was rejecting her or she him was only balanced by the unhappiness of estrangement from her family.

Beatrice noticed her tiredness but finally put it down to overwork. Mark in terms of interest more than compensated for Bess's energy slump. He'd become more sharply aware - quicker, focussed, expectant, and she was excited again.

Even Tom reacted to the new 'buzz' he was giving the place, which made it easier to forget or at least balance against Bess's moodiness. These days Mark was ready for a chat, Sheila cool but on her toes and Beatrice a joy to be with - full of the life he couldn't find for the moment in his wife.

By the end of the week the group was 'high' and looking for outlets. One evening the children were playing a card game called Liar and the adults, put off at first by their screaming, ended up excited by it. The structured way their antagonisms were working out - it could turn into a battle any moment but never did - attracted first Bess then Beatrice and Mark. They were joined by the others, including Lionel who had been invited for a meal by Sheila since Mark had forgotten, and within minutes the children had become progressively more disgruntled intruders on adult fun and were fighting in earnest. Sheila came over to control them and was persuaded by Lionel to join in and sit next to him. Mark, who had conscientiously sat opposite Bess, made up for it by watching her every move and not letting her get away with anything. He challenged every time she laid a card.

Beatrice, as keen as everyone else to let things out under the rules of the game, shouted at Mark the next time he laid, "You've got two there, you sod!" and grabbing his cards made him take the pool.

Sheila kept winning - the result of a defensive game and telling the truth when the cards let her. On her third win Lionel put his arm round her: "So you should, so you should," he said, "goodness and virtue will triumph!" and brushed his lips against her hair in paternal approval.

The children, forcing themselves back into play, became hysterical at winning and tearful at losing.

"They're getting over-excited, we ought to stop," Sheila told Mark who, glancing at Lionel's arm still round her, sat in stiff silence moving only to slap down his cards. Tensely aware and supervisory of his own moves, he was in a mood to sit in judgement on others. He'd become rigid with jealousy at Lionel's familiarity with his wife and furious at his self-enforced separation from Bess. He banged the cards hard enough to make the table shake and covered the blast with intense irritation at an outburst from the children. Peter had won. Claude was punching him and Mark, screaming at them all to get to bed, reached over to haul Claude off his seat. Sheila was so preoccupied with Lionel that the incident took place without comment and Mark was reabsorbed instantly. It was a brief shock to the nerves, having on the adults as much effect as a sneeze. Bess, the only one attentive, interpreted it - as she must - as an expression of tension and frustration that gave more fuel to her fire.

Mark now caught the game fever a second time but in a different way. The whole objective became the lying. He put the wrong suit down every time whether he had the right one or not, and being challenged was a small price to pay.

Sheila, aware of this new excitement and tension, shook herself free of Lionel's arm and stood up. "This is a kid's game and they're not playing!" she said angrily. "Go and see what they're doing", to Mark. He got up instantly. "Help me get the supper?" to Lionel. He did the same.

Bess was furious at her success at breaking up the game and looked for relief in silent abuse. 'Pompous, bossy, not able to enjoy anything that didn't invite self-approval' came quickly to mind but she remembered her part in Sheila's tension and leapt up penitently to lend a hand.

At supper similar action took new forms. They'd pushed a bench against a wall for a back-rest and the table was laid in front of it. Drawing up the other bench they added a single chair at one end - the Welsh dresser was in the way at the other. Bess slid along the wall bench and beckoned to Mary but Mark managed to squeeze in ahead.

Beatrice found herself on the single chair and between Tom and Paul. Tom admitted to himself with unusually careless spontaneity how much he liked the arrangement and Beatrice, ever responsive, warmed to his attentions. Within seconds Paul felt left out. His silent disgruntlement forced the other two to be more exclusive. When the situation grew difficult Beatrice took Paul into account just enough to make Tom feel her handling of it was masterly and for Paul to feel he was being patronised. Tom was dazzled. Even when focussing on Paul her actions seemed to have a delightfully devious way of concentrating on himself. He blushed and glanced down the table to see if Bess was watching. She wasn't. She was bright-eyed from the pressure of Mark's body and looking restlessly over the table as if for food.

Joan who was opposite passed her plate of meat but Mark pressed harder against her at that moment and her other arm was flattened against the dresser. She looked pale. Joan served her, forking meat into her plate and looking questioningly at Mark to see why he didn't move. His face was turned to Mary as she and John were settling in and was full of that extravagant concern to make room and be hospitable she found so typical. He was so totally at their disposal with a crowd-relish she envied. At that moment even to Mark the source of his fanatic pressure on Bess's body was indistinguishable from its cover.

Raised voices from the other end of the table drew his attention away. Beatrice and Paul were now shouting - half fighting, half playing out a game that involved the others. Paul had embarked on a wife-swapping story and was concentrating on the delights of bedding a stranger. Mark heard Sheila say:

"I didn't know you were married."

"Neither did his wife!" The answer came from Beatrice who directed it at Tom - intimately but audibly.

Sheila giggled.

"I left her about a year ago." Paul tilted his head slightly towards Sheila and the bare fact created a momentary seriousness no-one wanted to encourage.

"You'd never get the stuffy lot round here to do it!" Sheila said smiling. Joan couldn't believe her ears. She saw Lionel having the same problem and glancing first at Sheila then at her empty glass.

Mark had turned to Bess while Sheila was saying it and raised his eyes in longing. The look, as intimate and sensual as slipping a hand up her skirt, was over in a flash. Having reached the point where no response other than desire existed Bess was amazed at so much objectivity. Was it a game to him? She regained enough consciousness to look closer and thought she saw an element of self-indulgence in the expression. He was taking comfort. Was it from the fact that he'd made thought contact only, something controllable, removable - deniable even to himself? He'd decided to read the body pressure as unavoidable - was he also asking for sympathy for the torment it caused?

Making nothing of her blank face Mark turned to listen to Beatrice's voice raised higher still:

"So what fun can you get out of making love to someone you don't know?"

"Straight sex. No frills." Paul's voice was excited.

"Why bother? Do it yourself!"

"Not so much fun."

She moved her head closer and lowered her voice: "You're so primitive!" The sexy mockery was to amuse Tom who glowed approval. "For some of us mating's got more sophisticated." Her body was almost leaning on Tom's but she was still facing Paul. "We've grown less dependent on the right smell at the right time. Something to do with more complex social conditions, do you think?" She'd turned to Tom.

The heaviness of the mockery at this point was so close to open war it brought in Bates. "Don't you believe it," he shouted, "it's women who make up the trimmings. It adds to their pleasure not ours - all part of the persons-and-personality consciousness of the female mind!"

They went quiet and everyone looked at Beatrice.

"Let me see..." There was a new openness in her voice that sounded like relief. Joan wondered if it was at the opportunity to lay off Paul. "As distinctly female this persons-and-personality consciousness must be developing at roughly the same time as our tits!"

During the giggling she turned back to Tom: "You're persons-and-personality conscious, aren't you?" She was smiling into his face while he nodded energetically, then to Bates: "If sex has no trimmings why are you handing out roles to play?" Her tone was changing again. "You move me, George, you really do. You're one of those men who modestly disown their understanding of the facts - almost as if they felt unequal to them. How do you get such a sense of incompetence? Just remember how well you understand the human factors at play when you want something. That's being persons-and-personality conscious. You'd be seriously disadvantaged if you weren't, and you don't look underprivileged to me. It's not ability you lack, only skill."

He couldn't make up his mind how to deal with it and the pause gave her time to redeploy:

"You may have mixed up your labels," she said, "p'raps you're calling some of your approaches objective or impersonal. We all do it" - looking round the table for compassion - "it makes us feel better while we're worsted by situations we can't control."

He looked angry now and uncomfortable but before he could attack she was smiling at him: "Our needs are objective of course but then people are always involved. It leaves only one way to an objective - by a subjective route!" He started to blush and she looked uneasy. She hadn't intended so personal at attack and changed her approach: "It could be the reason," directing her remarks to Sheila, "why some middle-class families try to even up the score by sending their sons to public school."

Nobody knew where she was going now but Bates perked up waiting for the right place to pounce. Tom was relieved she'd eased herself out of the fight and Beatrice, sensing it, turned appreciatively:

"You know what I mean," she said affectionately, "they're choosing a protected, confined environment for their males much like the one most females get - subjecting them day and night to the pressures of living in a family group with little contact with the outside world and only ideological reference to it. There's no escape. It forces them to develop social skills they wouldn't any other way."

Tom said nothing, waiting for her to back it.

"Well," answering his look, "few members of a family - public or private - are wholly congenial to any one of us. With the rest, in order to survive you work at understanding what's going on and why. Surviving guarantees the expertise you think you haven't got" - smiling at Bates - "and breeds a lifelong respect for the mental trimmings you imagine you're doing without."

Sheila laughed and Beatrice said to her: "You'd be surprised how much of the so called female mentality comes out under Public School conditions. I was reading the autobiography of an old Etonian and the author used the phrase as glibly as you" - glancing at Bates - "but applied it to his fellow Etonians. It brought out lots of interesting things. He began to see 'charisma', for example, as the perfect marriage of personality with the code it operates, and to see that all achievement of any kind had to be submitted before the supreme court of unwritten social laws. Most of all it was clear that to think of personality consciousness, morals consciousness, appearance consciousness, fearfulness of codebreaking or gossiping (which kept them all abreast of the endlessly changing social scene inside and out) as predominantly female characteristics was absurd. He realised - I can't remember if it was consciously or not - that it wasn't innately natural to either sex but very natural in the circumstances. There are toughies on both sides finding it hard to learn the skills but for socially rather than physically hard-pressed survival, which is what the world's up against now, we've got to. Ignorance about the way people think and feel and the reasons for it can wipe us out, so it's a skill we'd better take seriously."

Sheila glowed approval but there was something in it that made Beatrice add: "When you remember those boys must also do a deal with the macho image of ignorance about personal relationships filtering in from the world outside you can see their potential for understanding and diplomacy must be as good as ours. Fists and compartmental thinking are still seen as bringing in the biggest rewards."

Sheila was responding with everything she had - her elbows on the table and staring at Beatrice with a delight that when turned on Lionel produced a loving squeeze of her shoulder. She thought he too must be a hundred per cent behind it all but when she looked at Mark her fire went out. His face, tired and expressionless, seemed not to have heard.

"Go on," she said angrily, turning back to Beatrice.

"What about?" Beatrice smiled, "dreams of the future?"

Sheila nodded.

"I should think horizons (men's and women's) have got to come closer in before they move out. If we put just half the energy we've been encouraged to give practical matters into scrutinising ourselves and immediate groups we could be on the road to a new world - these after all are the new practicalities!"

"But men don't like that! They think their stupid codes will do," Sheila said resentfully. "The fact that codes change according to jobs and nations doesn't seem to bother them! Businessmen's are different from lecturers'" - darting a glance at Mark - "but it doesn't tell them anything. What's considered smart work and a sign of intelligence in one looks unethical and basically stupid in another. They're only similar in being equally sure they're right."

Beatrice nodded.

"Well, how do you teach them life? Life's relatively unimportant to them. They like being brainwashed."

"You don't mean that!"

"Don't I? The only family they work at understanding is the professional one. In that they get into such a lather over rubbish it uses them up. Sometimes it ends up meaning more to them than reality. Codes have got little to do with life but a lot to do with status quo and that's what they want to keep!"

"But we're no different. We get sensitised to specialist achievements and dishonours. It's easy to forget they're only that. If we ever work Mark's three-day week things'll look up, we'll have to look around and see what else there is. We'll get to know each other in different contexts. It's all this identification with groups that's a killer. The only thing it's good for is 'oohing' and 'aahing' over the garden fence. It makes members of a group more obvious as such than as individuals and that's so off-putting to outsiders that we can't be bothered to break them out of it. We tend to recognise each other by a fearful following of simple patterns and behind it the real contact, person-to-person, stays so primitive and stunted it can look like an impediment to higher and safer objectives. Recognising members of a group shouldn't be more important than job or nationality description but we use it to shield our dwarfed personalities. It's the simplification that makes groups ignorable or irritating. Either's dangerous."

"Well, what do we do about it?" Tom said.

"What we do without realising, I suppose, but it's time we did realise - our organised thinking won't be affected till we do. We ricochet from the various group rules operating in our lives till we come to a unique rhythm suited to ourselves. The conscious ingredient pushes down the barriers between them."

"I can do that already," Sheila burst out - "better than Mark anyway!"

Mark heard his name, looked up and smiled. It was the last straw. Sheila got up - "for more wine," she told the others but there were tears in her eyes. In the sittingroom she took wine out of the cupboard but put it on the table and sat down looking at the gap it left. In recoil from Mark her feelings for Beatrice were nearing idolatry. Everything Beatrice said seemed right but was producing a turbulence separate from her anger with Mark. She'd always kept her rhythm better than him, no question of that, but mostly by treating other people's experience like scenery - something that made life varied and exciting and where she could find things to identify with. Beatrice's responses had a different effect. For the first time someone else's experience had totally fitted her own and she was so alarmed at the violation of privacy she began to feel 'set up'. But for what? Feeling as suspicious as this was the result of experience and it was obvious who'd taught her! Set up and judged in her relationship with Mark, she expected it everywhere else. The thought that failure in close relationships, whether your own fault or not, made every contact stressful and that this, more than anything else, would be a barrier to Beatrice's new world, left her stranded and she found herself looking for a way out. It suddenly presented itself. If she finally agreed with Beatrice that we're all equally victims it made us all equally able to do something about it. Attitudes did change over the centuries so some of us must be active on our own behalf. She was surprised it had taken her till now to admit it.

Another idea pushed itself forward. All this time she'd been wasting her energy in fears of losing what she'd got when really she'd wanted something different. For several seconds she sat with a grin on her face enjoying a sense of wonder that became one of power - and not just her own. She was excited partly because admitting complicity gave her an active role (what she condoned needed her co-operation to succeed) and partly because it helped her see how things happened. Why for instance had she ever accepted his judgments when she'd had her own equally valid responses to build on? A trap can't work if you watch it being set. Part of her had always known what was going on but she'd never used the information because she hadn't trusted her judgment. On the other hand all she'd achieved by accepting his was a waste of time trying to live up to it, along with resentment that it wasn't hers. She'd gone along with it imagining it would make for less friction or greater closeness. What a joke! The line of least resistance led away from not into a relationship and if you took it you were being evasive and deserved what you got!

Underneath it all she'd always agreed with Beatrice. Your only power for good lay in your own unique response - and that she'd let rot. How could someone like that be good to live with? If he wasn't challenged by her irritability then he wasn't able to contribute - as a pair they couldn't adapt or change. It had been a way of ignoring or even using him and preventing him using her. Giving him his way at one level meant at a deeper one he'd be impotent because he'd never reached her and she'd be left with her inner world intact and in peace to go about its secret business. Not much movement to be had like that and the punishment was cramp. The secrecy meant she'd opted to go it alone, so he'd had no choice but to do the same. All her impulses had been to deactivate. Was he supposed to be grateful for that? All it achieved was mutual sacrifice.

Beatrice's view of simplification - that it was dangerous - came back to her and she saw it was she herself who'd most passionately insisted that their lives should be simplified and who'd always been bringing the rules in that pushed people out. It was even uglier than it looked because she didn't do it just from fear, which was understandable, but from contempt of life. She'd been really proud of her superior ability to stick to a moral diet of bread and water. She didn't trust life because it didn't live up to the rules she'd imposed on it, and as the rules looked fair she'd despised its failure. With contempt of this magnitude how could you feel you belonged except through self-disgust? Self-disgust made you lash out, not think out, and she'd been doing just that - at herself because she too fell short, and at him. She and he had always been at loggerheads without ever understanding why. Was it because they only appeared to have the same values in common? If things were as wrong as all this why had it taken Beatrice to make her see it? Perhaps she'd been wrong about everything. Perhaps it was she who'd turned Mark into a treacherous partner in a moral game and so caused her pain. Not even a game - 'ideal' would be a better word. Barter gave few grounds for respect and less for understanding. Her attitudes made any deviation from the bargain look like going back on it. She'd been sticking to it as if her life depended on it. She'd thought herself stronger than him at playing by his rules. The ugliness of the word 'play' struck her. She'd even believed it was the only way, finally, to belong. As if anything but reality could do that for you! The truth was he'd never once been valued for what made him as unique as his own thumbprint and she knew from experience it was the only kind that counted.

Her whole conscious view of herself had been wrong. She should have seen it years ago - there had been enough evidence! The only world it made her feel she belonged to was the practical one. In that she'd made herself useful and seen to it he did the same. The most staggering blow of all came in seeing that the only comfort she'd ever got out of her roles was the glamour she'd put into them. She'd been alone all the time because she'd been dealing in symbols. Company was the presence of other symbolists. She'd always seen herself as more sociable than Mark because she demanded less from others - and the opposite was true.

If the new way ahead lay in challenging herself and others she'd have to begin with Mark. The thought knotted her stomach. It felt like destroying. The old relationship had to go so why angst over it? She wasn't trying to lord, only love. Genuine self-expression made room for others because it depended on them.

In the comfort of this thought her mind went blank. When she came to she felt like a changed woman. Life was suddenly so exciting she didn't know what to do with it - full of the power and promise she'd always known it should be. Now she'd have real situations not constructed ones. In those you couldn't be bored or neglected, because you didn't bore or neglect. And it was all so obvious! Was this marvellous sense of freedom no more than coming to terms with it - the 'conscious rhythm' Beatrice was talking of? She shot out of her chair grabbing the bottles and made her way back to the kitchen.

Surely it couldn't be this easy to make an advance? Wrong word! Judgemental words defeated you before you began - prisons for the self-condemned. All the rules she'd made up for life had denied its existence. The real thing got shaped by a combination of deliberateness and spontaneity so compounded you didn't know where one began and the other ended. After all, what had felt like passivity had led her to this!

She stood still in the kitchen doorway staring at Mark. He seemed different. Less threatening, more exciting. She saw she'd never been either victim or victor. The bliss was in knowing it. She took her place at the table, looking round. What a survivor! Drop her into any situation and she'd land on her feet. Mark was a baby by comparison - ill at ease everywhere.

Beatrice and Joan were staring at her. They'd noticed a change and she drew them off by looking at Bates who was in full flood. She listened for the first time to what he was saying - something about biological reasons for male dominance. It sounded so juvenile she laughed - not annoyed but waiting for Beatrice to deal with it. He was winding up and looking rosy. The last remark was, "Real women don't try," spoken emphatically.

"Now George," Beatrice said, and Sheila laughed again, not because of the tone but because everyone called him Bates and this was the second time she'd pricked the impersonal bubble, "you know that isn't true. You keep equating sex with personality and they've got nothing to do with each other. Dominance depends on dozens of factors

- none of them sexual. Even your favourite monopoly, aggression, has no more to do with testosterone than oestrogen. You've only to look at the natural world - a male lion's a bluffer by comparison. It's the females with young who are totally unpredictable and manic enough to attack at any cost to themselves."

Bates opened his mouth but she'd already turned to her glowing listener, Tom. "There are so many myths around," she said. "I saw a TV programme the other night on a pack of females with young hunting at night and rearing without male help or protection. The scriptwriter, male no doubt, assumed the reason lay in what was seen to have happened, the lion had found a younger pride. It never crossed his mind he'd been elbowed out."

Sheila's guffaw drew attention and Beatrice directed the rest to her: "There were so many young, you see, it would be tough supporting a comparatively idle greedyguts and sex isn't a priority if you're hungry. If the younger pack had fewer cubs they'd make themselves available but if the pattern repeated itself he might find himself having to move on - unless he pulled his weight of course. We all do what we have to do. He wouldn't budge if he were comfortable."

Sheila's voice came in, strident but amused: "Female urges to support life are the strongest, that very fact makes them the more dangerous."

Beatrice, always steering the argument away from confrontation, took over again as soon as she stopped. "As far as individuals are concerned," she told Bates, "there are just as many forceful personalities among women as men. Aggression takes as many forms as there are people to feel it. Most intelligent men, like intelligent women, avoid an open fight unless they're hysterical or brainwashed and when aggression is a way of working off frustration we're equally dangerous. The only difference is that men's aggression has been encouraged for its social usefulness and it's no longer useful - it's a disaster. When it was useful it was a factor in sexual desirability. The opposite's true now. A randy pacifist outstrips the lot in the sexual stakes. If you think mindless self-assertion is a characteristic of high testosterone levels you can't think as much of your sex as I do! If it were true the race would have been wiped out before it got started. Whichever way you look at it we're in a better position now than we've ever been to enforce control in ourselves. Big fears override smaller ones. Sheer aggression now, for whatever reason it's provoked, can be massively organised and universally fatal. Even if your view of testosterone were correct, the danger would subside over the generations through natural selection. The high levels would find themselves sexually and socially disadvantaged which would limit their desire to give it expression, and genetic development depends as much on the principles of 'use it or lose it' as 'need it and grow it'. Think of Mark's dolphins living and working as a team! Danger is averted as a team and wherever possible without loss of life, even the enemy's. What's more they're always on the move and shift roles and positions in their society at will. They don't rely on your absolutes, George - they're too bright!"

It wasn't Bates who answered. Sheila had been staring at him - ready to pounce if he interrupted and now, sensing Beatrice had finished, moved in, preventing him. The ringing note in her quiet voice got their attention. "Up to now," she said, taking her time, "we've dominated best by pandering to your image of yourselves. But in one respect you're right, we are different from you. It's our total responsiveness does it. Men have either lost or never had it." The delivery was still easy but they felt the mounting intensity.

A general stirring of alarm fed rather than checked it, giving her next remarks an extra thrust. "You could say it's this responsiveness that prevents us taking over every aspect of your lives that finally has any meaning. Life-ignorance of the sort you describe could and sometimes does put you completely in our power. The kind of male you favour" - she was smiling - "doesn't know how he got there or how to get out of it or why life's such a battle. Finally he's got no hope but dependence on the generosity of unearned affection."

They were ill at ease, attention broke up but the burst of chatting stopped the moment she spoke again. "If we wished," she added thoughtfully, "and some of us do, we could seal him off from the sources of renewal like a dying leaf."

Beatrice suddenly found her tongue but her words were lost in a clatter of plates. Sheila had stood up and was clearing away - her mounting outrage retreated behind the noise she was using to prevent further challenge. The others were forced to get up and help and behind the din it came to her it wasn't just her relationship with Mark that had been an endless constraint but her passion for the commune. It had structured her life more, not opened it up! The interaction Beatrice had taken for granted she herself prevented - and how magnificent Beatrice's assumption was! The marvellous egotistical fairness of it!

The sense of power and freedom she felt over the next few days made her a stranger to the others and herself. Manner and moods were so quick-changing no-one could trace the logic behind the switches, least of all herself. Sometimes she felt she relished Beatrice's friendship more than anyone's in the world, but knew it wasn't true. Sometimes it seemed that for the first time she'd been treated with the total equality and frankness of one human being to another that should have been her birthright, and knew that wasn't true either. When tired she became uncertain and the new consciousness looked more like bondage than freedom. At these times it seemed she'd only herself to rely on - that tools had been put in her hands but it was up to her to use them. She felt Beatrice's influence then like a skiff caught in the sidewash of a cruiser.

Almost the worst aspect of the change was that it stripped away old defences. What she saw going on now between Mark and Bess - no matter how restrainedly - made her furious, and not just at them. She recalled the schoolgirl way she'd giggled at her responses to Lionel. It didn't seem possible she'd been so simple. The world was suddenly full of desires - not only sexual - and full of pain to self and others. The increased hungers and frankness about them sometimes made her so miserable she wanted to go back but found herself pursuing a relentless attack on anything blocking her way forward. The one escape was ahead.

The stress made other demands on her too great and here the children came off worst. She couldn't escape into the old role with them either. They were suddenly like herself, neither diminutive nor different. Now they were really reaching her she couldn't handle it and started behaving like them, screaming and lashing out. She panicked and lost confidence but was rescued by seeing the alternative. She watched herself doing what she'd so often done in the past - punishing in them the expression of what she'd been afraid to understand in herself. She wasn't any longer interested in handing down rules, only skills, she couldn't go back to being ignorant when she wasn't. All the stances she'd adopted for the sake of humanity now seemed terrifyingly indifferent to it. Passing on her own constraints might look inevitable but it wasn't, she only had to give up her emotional investment in them. Another possibility was equally unacceptable. If the next generation got free without her she'd be forced to see her loss in their fulfilment. She couldn't bear it.

Swinging back into power she felt as at first so different that the change was almost physical - like glowing after a run. On such a 'high' she had the resources to face up to whatever she found, and letting herself watch the behaviour of Mark and Bess more closely met another defeat. This time what came across was something she hadn't bargained for - a restrained but unbroken awareness of each other that was never completely usurped by other interests. They did and said things independently, even in opposition, but while seeming to ignore each other were testing the ground between them or building bridges. A helplessness emerged that filled her with pain. She was watching the responsiveness and sensitivity she'd longed for - something weathering anger and argument and drawing them closer. Their manner, neither purposive nor secretive, looked like a process of natural bonding. All the characteristics of the relationship that before had helped her ignore it now gave it greater significance. It hurt and confused her almost beyond endurance and looking for a way out only sent her round and round the emotional cage.

12

The group, trying to get into the old rhythm of work and leisure, found it more difficult over the next few days. They felt the need but were ill at ease with the old shape of things which now seemed somehow irrelevant or a distraction - not the real thing.

The real thing turned up a few days later unexpectedly when the children, responding to the general restlessness, got a wild ballgame going in the boxed garden. The noise first attracted Bess then Tom, with Mark and Beatrice joining them almost immediately. Within a few minutes Mary and John heard shrieks sounding like hot people jumping into cold water and dashed over to see what was going on. When they got there Mark was stretched on the grass at Claude's feet, purple-faced grabbing the ball. Claude fierce with excitement kicked it away. Bess grabbed it, ran with it, was tackled by Tom but Mary dashed in and took it from her and passed it to Beatrice.

It became women versus men. Mark hurled his body like a missile over Bess's feet and Mary, standing close to her mother, dropped back. Instantly the women, grappling and falling, were outnumbered. John had gone mad, throwing himself on top of anyone at random. Bess, already on the ground, shrieked when he crashed on to her hips. Mary came back in, hitting and pulling him off, freeing Bess to grab the ball to throw to Mark. Beatrice, shadowing him, assumed it was meant for her and knocked it out of his hands. Claude saw his chance. He nipped in dangerously to grab it briefly before John whisked it away. Mary stepped back, dismissing the pack of them, and went to comfort Simon. She saw Peter's expression was ambivalent - excited like Claude's and anxious like Simon's - and stood between them, a reassuring hand on each.

The game speeded up. The women, blinded with action, excited the men further. John, momentarily left out of the scrum, plunged back in, colliding with Tom and being lighter was hurled on impact into the bushes, carrying Peter with him. Simon burst into tears and the others took note.

John's comeback was checked by a transformation and marked a new tempo. Faces had taken on a reliable look. Excitement draining away made even Peter look disappointed but the compensation for him was finding a place in the game, where frail and nervous he let rip. Playing more gently, more consciously they found consciousness wasn't so much of themselves as of their bodies. Hands thick with blood and the rest of them doused with sweat they moved with amazing ease among inflamed, green-streaked torsos all looking different. Seeing it produced a new excitement and blending in it and subsiding as one they streamed through the back door looking for drinks and lapping round the inmates, Sheila and Joan. They drank, cooled off and drifted out leaving the others disappointed - but by evening the mood was back.

All of them were excited at the approach of dark. For Bess it made work impossible. When supper was ready she couldn't eat. The meal was quiet with unexpressed action - a communal pulse overriding individual initiative. She was tormented by Mark's eyes following her and blazing with life. Fear and desire had knotted into an unrelieved ache round womb and thighs that she carted from act to act like a separate consciousness. After a sleepless night she saw excitement had subsided but that they were still in touch.

Things had changed since the flood. All signs of fight between Sheila and Mark or Beatrice and Paul had disappeared, which left Beatrice restlessly looking for something to take its place. Sparring as a way of life was temporarily unavailable, her lust for Mark had died in his absence but hunting for a new absorption she found it taking place in Tom and Bess. Concentrating on them made her feel she'd been off-beam earlier. What was exciting here wasn't just sex but the interplay of powerful natures. Small talk or exchange of ideas in this group came over as strictly personal. Listening to them was actually a way of getting to know them, rather than an obstacle course. Like everyone else they tried to conceal themselves but failed more spectacularly and it was their subtleties gave them away. The more they spoke the more they gave. Silence concealed - it was a deadly success and this place was alive. The failure was drawing them closer. Perhaps it was this, unusual and exciting, that her senses had translated as erotic.

Bess, of all of them, gave most away and she found herself chatting most to her. In a short while she was talking openly about her public and private life and when she mentioned her ambition to be a publisher with a firm of her own the relationship took on a new dimension. Bess was captured. The workable mix up of idealism and materialism she'd seen and enjoyed in London began to take shape as a possibility for herself and she got excited.

The new activity between them started affecting the others - mainly through Sheila who grew tense as the friendship took off, partly from irritation at an intimacy she'd never had, partly feeling cheated of the little she'd enjoyed. She turned to the old source of comfort and worked harder than ever. This time it was the activity not the outcome she valued and the loss of faith made it manic.

Mark watched her go about the place scarred with exhaustion, seeming to approve herself for it and reproach them for inflicting it, and moved emotionally further away. He saw dissociation at one level and over-reaction at another and read it as a personality flaw. He knew the stress she was under but to him it was the stripping agent revealing her as she really was. In the new light all her relationships looked fake. The fact she didn't see it made her stupid - irritability resulting from her failure became disappointed egotism. It was a relief to admit to the revulsion that found its clinching justification in her handling of the children. She acted out that relationship as if they were dolls.

He found, within a few days, everything she'd been passionate about had become suspect and started to lose his own sense of purpose. Physically and mentally he became less accessible and Beatrice took note. With the group he'd found a way of being faultlessly sociable that made her desperate, so that she ended up leaving the room whenever he entered it. She became angry, as if he'd lost presence deliberately, and was so convinced of it that the stench of animals on his clothing acted on her like a stink barrier put there on purpose. In the Spring it had been a sensual message.

The contradiction made her follow him on his rounds one afternoon hoping to adjust the balance and in the long unsociable silences she watched what he was watching out of boredom. She noticed he'd mixed some new grey hens with the red. They were larger and more arrogant and hadn't settled the pecking order - there were several raw backs among the reds. Gurgling communication between the greys and obsessive scraping had such threatening overtones she looked up to see what he'd do about it but a mixture of admiration and disgust in his face was as far as he went. They moved on to the stable where the horse was almost asleep, blinking at him over the half-door. He ignored her and hosed his boots, Beatrice was suddenly overcome with compassion and stroked her nose. The short matted hair rubbed the wrong way and nipping yellow teeth set going the flow of life and warmth she hated him for lacking and she gave him up, turning her attention to the group. The flow had gone here too, or retreated to smaller groups. They'd broken apart and at first glance only Bates looked more at home - his insularity seemed to have found a more prominent place offering better opportunities.

He hadn't given up with Mary though the failure was rankling. He'd found before that young and ignorant had its disadvantages - it didn't know what it felt or which way it would move. Things looked unpromising but he persisted not because it was the only sport available or because she'd been interested earlier and might be again (that might have been vanity) but for the feeling that he was still in the game. He found being in his forties unnerving and with nothing to offer had a lot to prove.

The biggest drawback to proving it was the cover she still had. He hated the way the Blakes hung together after outrageously independent activities. They had astonishing tolerance of each other and were always in touch. Tom was a mystery to him. He disobeyed so many rules of the game he'd have thought his chances negligible but he looked happy. Was he half-witted not to see what his wife was up to or did he have his own fish to fry? The whole set up was irritating, giving an independent little room to manoeuvre. The commune had seemed promising but was proving a worse than average hunting ground. 'Togetherness' as an ideological move should have brought to the surface such rampant individualism he'd have had good pickings but the Blakes had a sub-community of their own that was affecting the rest and leaving him stuck with communal strains and no personal rewards. Sheila was a menace. Unpredictable emotionality over trivial issues was worse when she suppressed it. It was a form of stupidity he'd normally steer clear of but couldn't here - nor from Mark's brutal disregard of everything but the current mood! Finding a profitable course was so difficult the mere presence of other personalities was sometimes offensive and Beatrice's good-humoured approach one afternoon sent him over the top.

She'd come to plant radish seeds in the space he'd been hoeing and her confident scattering made a vassal of him. Inflamed, vindictive, he let fly the moment she mentioned Mark and his difficulties:

"If he'd fuck the woman he'd solve them!" - his voice was loaded. She started, pretending not to know what he meant. Bess's approach stopped him following through and screwed him up further. Looking at Bess, pressure mounting, "He's so moody," he said, "it's a wonder we stand for it."

He could tell by her colour she was with him - her weak "Who?" spurred him on:

"Our man of honour and leading light."

Bright-eyed, colour deepening, on the brink of angry tears she made to go but his next remark stuck its foot out:

"What's wrong with malice and lust? - we all feel it - only a fool thinks he's got it licked!" He watched her pick herself up. The pressure was easing and he was ready to take his time. "Control and fairmindedness - why waste your time? - it's dangerous too. A person like him gets his way - makes it easy for us to trust him, as if love not fear were behind it! We read him wrong - he does it himself - has to or cut his throat. Somewhere he knows it and it makes him vengeful."

"What about you?" Beatrice moved closer, blocking him off.

"Sure, but I know it, he doesn't. He's petrified by his own rules - never obeys one more than another, leaving no clues for himself or anyone else. His type gets tempted and suffers but never falls - at least not in the direction they're looking. Their motives look vital. No clue to their natures but one and it points in the opposite direction. Dictating to life's not living it, it's hate not love we're looking at."

"It's both. In some of us that's constructive! Mark's got his hang-ups but 'man of honour' isn't one of 'em." Beatrice edged closer to Bess as she spoke.

"So how do you think he justifies himself to himself?"

"He doesn't." The small voice was Bess's and could hardly be heard.

"Oh he does! Listen to him carefully some time - not to what he says but how he's feeling when he says it and why he says it and who to. What he won't take one way he'll make certain of another - he favours the moral web that lets him do it without knowing, and we're the victims. With no pattern to follow we can't defend ourselves. There's only one emotion he can't suppress, it's fear."

Beatrice had pushed herself between them. "You're right in one small point and that's distorted! If a loving man's driven to torment and be tormented he's not fearing the right things."

"Can't help feeling it's loving, can you - but think, all this re-routeing of animal energy on compassionate grounds -

what a bloody cheek and what self-deception!"

Slipping the packet of seeds into her pocket Beatrice took his arm, turned her back on Bess and drew him towards the house. "What's your suggestion, a free-for-all?"

"Why not? Love, friendship, even common humanity go down as fast his way, and to a fanfare of trumpets!"

"In your free-for-all how do they get born?"

He looked at her seriously but as if his next point made answering unnecessary: "If Mark knows, and he does, that thinking accurately about ourselves is impossible, what kind of man's got the brass to think for others? As for feeling for them, it disappears with the first whisper of inconvenience."

"And comes back with the first prompting of need."

He gave a slight smile, asking if she put her faith in "a sort of generous egotism". She shrugged and raised her eyebrows.

"It's not as easy or clean as you make it sound", he said. "People fear and despise themselves more than anyone else. Look at Selby and Mark - that's mutual recognition based on self-knowledge. And don't think Mark's rules slow him down - they egg him on! Straight fear would do a better job. Calling fear and aggression something else is only freeing yourself to act. It may seem a touching state of affairs but the social approval it's aimed at makes things more dangerous - the additional stimulus makes murderers of us all. In the light of it we look strong and generous, because of it we're neither - it prevents us facing facts!"

"Some of us!"

"Mark then. If he accepted his lusts or objectives for what they were he'd accept his antagonism to what got in the way. That way it's a straight fight and he's got to decide if it's worth it. Such a man's brought in range and can be dealt with in any one of the million ways a victim escapes a predator. If he disguises it to himself we're done for. He doesn't recognise his moves so we don't. He's not prepared so we're not. The signals are confused. If he actually succeeds in self-suppression things are worse. Lust for life is converted into a power to control it and the explosion of will that's been necessary exposes us to fallout we never survive. The effects take a lifetime to show. Perpetual contact is a killer that escapes detection even after its victims die of it. We're contaminated by those particles of will that should have held him together as an egocentric unit and are disseminated by the explosion that's changed their structure. Against the new structure we've no defence. We know something's wrong but there's nothing to fight but ourselves. It produces a leukemia of the soul and death is attributed to other causes. How can success of that sort be either protective or love-induced? It's inimical to life."

"You've got it back to front!" The voice, coming from just behind them was Bess's. "If your view of life were right we'd still be single cells." She'd gone away like a whipped dog and come back, driven by anger and a fear that dictated she deal with him now if she didn't want him a threat for the future. "Everything you are is inimical. Being limited to a limited self with an even more limited view of itself is more dangerous than anything. Mark wants things you've never felt the need of, taking risks to get them you know nothing about. The only failsafe he's got is love, which was the driving force in the first place. Love's a form of interest and curiosity that momentarily puts the object of it before everything and can do it again and again, but it comes from an appetite sharper than yours. Yours is so small it brings in just enough to keep you ticking over. If that were enough for the rest of us we'd still be single cells. Hungers, attractions, curiosity amounting to desire is the only thing exposing us to change. Snapping up what's easy keeps the status quo. Timorous wills go nowhere and those on the lookout for richer sources have to manage the journey as best they can. It's these that are supportive. They find more than they need or expect, and we profit. Your sort are a menace for their lack of sympathy and the blindness caused by it. It can't value what it doesn't understand. All of us need challenge but for simple souls the challenges are simple. In most of us more complex emotional demands evolve from satisfied simpler ones. Yours are only useful for keeping going what *is* long enough for it to become what *might be.* It's your kind of fear and passivity that puts the moral abstracts you hate in power. It can't understand that real action's driven and rewarded by love. Love's so important that if you remove it from people it'll attach itself to objects - even ideas. It's so basic a force it'll convert to anything to get expression, even its opposite. The will to live is the will to love."

Bates made an angry move that Beatrice countered by putting out her hand and speaking in a way that identified with his feelings while bringing back the original target. Trained like a bullfighter she offered him a chance to score without damage:

"An oddball, Mark" - she was walking away again - "fearful and powerful in equal proportions."

The interruption took him by surprise. With no answer ready and only anger to express he followed her.

"No need to despise him" - deflecting it had made her sound contemptuous - "for not recognising what he's up to. Not recognising one's animal behaviour is thoroughly animal. We all need cover to protect our idle moments and conceal our active ones. Take away our old, we look for new!"

"If you burnt all the bushes there'd be nowhere to hide!"

"So Bess was right." She paused and smiled. "You are the moralist."

They reached the house and separated. Beatrice, who'd been interested and moved by what Bess said, had personal disappointment to deal with first. She realised, in much the way Sheila had, that she'd known all along about the relationship between Mark and Bess. Bates' comments only put it in a new perspective. She'd even assimilated it in a similar way as a source of lively disturbance not to be treated seriously. Even now she felt Bates was so crudely right as to have missed the point. Mark had been sexually dead to herself and she had to get over the disappointment of finding him awake somewhere else, but the new perspective didn't deeply disturb her. It was interesting that Tom seemed to have reacted in a similar way and she found herself transferring attention for the while to him.

Tom, missing the old Bess, found himself getting more and more from his Bess-substitute. The mixture of love and irritation in Beatrice's responses to men delighted and brought him closer than he meant. Her militantism was accepted because he felt it was basically gentle and constructive - in any case he felt supportive of people having a hard time making society see sense, his own predicament made him highly sympathetic. Her play and attack felt like the ball-game all over again. There'd been something in the women's tackling - a close assiduity with undertones of irritability making it impossible for any of them to react in a controlled way - and it had been wonderful! They'd all wanted contact more than competition.

He'd learnt to love this kind of challenge - restless, not inimical - through Bess, with her it had developed into an active intimacy he couldn't live without. Beatrice seemed to pinpoint its universality and in making him more conscious of its value reinforced his sense of security. All the battles with Bess that could have been threats had turned into promises. Even her interest in other men found positive outcomes. Earlier, when his jealousy had made her clamp down, her quietly angry rejection of himself and life in general had frightened him more. He'd felt she could only control this aspect of vitality by dismissing the lot. Her withdrawal from himself, more painful than the threat, had made him look for ways of accommodating her nature without being damaged by it. It was easier when he realised that without sex those relationships could even be rewarding. Mark was a man who couldn't handle the attraction and so not much to be feared - and now in his own feeling for Beatrice he was for once following the course he'd learnt to live with.

Unlike Bess, Beatrice was mistress of her sexual world and could carry her feelings to their logical conclusion. The likelihood of his following through was slight but the possibility added spice to the friendship. She was more independent than Bess, less interested and involved with others but replaced what was missing with a warm academic involvement, which was something he could identify with. He'd seen himself like that before he met Bess. Beatrice's confidence could take accident in its stride. The odd shaken marriage was an acceptable hazard - if it were living it'd survive, if not she'd have done it a favour. Her ease in the world was greater than his own and the opposite of Bess's. In fact she was so easy she could handle Bates without making an enemy of him - no mean achievement - and Paul looked happy with her attacks and defections.

Over the next few days Beatrice and he consolidated the interest neither was afraid of. They spent more time together and Bess, unconsciously aware of the slackened attention went headlong for Mark. One night she found herself chasing Simon to let off steam. The other two children were already in bed reading - he'd avoided capture. She made her pounce at the foot of the stairs where Mark, waiting for his goodnight kiss, was half leaning against the wall watching. As Simon was lifted Mark's head went back - eyes shut and mouth opening in anticipation of the wrong kiss. He came to and gave the peck the boy expected but Bess was so weakened by desire while carrying the boy upstairs that Sheila took pity on her exhaustion and sent her back down.

Mark was as she'd left him. She meant to pass but scooped his hand and they moved to the shadows where she hugged him hard, frightened he'd pull away and trying to wear herself out in the grip. He pulled back to reach her mouth - swerving at the last minute and just touching her lips with his beard, so she transferred expectation to her hands moving passionately over his bottom, but now pleasure turned to hunger so fast she had to stop and they separated. Exhausted by defeat they only glanced back long enough to reassure themselves of the other's need.

The following morning after a sleepless night, guarded and saddened they were evasive of contact but alive to every possibility of it. Mark's plottings to 'have' her became a form of consummation allowing him a sense of action. He made up pretexts for leaving the farm and collecting her on the way like an afterthought. Others always joined them. He showed no surprise or irritation and Bess knew how to interpret it.

After a while he spent most of his time on his own which better served his alternating purposes of pushing her out or locking her into his mental world. Long hours in the heat were a hated joy and the obsessionalism communicated itself to Sheila who once she noticed a work fever matching her own sought it out. In a very short while her hard work put him off his own. He saw it as a blind mania for their 'cause' that put him in touch with something similar in himself. Sacrificing specific desires for all-embracing ones had been automatic and in the light of her trivial catechism looked it. Having to face up to real choices for the first time in years drove him wild.

Sheila's presence began to suffocate him and tension reached a head when after lunch one afternoon Paul started talking to him excitedly. While clearing cups from the sitting room Sheila had caught the drift of the conversation. The two men were facing each other on the sofa - Paul passionately interested in the new technologies being developed in his physics department, Mark listening. It was Mark's expression that made her pause as she reached between them for a cup, then grabbing it suddenly she spilt the dregs down his trousers. He steadied her wrist, annoyed at the interruption, and the fierceness of the grip felt like a warning. She turned pale with rage.

"Don't you see what he's saying?" Her tone, sneering and quiet, stunned them to silence while they recovered from the violence in it.

Paul apologised: "Nothing bad, I promise. I want the same things you do." He was lost. Mark, looking contemptuously past her at Paul, puckered his mouth. Paul's instinct to get out was checked by guilt and feeling responsible made him doubly defensive. He stood up and put his arm round her. "Nothing's wrong." He was anxious and emphatic. She allowed the arm, stiffly. "My technology wants what you want but think you only achieve by cutting it out." He was desperately searching for a way of convincing her. "When all's said and done you've cut yourself off." Regretting it instantly and covering his tracks: "Telly and travel for instance, in keeping us informed are really drawing us closer!" - he gave her a symbolic squeeze - "and if you think about it, it forces us to be more of the open, sharing society you want."

She said nothing.

"Cutting yourself off from something," he said, "only makes you a potential victim of it - it's best to take it on board and find a balance with it. A sort of restless balance gives potential for change without dangerous lopsidedness, and fanatics find that politically impossible to exploit. Dangerous people become a minority - Mark agrees!"

What he thought would be the clinching argument drove her out of the room. Barely listening she'd been staring at Mark. On her own in the kitchen, cup in hand, she realised it had become a habit relying on his singlemindedness about the commune and now she thought about it it seemed even her sexual feelings had been linked with the idea of his purity of purpose - it had seemed to give him power and made the cost to herself worthwhile. Seeing herself left as the sole custodian of the values they'd started with didn't seem to matter. She didn't need him. She'd felt for a long while his emotional needs trivialised and endangered the enterprise. What she'd seen a moment ago hadn't even been conversion - just subversion.

By evening she'd reached a balance and calm they hadn't seen in her for a long while and as the group relaxed she took things a step further, suggesting they take the following day off. They jumped at it. Even Mark came alive at another stillborn opportunity.

Joan decided when they set off that this picnic was going to be pure pleasure. Sitting next to Mark who was driving she gave herself up as usual to the view. This time the roads took her eye - dominating the hills, streaming in the valleys, their gleaming corpuscles crisscrossing at speed, dispersing not concentrating energy. On the high roads roaring winds beat back conversation and the impact of the outer on the inner world made her so 'high' she had to get free of the others at the first opportunity to feed it.

They paused at a village post office. On the other side of the road a man sat on a low wall reading a newspaper and thrust-out sunburnt legs focussed her excitement. She crossed, saw their position tensed but easy and smelt the hot thatch over his head. A surge of new energy took her past him and along the cottages towards five house-martins nests at eye level under the eaves. One was occupied, with two heads jammed in the gap between eaves and nest, pointing over her shoulder. Obsessive, vivid, suspended in mud and stick a couple of yards from the road, their heads moved synchronised towards a sound she couldn't hear - uncluttered energy, in each moment of expression stronger than forces in and around it and altering what caused it. She couldn't get past it. In a confusion of feeling she went back to the car and when they drove off found she'd become more objective towards people and place.

She noticed for the first time that Autumn was close and her downward rush of response made her look for the weeds that had dazzled her earlier. A forest of skeletal stems rigid on the banks moved her eyes to the hill slopes where scorched gorse was now balanced by ploughed fields gleaming in a slanting light. Random impacts were suddenly manageable. Strips of stubble burnt and burning were cancelling summer but blazing with life. A buried excitement stirred. Part of her wanted the visit to be over but a sense of loss too strong for it made her loathe the old refuge she looked for in loneliness. She watched Mark's shoulders tensed at the wheel and thought of Matthew and in the blaze of life that followed saw decisions she'd made without knowing it. Now it didn't seem to matter if he were attached to someone else or if nothing came of it - what mattered was what she felt. Presenting itself as energy she'd understood what released it - an acceptance of the relationship as more important than the pain and confusion it could bring. The unexpected bonus was confidence. Releasing feeling had released the ability to deal with it.

Over the next few days she found herself looking round happily for corroboration - not from people so much as events - and found she was drawing closer to Bess. The shift of perspective made her see her, Beatrice too for that matter, in a new light. The mental and physical horseplay they loved began to have meaning for herself. It was more than a way of waiting on or sifting events - it stirred them up and disturbance made room for possiblity.

Beatrice noticed the change and commented, "You look happy!" as they passed in the hall. The loudness of it drew Bess's attention, she had one foot on the stairs - and Sheila's too and she came to the kitchen door to say, "Come on, you three, give me a hand." Beatrice and Joan went instantly but Bess hung back, assessing the chances of nipping off without offence.

"Are you coming?"

She followed, muttering something about promising the kids a game. Sheila raised an eyebrow and in allotting them their jobs paused to watch Bess fussing in a drawer for a sharper knife.

"You'd play your life away, wouldn't you?" She got no answer but needed one. "Don't you need work? I'd drift without objectives."

Beatrice was pounding the dough that had been pushed her way and grinned at Bess over her shoulder.

"I need fun," Bess said apologetically.

"We all do!" The slight impatience in Sheila's voice gave Bess an unexpected ally:

"She looked low when I saw her earlier," Joan said gently. "We can manage on our own, can't we?"

"You're dreadful, all of you!" Bess's assiduous chopping told Sheila she'd won, which made her happier and even more confident. "I expected you to support her," she said glancing cheerfully at Beatrice - "but not you," to Joan. Joan's look of alarm made her redirect: "Fun's as good as happiness for those two!"

Beatrice let it ride but the kneading grew more energetic, bringing her to the point where it was a stimulant not a sedative. "Well, what's the difference?"

The scoff from Sheila was only half playful.

"Happiness is better?"

Now Sheila didn't answer.

"How can a permanent state be on? If you want an objective, fun's all you can arrange for - happiness is an accident." The dough, stuck fast to the board, started thumping. "Anyway, what makes you think fun doesn't make us happy?"

"Some of us need some reason."

"Then some of us are done for!"

Joan smiled.

"At what point do you tell yourself you've reason?" Beatrice said, half directing it at her. "Wellbeing's all that counts. Look, Joan can feel it and she's only peeling spuds."

"I'm not taking part - you're on your own," Sheila told her crossly.

"Well, your rotten objectives give me a sense of failure"

Sheila frowned, feeling the centre of activity slipping out of her control. "I mean," she said in an effort to bring it back, "some of us need more than mindless wellbeing to be happy."

"I know what you mean and you're wrong. A stampede to objectives crushes our chances. What if my one objective's to be happy? For that I've got to take on something real, and real people and real events are great killers of objectives. It means objectives change so much there's no point in calling them that."

No comment.

Beatrice glanced at Sheila's squared shoulders. "You know happiness isn't different. It's anything and everything and if it's not permanent it's renewable. It's the afterglow of involvement and involvement's riddled with pain and discontent." Sheila was set against her and she turned to Joan: "I hate her angle - ideals, duties and suspicions! Time off from judging your progress is for indulging the sins you see as obstacles. She's a romantic which is the same as calling her a cynic - two sides of one coin minted by self-love and ignorance."

"Now you've done it, you know-all spouter!" Sheila sounded angry but hardly more than a moment ago. "You think you know, but nobody does. Nobody knows what they need to be happy."

"Exactly! That's why I am."

Joan's laugh was a noisy event forcing her reluctantly into it: "Part of me agrees but I'm never that sure. Not of what I'm seeing, interpreting, even feeling - so it's all qualified."

Sheila looked grateful.

"Don't you believe her," Beatrice said to Sheila, "she's making it up. A baby - a dog - knows and reacts accordingly. The only difference is you're bogged down with guilts and confusions associated with your objectives. We all know what we all need and how we all operate. When you don't block it happiness is easy because identification and involvement are." Sheila, not ready to give an inch and keeping silent made Beatrice defensive: "I haven't got your confidence," she said, staring at her back - "how do you find the guts to live off symbols? - because that's what you're doing. Images of relating. They're too insecure for me, specially since men and women use different ones. I can't link happiness to attitudes." She'd ended up looking at Joan who was still with her, but it wasn't her voice that answered:

"You make it sound easy but it isn't." The abstracted tone was Bess's. "When we carefully adapt the machinery of attitudes we grow up with to be 'in sync' with our own, changing can immobilise us - for a while anyway. It's not because we're lazy or frightened but because they were part of a growth pattern that takes time to reshape. For a while nothing seems to happen. It's a matter of redirecting energy and exploring the new space. Failure to move out of a mental rut is a physical one made worse by being linked with a physical need to sustain habit. Physically we need a status quo to survive. We're millions of cells and viruses locked in a self-renewing pattern to which rhythms of repetition and dependence are basic and keep us from breaking up and flying into separate molecules. Our bodies work with what is, as it is, which predisposes us to be subject to both - even to maintain them when they're losing their value. We're capable of perpetuating misery because it's known and, however badly, been adjusted to." She seemed to be talking to herself and the others felt like eavesdroppers. "A temporary mental-emotional paralysis sometimes seems to need superhuman effort to break. Anti-change and retention go deep. We can make our reality out of anything - even illusion."

"But we don't have to feel trapped," Beatrice got in fast, "we're in control, which though it's the cause of our trouble is our only way out of it. If we were totally victims of training and biochemical patterns the next jolt from either source would shift the balance. What's more, all our chemical blueprints are slightly different, which means in affecting each other we're changing ourselves all the time. We're used to adaptation! What causes the problems is the masterplan - the built-in override that lets us act consecutively rather than together. It gets in where it has no business." Her suspicions were aroused again of a certain passivity or indifference in Bess's responsiveness and Bess, hurt, wanted to bring her round:

"I'm only saying it's not as easy as you'd like it to be because we're on the lookout for condition-sustaining environments. Look at Selby - it's no use writing him off as vengeful and destructive, he's that because he's sustaining the environment he's learnt how to live in, and doing it by producing it in others. It's not just your own pattern of struggle and adjustment that gets established but dependence on the specific conditions producing it. Even if your overall feeling is of defeat and misery you've still established a workable balance or you'd be insane or dead, and it includes the triumph of achieving it. There's positive encouragement in coping negatively. The most confined experience is studded with real rewards and our bodies have a chemical memory of every one of them. As physical beings it's the chemical memory that counts and dictates the next step. The only feelings we can hanker for are the ones we've had. Ideas - however well they fit our natures - even if we're adapting and working them out as we go along - aren't valid till we've felt them. Decisions have to be stillborn unless circumstance gives them life - nothing grows in arctic acts of will."

"What if we're desperate and totally believe in them?" Joan's nervous voice brought out a warmer tone:

"If we're desperate it'll work. Desperation means there's a lot of life-energy still available and we're ready to take chances. Otherwise we need 'pulse' experience to verify every step of the way. Without it we're asking ourselves to make a leap in the dark similar to another leap or transition where nothing's proven - and unless we're desperate we avoid that just as hard - real change is always a matter of life and death." She felt apologetic and that she still hadn't squared it with Joan enough. "Beatrice seemed to be asking for some kind of abstract decision-making, and that's so useless that new convictions end up as new descriptions of old habits. Living things only make radical changes if they feel the present situation's killing them. Most of us, most of the time, try not to. If the stress is endurable but restrictive of what's unique in us we start imitating those feelings that haven't been naturally generated. That's when happiness looks impossible and seems like an unreal objective."

Sheila came over wet-handed without speaking and Bess, looking at her frightened expression said quickly, smiling: "I agree with Beatrice really - I wasn't easy with her confident tone, that's all. Understating a difficulty makes a new one. My feeling is that we can all be happy but we've got to know the strength of the enemy."

"Our physical selves?" Beatrice was half shouting, half laughing. "Now where've I heard *that* before?"

Bess pressed her lips together and after a moment said, "You're obsessed with the idea there's something anti-physical in me - that these are my old habits dressed as new convictions but honestly I think you're wrong. My physical self is the only bit I trust. Constriction of it in some form or other is the only thing that makes me move. You should be the last to doubt me. As women released from 'confinement' and newly on the move we're changing social attitudes faster than anyone could have dreamed, but as individuals how do you completely separate impersonal from personal drives? Our different mixtures of them make up unique response and in that you're no different from me. The experience we've got in common as women is our sex's concern with what's living and changing rather than fixed and dead, and the active inclusion of it in a new society marks the beginning of its adulthood. Our adolescence hasn't just been a matter of undeveloped capacity but the shortage of experience in part caused by it. As a result we've all had to rely on the glamour attached to attitudes to get us going. The extra, highly developed experience we're releasing into society is making it possible for us all to capitalise on endowments we all start with. The sexes are born with equal potential for associative and dissociative intelligence but when sexual rewards are identified with one or the other we find ourselves constantly assuming the reward position - as far as racial maturity is concerned we can forget it! Sex and life are so *one* that from whatever circumstance gratifies it, however indirectly, we get a pulse training near impossible to move beyond while carrying the same needs with us. Men and women have been approaching the world from opposite angles. Mark's dissociative approach makes him a compartmental thinker with associative hankerings. It's not the dolphins he's most interested in, it's us. We're closer to the dolphin objective."

Beatrice had to have one more jab to be sure the structure was sound: "I'm still not sure about you! That retention theory could only come from a 'depersonaliser' - someone already half way to breaking up into the precious molecules that get her eyeing death with lust. How else can the ultimate flexibility be achieved? How else do we finally realise our potential for re-forming as something new? You've got the physical and metaphysical too mixed up."

"They are mixed up."

"Haven't you noticed how like Mark you are?"

"We want the same things, that's all. He sees it as something to organise - I don't. Getting the right balance is a private, personal achievement - a dissociative viewpoint but one that emerges from an associative lifestyle. Because it means being given up to everything, structure defeats it. In my view there's no need for self-preparation more than recognising need. Our approaches couldn't be more different." She gave Beatrice a worried look. "Your anxiety about me, why's it there? If spontaneous response to unavoidable impact brings in the goods, it's not surprising if my view of death gets included. Even so all it does is make me want to live longer and more. Exposure brings in more to live for. Having things to live for is security - nothing else is! I'm always after interest and affection and never know how they'll arrive. My faith in the impersonality of events is for that reason. The only constant for me is interest and it's the only form of love that breeds. If the terms I use put you off, forget them. See me as like yourself having to reach unconscious knowledge by a conscious route but in so far as I'm not you, taking a different one. We want the same thing - more life."

"And your fear of more?"

"No worse than yours. I go under so easily fear's almost as strong as need - sometimes stronger. In me passion threatens everything. I fight for balance every minute and chart my life through losses."

They accepted what she said. Beatrice and Joan felt released and reassured but for Sheila understanding Bess was another trap and got in the way of caution.

Joan was excited because her own experience corroborated what she'd said. The games Bess played were for Bess a serious business - a life-necessity. Mental or physical play put the components in flux, changing their shapes and energies long enough for a new interactive life to emerge which could develop as opportunistically, given the space, as life itself.

Beatrice felt at home for the first time because she felt she could take this friendship on trust as she had as a child. It no longer mattered that Bess was different - suspicion of what she didn't understand could be dealt with moment by moment, as then. Bess's honesty made her visible. Being able to see she was dangerous made her trust her - and there was something more. Most of us carried our cages in our faces while hers, even as she spoke confusion and confinement, looked ready for anything. The sense of release in her company set free the old dream of finding a suitable partner in a publishing business. Suddenly it seemed not only a possibility but an immediate one. She could work with this woman - especially if Tom came with her. What she needed now was to get back to London, look up friends in the business and see what the possibilities were before mentioning anything to Bess and Tom.

Paul had been ready to leave for some time and the next day they told Sheila they were going. The others, especially the Blakes, did their best to keep them and when faced with their obstinacy decided to share part of their journey - at least as far as Paul's aunt's where they'd arranged to stay overnight. When the time came something in Mark's manner made a group trip impossible. In the end it was only Joan who went and she felt pressurised into it.

It was at Paul's aunt's she first noticed uncomfortably that Mark wanted something from her. He was more interested in watching her than saying goodbye. She wasn't able to give anyone anything and could only reflect in her face the vague well-meaning interchanges going on round her but for him it seemed enough.

On the way back he stopped the car at the top of a slope to the sea. They were looking at a wide flat watersoaked place where an enervating merger of sea and land made the sea look still as drainage. The indeterminate under an empty sky made her uneasy - he felt the same but it was looking at her that released it. He followed her back to the car feeling an affectionate almost passionate familiarity that seemed to have all the advantages of love and none of its pain. The peace and closeness between them had a similarly releasing effect on her. She felt freed to take in the world for herself and suddenly recognised a hill slope she'd seen earlier in the year when it was pink with ragwort - now it was bristling with the dead energy of its sticks. In spite of a sense of loss her feelings had moved on and when she got back to the commune she sensed that something similar had happened there - the removal of Beatrice and Paul had let it flourish.

It was a few days later that she walked into the kitchen and into a battle between Sheila and Mark they now seemed to be making no effort to conceal.

"So where are they?" she heard him ask.

"Frank and David took them fishing."

It took a second for the information to sink in and he was in the hall, his back to Sheila, when it did. Sheila, looking triumphant, was in fact a little amazed at the ease with which she'd asserted herself. She started humming. He heard it at the same moment as seeing Bess and Tom come down the stairs relaxed and flushed and with their arms round each other. Joan saw Bess smile at him with a freshness and ease that seemed to hurt him to frenzy and then walk past him to the source of the cheerful notes in the kitchen. Sheila was joyously out of reach. In fact she felt she'd not only won a battle but that the victory had romantic undertones. The children had gone with the Selbys to Lionel's town like undelivered messages.

Joan heard the street door slam and the Landrover start - it was followed by a brittle cracking sound that drove her to the window where she saw him swerving away from the rhododendron bush. A branch of it fell off the bonnet as he turned the corner.

Mark's fear and sense of loss overwhelmed him on the way to Warford, where he knew Selby did business every Friday. Pain and anxiety had fixed on the children and terror had turned to guilt. If he'd told Sheila about his fight with Selby even she wouldn't have let them go. Worst of all he'd killed the dog! He'd set the terms. Mutual destruction conducted in secrecy with the naturalness of life. He pictured Selby needing to say no more to David than "Be extra careful with the baby" - the machinery of violation and violence would do the rest.

When he came to the place where they'd fought he was so deafened by terror it took him seconds to hear the splashing and laughing and Claude's voice over it. He saw their heads in the river bobbing and ducking. Claude caught a frightening image of his father on the bank and swam towards it. Simon, up to his chest in muddy water, looked and started to cry. One by one they came out and stood shivering in the sunlight. Claude fetched their clothes, expecting punishment and within seconds longing for it.

David dressed and waited for them. Indifferent or ignorant of the strain he followed them back to the car and as its doors shut him out shouted, "See you tomorrow!"

13

Out of relief Sheila accepted the return of the children without question - neither of them spoke about it and when Claude asked why they weren't supposed to go swimming she pretended she hadn't heard.

Confused, guilty, unsure if there'd been a danger except of his making - seeing the more alert to it he was the more he created it - everything in Mark's life seemed suddenly to have lost purpose. The only living feature of it was his passion for Bess and he was more afraid of that than anything. He spent the next couple of weeks haunting Joan - constantly looking for her, working with her, sitting with her at mealtimes and talking to her - assiduous for her opinions as if he'd found an oracle. She was the only one he really listened to, which quickly made the obsession irritating to the others. Bess watched him frowning with the effort of tailoring his responses to fit Joan's in an attempt to adopt her viewpoint. When he achieved the kind of understanding he needed he looked relieved - lightened in face and conduct. For him Joan had a balance, a warm and now lively dissociativeness that he wanted more than anything - far more than passion. She had a place in the commune he couldn't achieve, one that seemed to keep her free at the same time as holding her poised in the middle.

Part of him knew Bess was better at it than anyone but mistrusted what it knew - it wasn't dissociative. He saw the intensity in her and potential for it in himself as burning away the surface sensitivity that kept us more vividly alive than passion - not just to others but ourselves. He'd begun to feel his relationship with Joan was the ideal one. It was what love should be - a couple balanced and in tune, undemanding yet offering everything in an ultimate refinement of consummation without the alcoholic poison of sexual possession.

The protection the relationship gave him was perhaps what irritated the others most, especially Bess. To begin with she'd seen it as comfort-seeking and in that context a reaction to her own phase of withdrawal. She'd been trying to get on top of her feelings by consciously holding back from answering the demands he did make, on the grounds of his refusal to meet her answer, but after several days she started to see the new refuge as a threat .

One evening, hearing him playing his violin, she came into the sittingroom from supper to find Joan there lounging against the table absorbed in the sonata he was wrestling with. She saw her face soaking up the effort and emotional determination - saw it accept the dedication of the experience to herself - saw not only the pleasure it gave but the sympathetic identification it aroused and saw in his swaying towards her a physical and emotional gift of himself that made her walk out cold, blasted with jealousy.

For a while it killed all response. Her behaviour with him became mechanically friendly, but that dictated she take part more, almost in the old way. The apparent speed and flexibility of emotional movement seemed to make things better for him. He seemed grateful. It irritated her further. He kept Joan by him. More than anything he seemed to himself to be concentrating on halting the relentless swing of interest and concern away from Sheila.

Sheila and he, having spoken to each other little about the things that most affected them, now didn't speak at all. Limited discussion on running the place was conducted with neither side interested enough in the outcome to put up an argument - first one backed down, then the other. The seesaw struck up a rhythm between them that at times successfully excluded everything else. At those times their lives seemed to be going on as usual and with an amazing mechanical efficiency. For Sheila the achievement, based on a bleak democracy, surprised but bitterly satisfied her. It was a matter of obeying the obvious rules and in that direction she felt he could always be relied on to do his best. What made her bitter was that life wasn't letting them down as a result of it but living up to them. Her feeling of emptiness showed more in her dulled eyes than her behaviour, while his inner negation of her enabled him to brush past her in the kitchen as if she didn't exist and in the resulting moment of paralysis she found herself welcoming the draught.

Bess saw her total defeat and in spite of shame and compassion rose in triumph. In the power of it all her problems seemed smaller. Sheila was no obstacle now but neither was Joan - only Mark himself. She was released from jealousy to find herself back in the straitjacket of embargos. In fury she imitated his behaviour with Sheila and used it against him. Her apparent friendliness ceased. She walked past ignoring him, honestly forgetting he was there when larking with her group. Within a couple of days she had all her old energy back and, to him, every bit antagonistic. The onslaught was so strong and relentless Mark felt he was being beaten up by a professional out to leave no surface bruises. Day after day she seemed to hate him and, balance lost, day after day he became more miserable, directing his general conduct by a thin beam of lucidity that kept him in touch with his pattern of activities.

One evening on the sofa watching a play on television that was based on a novel Tom didn't want to include in his book but wanted to review again in his head, Mark found himself sitting by Bess. The dreary, death-toying, life-dreading piece spread itself out with elaborate artifice sending the three of them further back into themselves and capturing only Mark with its occasional black humour. His explosive, hard-edged laugh at a dismissive suicide joke penetrated Sheila's silence. She was sewing in the corner and looked up puzzled. Her stare made Bess look at him and catch a glance of intense unhappiness directed at herself. A gentle tentative pressure of his knee against hers seemed unconscious - and could have been - and the whole chaotic torment of passion was back.

This time the avalanche took her shelters with it. It set the conditions of a phase so painful and immobilising she lost her route back. She kept glimpsing it in her contact with Mary who, forcing her to be aware of her, prised out a measure of sanity. Bess's habit of pushing everything aside on Mary's behalf came back erratically. What Tom saw as moodiness and tiredness Mary couldn't begin to define in terms separate from her needs. No mood or ill-health took precedence. Confidence in Bess's availability was as unquestioned as having air to breathe. She saw her mother was dammed up and as there was no separate charter attacked the blockage. Ill will and irritation if she failed to reach her drove Bess further into herself, but coming out was rewarded as an excursion to normality and helped her realise that Mark's refusal had never really been a shared one. The sense of helplessness was one he'd engendered. It was destructive and against her nature but seeing it didn't help - he didn't see it and she couldn't fight free of him.

The days, exhausting and repetitive, moved between extremes of feeling. An afternoon of touchless, passionate contact, leaving her sick and tearful at an emotive experience as slight as Simon's hair brushing her hand while he reached for his father's, would be followed by being 'high' on possibility equally lightly engendered. Squeals of triumph and laughter as the other two romped and thumped the floorboards could be translated by her ears and feet as conquering energy. The passion had its own momentum whether she fed it or not. If she smiled at Tom when Mark's eyes sought contact or held his gaze the result was the same. Making love with Tom so intensely should have freed her but often as not left her stranded in tears.

Deciding she wasn't fighting hard enough she began to feel better only if she succeeded in hurting him, but punishment and dismissal became the routes by which temporary loss stimulated stronger passion. His stony face under her assaults of silence looked alive only in its breathlessness. His gasping for air rewarded her like touch. They were sounds closer to hysteria or illness than suffering and led to another triumph of rejection in making love with Tom, where Mark's presence found its place in the climaxes with the word 'suffer' coming helplessly to mind as an aphrodisiac.

Occasionally there was a point where she could slow things down. An accidental concurrence of events inside her and out gave a moment of wellbeing when she felt she had things under control. At those times she seemed to see the situation as it really was. She was a casualty of his war against himself and in that light his suffering and sensitivity looked brutal and sick. A normal couple would have become lovers long ago. He refused chaos and accident but took on pain of his own making and it became loathsome to her. Weakness and insularity disguised as control taking its canon from rejection. In the long run seeing it 'clearly', as she thought, was no more useful than fighting it. Its value lay in sticking in the memory long enough to mark a pause, reminding her pause was possible.

The commitment or passion he sought was a terror to him but it helped her identify further and strengthened the trap, and a sense of helplessness again became something they shared. His experience was unique because he was, and it was what he was that attracted her - the warring, defensive, coldly passionate totality. She wasn't interested in a manageable part of it. She stared miserably at his baggy clothing and pale face, its skin ageing and tight over the bones had an ugly set of misery that didn't care about her or anyone else. Shut down, negatived, he inspired an agony of desire that made her feel she was the one who was sick or going mad.

In spite of the obsession her love of Tom kept surfacing unexpectedly. Sheila put on the radio and an Italian tenor voice streaming from the open window reached where she was working. Uninhibited feeling and sensual generosity brought him vividly to mind. Patterns of desire and restraint, pleasure and pain were made subtler through flesh. It was simple music made complex by the singer - the unashamed openness transformed everything in its alchemy.

But the hunger never let up. In using up her sexual energy the pool of it filled faster. Exhausted, she felt on the verge of physical illness - feverish and her head wouldn't clear. She sat on her own for long spells, head dropped on her arms, resting on a table - waiting.

Her exhaustion didn't seem to alarm Tom, nor did the frequently 'snappy' preoccupation. Her increased sexiness put him in a dauntless, joyous mood that was difficult to penetrate - he'd no intention of trying to. The sense of strain occasionally made him uneasy but he explained it first one way then another and general conclusions gave rise to a general protective guardianship. All the physically demanding chores he did for her - even trying to cut down her sexual appetite though he revelled in it - but one morning he got a letter from their publisher making it clear they'd reached the end of their bargaining and he was plunged into insecurity. He told Bess. She was upset but only the change in his attitude towards herself really drew her attention. Any sign of imbalance in him frightened her - at those times his generosity became reckless impulsiveness. Sudden craters in his nature - boiling with insecurity - made his abandonment to them look like mini-suicides. She moved closer.

When he wasn't around she kept close to Mary and John. It wasn't just Mary who reacted well to her return - John developed a habit that carried on long afterwards of coming in on them suddenly and flinging his arms round all the Blakes he could find, saying "Hi, team!"

As Bess moved out of orbit with Mark he found himself interpreting his stress almost entirely in terms of his failure with Sheila and re-establishing his old pattern of defensive retreats - including Joyce. Whenever he thought of Joyce he managed to forget the other two. In her recent letters she'd made her relationship with the man she lived with look shaky and there was a suggestion that with encouragement she'd leave him. At this time it felt exciting. He was reconvincing himself (he'd done it before) that since Sheila couldn't be his whole life, even with the children, then he was a man who needed more than one woman. The opportunity to skirt all issues and climb back into the driver's seat transformed his view of himself. For a while it turned failure into triumph, lightening his dealings with the others.

Sheila, making the most of it, summoned them all together one afternoon for a session of yoga. She was pleased to see them in the lounge at the appointed time waiting for her - she'd expected to have to chase them up. John and Mary wandered off before they started and Bates hadn't arrived but it didn't matter - it was the first time Joan had been there and Bess had actually been looking at the door expectantly.

Bess had surprised herself by remembering a pamphlet - a European version of the Worship of Krishna - someone thrust into her hand a while back. There was nothing mealy-mouthed about the longing for peace but another memory came back with it, as if it had made an outright statement on the impossibility of life without help. Personal incompetence, the need for assurance, were not only accepted but the cornerstones to a spiritual structure the body helped build. In memory it seemed to involve a conscious resetting of body and soul in a way suited to your own unique machinery. She'd always relied on the accident of wellbeing. She saw now that balance had to be worked out in a practical way to be a practical commodity. If it was a way to get peace and dissociation at one level and return to life refreshed at another she wondered if eventually you'd achieve it at will - at the instant of need. The idea of reaching it through a semi-physical route seemed suddenly wonderful.

While waiting for Sheila she'd been watching Mark and imagining its appeal for him. To her, taking simple steps to complex rewards might seem possible, not to him. She was over-aware of the mind's dependence on physical resources - knowing it and knowing that experience was always more than could be structured made the biggest gulf between them. His only answer was rejection. The bit of the idea likely to appeal to him, apart from the flexible control of his body, might be a looking towards the time when sensual and material anxieties could be overridden at will or all the time. She watched him limbering up and saw vanity keeping its clutch. Self-mistrust, self-removal hadn't damaged it much. The booklet had sometimes tried to reach its readers by a similar route, saying you'd feel better and look it. In his case energies for life were privately owned, on loan only to a few ideas about it. Anything that could be used in the fight of self against the self would be. She supposed he felt it limited the casualty area.

Sheila, being pleased with the size of the group, encouraged the new ones by giving beginners exercises. Joan was allowed to watch for a while and build up her confidence. Bess put herself into it with too much energy and was reminded the objectives were ease and tranquillity. She tried but failed, at best achieving nervous insistence on taking it easy.

"You'll learn," Sheila said. For Tom, equally inexperienced, no consolation was necessary. He was enjoying it naturally and naturally taking it at the right pace. Joan found watching him delightful. He was more fun to watch than the experts - her idea of normal response was easier to trace in it. She envied his frame of mind and its robustness. Surprisingly she found the experts' movements attractively accomplished in one way and repellent in another. When she forced herself to watch them she found herself making mental comment. 'Push-ups' from an inside-out position got labelled 'voluntary self-sacrifice,' a position on all fours with 'neckroll' was another act of self-submission. Full lotus became 'sealed circuit' and posture clasp 'self in half-nelson'. The structured knotting of the full twist made her slip on the floor beside Tom, where there was space, and concentrate only on her own movements in congenial company. After a while she felt so physically released she was momentarily let out of prison and a match for anything. It reminded her of swimming. The freshness and sense of freedom was more than she'd bargained for and she looked more at home than Bess.

Bess, though concentrating hard on her own movements, was conscious all the time of the movements of others. It was a physical sharing certainly, but without touch. This kind of closeness demanded you keep your distance for space to move - she wanted it but because of Mark it wasn't enough. Looking at the experts she saw the weight and sensual presence of real bodies converted into something like a product of genetic engineering, combining the flexibilities of amoeba and fine steel. She enjoyed it just the same - the interflow and vitality, the sense of wellbeing achieved without sex or games - and not even all the fun missing. She was beginning to like the idea of getting results on her own. Looking at them - isolated in unison - it moved her so strongly she stopped and watched. Sheila's exultant look doubled her pleasure. It was working for Mark too. She saw how beautifully he moved - how responsive to the purpose of the exercises and how he retained his power. The beauty and independence so matched his purpose it left him untouchable. He was near Sheila. With the slightest inaccuracy of movement he could have touched her but kept his space. It was so faultless a plaiting of acceptance, reconciliation and rejection it had

Sheila responding gratefully. For her, it seemed, the moment was everything - there was no real evidence to work on but the moment's.

When she started again Bess was so unnerved she made mistakes that called for help. She was wobbling on one leg, the other foot stuck in her groin and her arm stuck out to steady herself. She refused Mark's offered hand and balanced herself lightly with her fingertips against his arm. He was hurt but watched - partly puzzled by her clownishness, partly envying the dedicative openness that let her body take her by surprise.

At the end of the session Bess went outdoors and looked round in the twilight - more chance to pick up suggestions of composure eluding her in yoga as everywhere else - but the light sprang on behind her in the kitchen and she heard the curtains being pulled. She looked through a gap and saw Mark about to go into the hall but stop at the doorway. He stepped aside and leaned his head on the wall, moving as Sheila came and standing facing her, hands dangling at his sides. It looked as if he were saying he didn't feel well. She moved closer and kissed him lightly on the mouth. He received it inert, much like a sick child. As he left she saw him turn towards the stairs, and stepped back far enough to see him pass the landing window and to catch the outline of a bent head.

She came indoors looking for Tom and found him still in the sittingroom. John and Mary were there and in a noisy mood. It was just what she wanted. Within seconds the three of them were screaming with laughter. Falling off chairs, tickling and getting caught in physical traps bred overtones of bad temper and were too much for Tom who went upstairs to work.

Spontaneous release became rarer but there were still

"A Woman's Press basically and to cover all areas but not just women writers."

His memory of Beatrice, momentarily releasing his hold on Bess, let her take him. She felt freer and excitedly herded his responses in a direction that let him feel the unquestioned underlying assumption of a shared future. It released her more than she thought - she felt genuine excitement at the thought of a job. The change reflected in her face transformed his. But the threat involved in even this much freedom caused sudden panic - passion for Mark and for life had become interwoven. In spite of this, on the way back things were better.

Tom caught only the positivity. The idea opened up a new world while including and expanding his old. When she was staring round he was staring at her. She'd given the answer he needed. She told him John wanted to be a science journalist and be included in it and he laughed with delight. She said he'd mentioned the idea of a science magazine to Beatrice who seemed to like it. Remembering John's "Hi team!" he now thought of it as prophetic rather than schoolboy. He'd been looking anxiously behind him and a new future had been opening up in front of him.

14

Mark had it fixed in his mind that harvesting the north wheatfield would be a main event and a way of celebrating the year's work. Last year it was full of promise and he couldn't forget it. Under recent stress he'd once or twice been tempted to hire a combine harvester but had come to his senses in time. If his body couldn't feel the achievement then it wasn't one. He fell into a warm-up programme consciously encouraging undertones of ritual in which everything could be wiped out in a run-up of successive days of fast hard work. Symbols worked for him, even the amount he sweated measured release and flow, becoming proof of the interchange between himself and his chosen way of life. Only vigorous work helped, not the slow drag. Banishing thought was an obstacle but in the end there'd be no room for it.

He'd had more than enough of what he thought he'd come here for. Spiritual, physical, mental, social needs being satisfied in one was not only a dream but the wrong one. Recently all his needs had been working against each other as well as the group. In a passion for association he'd allowed too much. As far as hope and understanding were concerned he'd have been better off if he'd stuck to music or literature. The interchange of real lives he'd so badly wanted was causing all the trouble. We had needs in common but they couldn't be shared - they kept rhythms different from each other and, through the resultant stress, from an impersonal environment that perhaps could satisfy them. The 'dissociative' hadn't been given enough play. Keeping a distance would let you get back by a different route - one demanding less of the impossible. If he'd kept himself alive to that he'd never have got into this state with Bess. Fulfilment was for those who saw what could be achieved. He'd often reached a state where body and mind felt like one and at those times nothing was missing. We needed what was possible and it was so easy to get that it made the rest look like insanity. After he'd been working hard for a couple of days a cup of sweet tea felt like alcohol, sitting was a longed-for reward and lying down a sensual luxury resolving everything in oblivion.

Back on target he achieved a dependence only on finishing jobs - freedom was the autonomy of self-appointed goals, satisfaction achieving the achievable. In that world mistakes and regrets had a chance, developing skills that had a future. He felt he'd now put himself in a context where he glowed and burned in dependent competition with the impersonal. It was the final justification of isolation since the only way to discover the rhythm allowing such an interchange was to block interference. He could do without others altogether if he got a smaller place and worked it with Sheila and his sons. What he was feeling during these days made him see it would have a valuable social outcome. When the balance between assertion and submission was really confined to the self, others became relief and refreshment. Being with them occasionally was reward enough. Like drinking and eating they warmed and braced him - food and drink had a life of their own fusing with his and converting to social energy in a way sex never had.

In the evenings with the others all sense of problem had

gone - each evening was a mini-celebration leading up to the big day and everything in it touched or was touched by him. To the others the unexpected peace felt unreliable in the context of his growing excitement as the day approached but on the day itself his symbols took revenge. Dug earth exhaling life in the morning by evening was breathing decay.

The scything had been the turning point. A brief, exuberant, sweaty excitement followed by stooking sheaves head to head had a symbolism he couldn't convert. He found himself looking at Bess's flushed face and scratched arms with a hopelessness that felled him. Betrayed, cheated by himself and life - even of refuge in himself - he waited days for a return of response but nothing happened. Most days were spent wandering rather than working - looking for meaning or intimacy to appear in work or with people. He slept little and getting up one morning saw a blazing sunrise in which there was relief in knowing its colours were only his body's identification of certain lengths of light. There was freedom in the mathematical relationship. He went out afterwards and hung around the stream at the southern edge of his land waiting for Polly to nose her way through the bushes and afterwards felt restored enough to make a simple move. He spent the rest of the day away from home taking eggs to his regulars.

Bess was freed by his absence. She noticed how tired Sheila looked - not so much through her dark eyes and pallor as the hunched desolateness or bewilderment that seemed to remove her completely from the centre of their lives. She was no longer even a practical presence. She wanted to comfort her but something in the misery made her steer clear. Over lunch she mentioned it to Joan who, encouraged by the conversation, tried to talk to Sheila but she was unapproachable. At the suggestion of contact she gave off signals of outrage and desperation that made Joan back off but she thought anxiously, later, she'd seen her nervously fingering something in her pocket.

When Mark came home he ate with them and as it started to get dark went to the cowshed - something he'd been doing regularly since the harvesting. As soon as he smelt the warm hide and sweetish breath he was plunged into another world. A vigorous, different life-energy made real to him in the suddenness of her moves came over as totally independent of him even though he was dictator and provider. The experience was so concentrated it freed him and so impersonal it relaxed him - so much so that one hot night he fell asleep there. When he turned up for breakfast stinking, Sheila's outrage, silent and impotent, barely matched the incredulous half-contempt she recognised as becoming his habitual response to the gap in understanding between them. The occasion was new to her in one respect - she noticed Bess showing an outrage and tension similar to her own.

A couple of mornings later, feeling vicious cameraderie, she showed Bess what she'd been carrying in her pocket and the effect surpassed her expectation. It turned into something she hadn't quite looked for - not just triumph but relief. The letter Bess had been given dropped on to the table from her hand and now to Sheila it was dead. She found herself watching Bess as she bumped into a couple of chairs on the way out - amazed and almost grateful.

She picked it up without trembling. For the first time the sight of Joyce's handwriting wasn't an obstacle to understanding. She passed the introductory "Darling" almost unscathed and found the new reading revealing undertones of complaint. The sentence describing Joyce's confusion and loneliness with its plea for a meeting to clear things up felt like her own.

Bess dropped out of the picture for her. Ill with sickness and diarrhoea Bess spent days in her room with Tom and Mary. When she was beginning to feel able to come downstairs and face Mark he started feeling unable to face her. Having heard she'd be coming down his tension was so great he made a snap decision to clear up his other mistake, getting him out of the house. He told Sheila he was going to London to settle things once and for all with Joyce. The grim delivery and lack of reassuring detail terrified her and if his saying "Don't be silly, I'll be back" was meant as reassurance it failed.

Some hours after he'd gone Bess came downstairs and Sheila, finding her alone, told her he'd left. She expected instant understanding and getting it released her tears. There was little appreciable change in Bess's expression - to her he was lost anyway - but she asked for Sheila's sake where he'd gone.

"To her."

There was no answer and Sheila, desperate for anything, pushed on: "To straighten things out - if you can believe him." Her crying grew louder. "He won't come back, he won't come back!"

Bess took Sheila's hand. "Did he say he would?"

She nodded.

Bess held it tighter. "The letter, did you find it?"

Sheila shook her head with a new expression - "He gave it me" - and waited for Bess's response. Bess's face brightened.

"When did he say when he'd be back?"

"Sunday."

After a long pause Bess said, "I'd believe him if I were

you."

"You didn't see him leave," Sheila raged, "as if his life depended on it - couldn't wait to get to her." But the new calm in Bess had an effect and she left the room to look for the children.

From Mark's point of view the manoeuvre was successful. A remarkable access of clearheaded decision-making on the train made him feel he'd blasted himself clear of both women at once. For the first time in a long while he felt not only free but indomitable and it built up a restless excitement preventing him from sitting quietly at his table. He walked the gangways. Speed pulsing through his feet gave him a fresh curiosity about everything he saw. He was responding to faces openly like a child. He'd been right then. Close attachments clogged. The blockage meant you couldn't take in as much. Like this he could take on anything.

He sat down again. Out of the window he saw himself travelling in England and abroad - especially abroad. He was the paralysed man who'd got up and walked. The new sense of power took expression before he knew it, in eyeing the women. And that was all right too. It was impersonal - all-embracing not person-embracing. That was the clue. If he fed his appetites they'd tear him apart.

The task he'd come for could be done gently and finally. Joyce had been living with someone for the last couple of years, she'd had a baby by him. She'd be relieved eventually that their intimacy wouldn't be a threat. Out of need of a friend he'd confused her.

Searching the maze of back streets for her flat felt like a quest for peace - hers as well as his. Just the same when he got there and found he couldn't do the job he'd come for he was momentarily pleased. She'd gone away. The girl coming out of the room opposite told him, "Taken little Mark to her mother's for a week."

It took seconds for him to take it in. How could she - how dare she call the baby Mark? In the streets he now found himself raging at not being able to see her and see in her face she'd let him go. Like acid the name burned through his new confidence. He couldn't get his balance.

He remembered some London friends he'd just about kept in touch with and made for their house in the suburbs. Sitting in the underground stiffly facing pale stressed faces as determined to cancel him out as he was to be cancelled, he avoided contact with the legs of straphangers and new arrivals. He became obsessed with the idea that everything Bess stood for was wrong. Setting a course and sticking to it was all that mattered. It had to be done whatever the cost. What was making the situation at home unbearable was her endless ability to take things on board - as if her immune system were no good. In her case, whatever happened she responded to, and it wasn't as if she didn't know what she was up against. She knew what *he* was and what the situation was and reacted as if positives were involved. Years ago he'd felt his problems arose from a lack of understanding - excess of it was worse, for her as well as for him. Whichever way he moved she adapted, and he'd been trying to move with others in a similar way. He'd grown dependent on it. It was the worst move he'd ever made.

At his friends' house he was lucky enough to find them in and in a mood to make a fuss of him.

When Bess woke the following day she was amazed at her recovery. A feeling of weakness sensitised the relief, turning it to gratitude and tenderness. Her blocked responsiveness melted in an outflow of interest and susceptibility, making her more than usually conscious of feelings around her. At the first sight of Sheila's puffed and blotchy face her own tears flowed in sympathy.

Sheila, coming across the room to be near it, asked her to take her for a walk: "I need to be moving."

"He'll be back, I know it," Bess said, throwing her arms round her, "he's not weak, nor that kind of liar."

"We all are, " Sheila said, letting herself be coaxed to a chair. When she was ready to talk it was to think out loud. "We've nothing in common any more. We're guessing about each other all the time. Lies are as good as the truth. If we started talking things through the real stuff wouldn't come out - we'd take short cuts - neither of us knows who we're talking to. He's as incapable of doing anything about us as I am." She was crying again, "Joyce might look like a safer bet or at least a change of scene."

Her louder crying brought the children in, Claude first followed by Simon who kept himself at a distance. Claude cried as soon as he saw his mother's face and Simon, dull-eyed, looked on sucking his thumb. Claude climbed on her lap but Sheila pushed him off. He climbed back on and she threw her arms round him this time, burying her face in his neck.

"He's been in and out of my bed all night," she lifted her face and cupped the boy's in her hands, "he's the only one - the only one who's mine - the others are his."

Bess watched Simon leave the room.

The idea of a walk had lapsed. Instead Bess made endless tea and gave idle reassurance. In the evening when she and the others had made a meal Peter turned up for the first time. He ate his lamb and rice clearing his throat with water occasionally to ease out snatches of quiet singing - he had a choir practice that evening. For Bess this response was the most frightening. She felt hatred for Mark for the first time. This boy was his favourite - in him he could see the acceptable face of fear, conformist, unexacting and ungiving.

Sheila sat chin in hands over her food with nothing touched. "I'm going to phone them," she said in the middle of everything, but did nothing.

When they'd cleared away Bess found her sitting on the livingroom floor listening to the phone ringing. As soon as Sheila saw her she told her, "They're not answering."

"They're not in."

She shook her head, "They've got the phone off the hook!"

"It doesn't make that noise."

Sheila rested the phone in her lap, "I'm going to sit here till they answer." Bess persuaded her to try again later.

Looking for something to fill the gap Sheila said, "I'd like to see a priest."

"You don't go to church."

"He'd be a comfort." A moment later she was back on the phone.

"There's nobody in," Bess said.

"They're in bed and not answering."

"Sheila, listen: he can't. He can't act on impulse."

Sheila looked up as if it made sense.

Claude coming in sat on the floor by his mother. "When's Dad coming back?"

"Very soon," Bess said, but he was staring at his Mum's foot, not listening.

On her way out of the room Bess passed Joan. Joan knew something of why Mark had left but, like the others, nothing much. The men had been working outside all day keeping their distance so this was the first time anyone else had entered into it.

Joan asked Bess about Sheila adding, "I found a note in the Spring - I think it must have been the same woman."

Bess tensed, "Perhaps."

"Perhaps they met on the days he went selling eggs?"

Bess walked away. When she was over the impact she wondered about Joan - there'd been so much fear and intensity in the question. She'd dismissed it by assuming it reminded her of her own trouble but a flare of jealousy suggested other possibilities.

For the rest of the evening Joan sensed the tension, even hostility, and kept her distance. Later, coming across Bess and Sheila talking she stood well back to listen. She heard Sheila say "Why not?" viciously in Bess's face and watched Bess lean over to prise her fingers off a tiny bottle. There wasn't a struggle. Sheila burst into tears.

Joan went up to her room, failed to distract herself, failed to come to terms with what was going on or to forget it, and came back down again.

Sheila was now given up to grief like a cork on a sea - totally abandoned, face streaming and answering Bess with "No I can't - I need him - I want him back!"

The tears leaping to Joan's eyes were checked by such abandonment. Sheila'd given herself up so completely Joan's feelings were first shocked then positive. There was nothing for *her* to cry about. Sheila's crying was almost exultance. There was much more than relief in it. It was demanding a support being given as naturally as it was claimed and she started envying what she saw.

Peter came in to ask if his Mum would take him to choir practice and Sheila, now instantly responsive, said, "I haven't got the car."

"I'll ask Bates to do it," Joan offered and the boy looked grateful.

By late evening, drained, Sheila found herself talking more and crying less. Claude, still with her, kept interrupting and saying, "We need a lie-down." He'd climbed on to her lap and drawn up his legs, gripping her round the neck.

Mary and John weren't seen till nightfall. When everyone was indoors and things seemed quieter it drove Joan wild to see Sheila go to the phone for the hundredth time but in a short while Sheila and Bess were again alone together - herself still hovering. The others had gone to their rooms. Now she heard Bess say, "Be patient with him, perhaps you're stronger than he is."

She was amazed but Sheila looked interested, saying, "She's a cold, bloodless, hateful woman - considers herself intellectual. I can't be like her if that's what he wants."

"It isn't."

"She was slimmer than me - I've put on weight."

They looked at her skinny body hunched on the sofa.

"She's got lovely hair and wore it long. I'm so thick I wanted to be liked even by her. She can't make real ties - I don't think even the baby will make much difference - she'd suit him in a way. You really think I might be stronger?"

Bess nodded.

"Why?"

"More resilient." Joan made a sound in her throat making Bess look round but she turned again adding, "Accept it and the responsibility of it."

Sheila wasn't listening. "When we were married I thought he was because he knew more. I got disappointed. Couldn't see the value of what he knew - but I was happier then."

"Were you?"

Sheila nodded emphatically, "That had nothing to do with loving him as a person though, did it?"

On Sunday Mark came back so late only Sheila knew about it. At breakfast they all tried to greet him as if nothing had happened and he, apparently more in control than when he'd left, acted up to it successfully until the children came in and he could see his action in their faces. Taking his coffee to another room he blundered into Claude and trod on his foot, getting a vicious blow on the hip for it. His eyes were blazing with hatred.

A few days later they began to feel it was over. In some respects things were even a little better than before. Mark worked harder than usual at slipping into the moment-by-moment life of the group. For Bess it wasn't reassuring - it had the feel of an outsider trying to keep in touch.

He had no further anxiety about Joyce. A letter explain ing it was over and that it had all been a selfish mistake on his part had already been posted. The days at home became more difficult as the others slipped gratefully into routine. As tiredness and inertia turned poisonous, life started feeling like a life sentence. Tom and Bess were leaving when term started, thank God, and it felt as if he'd willed them away. What he couldn't prevent was a feeling that they were taking his life with them. His old interests in plans and ideas - even desires - disappeared as if they'd been misleading fragments looking for the whole. Ideas were hieroglyphics with such an infinity of translations there was nothing left for him now but acquiescence. Love was the only positive and in him more perplexing than anything - so fraught it made every move a wrong one.

He started to watch Bess, impersonally as he thought, making the most of her while she was there. He found her changed. He wondered if leaving the commune and heading for the new life he'd heard her talking excitedly about were behind it.

Bess, having seen his sexual rejection in its inexhaustible variety of evasions felt the only thing left was work. Even now she couldn't hate him. He noticed a tenderness and sensitivity in her manner with him not so unlike her offerings to others - it seemed not to have lost intensity so much as purpose.

One day, whichever direction he turned there seemed to be nothing. No outlet, no movement of any description - not even in himself. He watched his family and found they'd already adapted to the circumstances, pursuing the old course with less reference to himself.

Sheila took the opportunity his stillness gave to mother him. She seemed a little happier and Claude's resentment deepened - he went outside most days and wasn't seen till hunger drove him in.

Mark began to see them all as if they were on a screen where occasionally he'd find himself moved in predictable ways but entirely without relevance to his life. "Run down - moody" were descriptions of himself he heard more often when he started to take more notice, not of people but the world outside. He became excited by changes in the weather and light. In his copse one afternoon he was caught by the light's changing focus. A storm was brewing. Blue-black clouds closed in on a freak gap blazing with radiance. Birds in excited twos and threes tossed up white bellies and he looked from the feathers to leaves stirring to crescendos of activity. He wandered, floating in light as if it were water, flowing as if weightless wherever he looked.

For the next few days the weather grew hotter and they spent more time indoors. The air, humid and heavy, left them no energy. Sheila, still drawing Mark to her by arranging his outer world, suggested they get out when it let up a little. Another walk and picnic before the group broke up, she said.

He received the idea with his current passivity, feeling she was right - they wouldn't be doing anything like it again - but found being out with the others too much for him. He looked on their easy, relaxed manner with each other, as it seemed to him, as if he'd never felt it and wondered if he ever had. He watched Bess walking with and talking to Tom - later she was walking with John, letting him hand her over a stile. All right.

The beach with the tower on the cliff edge was their objective - though the cliff on the other side of the bay had a nodding donkey oil pump going day and night with metronomic regularity like an insanity. They spread their picnic on the beach, turning their backs to it and looking up at the tower. The kids rushed to the water. Joan wandered off on her own - then Mark.

Joan finding the heat oppressive was looking for shade and made her way through the graveyard of fallen rocks under the cliff. A scrap of cliff face slid idly as she passed. Warning notices every couple of hundred yards put her off and she turned back. Reaching the others and standing further off she thought she caught a glimpse of Mark near the tower. Another figure, Sheila probably since she hadn't seen her yet, toiling after him.

Mark felt good on top - impressed with the conflicting winds at the corner. They weren't refreshing but violent, letting him trace the currents in channels of bowing corn that hadn't been cut yet. On the other side the water repelled him - a bleak glare, but if clouds passed over pressed flat like dogs ears before a leap. Surges of wind like an attack from a bodiless force made him step back from the edge. He liked the consciousness of his own energy the battling gave him.

Sheila shouted when she reached the top but it was lost in the wind. She held on to the wire round the tower, frightened and fascinated. His back, tensed against it, held her in silent sexual longing till the wire bellied in a gust and she lost balance. The sound she made, penetrating and totally intimate, made him turn and seeing her, step back. It looked like perfect balance but he disappeared.

He died on the way to the hospital.

Bess stayed on alone with Sheila for a few weeks after the others returned to work. With Lionel's financial help she organised part-time workers for the farm. He visited regularly and as a new security took shape in Sheila, Bess's own grief hit her. A growing hatred took its place finding its justification in what she now saw as his feeding of her love without returning it.

One evening when Lionel had put the children to bed and was sitting with his arm round Sheila's shoulders she saw in his face for the first time a response more vital than comfort. It was time to go. Her new life was already claiming more space in her mind. She waited long enough to be quite sure Lionel would take her place, perhaps even Mark's, and went home.